D0790524

"What's wrong?"

Ryan noticed the shadow that fell across her face. "I thought you wanted to marry me."

"I do," she quickly confirmed. "But you have to understand why I think we should wait awhile. There's a war going on. Like it or not, we're both now a part of it."

"*I'm* a part of it," he tersely reminded her. "Not you. It's no place for a woman, and I'm getting you out of it."

"But I don't want to get out of it."

He released her, sitting up to glare at her with rising anger. "Belinda, you don't know what you're talking about. You got into this by accident. Surely you've got sense enough to realize the danger you're in. I'm taking you home."

Firmly she shook her head. "No. I might have got into it by accident, but now I'm staying."

Dear Reader,

This month we bring you award-winning author Patricia Hagan's latest Harlequin Historical, *The Desire*. The novel is the sequel to *The Daring* (HH#84) and tells the story of Belinda Coulter, a troubled young woman who finally finds happiness as a Confederate nurse, only to come face-to-face with a man from the past.

Columbine is the second book by Miranda Jarrett, one of the first-time authors introduced during our 1991 March Madness promotion. The story sweeps from busy London to the wilds of Colonial New England, where a disgraced noblewoman finds a new life full of hope and promise.

Theresa Michaels's *Gifts of Love* is an emotional tale of a grieving widower and an abandoned woman whose practical marriage blossoms into something far more precious than either of them could ever dream.

Lucy Elliot has been writing books for Harlequin Historicals since the introduction of the line. *The Conquest,* her eighth book, is a sequel to *The Claim* (HH#129). It's the story of a tempestuous Frenchwoman and a cool-headed American soldier who fall in love against the backdrop of the American Revolution.

Four intriguing heroines. Four unforgettable heroes. We hope you enjoy them all.

Sincerely,
Tracy Farrell
Senior Editor

The Desire
Patricia Hagan

Harlequin Books

TORONTO • NEW YORK • LONDON
AMSTERDAM • PARIS • SYDNEY • HAMBURG
STOCKHOLM • ATHENS • TOKYO • MILAN
MADRID • WARSAW • BUDAPEST • AUCKLAND

If you purchased this book without a cover you should be aware that this book is stolen property. It was reported as "unsold and destroyed" to the publisher, and neither the author nor the publisher has received any payment for this "stripped book."

Harlequin Historicals first edition October 1992

ISBN 0-373-28743-7

THE DESIRE

Copyright © 1992 by Patricia Hagan.
All rights reserved. Except for use in any review,
the reproduction or utilization of this work in
whole or in part in any form by any electronic,
mechanical or other means, now known or
hereafter invented, including xerography,
photocopying and recording, or in any information
storage or retrieval system, is forbidden without
the permission of the publisher, Harlequin Historicals,
300 E. 42nd St., New York, N.Y. 10017

All the characters in this book have no existence
outside the imagination of the author and have no
relation whatsoever to anyone bearing the same name
or names. They are not even distantly inspired by any
individual known or unknown to the author, and all
incidents are pure invention.

®: Trademark registered in the United States Patent
and Trademark Office and in other countries.

Printed in the U.S.A.

Books by Patricia Hagan

PATRICIA HAGAN,

New York Times bestselling author, had written and published over 2,500 short stories before selling her first book in 1971. With a background in English and journalism from the University of Alabama, Pat has won awards for radio, television, newspaper and magazine writing. Her hobbies include reading, painting and cooking. The author and her Norwegian husband, Erik, divide their time between their mountain retreat in North Carolina and their home in Bergen, Norway.

Chapter One

The smothering heat of day had melted into sweltering night. Not a breeze was stirring, but any movement at all on the streets of Richmond, Virginia, lifted clouds of dust from the parched earth. There had been no rain in weeks, and the summer of 1861 seemed like a miserable glimpse into the veritable ovens of hell.

Belinda Coulter felt as if she was being crushed by her tight-laced corset. Every breath she drew was agony. And how was she supposed to sing when her ribs were aching? She had said as much to Frank Barco, the saloon owner, the night before, when he had first made her wear the awful dress, but he had merely laughed and said she'd damn well better be able to, or she could hit the road.

She pulled the dress over her head and adjusted it into place, and a furious glance in the mirror confirmed once again why Mr. Barco insisted on the scandalous costume. Thanks to the tight corset, her bosom poured from the dipping bodice of the garish purple satin gown. The skirt fitted tightly, molded to her hips, with a revealing slit cut all the way to her thigh.

She had told him it was scandalous and indecent and also complained about the way he'd had one of his saloon girls make up her face. Shiny purple paint on her eyelids. Bright splotches of red on her cheeks. Coldly, indignantly, she had reminded him she was a singer, not a *lady of the evening*.

He had stepped back to scrutinize her, amid the boxes and barrels in the tiny storage area he had rearranged to serve as her living quarters. Rolling the stub of his cigar across his lips, he'd swept her with an approving gaze and said with a grin, "Yeah, yeah, you do." Then, with a flash of annoyance, he had snapped, "And that's fine and dandy, girlie, 'cause this ain't no church. It's a saloon. And men ain't comin' in here to listen to hymns. They want to have a good time, 'cause in case you forgot, there's a war goin' on and all of 'em know this just might be the last good time they'll ever have, and you're gettin' paid to give it to 'em."

She had dared argue with him. "Then let me give them a good time, but in a nice way, Mr. Barco. Let me wear a pretty gown and sing them a pretty song. Why do I have to look this way?"

He snickered. "Maybe you'd like to go out there lookin' like you did the first time I saw you—wearin' dirty rags, starvin' and exhausted. Hell, you were desperate, girlie. You'd been all over Richmond and couldn't find a job singin', remember? You couldn't find a job doin' *nothin'*. If it hadn't been for me, you'd have wound up workin' at Miss Lucy's. *On your back.*"

Belinda had turned away so that he couldn't see her tears of humiliation. Maybe he was right about her being hungry and desperate, and, yes, she had been all over Richmond looking for work. First, as a singer, and then, ultimately, she'd been willing to take almost anything. But never, she clenched her fists in furious resolution, would she have been driven to prostitution. She would have starved first, by God.

She dared take a deep breath and felt a sharp pain in her ribs. There would be no high notes this night. She had given Edwin, the piano player, a list of songs she could sing in a lower key, and that was the way it would have to be. She only hoped Mr. Barco didn't get mad, because he was right when he said she was desperate. It was this job, or nothing.

She paced up and down in the tiny room, waiting to go out and perform. There were no windows and it was stifling, and the misery made her think once more of the cool, refreshing air of her beloved Blue Ridge Mountains. Yet, no matter how hard she struggled against it, bad memories took precedence over good, and the sadness came flooding back.

Her mother had died giving birth to her, and she had been raised by her older sister, Jessica. Her father, having lost three wives, had believed he was cursed, and he had become a drunkard as he fought the demons within. Times had been hard when Belinda was growing up, but she had dared think her future bright when Harmon Willingham came into her life.

Without conceit, Belinda knew she was pretty, and she had her pick of beaux, but none of the young men of Buncombe County could turn her head. Harmon, however, had stolen her heart from the moment they met. With hair as black as crow's feathers and eyes as blue as a spring day, he had set her heart to fluttering. Well educated, the son of a wealthy doctor in Raleigh, he had sworn to love her forever, promising a life of wealth and leisure. With war clouds hovering, he had proudly joined up with the First North Carolina Regiment, but still they had planned to be married. She would live with his family while he was away fighting in what was sure to be a very brief conflict between North and South.

Her father had ruined all that, she recalled with a bitter frown. Unlike his neighbors, Zeb Coulter had sided with the North, and he had rather unwisely made no secret of his loyalties; he was forever getting involved in arguments, even a brawl from time to time. Then, when a particularly ugly incident caused a bully by the name of Culver Hardin to be blinded in one eye, Belinda had wound up being the target of Culver's sons' revenge against her father.

She squeezed her eyes shut against remembered anguish.

After the fight in town between her father and Culver, Deputy Dan Cowley had come to the house late in the day to warn there might be more trouble, and if Zeb was smart, he advised, he'd lay low and keep his mouth shut. But Zeb had said that he wasn't worried, that he had a right to his views on the war, and that Culver had started the fight, anyway.

Adding to Belinda's embarrassment over her family had been the scandal concerning Jessica and the circuit rider, Derek Stanton. Jessica had lost her job as a schoolteacher as a result of all the terrible gossip.

Belinda had decided to declare her disapproval of her father's and sister's behavior. Sooner or later, she knew, Harmon would hear about all the shameful things that had happened and perhaps decide he didn't want a wife from such a disreputable family. Her mind made up, Belinda had set out for his aunt's house in Asheville.

She hadn't made it.

They had been waiting for her—Culver's boys, Jake, Rufus, and the man she didn't know but would never forget. *The man with the eyes of a cat.*

She had been raped, battered and bruised, but the physical torture was nothing compared to the aftermath of the savage attack. Her father had shot and killed Rufus, wounded Jake, maybe killed him, too. She didn't know and didn't care. Her father had been arrested, and Jessica, it was said, had helped him escape. He had gone away, everybody figuring he'd headed north to join the Union army. Again, Belinda didn't care. She had clung to the foolish hope Harmon would not hear about any of it. They would be married and later, if need be, she'd tell him.

Then had come the fateful day, a day Belinda would never forget. It had been two weeks after the bombardment of Fort Sumter in South Carolina, which everyone had been sure meant the war had finally started. Harmon had arrived at the farm, wearing his new Confederate uniform, resplendent in gray coat with two rows of gold buttons and gray trousers with a crimson stripe running up each side. Spit-polished Jefferson boots, and a saber hanging from a shiny black leather scabbard. He had even worn a wide-brimmed gray felt hat, sporting a bright red feather.

She had been in the root cellar, gathering turnips and potatoes for supper. When his shadow fell across her, she'd jumped, startled, then whirled about to give a shriek of joy in recognition. Dropping her apron full of vegetables, she had attempted to fling herself into his arms—but he had held up white-gloved hands to fend her off. In that frozen moment, she had known he had heard about what had happened.

He told her as much, bluntly and coldly. He had also been angry that she had not written and told him herself, for he was humiliated, he said, to have to hear it from others. The marriage would have to be postponed. He needed time, he had said, to decide whether he could accept a wife who was soiled, from a family of traitors.

And when he had ridden away, it might as well have been her heart trampled beneath his horses' hooves, rather than mountain clay, for he had destroyed her spirit as well as her will to live.

Unable to bear the misery of her home, Belinda had fled to Richmond.

Richmond was a different world, crowded and teeming with anxiety and excitement over the war. Virginia had seceded, and the Confederate capital had been moved to Richmond. The Rappahannock River had been blockaded, along with the ports at Mobile, Alabama, and New Orleans. Despite the tension, there was still a flurry of social activities, dances and concerts, receptions and theatricals. But no place or job, Belinda had quickly discovered, for an unknown girl from the mountains of North Carolina.

The money she had saved for her wedding had quickly disappeared, and she had found herself sick with hunger—and with nowhere to go. In desperation, she had gone to Frank Barco's saloon and asked for a job as a singer, offering to work in exchange for room and board. Reluctantly, Barco had agreed. That had been nearly two weeks before, and Belinda had hated every moment she was onstage.

The saloon was situated on a side street and was not as large or as richly decorated as many others in the city. A long bar ran down one wall, with mirrors behind it. The rest of the room was filled with tables and chairs. The stage was nothing more than a small platform at the rear, with tattered red velvet curtains framing it.

There were other women working there, waitresses in gawdy costumes much like hers, though she suspected they served up something besides drinks. Unlike her cramped quarters in a storage room, the others had rooms upstairs, and she had seen them leading customers up there from time to time.

Almost all of the men were soldiers, rowdy and rough, and the more they drank, the worse they got. The first time one had reached out and touched her, grabbing her ankle, she had panicked and screamed. Others, rushing to defend her, had wound up in a brawl with friends of the offender. Afterward, Frank had surveyed the damage, the broken tables and glasses, and furiously blamed her, saying she needed to grow up and learn how to laugh her way out of such situations instead of inciting a riot.

Belinda tried. She fought back the waves of hysteria when a man clutched at her, kicking at him or pushing him away. But always her flesh crawled at the touch of a man's hand, for it reminded her of the horrible night she'd been ravished.

A loud banging on the door brought her abruptly from her reverie. Frank called, "Hey, get out here before they tear the place down. What are you doin', anyway?"

"Trying to breathe," she snapped, jerking open the door and moving past him. "I feel like I'm smothering, thanks to this corset and this choking dress."

"Better than starvin'," he fired back, pointing toward the curtain separating the back hallway from the main room of the saloon. "It's full tonight, and I want you to give 'em a good show and keep 'em drinking. That new place up the street opened today, and I've got to give 'em a reason to keep comin' here—or I should say *you* do."

Only with great effort did she muster a dazzling smile as she stepped onto the platform, having to swallow against her rising disgust at the sight of a sea of drunken, leering faces.

A roar went up from the crowd—cheers and clapping, along with the stamping of booted feet and glasses banging rhythmically on tabletops.

Belinda walked to the edge and nodded to Edwin. He started playing and she began to sing. Then, with eyes closed, she lost herself in the music, no longer seeing the staring, lustful gazes of the soldiers. Neither did she hear the inevitable taunting invitations to come down into the audience, to sit on their laps, to share a drink, to sing only to them....

At last it was over. She always sang six songs, one after the other, standing in the same spot, then rushed from the stage, dreading having to return an hour later.

In her haste to reach the sanctuary of her room, Belinda did not see the man standing in the shadows of the hallway. When he spoke, she gave a little cry and instinctively backed away, for she now considered all men threatening—especially when no one else was around.

"Hey, don't be scared!" he said quickly. "I'm not going to hurt you. I just want to talk to you. The name's Starkey. Bart Starkey. And I think you've got a real fine voice, little lady," he added hastily.

Belinda felt a wave of relief. Now she could see him in the light from the lantern hanging on the wall. He was older than most of the men outside, maybe the same age as her father; unlike her father, however, he was clean and neatly dressed. He had nice eyes, friendly, not grinning insolently the way the overbearing Frank Barco did. Still, she felt uncomfortable and she dismissed him with a murmured "Thank you" as she opened her door and started inside.

He was right behind her. "Wait, please. I really need to talk to you. Can I come inside? As I said, I'm not going to hurt you."

Belinda gave a bitter chuckle. "There's hardly room for one in here, much less two, Mr. Starkey. Even if I *were* the sort to entertain in my dressing room," she added sardonically.

"Oh, I didn't mean to insult you, Miss Coulter. Please believe me," he said in a rush. His eyes were wide and he was twisting his hat nervously in his hands. "We can talk here, if you'd like. I just didn't think you'd want Mr. Barco to hear me offering you a job—"

"A job?" She blinked in disbelief, then felt her guard go up again. Dressed as she was, working in a place like the Wild Dog Saloon, she could hardly expect him to have anything propitious in mind for her. Curtly she said, "I don't think I'd be interested in whatever you have to offer." She started to close the door in his face.

"Not even touring the country like the Swedish Nightingale?"

She opened the door again to stare incredulously at him. "What did you say?"

"The Swedish Nightingale," he repeated. "You have heard of Miss Jenny Lind, haven't you?"

Belinda stammered, "Well—why, of course I have. Hasn't everyone? But what has she got to do with me?"

His smile was mysterious. "You mean, what have *you* got to do with *her?* A voice, that's what. I've traveled all over the world and believe me, you're the nearest I've ever heard to sounding like her. With the right kind of handling and promotion, why, I've no doubt you can be the American Nightingale, for sure.

"I've worked for P. T. Barnum himself," Starkey revealed proudly, now clearly confident of having her attention. "Back in the fifties, on Miss Lind's concert tour. Oh, I didn't have an important job, I admit that. I took care of packing and unpacking stage props, cleaning up, that sort of thing. I was just a lackey, to be sure, but I learned a lot, enough so's I was able to finally take off on my own and start up my own traveling show. Oh, it wasn't big like P.T.'s, but I made a good living, with freaks of nature, magicians and seers and the like. It's always been my dream to discover my own singing angel, and I never did—till now. *You*, Miss Belinda Coulter," he said with a bow and a flourish, "are that angel."

"I'm flattered you think so, but I'm afraid I don't want to share a stage with freaks and magicians." She started to close the door again.

He stuck his foot out to block her. "But it's not like that now. I don't have a show anymore, but I'm trying to get one started, and that's where you come in. You'll be my star and we'll travel all over the country. I'll make you famous—and rich," he added.

Perhaps once, long before, Belinda might have been intrigued by such an offer. But when her innocence had been lost, so too had her optimism and zest for living. Now she merely took one day at a time, trying to survive. Beyond that, she really didn't care what happened anymore. Besides, she was not about to go traipsing off to God knows where with an absolute stranger.

With a wistful sigh, she again declined, regretfully warning, "If you don't take your foot out of my door, I'm going to have to call for help. You seem like a nice man, and I'd hate to see you thrown out of here, but I don't have long between performances and don't intend to waste time listening to nonsense. Now, good evening, Mr. Starkey."

Reluctantly he stepped back, but it was obvious that he wasn't about to give up. When she closed the door, he leaned against it to say softly, "Think about it. That's all I ask. Just think about it. I assure you, I have the most honorable of intentions. Never would I attempt to compromise your virtue. We could even hire a woman companion to travel with you, if that would make you feel better, and everything will be quite proper. We'll start off entertaining the soldiers.

We'll go from camp to camp. I play the banjo and a little guitar, and I'll accompany you. Later, when we're making money, we'll buy a piano and hire somebody to play it. It doesn't matter if there *is* a war going on, people are still going to want to hear music and singing.

"And before you know it—" his voice was rising with excitement "—you'll be singing in concert halls in New York, Philadelphia, even London and Paris, just like Miss Jenny Lind."

On and on he went. Belinda listened without responding, and finally he went away. She continued to think about everything he had said, deciding it would be crazy even to consider such an offer. It might not be cozy where she was, but at least Frank paid her room and board. Maybe the room was little more than a closet, and maybe the food was only one meal a day at Maude Sutton's café down the street, while the rest of the time she had to nibble on the offerings at the bar. But at least she knew what to expect and felt reasonably safe, because, despite Frank's temper and the way he made her dress, he wouldn't let anything happen to her as long as she worked for him.

The truth was, Belinda sadly acknowledged, her ambition had dissipated along with her spirit. The future no longer mattered. The past was too painful to think about. All she had was the here and now of each day. Thoughts of another kind of life, especially with a war going on, were disturbing, almost frightening, to contemplate.

The war!

Belinda, like so many other Southerners, was beginning to fear that peace might not come as soon as everyone had predicted. Since arriving in Richmond in May, she had felt tension steadily building among the city's residents. There had been a minor skirmish in the northern part of the state, at Arlington Mills and Fairfax County courthouse, in which a Confederate captain had been killed. Then had come a victory by Union forces on the western border, followed a week later by a battle at Bethel Church. Now it was being said that the settlement at Harper's Ferry was being abandoned by Southern soldiers trying to keep from being cut off by the Yankee general, McClellan, who was reportedly advancing from the west and north.

Where would it all end, she sadly pondered, and where would she be afterward? She didn't plan to ever go home, even though she missed Jessica terribly and felt guilt over having been so quick to condemn her. After all, Jessica had never had any real joy in her life, and certainly no romance, because her responsibilities to her family had robbed her of her youth.

While Belinda had enjoyed picnics and parties, often traveling to Asheville for the constant social activities there, Jessica had been the one to do household chores—cleaning, cooking and baking. Belinda had offered to help, but Jessica would shoo her away most of the time, urging her to go her way and have fun. And Belinda had not missed the wistful gleam in Jessica's eyes when boys came calling, as Jessica was forced to witness yet another part of life passing her by.

Perhaps, Belinda reasoned, the circuit rider, Mr. Stanton, hadn't been all bad for Jessica. True, he had gone off and left her, breaking her sister's heart. But most of that was due to Reuben Walker, that sanctimonious hypocrite, Belinda thought, fuming. All he had wanted was a wife to replace the one he'd sent to an early grave by making her work like a mule from sunrise to sunset. Of course, he was also after someone to warm his bed and take care of his child. Rejected by the younger girls, Reuben had talked Zeb into making Jessica, considered a spinster, promise to marry him. Infuriated when he found out about her and the preacher, Reuben had wasted no time in getting revenge by spreading the tale all over the Blue Ridge.

Maybe, Belinda pondered, despite everything, Jessica had been left with memories to last a lifetime. Perhaps her sister might even go through it all over again for just the chance to be held in the arms of the man she loved.

Belinda wished she could say the same about her own past tragedies. The memories were ugly and harsh, a painful torment. Thoughts of a man ever touching her that way again made her want to scream.

One day, she firmly vowed, when there was peace across the land, she would write to Jessica. Maybe she would even ask her to come and live with her, if she had a decent job by then, a nice place to live, and—

"Am I gonna have to come get you every time the show's about to start?" Frank bellowed from the other side of the door. "We got a real rowdy bunch out there tonight, damn it, and it agitates 'em even more when they have to wait for you."

Resolutely Belinda stepped out, started to make her way to the stage.

"Wait a minute." Frank was right behind her, irritably commanding, "I don't want to hear you stoppin' after six songs, understand? I've already told Edwin. You keep on going till I give the signal you can quit. Long as you're singin', they'll just sit and drink and listen." He went on to say that he'd sent word to some of his friends to come over and help keep things under control, but it would take time for them to get there. "Till then, you keep 'em happy."

From the moment she stepped onto the platform, Belinda knew trouble was brewing. This time, when she began to sing, the audience did not settle down; they continued with their revelry. She looked down at Edwin, who could only return her miserable, worried gaze with a helpless shrug.

There was one man in particular that disturbed her more than the others. Big and burly, with a full beard, he wore a gray uniform bearing a sergeant's insignia. He called out boldly to her, beckoning for her to come down off the stage and sing especially for him. He kept leaping to his feet, blowing kisses and yelling her name over and over.

Dear God, she prayed, let her get through this night and tomorrow she vowed to hit the streets again in search of any other kind of job but this. Surely she could find something, anything....

Her eyes flashed open when she felt clammy fingers wrapping about her ankle. It was the sergeant, and he was tugging at her, calling, "Come on down, sweetie. Sit in my lap and sing just for me. Pay you good, I will...." He was waving money at her with his other hand.

Struggling to remember the words to the song Edwin was playing, she looked down at him with a patient smile, at the same time sharply kicking away his hold on her leg. Frank saw what was happening and rushed forward to lead the sergeant away with the promise of a free drink, so anxious was he to appease his customer.

Belinda stepped farther back on the platform, trying not to think about how narrow it was, how if she wasn't careful she'd topple right off the rear edge.

Deciding she had to keep alert, lest someone else be so bold, she swept the crowd with a wary gaze.

Suddenly she felt her heart slam into her chest as she saw the strange eyes staring up at her.

Cat's eyes!

At once she was jolted to remember the last time she'd seen those strange gold-green eyes looking down at her, just before...

A shudder shook her from head to toe.

It all came flooding back. Her clothes torn off, her arms pinioned above her head, her legs held down and spread apart. Pawing hands, probing fingers, wet lips upon her flesh, and then the pain.... Dear God, the excruciating, stabbing pain.

A great roaring began from deep inside her. Belinda had fallen silent, stumbling, staggering, all pretense of singing swept away amid her rising hysteria.

Anger and rage erupted among the irate onlookers, and they began to jeer and shout, demanding to know what was wrong. Edwin, alarmed to see the expression on Belinda's face, abandoned the piano to leap onstage and grab her just before she fell.

The sudden silence only fed the impatience of the mob, and they began to surge toward the platform.

From the corner of his eye, Edwin saw a bottle flying through the air just in time to yank Belinda out of the way. It broke against the wall, showering them with glass.

Someone roared, "Hey, you son of a bitch, you almost hit her!"

"Who you callin' a son of a bitch, you son of a bitch?" came the furious response.

And the fight was on.

Half carrying, half dragging her, Edwin managed to get Belinda off the stage, assisted by a stranger who had suddenly appeared. Behind them they could hear the sounds of the riot—flesh striking flesh as fists wildly flew, chairs and tables being broken, and more glass shattering.

Once inside Belinda's room, Edwin bolted the door before worriedly asking her, "Are you all right? Are you hurt anywhere?"

She shook her head, not about to confide that her pain was mental, not physical, for in that frozen instant she had experienced true terror.

Those eyes!

Those horrible, but beautiful, cat's eyes!

And, worst of all, he had been staring at her as though he *knew* who she was.

With a great shudder, Belinda lowered her face to her hands and wept.

"Miss Coulter?"

She looked up at the sound of the kind and gentle voice and recognized Bart Starkey.

"Miss Coulter, what happened to you out there?" he asked, his expression one of genuine concern. "Something frightened you. What was it?"

She tried to take a deep breath but the constricting corset painfully prevented her. Suddenly she was terribly hot and felt sick to her stomach. "Please, leave me now," she begged both him and Edwin as they anxiously hovered over her. She wanted to get undressed, hoping that when she could again breathe freely, she could figure out what to do next.

Starkey was plainly reluctant to leave her, but Edwin gestured for him to follow. At the door, Bart made one last attempt to get her to change her mind about his offer. "Maybe it would be good for you to get away, Miss Coulter. Maybe you just need to get away from this place—"

Just then, with a roar, Frank Barco appeared. He lunged between the two men, knocking them aside. He seemed to fill up the doorway with his wrath. Eyes bulging, lips twitching, fists balled at his sides, he towered over Belinda. "What in the hell happened to you out there? I told you to keep them happy till I could get some help over here, and now my place is a shambles, 'cause you just quit cold! Are you crazy or what?"

She tried miserably to apologize. "I'm really sorry. I don't know what happened—"

He cut her off. "You ain't got your mind on what you're doin'."

"I think she's sick," Edwin suggested. "I mean, she looks kind of sick, don't you think?"

"I think she's worthless, that's what!" Frank shouted at Edwin, then shook his fist in Belinda's face. "I want you out of here first thing tomorrow morning, understand? Or so help me, I'll toss you out myself."

Again Edwin attempted to intervene. "Listen, Frank, why don't you give her another chance? After all, you said yourself they were extra rowdy tonight. She's just a kid. Got scared and forgot the words. It wasn't her fault they went crazy. And besides, where's she gonna go?"

Frank sneered. "That ain't my problem."

Bart saw his chance and took it. "It isn't a problem at all."

All eyes were upon him, including Belinda's.

He directed his words to her. "You've got a place to go, Miss Coulter. You can take my offer."

"I don't know what in hell he's talkin' about," Frank snapped, turning away at the sound of more furniture crashing in the distance. "And I don't care, 'cause like I said, you got till mornin' to be out of here."

When he left the little room, Edwin followed after him. Belinda knew he had good reason to fear for his own job should Frank accuse him of displaced loyalty, so she understood why he didn't speak on her behalf again.

Starkey looked at Belinda in the awkward silence that followed. "Well?" he prodded with a coaxing smile. "What do you say?"

Fingers of terror still clutched her spine. It had to have been someone else, she told herself. Surely the man who had raped her was not the only one in the world with green-gold eyes. She had to stop brooding over that awful night, and maybe Bart Starkey held the answer, with his offer of challenge and adventure. Still, she needed time to think and decide if it was really what she wanted to do. After all, he *was* a stranger.

"What do you say?" he repeated.

Diffidently she asked, "Can you give me till tomorrow morning to decide?"

He grinned. "Sure thing, Miss Coulter. I'll be here at first light, and I sure hope the answer is yes."

Belinda could give him no hope that it would be. She knew only that she had her whole future to consider during the long, hot night ahead.

Chapter Two

Ryan Tanner had wasted no time in leaving when the fighting broke out. He was no coward, and if dead men could talk there'd be a few who could attest to that fact, but the brawl at Barco's place didn't concern him. What did was wondering how much he actually had to do with it starting in the first place. He had been sitting there having a drink and listening to the girl singing, like every other man in the room, probably sharing the same thoughts as the others, thoughts about how damn pretty she was. Hair the color of sunrise, and the face of an angel. She had a nice body, too. Her breasts had practically poured out of her dress, which had been molded to the shapely rest of her. And the sight of her long, slender legs, revealed by the provocative slits in her skirt, had made his breath catch in his throat. A fine-looking woman, to be sure.

As he had continued to stare, he had started thinking how she just didn't look like the sort of girl who would be singing in a saloon in front of a bunch of gaping, insulting drunks. Beneath the heavy rouge and lipstick, Ryan had sensed her anxiety and reluctance. He had seen how she held her hands in front of her bosom, as if she was attempting to cover up some of the flesh that was revealed. And she had been squeezing her hands together, so tight that he could see the whites of her knuckles even from where he sat.

He had been wondering what color her eyes were as they swept the room, and that had been when it happened. Her gaze had fallen on him, and all at once it had been as though she'd been hit with a pail of ice water, and he had seen the pure terror flashing in those smoky emerald depths. She had stopped singing, had begun to sway to and fro, staring at him in horror all the while. Then she'd begun to stagger backward, and everyone had leapt to their feet. Ryan hadn't really been able to see what was going on. The fighting had started and he had scrambled to keep from getting his head busted by a flying bottle.

So he had gone down the street to another bar and nursed a drink as he tried to figure out what had provoked such a reaction.

Something else was also needling him, because he had the feeling he'd seen her before—but where? If he had indeed met her at some time or another, it didn't stand to reason he could ever forget one so lovely. He wished he'd had a closer look at her face.

It was getting late. Everyone was starting to leave and head back to their camps. Though most of the soldiers did have a curfew, Ryan was on leave and didn't have to report anywhere for the next few days. He had thought about going home, but had realized there was no reason to go back there. He had no family anymore. His parents had died when he was just a tyke. With no brothers and sisters, he'd been raised by his aunt and uncle, but now they, too, were dead. That left his cousin, Tully Hodgkins, who'd so proudly marched off to war with him as part of the regiment they'd formed in western North Carolina. Gradually, their small group had been divided into other companies. It saddened Ryan to think how Tully had died of dysentery in the first month.

Now Ryan was proudly looking forward to his new assignment with General Pierre Beauregard. Beauregard had been appointed the first brigadier general of the Confederate army and had commanded the troops that took over

Fort Sumter. Ryan was honored to be heading up one of the general's cavalry companies.

One of the bar girls came over to ask if he'd like something else. They were getting ready to close. He said he'd have a shot of her best whiskey, smiling absently and adding, "Might as well end the evening right."

Leaning over—providing a better view down the bodice of her clinging red satin gown—she boldly whispered, "I know a better way to end the evening, Captain, and I've got a real convenient room to do it in upstairs."

Ryan knew her. Viola was her name. He also knew that Ethan, the big gorilla of a bartender, claimed her as his private stock. He'd heard someone say that Ethan's mother had died in Fredericksburg and he'd gone to bury her. No doubt Viola was lonely, but Ryan was no fool. "Thanks, but I've seen one brawl tonight, honey, and I sure as hell don't want to be part of another when Ethan gets back."

She threw back her head and laughed to mask her disappointment. The truth was, Viola would have sneaked him upstairs for free, good-looking as he was. She'd had her eye on him for quite a while. "Well, it's your loss," she told him flippantly. Then she asked, "What happened over at Barco's tonight? They say it was quite a riot. What started it?"

He told her all he knew—the girl stopped singing, and the men got mad.

"Oh, *her!*" Viola snorted. "Yeah, we've heard how Barco brags about how she packs 'em in. Serves him right, after he stole our piano player."

"What do you know about her?"

Viola put her hand on her curvy hip and smirked. "Not much. Her name's Belinda. She came in here lookin' for work and Josh laughed in her face. Said he wasn't hirin' babies, that she was nothin' but trouble. He'll be glad to hear he was right."

"Is she that young? I couldn't tell from all that war paint she was wearing."

"Not so young. Just dumb. Her kind always thinks they're better than anybody else, anyway, and Josh was right when he said she didn't belong here, 'cause she'd just be lookin' down her nose at folks the whole time. I'll bet Barco would agree with him now."

"Do you know where she stays?"

Viola shrugged. "Maybe. What do you want with her?" Before he had a chance to answer, she giggled. "Oh, I get it. You're scared of Ethan, but you figure she'll be ripe for the pickin', bein' in trouble and all. But don't bet on it."

Ryan didn't say anything. He didn't care what she thought.

"I heard Barco put her up. And the reason I know is 'cause I've heard talk about how he's told soldiers who went to him wantin' her favors that she wasn't givin' any out. He also told somebody he'd fixed up his storage room for her, 'cause if she was such a little prude he wasn't giving her a nice room upstairs like the other girls that work for him. You know he tries to compete with Lucy," she added derisively.

Ryan didn't know, didn't care. All he wanted was to find out what had caused the beauteous lady known as Belinda to panic at the mere sight of him.

He paid his bar tab and left, with Viola staring after him in longing.

He took a room at a hotel, where he spent a restless night. The suspicion that he'd seen Belinda before continued to nag at him like a toothache. Perhaps if he saw her up close he'd remember exactly. If he couldn't, maybe she would tell him. Damn it, maybe it was all his imagination. But one thing was certain. He was going to find out.

At first light, he was up and out and heading for Barco's place. A crew was already at work cleaning up the mess. He found Frank Barco at the bar, having a stiff drink to try and ease his misery.

"What do you want, Captain?" he said tonelessly. "We ain't open, and thanks to the little bitch, we may not be open for a month or more."

"*The little bitch...*" Ryan repeated, amused. "Where can I find her?"

Barco pounded his fist on the bar for emphasis as he roared, "She damn well better be on her way out of here. I'm going back there and see when I finish this drink. I knew if I went back there stone sober I might kill her."

Ryan raised an eyebrow. "That bad?"

"That bad!" Barco confirmed, repeating his tale of woe, and how he'd emphasized to Belinda the need to keep the men happy last night. Then, looking at Ryan suspiciously, he asked, "What's your business with her?"

Ryan nodded curtly. "It's just that, Barco. My business."

He went to the rear and found a narrow hallway. There was only one other door besides the one leading to the alley. It had to be her room. He hoped he wasn't too late.

He knocked, waited, hearing the sounds of stirring within and, finally, a soft voice sleepily calling, "Just a minute, Mr. Starkey."

Ryan frowned. Who the hell was Starkey?

Inside, Belinda looked at herself in the cracked mirror on the wall and saw the dark shadows beneath her eyes. It had been a long night, and she hadn't slept at all as she tried to decide what to do. Finally, as the first light of dawn had come through the one tiny window in the storage room, she had reached the conclusion that she could not go away with Bart Starkey. Even if he was legitimate and trustworthy, she'd have no way of knowing—until, perhaps, it was too late. Rather than live in a state of panic till she found out, it was better to remain in Richmond and try to find other work. Surely there were churches, with ladies' aid societies, that would give her temporary shelter.

One thing was certain, she vowed with a stern look at herself in the mirror, she'd take any kind of work, no matter how hard, before ever again working in a saloon.

With head held high, fired with renewed spirit and determination, she unlocked the door and yanked it open. "I'm sorry, but I've decided—"

Cat's eyes!

Green and gold and burnished orange, eyes that almost glowed.

"Oh, dear God!" She choked, swayed, caught the doorframe and held on, knees trembling, legs suddenly weak. It was *him.*

"Dear God," she repeated, her voice a faint whisper.

Ryan was staggered, for now he knew he hadn't been imagining anything. "I think we need to talk," he began, unable to keep the irritation from his tone. "My name is Captain Tanner, and I don't mean you any harm, believe me. I understand your name is Belinda. Have we met before?" Damn it, he silently cursed, he just could not remember ever having seen her before.

Belinda began to rally from her stupor, her instinctive will to survive prompting her to try and close the door, but he moved to block it.

"Woman, what's wrong with you?" He was losing patience. "If I've done something to offend you, I want to know it."

"Get away from me. I'll scream!" she warned.

"Why?" He threw up his hands in a gesture of surrender, but continued to block her from closing the door. "Why would you do that? I told you, I'm not going to hurt you. I just want to know why the sight of me makes you go crazy." He was really starting to get mad, riled by how she was staring at him as if he were some kind of murdering monster.

With a jolt, Belinda realized he actually didn't know who she was, and that it was to her advantage to pretend likewise. "I don't know you," she told him. "So what business do you have coming here at this hour?'' She was able to glare at him with fury, blinking against the fright boiling within her.

''Last night,'' he began, relieved that she seemed to be calming down, though he could feel her hatred, ''you took one look at me and you were paralyzed. With fear. Revulsion. You did the same thing just now, when you opened the door and saw it was me. I want to know why, and I'm not leaving here till I find out.''

Belinda reasoned that she was safe as long as he didn't know who she was. Otherwise, he might kill her to keep her from charging him with rape. And, she thought furiously, he probably had so many women he couldn't remember them all, anyway. Still, she couldn't help wondering why he'd resort to force. He was a handsome man. Extremely so. Looking at him with her terror quelled for the moment, she found his eyes almost beautiful. Fringed with thick lashes, they were mesmerizing. He had a nice set to his jaw, too. Firm. Strong. And he had a good nose. Roman, some people called the shape. His hair, a soft chestnut brown, barely touched the collar of his uniform, and he had a neatly trimmed mustache that gave him an authoritative air. But even if he was good-looking, she knew him for the brutal beast he was, and she had to clench her hands together to keep from raking her nails down his face.

Taking a deep breath to firm her resolve, she said, ''I thought you were someone else. I was mistaken. I'm sorry.''

Ryan relaxed, but only a little, for he could still see she was angry and upset. ''Well, I'm glad it's not me,'' he said. Then he smiled. ''But I can't help wondering what anyone did to upset you so.''

''That's none of your concern,'' Belinda stated curtly. ''Now, if you'll get out of my way, I'd like to close the door.''

''Would you mind telling me where you're from?'' Ryan asked. After all, she might have him mixed up with someone else, but he still had the strange feeling they'd met before.

"Yes, I do mind. That is also none of your business." *Oh, Lord*, she thought, heart pounding with fury, *I do hate him so....*

Ryan wasn't giving up. Maybe he couldn't place her, but he was certain of one thing—she was the loveliest girl he'd ever seen, and he wanted to get to know her better. Trying to put her at ease, he offered, "Look, we got off on the wrong foot, and though it wasn't my fault, I'd like to make amends for what happened last night. I understand you've lost your job and Barco ordered you to leave. Let me buy you some breakfast, and we can talk, and maybe I can help you find a place to stay."

"No!" She all but screamed the word at him, attempting to push the door shut, but he held his ground. "I don't want anything to do with you! Now this is your last warning! Get out of here, or I'm going to scream!"

He shook his head. "Barco would love an excuse to come back here, Belinda. He's at the bar now, having a drink, in hopes it'll keep him from killing you. He's pretty hot. I'd leave him alone if I were you."

"Will you leave me alone?" Tears stung her eyes, and she blinked furiously, not wanting him to think her weak. "What do you want from me?"

"Friendship," he replied in his humblest tone. "I think you're beautiful, and I hate to see you in trouble. I want to help."

"You've done enough—" She caught herself and bit her lip. She could not give herself away. "Please," she begged him. "Just go."

"I'm Captain Ryan Tanner. I'm from North Carolina," he volunteered. "The western part. A little town called Franklin. They mine for gems there, rubies, garnets—"

"I don't care!" she screeched, silently crying, of course he was from North Carolina, the bastard! That's where he had raped her, along with those other two monsters, and if he didn't go away and leave her alone she would give herself away, because it was all she could do to keep from leaping at his throat!

This time, Ryan shook his head in frustration. Maybe the girl was deranged. Sad, for one so lovely, but those things happened. "All right," he said finally. "I guess it's no use. But I wish—"

As he stepped back, Belinda leapt at the chance to slam the door and throw the bolt in place.

With a sigh of finality, he walked away.

Belinda pressed her ear against the door, listening till she heard his retreating footsteps. For the moment she was safe, but if—or when—he remembered who she was, no doubt he'd come after her.

And she was taking no chances.

She knew she looked a fright, but there was no time to worry about that now. Grabbing up the small satchel containing her few belongings, she decided to leave at once. She could go out the back door, to the alley, in case Captain Tanner was lingering in the saloon. She'd find a church somewhere, as fast as possible, and she wouldn't venture out of it for a long, long time. Surely even if he did look for her, sooner or later he'd have to give up, go back to the fighting, and she felt no guilt at the hope that he would die a horrible death.

She froze once more at the sound of another knock on the door. But this time the sound was hesitant, almost apologetic, and just as her heart leapt to her throat in apprehension a gentle voice called out, "Miss Coulter? It's Bart Starkey. I hope you've changed your mind—"

"I have," she snapped. Then, suddenly, she realized there was no need to run and hide in Richmond—not when she could quickly get out of town. And, by God, she'd rather be with a perfect stranger than risk encountering a known rapist.

She unbolted the door and flung it open. "I'm going with you," she announced breathlessly.

"Why—why, that's wonderful," Bart stammered, astonished but happy. "I swear," he assured her, "I'll make you the American Nightingale."

She picked up her bag and handed it to him. "I'll worry about that later, Mr. Starkey. Right now, I just want to put some distance between me and Richmond."

With a bewildered shake of his head, Bart hurried after her.

Chapter Three

Bart was apologetically explaining to Belinda that it had never been his intention to leave Richmond on such short notice. "First, we need to get you fixed up with some decent clothes, 'cause frankly you're a sight." He swept her tattered muslin dress with a disdainful glance.

"Then can we leave?" she asked anxiously. He had rented a room for her at one of the nicer hotels, and they were having breakfast in the dining room. She hadn't realized how hungry she was till the platter of fluffy scrambled eggs and thick slices of country ham was placed in front of her.

Bart explained that he'd like to stage a concert in Richmond to introduce her, reminding her that there was, after all, a war going on. It was not going to be easy to plan a successful tour, but he was determined to try, and he needed her cooperation. "I get the feeling you're scared of somebody," he said with eyes narrowed thoughtfully. "Something happened last night. Don't know what it was. But it's got you as jumpy as chickens in a henhouse when a fox is creeping around outside. If we're going to work together, I think you ought to tell me what's going on. You aren't running from the law, are you?"

"No, no, nothing like that." She shook her head firmly, then stared at him in contemplation, trying to decide how much to tell him. He did have a right to know something, but not everything, for God's sake. She had no intention of telling him the whole story.

"There's a man," she began hesitantly, "who frightens me, because I knew him a long time ago and he can be terribly mean. I saw him last night in the saloon, and it unnerved me so bad I was almost paralyzed. That's why I want to get out of Richmond as quick as possible."

"What's his name?"

She told him.

"I'll see what I can find out. Maybe he's not around anymore. All these soldiers and officers come and go. None of them are around very long, so I don't want you to worry, because we do need to stay here a little while, at least long enough to have you sing in a decent place.

"Besides—" he leaned over to pat her hand in an almost fatherly gesture of comfort "—I'm not going to let anything happen to you, dear. You can be sure of that."

Belinda hoped he was right, because, for the time being, she had no other choice.

Over the following week, Bart Starkey directed a complete transformation for Belinda. He had her fitted with a small wardrobe of gowns, lovely but demure in style. He had a hairdresser create an elegant coiffure for her flaming red tresses.

When it was all done, Belinda was stunned and hardly able to recognize herself. With her hair caught up at her crown, ringlets dangling about her shoulders, and with the elegance of the gowns he'd had made for her, she looked nothing like the drab little mountain girl of the past. If Captain Tanner were to see her, she realized with relief, he'd never recognize her from the Wild Dog Saloon.

Bart was ecstatic at the results, and he was even more pleased when he was able to arrange for her to sing at a tea dance hosted by one of Richmond's social leaders, Mrs. Gertrina Tyson. Afterward, however, he was disgruntled when Mrs. Tyson did not share his enthusiasm over Belinda's future success and declined to assist him in arranging a large concert.

"She has a lovely voice, Mr. Starkey, but I'm afraid I don't share your opinion of her ability to compete with the talent of Miss Jenny Lind. I had the pleasure of hearing Miss Lind when she performed in Vienna several years ago, and by comparison, your protégé will shine only in a church choir."

Bart had argued, even offering to donate half the proceeds of a concert to the Confederate cause, but Mrs. Tyson declined to be involved. Airily she explained that, due to her position in Richmond society, she could not lightly endorse anyone.

"My suggestion to you," she advised with a patronizing air, "if you're so insistent on exploiting Miss Coulter's talent, is to travel about and entertain our brave troops. It would be a charitable, worthwhile cause, and I'm sure the soldiers would give you token compensation."

Discouraged but not defeated, Bart set out to do just that. Belinda, surprisingly, did not seem to mind. He had noticed in the past days, since her transformation, that she seemed more poised and self-assured. He did not tell her of Mrs. Tyson's rebuff, not wanting to hurt her feelings, but he found himself wondering whether Belinda would truly care. More and more, as they spent time together, she seemed to be concerning herself with the war.

"Nothing for a lady to fret about," he advised her irritably one evening during dinner. He had spent the day at the Confederate headquarters, asking for assistance in mapping the safest route for their tour, and he wanted to tell her about it. She, however, had gotten hold of a copy of the *New York Times,* dated June 26, that had found its way to the hotel lobby. An article headlined "Forward to Richmond!" had her dander up, and that was all she was interested in talking about.

"They're saying the Rebel Congress mustn't be allowed to meet here next month, and Richmond is to be taken over by the Union army by the twentieth of July. Do they really think they can charge right in here from Washington?''

Wearily he responded, ''I suppose they think they can, my dear, or else they wouldn't have started the war in the first place, would they?''

She wasn't listening to him. She scanned the paper, then cried irately, ''And listen to this. Tennessee has already voted to join the Confederacy, but Kentucky is trying to stay neutral. The Yankees are there now, recruiting for volunteers—''

Bart reached across the table to rudely snatch the paper away and toss it to the floor. As she stared at him in astonishment, he curtly apologized. ''I'm sorry to have to do that, but I'm trying to talk to you about your future, Belinda.''

Indignant, she snapped, ''My future, as well as yours and that of every other Southerner, depends on the outcome of the war.''

''Maybe. But you can't do anything about it, and neither can I. So why worry about it? Just concern yourself with getting ready to leave by the end of the week. I'll have our wagon ready, with all the supplies we need.''

She supposed he was right. ''So where are we going?''

''We'll travel around Virginia and try to stay out of dangerous places where there's liable to be fighting. I figure by fall you'll be so well-known, Richmond's social leaders will be after you to sing at every event this winter. They'll be looking to get some entertainment going during the cold-weather months, when the fighting is sure to slow down.''

''It'd suit me fine if we could stay out of Richmond.'' Thinking about Captain Tanner, she shuddered involuntarily.

Bart saw her shudder and knew what she was thinking. ''I checked on that officer who has you so spooked.''

''And?'' she prodded, eyebrows lifting. ''Go on.''

''He's left town. You've got nothing to worry about. And what I can't figure is why you'd be afraid of him, anyway. From what I was able to learn, he's fast getting the reputation of one of the best damn cavalry soldiers in the whole Confederate army. I heard General Beauregard specifically asked for his assignment to his army. They say he's not only a fine horseman and marksman, but he's also invaluable when it comes to keeping the horses up. Seems he has some experience in blacksmithing, so he's able to keep them properly shod, which is real important. Didn't hear anything bad about him at all," Bart went on. "He's from western North Carolina. Mountain boy. So—"

"I don't care about any of that," Belinda snapped, rage washing over her once again at the thought of what he'd done to her. "I just want to make sure I never see him again."

"Well, for your sake and his," Bart said, dismissing the subject, "I hope you don't, either."

They were well received at the first camp they went to, a few miles north of Richmond. The soldiers cheered when Belinda stepped out of the wagon wearing a dress of green silk, soft and flowing, with no hoops. She took Bart's hand, and he led the way to a little platform that had been hastily constructed especially for her.

"Anybody here got a guitar that can play for her?" Bart flashed the eager crowd a coaxing grin.

A tall, skinny man came forward, carrying a guitar. With a polite nod for Belinda, he introduced himself as Seth Cochran and said he'd be glad to do the best he could. Belinda gratefully conferred with him in private a few moments about what she wanted to do. Then, with him settled at her feet, she began.

"Dixie" was her first choice, and the soldiers went wild, clapping and stamping their feet. A few got up to dance a jig. Things quieted down as she offered the sad refrains of "Annie Laurie" and "Juanita."

She'd planned to sing only a few songs, but the men sat mesmerized, obviously enjoying her performance and very grateful for the evening's entertainment, so she continued.

Finally Bart noticed a few of them drifting away, weary from the day's drilling. He knew that as the crowd thinned, so would the contributions. He took off his hat, interrupting Belinda to shout out a reminder that they had traveling expenses, and while they weren't looking to make a profit, only wanting to do their part to ease the soldiers' discomfort, any amount donated would be greatly appreciated.

Belinda hated having to beg, and she watched with remorse as Bart moved through the group.

Afterward, despite what he'd collected, Bart was disappointed. "Not near as much as what I'd hoped to get," he grumbled. "They got money for gambling and whiskey. I know for a fact there's some prostitutes slipping in and out of here, and they don't come cheap. Least they could do is pay to hear a lovely songbird like you. We'll do better the next place we go."

Belinda didn't share his optimism. To the men, spending money playing cards, drinking and sharing the company of immoral women was more appealing than listening to her. Unlike Bart, however, she really wasn't upset. After all, they had plenty to eat. The officers were nice about inviting them to dine with them. They had the wagon for shelter. What more did they really need? Besides, she enjoyed what she was doing, and even if the soldiers didn't give as much as Bart wanted them to, they enjoyed her. She knew it because she could see it in their eyes, even when they weren't clapping and cheering.

For the first two weeks of July, Bart stayed within a comfortable distance of Richmond. He said he wanted to be close enough to retreat back to the city should heavy fighting break out, and he also wanted to be close enough for word to filter back of what a wonderful performance Belinda was capable of giving. Some of the ladies from Richmond's churches ventured out to visit the sick when they were close enough, and Bart always made sure he introduced Belinda and expounded on how the men adored her.

Word was spreading, so they were eagerly received everywhere they went.

"Made more money with freaks," Bart grumbled one night as he counted the money he had just collected. "Know what we got here? Fifty. Fifty lousy dollars."

Belinda watched him with quiet anger. Strange how she'd been leery of his offer merely because he was a man. That, she had come to realize, should be the least of her worries. What she had not known about, could not have known about, till after the experience of being with him over a period of weeks, was his greed. She was coming to realize that money was all that mattered to him. She was disappointed, but she told herself there was nothing to be done as long as the war was on, and she should be grateful for food and shelter. And, she cheerfully reminded herself, maybe she didn't have the talent of Miss Jenny Lind, but the soldiers didn't care. They made her feel appreciated, and, in turn, she was glad to bring a little sunshine into their woeful lives.

It bothered her when Bart started joining the soldiers in their nightly poker games. After her performance, she'd retire to the covered wagon, where she slept. Usually Bart bedded down on the ground beneath. Then, she noticed, he began to hang back with the men. Finally, when she heard him stumbling in drunk one night, she knew he was into something. Still, she didn't realize how serious it was till the morning he confessed he'd lost the previous night's donations gambling.

Belinda admonished him, but it was useless. Then, when he won a huge amount at the next camp, the gambling fever took hold, and suddenly he was more interested in cards than their little traveling road show. He'd win big and lose big, and instead of following the safest route of travel, he began to head in the direction of camps said to have the biggest gambling stakes.

He led them into the Shenandoah Valley. He'd been winning steadily, and he'd heard of a high-stakes game among

Brigadier General Joseph Johnston's army of Virginia volunteers.

"It's not my fault things didn't turn out like I'd planned," he said, attempting to pacify Belinda when she voiced her disapproval. "Folks just aren't interested in our kind of entertainment, what with the war and all.

"Even if you do sound like Miss Jenny Lind," he added with a consoling smile and wink.

Belinda had lost all her illusions, and had had to face the reality that her voice was only mediocre. Still, as long as the soldiers seemed to like her, she figured she might as well tag along with Bart. Where else did she have to go, anyway?

It was late in the day when they rolled into General Johnston's camp, and it was still blistering hot. The sun's intense rays rolled like restless waves across the parched valley, and not a breeze was stirring.

Pickets directed them to a grove beside a small creek where they were to wait for permission to go any farther. Tents spread in all directions. Campfires were burning and the air was pungent with the smell of coffee and frying bacon.

"Stay put," Bart told her, eagerly jumping to the ground. His excitement at the evening ahead was evidenced by his springy steps as he followed the picket toward a tent with a huge Confederate flag flying above it. That would be the commanding officer's quarters, and he would be the one to give consent for the performance.

Belinda took off her bonnet and began to fan herself. Every stitch she had on was soaked with perspiration, and the sound of the smoothly undulating creek made her long for a bath. Weariness played through her bones, and she wondered whether she'd be able to sing a note without benefit of a short nap beforehand.

She glanced about to familiarize herself with the surroundings, uneasy about being left alone, even though soldiers were within shouting distance. One of the pickets they'd met along the way had warned that skirmishes were going on all over the place and they needed to be very careful. He'd even told Bart he should settle in with General Johnston's army for a while. Rumors were flying of a big battle coming.

Little did the picket know, Belinda had sardonically mused, that Bart had already made up his mind to do just that. And not because of worries about fighting. Gambling was all he cared about these days, and she was starting to suspect that he'd only used her as a ruse to get into the camps in the first place.

Suddenly she heard rustling in the bushes down by the creek, and what sounded like an anguished moan. Leaning down from the buckboard, she strained to see into the clumps of weeds and shrubs, timorously calling, "Is someone there?" Dear Lord, she thought with a flash of terror, a bushwhacker could be about. Someone had definitely been hurt.

She was about to scream for help when she saw him—a man in a gray uniform lying on the ground. He was looking up at her with fearful eyes. "Don't call nobody, lady, please. I don't want anybody to see me like this," he pleaded in a hoarse whisper.

"But you're hurt..." Already she was scrambling down from the wagon.

"No, please, just leave me alone. I told you, lady, I don't want nobody to see me. Go away...."

Concealed by the wagon, she ignored the briars tugging at her skirt as she made her way to kneel beside him. She noted at once the ashen pallor of his young-looking face, saw he was hardly more than a boy.

"Lady, just go away," he continued to beg raggedly.

"Where are you hurt—?" She gasped and winced at both the sight and the smell of his wound. He had torn open his right trouser leg, and pus was oozing from the swollen, blackened flesh just below the knee. "Were you shot?" she asked sharply when she could trust her voice enough to speak above the rising nausea.

"Cut myself on my own bayonet about five days ago." He managed to choke out the embarrassed explanation. "Got drunk and passed out. It was propped on a rock, and I stumbled and fell on it."

"But what are you doing here? Why haven't you been to the hospital tent for treatment?"

"Thought it was gonna be okay, but then it started gettin' worse, and I wasn't about to let them butchers hack my leg off. That's all they do, you know, when gangrene sets in. Cut it off. And hell, I'd rather lay here and die than spend the rest of my life hobblin' around on a stump leg." His angry resolution seemed to give him momentary strength. He looked her straight in the eye and warned, "And don't you get no notions about tellin' 'em where I am, either."

"How long have you been hiding here?"

"Since last night. It started gettin' real bad then. Boys in my tent started grumblin' about the smell. I just got up and left after they went to sleep. Guess by now I'm a deserter." He grinned wryly, then grimaced with pain.

Belinda pressed her fingertips to his forehead. It felt clammy, but not hot—a good sign there was not yet fever. With a quick glance over her shoulder to make sure no one was coming, she offered, "Will you let me help you?"

"You?" he echoed in a wondering tone. "What do you know about doctorin', lady?"

She told him how she'd once spent a summer tagging after old Doc Jasper, back home in the Blue Ridge Mountains of North Carolina. "His wife usually went with him when he made his rounds, but her sister in Waynesville was real sick, and she went to take care of her.

"I learned a lot from him," Belinda went on, "and I also learned a lot of remedies from my sister, too. And the first thing we need to do is get that wound cleaned out—"

"I wash it in the creek. That's why I'm layin' here. I can lay it in the creek and let the cold water run over it. And nobody sees me here 'cause there's a big log I can crawl into if somebody comes."

"You weren't scared of me," she pointed out.

He frowned. "I was hurtin' real bad right when I heard your wagon. Couldn't move too fast."

She knew he was in more pain than he cared to admit, but she didn't press him. "Well, will you let me take care of you?" she repeated, adding bluntly, "If you don't do something, you're going to die, you know."

"And you won't tell nobody?"

"Not a soul."

The tense muscles of his face slowly relaxed. "What are you doin' out here, anyhow?"

She told him, teasing that he would miss her performance, but promising to get back to him as quickly as possible. "Now I suggest you scramble in that log, if you're determined to keep hiding, and I'd like for you to keep that leg out of the creek for a while.

"By the way," she softly asked, "What's your name, soldier?"

"Private Orlie Potts," he replied with a shy smile. "What's yours?"

"Belinda Coulter." She liked him already. He had red hair just like her own, and a sprinkling of freckles across his nose, and she caught herself thinking how if she ever had a son she'd want him to look just like Orlie. Only, she'd never have a son, or a daughter, because she'd never again have anything to do with a man. Not after Harmon, and then Captain Tanner and those other bastards....

She shook her head briskly to dispel the terrible images, then hurried back to the wagon.

She did not have to wait long for Bart to return, eager to share the good news of General Beauregard's willingness to have her perform. A soldier was with him to lead the way just upstream, where he said they could camp, explaining that the General thought Belinda should have as much privacy as possible. She was grateful for that, and also glad to be close to Orlie.

The performance went well, and Belinda acknowledged the rousing applause by singing three encores. By the time she had finished, Bart was nowhere to be seen. The young soldier who had eagerly accompanied her with his guitar said he'd seen Bart heading for the tent where the poker players gathered. Good, she thought. He was out of the way, would not be bedding down beneath the wagon till the wee hours.

Invited, as usual, to join the officers for supper, she declined, saying she was tired. When her tin plate of boiled beans was brought to her, she surprised the corporal who delivered it by asking for a slab of salt pork. "I just can't eat beans without salt pork," she demurely explained with a sweet smile, and he eagerly obliged.

Rushing back to the wagon after singing, Belinda took the beans and the salt pork and made her way down the side of the creek. No sentries were posted this close to the center of the camp, so she was not observed scurrying along in the shadows.

Orlie had not moved. In the faint light of the quarter moon, she could see him. When she whispered his name, his eyes flashed open. At first he was startled, but grinned with recognition. "You did come back. I thought you was just foolin'...."

"Why would I fool about a thing like that? I don't want you to lose that leg, either, soldier." She helped him to sit up and lean back against the log. Handing him the plate of food, she watched as he ate every bite. Taking a deep breath, she told him, "Now you've got to let me clean that wound. I'm going to pack it in salt pork to draw out the poison.

"And don't argue," she warned when he made noises of protest. "I'm trying to save your life."

He pressed his hands against his face to stifle the sound of his soft moans. Belinda worked fast, so as not to prolong his suffering. When the gash was cleaned as best it could be, she packed salt pork into the gaping hole, securing it with strips of cloth torn from the bottom of her petticoat. "I'll be back tomorrow around noon to change that. You just lay still and rest till then."

He thanked her, and she hurried back to the wagon, praying the remedy would work as it had that summer so long ago when Doc Jasper had treated Willie Bolton's arm. Willie had cut himself falling, and it had looked for a time as if Doc would have to amputate, but the salt pork had pulled him through. She prayed Orlie would be as fortunate.

The next morning, Bart was so happy to tell of his winnings of the night before that he wasn't the least concerned over the news spreading through the camp like wildfire that they were moving out.

"To where?" Belinda was desperate to know. "Bart, we can't go with them. They're soldiers going into battle. We're civilians."

"There's no place to run to," he said with a shrug. "It would be real dangerous to try to make it to Richmond on our own, with bushwhackers all around. Besides, you can cheer up the boys with your singing. They like you."

Belinda was worried about Orlie. He'd never forgive her if she gave away his hiding place and the surgeons decided to remove his leg. She'd just have to talk them into giving the salt pork time to do its job.

Telling Bart she was going for a walk, she went to where she'd left Orlie. No one was watching, because everyone had gathered outside General Beauregard's tent, awaiting orders which were said to be imminent.

With a gasp of surprise, she saw Orlie sitting up. He actually had color in his face. "You're better!" she cried jubilantly.

He pointed to the wound. He had unwrapped the bandages, and Belinda could see how white the flesh of his leg was. She marveled how the salt pork had turned green as it drew out the deadly poison. "Even the swelling is goin' down," he told her triumphantly. "And it don't hurt so much now."

She rushed to verify that, indeed, the pork had done its job. "But only because we treated it in time. Another day and it would've been too late. You're going to be fine now, but we need to get you to the doctors so they can bandage it proper.

"I hear you all are moving out," she added, "but I don't have any idea where you're headed."

"I do," he said grimly, his previous expression of joy turning to a look of dread and dismay. "Two of the officers walked by here late last night. They didn't know I was here, so they talked freely. I heard 'em say we're going to Manassas Junction to try and meet up with Johnston before McDowell's army wipes 'em out.

"We're going into battle, lady," he declared solemnly. Then he added, with a lopsided grin, "But I figure it's a blessing having you with us. If you can work miracles with salt pork in a creek, think what you can do in a hospital."

At that ludicrous idea, Belinda laughed. "I'm a singer, Orlie, not a nurse."

"Well, I ain't heard you sing, so I can't say you're any good. But I have seen what you did with my leg, and a doctor couldn't of done no better. I think you should stick with your nursin'."

Belinda scoffed at the thought. "All I want, soldier, is to get back to Richmond and stay there. I don't want any part of this war."

"You ain't got no choice. Ain't no Southerner got a choice no more. We're all a part of it now."

Soberly and sadly, Belinda could only agree.

Chapter Four

The Union general, Irvin McDowell, and his Army of the Potomac had moved out of the defenses of Washington and were on the move toward the Confederates at Manassas Junction. Morale was high—till they arrived and found nothing there.

They had expected to encounter Beauregard and achieve victory with the same ease with which McClellan had taken control of the western part of the state. McDowell was quick to realize the strategy of the Rebels; they had pulled back to the banks of the stream called Bull Run, hoping he would force his way through to Manassas, which would mean facing strong opposition. Compounding his woes was the harsh fact that in a few days he was going to lose a third of his force. Nearly ten thousand of his men had enlisted for only ninety days, and that time was about to expire. Consequently, it was imperative to achieve his goal without delay, and when a scout reported an unguarded ford across the Bull Run at a place called Sudeley Springs, he immediately moved to get into position to outflank the Confederates.

Meanwhile, General Johnston had been ordered to reach Beauregard as soon as possible. The element of surprise would be on their side, because Johnston was thought to still be encamped in the valley.

"They're leaving the sick and wounded behind," Belinda pointed out as Bart got the wagon ready to leave. "Why can't we stay here, too?"

"And do what?" he challenged. "Not me. This war is going to be over real soon, and I'm taking advantage of every hand dealt.

"I won big," he went on to boast, clearly intoxicated by the thrill of it all. "These men play for high stakes, not the small pots in saloons. A few more nights like last night, and maybe we'll have the money we need to head for Europe and have you sing at all the big places, like Paris, London, Vienna—"

"Bart, you aren't serious, and you know it," Belinda accused irately. "I think all along you were scheming to get into these camps to gamble with the soldiers. You never intended to make me another Jenny Lind, and I should've been smart enough to realize I don't have her talent, anyway. But I was desperate, and you knew it and took advantage of me."

With a scowl, he gave the horse's harness one last tug, then whirled on her to cry heatedly, "That's not so. In the beginning, I really thought we had a chance, but I don't care what you say, anyhow. Now I'm going with these men. There's nearly nine thousand of them, and I know I'll be safe. You stay here if you want, but I'll be back in Richmond within a week, rolling in money. Where will *you* be?" he finished with a sneer.

Dismally Belinda was again forced to acknowledge she had no choice, but this time, she fervently vowed, when she got to Richmond, she'd stay there. Looking back, she was ashamed to have panicked over the unexpected appearance of one of her attackers. What she should have done instead was pretend not to know him and be wary.

It was nearly four in the morning when the drums of the infantry and the trumpets of the cavalry sounded the general. The tent city collapsed as if at the stroke of a single hand, and soldiers rushed to roll and pack the canvases and stow them in the supply wagons. Water details moved back and forth from the creek. Companies formed as assembly blew, the voices of thousands of men ringing out in the blue-black stillness, answering roll call. The crisp voices of officers barked commands as formations appeared. Excitement and tension rippled across the land.

Belinda did not take exception to Bart lining up the wagon behind the ambulances and supply carts. She did, however, wonder why they were being allowed to go along with the troops. It didn't make sense that anyone should have entertainment on their minds. She said as much to Bart, who merely grunted and stared straight ahead, now and then popping the reins across the lumbering horse's rump lest they fall behind. They were last in line, she noted, except for the soldiers keeping watch at the rear.

Doggedly they moved all day long, the sun relentlessly beating down. They did not stop till absolute darkness fell. Hasty rations were prepared, and then everyone collapsed in weariness. Nothing was said about Belinda singing, and she didn't care, because she, too, was exhausted.

The next morning, they set out again. Now and then soldiers would ride up alongside Bart's wagon to chat as they moved, always falling in on Belinda's side. She was polite but aloof, for if there was one thing she could be sure of in her chaotic world, it was that she wanted nothing to do with men in a personal way.

It was midday when Bart glanced up to see a soldier approaching and grumbled under his breath, "Him again. Corporal Hewitt. How many times has he come by today? Three?"

"He's in charge of lining up the supply wagons," Belinda reminded him, greeting Corporal Hewitt with a polite smile.

He tipped his cap, slowing his horse's gait. "We're going to be setting up operations soon. I'm putting you folks with the supply wagons. I understand you'll be working at the mess tent, Miss Coulter."

It was the first she'd heard about it, and when Bart would not meet her questioning gaze, she realized he'd taken the liberty of volunteering her services. Now she knew why they'd been allowed to come along. "I suppose I am, Corporal" was all she could say.

"It'll be nice to have a woman's touch, though I don't imagine anybody will be thinkin' about food once the fightin' starts."

Bart spoke up. "And when do you reckon that'll be? Are we far from the battlefield now? I don't hear anything."

At that, the corporal chuckled. "And I hope you don't till we get there, and then I hope all hell breaks loose." When he saw Belinda's worried look, he attempted to soothe her fears. "You'll be safe back here. They always put hospitals out of reach of the artillery, and even them Yankee varmints got a little respect for the wounded. It's the safest place for you."

"The safest place would be back in Richmond, which is where I intend to go as soon as possible." Suddenly she was moved to ask, "What about you, Corporal? Are you scared?"

He didn't hesitate. "I'd be lying if I said I wasn't, but if I turn coward and run, I hope my own men will shoot me in the back."

"Have you been in battle before?"

"A couple of skirmishes. And I have to say, once I fired that first shot, I was like a new man. Wasn't worried a bit for myself, even when the soldier next to me fell dead. And if I thought at all with them minié balls flying, it was about getting revenge. I think by the time I got through the showers of bursting shells, my soul was dead to everything except killing the damn Yankees who'd dared invade us to start with."

Belinda was moved by how open he was with his feelings, but Bart gave a bored sniff and asked where the card tent would be when they bedded down for the night.

Corporal Hewitt laughed again. "Gambling will be the last thing on anybody's mind tonight except yours, Mr. Starkey. There are all kinds of preparations to be made, like cleaning guns and handing out ammunition, and there'll be lots of prayer meetings and talks with the parson, I'm sure.

"You'll even be spared having to sing to us, Miss Coulter." He swept her with an admiring gaze, thinking again how truly beautiful she was. "Though I hope to hear you again, real soon."

He rode away, and Belinda turned a deaf ear to Bart's annoyed muttering about the boring evening ahead.

While the wagons were directed to settle beneath a grove of spreading oaks, the troops marched farther on before stopping for the night. The only tents that were set up were for the hospital—it was likely to be needed—for the soldiers would be called to muster before daylight. Tonight they would sleep on the ground, out in the open.

The order was given that there be no fires for the enemy to see. Supper would be cold drap dumplings and hard, stringy beef left from supper the night before. Belinda helped pass out the rations, noting the men were too preoccupied with their anxieties over the pending battle to care what they were given.

She was helping clean up when a soldier came with orders for her to report to the hospital. Curious, she hurried to the area, which was situated a good ways from where the troops had settled in.

Directed inside a smaller tent, she found herself standing before a crude desk and staring down into the condemning eyes of a man who introduced himself as Dr. Wilkins, the brigade's senior surgeon. "I'll get right to the point, Miss Coulter," he brusquely began. "I understand you treated one of our soldiers, a Private Orlie Potts."

"That's right," she said. Then she asked anxiously, "Is he all right? He stayed behind with the other wounded—"

"Yes, yes, he did." He waved his hand for silence. "What I want to know," he demanded tersely, "is what made you think you had the right to administer treatment? Particularly with some ridiculous folk remedy—"

"That folk remedy," she hotly interjected, "saved his leg. The salt pork drew out the poison. It doesn't always work. I was taught it all depends on the depth of infection, but this time it did, and Orlie Potts still has his leg. As for what gave me the right to help him," she rushed on, not about to give him time to speak till she'd had her say, "I was trying to save his life. I found him in that ditch, and he'd made up his mind to die rather than have his leg cut off, which is what you or one of the other surgeons would have done, and you know it."

"Which is not for you to criticize!" he roared, standing and slamming his palms on his desk. "I won't have you playing witch doctor with our men, understand? Now, if you want to work in the hospital tent, there are plenty of chores to be done—changing bandages, cleaning wounds— but you will be supervised. You will not take matters into your own hands."

"Wait a minute," Belinda protested. "I never said I wanted to work in the hospital. I'm a singer. I'm here to entertain. Didn't you see my performance a few nights ago?"

He snickered. "A *singer?*" He dismissed her with a curt nod and sat down again. "Get out of here. I only called you in to tell you what is and isn't expected from a nurse, since Potts raved to anyone who'd listen how wonderful you are. I should've known you were just a meddler, like those simpering women who are always visiting the hospital, only to turn away with the vapors at sights and smells they can't tolerate. Out with you, now," he repeated.

Belinda was livid with indignant rage. "Wait a minute. I'd never faint over something like that. I worked with a doctor one summer back home, and—"

"Back home? Back home *where?* I believe someone said the North Carolina mountains? A backwoods doctor, Miss Coulter? I'm afraid I'm not impressed. Doctors who settle in primitive areas *have* to rely on folk medicine, handed down by Indians and the like. They have no exposure to the latest findings, and—"

"Why, you arrogant, pompous fool!" Her brows lifted over widened eyes. "I'll have you know I'm not impressed that you'd chop off a young boy's leg rather than try other remedies in hopes of a cure."

"We're at war, Miss Coulter. We can't wait and see what happens. We have to work fast and make room for other patients."

"Orlie didn't get injured in battle. And I didn't notice any emergencies when you all were camped back in the valley."

"I don't have time for this." He called out to the guard posted outside his tent, who promptly appeared to accept his order. "Take Miss Coulter back to the supply wagons . . . where she belongs," he scornfully added.

Belinda was beside herself. She shrugged away the guard's guiding hand and rushed out.

Bart was nowhere around—probably, she decided, trying to get a game going somewhere, despite the air of tension in the camp. It was twilight, and all around preparations for battle were under way.

She was still fuming a short while later, when Corporal Hewitt stopped by to ask whether there was anything she needed. "You're very kind," she told him. "But the only thing anyone could do for me now is get me out of here. Frankly, I never thought I'd wind up in the middle of a war."

He seemed to share her anxiety. "It looks like the first really big battle, for sure. They're handing out ammunition now, between forty and sixty rounds to each man. You know anything about guns?"

"Never had a reason to."

"We've got muzzle-loaders, and one round consists of a ball and enough powder for shot." He reached for the leather container hanging from his belt and opened it to take one out. "This is a round—lead and powder wrapped in a piece of paper. The ball's at one end, powder behind, twisted to keep the powder in place. To fire, you bite off the twisted end, so's the powder will explode from the spark when the trigger's pulled. All you got to do is drop the cartridge in the muzzle, ram in a piece of wadding, and then—'' he gave Belinda a wide grin ''—you can send a Yankee straight to hell.''

Belinda shuddered involuntarily, murmuring, ''It's all so senseless, so needless.''

''They started it.'' He ground out the accusation stormily. ''And we're going to finish it.'' Then he changed the subject. ''Are you going to help out at the hospital? I heard you were over there. I'm afraid they're going to need all they can get.''

''If called on,'' she murmured, hoping all the while she wouldn't be, not if it meant working for that dreadful Dr. Wilkins.

He held out his arm. ''Let's go for a walk. You look awful unhappy, Miss Coulter. Maybe it'll get your mind off things.''

She doubted it, but she supposed anything was better than just sitting in the back of the wagon, watching the soldiers and morosely wondering which ones would be dead by this time tomorrow. And besides, she reminded herself, it was good to be in the company of a gentleman, to be forced to remember that all men were not like Captain Tanner and his savage comrades.

Many of the soldiers, she observed, were busy writing letters, probably vowing love for their families on what might be their last night on earth. Some were intently reading their Bibles, while others sat with hands folded and heads bowed, obviously in fervent prayer. A few sat with jaws full of tobacco, staring ahead, lost in reverie. With everyone preoccupied with their own thoughts, not a one glanced at Belinda as she passed.

When they came upon a company being addressed by an officer, Corporal Hewitt suggested they turn back, but Belinda resisted. While she was secretly horrified by all that was going on around her, she felt compelled to witness everything. These were, after all, her fellow countrymen, and, like it or not, she was now a part of the conflict.

The officer was instructing, "Don't shoot till you're within good musket range. Fire deliberately. *Aim,* damn it," he told them fiercely. "Don't panic and shoot wild. Save your ammunition. And aim low and remember it's better to wound a man than kill him, because they've got to be taken off the field by others, who make good targets if a cease-fire hasn't been called by both sides. Try to pick off the officers—theirs, not ours. Try for the ones on horses. Remember to stay in your ranks, and don't huddle together if the firing gets heavy. When you're ordered to charge, make haste and *go....*" He struck the air with his fist for emphasis.

Corporal Hewitt gave Belinda's hand a tug and whispered, "Don't you think you'd like to go back now?"

She shook her head, intent on listening.

The officer went on to point out that they stood less chance of getting killed if they kept moving forward. "...even if your objective is a battery, don't panic. Artillery is never as deadly as it seems like it is. The closer you get up on it, the less its power to destroy."

He went on to command that under no circumstances should they pause to plunder the dead or retrieve any spoils. "Battles have been lost by this temptation.

"And above all—" he raised his voice "—don't heed the calls for help from your wounded comrades, no matter how tempted. The best thing you can do for them is drive the enemy back and clear the field."

He finished by curtly reminding them that straggling would be punished severely and cowards would be shot. "Now go," he brusquely finished. "And try and get some rest. We muster at 2:00 a.m."

Belinda gave another shiver and turned away, but just as she did so, one of the soldiers seated on the ground not far from where she stood boldly called out to her, "Miss Coulter, would you sing for us?"

She realized with a start that suddenly all eyes were upon her. Even the officer who had addressed the company was looking at her. Her hand slipped from Corporal Hewitt's crooked arm as he stepped back. She wondered if she could trust her own voice, for there was a lump in her throat, and she felt she would burst into tears any second.

But then something stirred within her as she gazed at all those expectant faces. Taking a deep breath, she began to sing "Dixie," motioning to them to join in. By the second verse they had all joined in, and the stillness and tension of the night were no more. As the sound reached the ears of others, they, too, began to sing the rousing song, and the singing finally spread throughout the camp.

And when it was ended, Belinda was not ashamed of the tears trickling down her cheeks, for there wasn't a dry eye in sight.

It was nearly midnight, but Ryan Tanner was wide-awake. With a bloody battle only hours away, he could not sleep. Neither could the rest of the men in his cavalry unit. They were all ready; they were merely passing time till the signal was given.

Beside him, Thad Staley lamented aloud, "The waitin' is worse than the fightin'."

Ryan chuckled at that. "And how would you know? You just joined up with us. You haven't been in a fight. You even got to miss that little skirmish at Mitchell's Ford day before yesterday. We might have lost fifteen to their twenty, but they pulled back, and Davis sent word to Beauregard praising him for a successful beginning. But I guess you had more important things to do," he added teasingly.

Thad Staley plainly didn't share his amusement. He retorted grimly, "Yeah, I'd say gettin' married was real important, bein' as I may never see my wife again. Guess that don't mean nothin' to you, you bein' without family."

Ryan shrugged. "No, I don't guess it does."

"Ever been married?"

Ryan shook his head.

"Ever come close?" Thad probed.

"No."

Thad grinned, anxious for a conversation to turn his mind from pervading thoughts of impending danger. "But you've had lots of women, right? Now me, there wasn't but one girl in my whole life, from the time I was a little tyke. Mary Lucille Abernathy." He sighed. "A real lady, through and through. She ain't but fourteen, and I know I'm a bit older, but with the war and all, we didn't want to take a chance on me gettin' killed without our ever having known each other, if you know what I mean."

Ryan indicated he did, not really interested in anything Thad was saying, but also wanting a diversion from the shroudlike tension.

As Thad droned on, wistfully remarking how he hoped he'd left Mary Lucille with child so that part of him would live on should he be killed, Ryan was moved to look back on his own past, especially where women were concerned. There had been a few. He had not fancied himself in love with any of them, and he had never led them to believe that he was. A couple of them had gotten marrying notions, and he'd found himself having to carefully extricate himself from delicate situations a few times. Still, he'd left no enemies, and there was even one he made a point to see for a night of romance whenever he chanced to be in her territory. And it wasn't that he was opposed to marriage. He just hadn't met a woman he'd taken a fancy to for any reason besides bedding her—till that strange night in Richmond.

And now he couldn't get those smoky emerald eyes off his mind.

He also continued to brood over why the sight of him evoked such god-awful fear in her.

But maybe none of it mattered. Maybe his life was about over, so what difference did any of it make, anyhow?

Yet, in the stillness before the fated hour of reckoning, Captain Ryan Tanner knew he'd fight like a tiger to stay alive.

And when it was all over, he'd go back to Richmond and search for Belinda Coulter.

Chapter Five

The sweeping stillness of the night was actually a deafening paradox.

No man slept in the final ominous hours before the First Battle of Manassas, July 21, 1861.

When the long roll of the snare drums finally began at 2:00 a.m., it was with a shadowed sense of relief that the soldiers leapt to their feet. Waiting for battle, some adamantly swore, was the real torment of war.

Captain Ryan Tanner, astride his horse, watched as the infantry proceeded to their appointed places in line. Behind him were his cavalrymen, all courageous men, skilled in horsemanship and proficient in the use of the special firearms they'd been issued—breech-loading Sharps rifles. They were accurate up to six hundred yards and could fire ten rounds a minute. That made them three times faster than the muzzle-loaders carried by the foot soldiers. Cavalrymen had to be quick, for they were perfect targets on their charging mounts. Each carried a sword, for once they plunged into the midst of the enemy they slashed and sliced as they went.

With only a hundred miles separating the capitals of the Union and the Confederacy—Washington and Richmond, respectively—both governments had been assembling armies to defend their capitals since spring. For some time Ryan had figured the clash at Manassas was coming, and he was optimistic that the South had the advantage. Thanks to privileged information, he knew General Beauregard had received a coded message from a Confederate spy five days earlier, informing him that McDowell had received orders to march on Manassas. Carried by buggy with a relay of horses down the eastern shore of the Potomac, the momentous dispatch had been in Beauregard's hands by nine o'clock that night, and within half an hour his outpost commanders had been aware of what was going on. So, while McDowell was on reconnaissance, Beauregard was making ready, with the arrival of General Johnston from the Shenandoah Valley with over eight thousand men, and General Holmes coming in from Aquia Creek with over twelve hundred soldiers and six pieces of artillery.

Rations of water and hardtack were passed out for breakfast, but Ryan and his men declined. They had no thirst or appetite, wanting only to get on with the ominous task at hand.

Ryan smiled to think how Beauregard had been able to efficiently muster nearly thirty thousand rank and file and fifty-five guns in such a short time. He held the general in the utmost esteem, and was proud to have been requested to serve with his army.

Finally, with the waving of colors and the stirring rhythm of fife and drum, they began moving forward.

They rode slowly, cloaked in the mantle of night. Ryan flanked the foot soldiers, wanting a clear field to charge when the order was given. No one spoke. Every man was locked in tense personal musings. Most of them had wives, children, families, that they cared about.

Ryan had no one.

He supposed that might have had something to do with why he had been given rank and authority. The thought was slightly vexing. After all, he'd rather think he was valuable due to his skills in horsemanship and shooting, instead of the rationale that his death would be a loss to no one.

But he refused to feel sorry for himself.

He liked to think that perhaps one day, if he did survive, he would meet a woman he could fall in love with and marry, and they would have a family.

And, with such profound thoughts in mind, he was startled as the image of Belinda's lovely face suddenly swam before him.

What, he wondered with a frown, was it about her that had caused such an indelible reflection? After all, he'd known beautiful women before, bedded most and forgot them later. So why did the memory of one, with whom he'd only had an encounter of short duration, and an unpleasant one at that, stick with him? And why now, in what might be his final moments on this earth?

He did not know, but he promised himself once more that he would find out—if he survived.

A dispatch rider approached and Ryan tensed to hear him brusquely advise, "Captain, General Beauregard wants to see you right away. I'll lead the way."

Ryan ordered his men to rein up and sit tight, then hurried after the messenger.

The general wanted Ryan to know of the latest word of the enemy's movements. Union troops were traveling by the Stone Bridge over Bull Run. The Confederates' advantage, he said, was that McDowell, situated at Sudeley Springs, was unaware Johnston had arrived to combine forces with Jackson. "McDowell is hoping to surprise us by striking us on the left flank at the Stone Bridge. I want you to take your men and move quickly to join up with Jackson to reinforce."

Ryan saluted and took off. He knew the area well, for he'd scouted the terrain in previous days, knowing they would have to move in the waning hours of night. His men, all handpicked, were disciplined and followed orders explicitly, asking no questions.

The Northern artillery began to retch and rumble and explode with fury as the first light of dawn streaked the sky. They were using grapeshot—shells filled with balls the size of oranges—and canister filled with lead balls the size of plums, deadly in close-up action. They also had Napoleon smoothbore howitzers, capable of much damage.

The rattle of musketry was heard as the skirmishers made contact with enemy pickets. A signal gun rang out and the Confederate artillery joined in with accumulating fury. Finally the awaited command rang out, "Forward," and with near-maniacal screams the infantry charged into battle.

Ryan could see the Yankee lines looming larger, a sea of blue. "Fire at will!" he shouted, and his men obeyed, guns exploding with hardly a pause for aiming.

Amid the roar of countless muskets, there was no time to be conscious of the noise or the kick of their weapons. Neither was there time to consider the effectiveness of the shot. They knew only that scores of Yankees were falling, as well as men in gray, but they could not attend to details of slaughter on either side.

All around, the infantry were falling to their knees, biting off and inserting a cartridge, ramming it home with a quick thrust of the rod, then rising and dashing along with their comrades. The exultation was a sweeping hand, urging them on, despite the fallen bodies and the screams of the wounded.

Ryan pulled back to appraise the situation. It appeared the troops on the right would be unable to get into position before the Union offense could make much progress on the left, so he made the decision to set out at full speed for the main point of conflict—the Stone Bridge.

He turned to wave to his men to follow, allowing himself only a split second of anguish when he realized that two of them had fallen, ordering himself to remember that it was the moment at hand that counted. There would be time later for mourning.

They came around between the base of a hill and the Stone Bridge, into a shallow ravine that ran up to a point on the crest where General Jackson had already formed his brigade at the edge of the woods. The Yankees were on the run, and the Rebel commanders were resolutely blocking further retreat and trying to restore order among their own forces. It was a scene of chaos, with more than two thousand men shouting back and forth to each other, their voices mingling with the noise of the shells hurtling through the trees overhead.

One of Ryan's men sprinted his horse alongside him to say anxiously, "It's bedlam, sir. You can't tell what's going on. Yankees running, and our men are stumbling over them trying to keep on fighting."

"Jackson's holding the bridge," Ryan pointed out, "but the disorder is going to cost some lives unless the men rally. Start gathering standards and carry them forward to draw their eye."

The cavalrymen rushed to obey, charging into the melee to gather up the flags and stab them into the ground forty to fifty feet ahead of the conflict. And it worked, for the troops fought their way forward to meet their officers, who had also seen what Tanner's cavalry was trying to do. With orders received to advance and form the line of their colors, they were able to obey with a general movement and charge ahead with full force.

Ryan saw a cavalryman from another unit rushing toward his. "Join us," he shouted tersely. "I'm Wade Hampton. I just came from headquarters, and General Beauregard says we've got to reinforce to the left. They're being hammered by artillery. He and General Johnston are heading there, and I'm taking my men to the right flank on Henry Plateau."

Ryan signaled to his men to fall in, and with sword in one hand, gun in the other, giving their mounts the reins, they dashed across the landscape beneath the blazing sun. They paid no heed to the sickening feel of hooves smashing into bodies as they rode, the dead paving the way. At the sight of wounded, they skirted about, but only if they caught a glimpse of gray. Blue uniforms were trampled without mercy.

Ryan saw another of his own troop fall. Another's horse was gutted by a Yankee sword as he attempted to leap over a revetment.

Morning turned to afternoon and eventually the Federals began to pull back. Ryan joined a rout by a recently arrived cavalry troop led by Colonel Jeb Stuart. Frenzy broke out in parts of the Union force, which began to retreat in panic.

"Look at that," someone called out, laughing. "Civilians! Looks like they came out from Washington to have a picnic and watch the fightin', and now they're runnin' for their lives."

"Serves them right," Ryan muttered under his breath, angrily thinking how soldiers on both sides were dying by the hundreds. This was war, damn it, not entertainment.

Word spread that the main road of retreat for McDowell's men was blocked when a shell destroyed a wagon. Those trying to force their way past the bottleneck caused a contagious panic, and soon the entire Union army was in full flight.

Ryan, along with Hampton and Stuart, rode forward with the colors of the Fourth Alabama, a courageous troop that had fought all morning, fled, been routed and disordered, but had rallied to advance and assist in victory.

"Look over yonder," a respectful voice called from somewhere. "President Davis himself!"

Ryan looked, and saw Jefferson Davis leaning out of a locomotive as it proceeded toward headquarters. Someone said they'd heard it had been detached from the rest of the train, because President Davis couldn't get a horse to ride to the field where the battle was raging and he was determined to find out what was going on amid the confusion. Cheers went up as the soldiers waved at their president, and Mr. Davis responded by cheerily greeting them in return.

"Sir, we lost three men."

Ryan wearily turned in his saddle as Corporal Stancock rode up to tell him what he already knew.

"Copeland, Kerry, and Burdette," Stancock advised him dismally. "All dead. No wounded, though."

Ryan bit out a command, "Help retrieve their bodies. See they're properly buried, their effects collected for their families."

Stancock, reining his horse about to obey, murmured sourly, "A goddamn waste..."

Ryan tersely called him back. "Wait a minute, soldier. A tragedy, yes. They were all good men. Fine soldiers. I understand Kerry's wife just bore him a son. But don't call it a waste when the Yankees' Forward to Richmond march was stopped in a matter of hours and turned into a triumph for the Confederacy."

Stancock contritely mumbled, "Yes, sir. Sorry, sir."

"And most of all," Ryan continued, more to himself than to the corporal, "The North will have to realize it's not going to be over quick, like they thought. It's going to be a long war. A costly war.

"For both sides," he added grimly, turning away.

Belinda had covered her ears with her hands against the sharp, eerie whistle of the minié balls, the hideous screeching of shells and the thunderous roar of cannon fire. Huddled inside the wagon, she knew the fighting was too far away to place her in danger. Still, the bedlam was deafening.

She had watched as the surgeons prepared their kits and the litter bearers and ambulances ominously waited for the signal to retrieve the wounded from the fields.

"I feel so helpless," she said to Bart, who was huddled irritably on the floor of the wagon behind some boxes. Unlike Belinda, he had no interest in what was going on outside. He was angrily thinking how he never should have gotten caught here, how they should have hightailed it back to Richmond when it became obvious they were about to be caught up in the thick of fighting.

He looked at Belinda. "Helpless isn't the word. Stupid is more like it. We shouldn't be here."

"But now that we are, I feel as if we should do something." Belinda squeezed her hands together against her bosom as the world exploded in the distance.

"Yeah, get the hell out of here, which is exactly what I'd do if I knew which way to go."

"That's not what I'm talking about. Those soldiers out there are Southerners, Bart, willing to die for what they believe in. There ought to be something we can do to help."

Incredulous, his brows shot up as he decried, "I suppose you think I should pick up a gun and run join them!"

"I wish *I* could," she remarked solemnly.

"Well, you go right ahead, lady. I'm staying here where it's safe, and first chance, I'm heading out."

"You were the one who wanted to come along. We could have stayed behind," she reminded him with an angry lift of her chin.

"I didn't know it was going to be this bad, or this fast. I thought there'd be time for a few games of poker, keno, along the way, and then I'd take my winnings and veer off before the actual fighting started. It all sneaked up on me," he concluded wistfully.

Belinda was no longer listening to him. Seeing one of the cooks, she scrambled down from the wagon and ran to ask, "Is there anything I can do to help?"

"You want to help?" he snapped, eyes wild and worried as he hurried along, Belinda trying to keep up. "Lady, they need all they can get at the hospital tents, 'cause the first ambulances are fixing to go out now. We've heard the number of wounded is running real high."

Belinda frowned as she remembered the earlier unpleasant scene with Dr. Wilkins, but she knew she wasn't about to let the incident keep her from doing what she could to aid the suffering. "I'll go with you," she told him, quickening her pace.

The cook glanced at her sharply. "I heard Dr. Wilkins got mad about you taking it on yourself to treat that soldier back in the valley. You'd be wise to remember your place, Miss Coulter."

"My place?" Belinda blinked, confused.

He slowed to regard her with narrowed eyes. "In case you don't know it, it isn't considered proper for a woman to work in hospitals and have intimate contact with strange men, especially a woman who's young and unmarried, like you." He nodded at her curtly. "You'd be wise to volunteer your services and wait to be told what to do. I don't imagine they'll be wanting you to do more than empty slop jars and haul out bandages and severed limbs, anyway."

Angry at bearing the brunt of such prejudice, Belinda irately responded, "I'll do whatever I'm called on to do, whether it's considered proper or not."

The cook sneered. "You won't last long."

Belinda didn't comment, seeing no reason to attempt further conversation with this unpleasant man.

She went into one of the hospital tents, and was relieved not to see Dr. Wilkins anywhere around. She figured he must be in one of the other facilities. She introduced herself to a Dr. Reid, who said he was an assistant surgeon in charge of the infirmary corps. He said he'd heard her sing and was grateful she'd remained at the camp to help out.

"Make sure each of the corp members has his knapsack. They were supposed to have been packed last night," he explained, "but one of our supply wagons was late getting here with the rest of the things we needed."

He indicated a section of the tent where boxes of supplies were stacked in readiness and rattled off a list of what was needed in each knapsack. "Pocket case of instruments. Ligatures, needles, pins, chloroform, morphine, alcohol, tourniquets, bandages, lint and splints."

He went on to tell her, "The members of the infirmary corps are unarmed, but they wear identifying bandages. Make sure they've got one litter to every two of them, a canteen of water and a tin cup. We're going to be leaving as soon as we get the blankets and knives loaded.''

Belinda understood the need for blankets. Men suffering from wounds and loss of blood were extremely sensitive to cold, even in hot summer weather. Knives would be needed for cutting away bloodied clothing to get at wounds and treat them.

Working feverishly, following all the orders she was given, Belinda assisted in sending off the first group of wagons. When they returned with the first load of wounded, Dr. Reid hurriedly told her it was going to be necessary to send out more workers with each wagon to try and bring back as many as possible in one load. ''You can't lift bodies, but can you handle the horses?''

She assured him she could.

''The fighting is almost over, but can you stand the sight of blood?'' he probed anxiously. She nodded, and he pressed on to make sure. ''Men with their faces blown away, blood and guts all over everywhere?''

Belinda swallowed hard. ''Yes, sir. I'm willing to do anything to help.''

''Then get on that wagon there—'' he pointed ''—and get out there.'' He rushed away at the sound of screams as a soldier was brought in with his legs blown away at the knees.

Belinda scrambled up into the wagon and took the reins, waiting for the infirmary stewards to unload the litters and make ready to head out onto the battlefield once more.

Bart came running up, waving his arms wildly and shouting, ''What do you think you're doing? We're getting out of here. Now. They say we've won, and the roads to Richmond are secure, and this is our chance to get the hell out while we can. Come on!'' He motioned frantically for her to get down.

Belinda shook her head. ''I can't. There's no one else to drive this wagon.''

Bart gasped in disbelief. Then, his hands on his hips, he glared up at her and issued his ultimatum. ''You either leave with me now, or you're on your own. I'm not hanging around here.''

Just then, the steward scrambled on board, urging her to move. With a pop of the reins, she called down to Bart, "Well, I guess you'll have to look for another Jenny Lind, because I'm staying where I'm needed."

Bart stared after her, but not for long. With a shake of his head, he headed for his own wagon.

On into the night, Belinda tirelessly held the reins. At first, the sights and sounds were unbearable—dead bodies strewn about, a scene every bit as horrible as Dr. Reid had said it would be. Wounded men screamed in agony, begging for either help or the quick, merciful relief of death. Her eyes stung from the acrid smell of smoke, and the metallic odor of blood was nauseating.

The battleground was also a scene of chaos, as soldiers tried to find their way back to their companies. Ambulances and carts from all regiments worked their way through the noise and confusion, attempting to pick up their own casualties but turning away from no man.

Finally, as Belinda reined up at the edge of a patch of woods, one of the stewards wearily declared, "Last load till morning. It's hard to see by torchlight."

Another chimed in with his agreement. "Yeah, unless they're strong enough to call out or groan, we're just wasting time when we could be back at the hospital helping there. Let's spread out and find as many as we can and then start out again at dawn."

"I'd like to help," Belinda reminded them.

"Stay here," the soldier in charge of the detail growled, annoyed. She would only be in the way, and would probably faint at the sight of blood, anyway. "And if you do wander off, and you aren't here when we all get back, we'll leave you out here," he warned.

She bit back an angry retort. It had been like that all evening, constant sniping and sarcasm at the idea that she, a woman, would dare go onto the battlefield.

Belinda did not like being left alone, for in the faint light she could see the bodies, so still...so dead. With an ache in her heart, she watched as the stewards moved among them, pausing to make sure there was no life before moving on.

They disappeared over a ridge. Someone had said they were near Henry House Hill, where the Confederates had made such a strong stand. General Jackson's brigade had held fast, and word was spreading that Jackson was now being called "Stonewall" after the way his troops had boldly held fast against the enemy.

But there had been many casualties, on both sides, and Belinda found herself wishing the stewards would return.

She stiffened at the sound of a soft moan from somewhere in the somber darkness.

She gasped aloud. Dear God, the stewards had missed an injured soldier.

Without hesitation, she scrambled down from the wagon and started toward the noise. It did not sound particularly agonized, she noted, but rather confused, as if someone was trying to figure out where he was, what had happened. A tiny scream escaped her lips when her foot touched a dead man. She stumbled, fell, landing on top of yet another casualty, wincing, shuddering, at the feel of soft, bloodied flesh against her own.

The sound came again, and she was puzzled as to the location. While it seemed close by, it also appeared to come from below her. "Where are you?" she called, frustrated. "I want to help you, but I can't find you."

"Here..." came the plaintive call. "Be careful. I think there's a ravine..."

There was—and she stumbled into it, clumsily rolling all the way to the bottom.

"Are you okay?" the voice asked anxiously, having apparently heard her fall.

"I think so." There were a few rips and tears in her dress, some scrapes and bruises, and probably a very dirty face, but Belinda detected no serious injuries. "Now let's see about you." She groped and found him in the darkness, though she could distinguish neither his face nor uniform. For all she knew, she was ministering to the enemy, but it made no difference. Unlike some of the stewards, who could so easily pass a wounded Union soldier by, Belinda knew she would not be able to turn her back on anyone who was suffering, no matter the color of his uniform.

"How bad are you hurt?" she asked him. "Are you bleeding?"

"Shoulder," he told her in a thin voice. "And yeah, I think I'm bleeding bad. Got something to pack it with?"

Belinda cursed herself for not having stopped to grab a medical knapsack. "I'll have to go back."

Scrambling up the side of the ravine, she again picked her way among the bodies of men, horses and mules to find the wagon. Searching, she was dismayed to realize that the knapsacks were being used. Then she remembered that the wagon had previously been used to carry supplies, and not everything had been unloaded. She began to feel around hopefully for whatever had been left, then gave a cry of delight to find what she was looking for—small bags of flour and salt. Taking one of each, she hurried back to the wounded man.

She called to him, and was relieved when he answered, though he sounded even weaker now. Probing with her fingers, she grimaced to feel the heavy flow from the wound.

Tonelessly he said, "I can feel my own blood running out of me, so it has to be bad."

"Not so bad," she lied. "You're lucky I found you. You'd have bled to death by morning. Maybe sooner. How long have you been here, anyway?"

"I'm not sure. I must've been knocked out when I fell off my horse, because I remember it was midafternoon, and now it's night.

"I recall we won the battle," he added, and suddenly there was a lilt in his voice.

"That's what I hear, soldier." She was busy ripping her petticoat to shreds for bandages.

"This will have to do till we get you to the hospital." She explained how she was packing the wound with equal parts of salt and flour.

"Hey, I remember my grandmother doing that once, when my grandpa fell on a pitchfork and got a nasty hole in his side."

"It's an old remedy, but sometimes it works. I think in your case it will. I'm already wrapping the third layer of bandage, and I can't feel it getting wet like the other layers, so it's slowing down."

They heard the sound of someone walking above them, and Belinda quickly called out.

"A woman!" someone said, surprise in his voice. "What are you doing there?"

Belinda realized it was not one of the soldiers from her wagon and felt a stab of fear at the thought that he might be a Yankee. Just then, however, the wounded man she was tending recognized the voice and shouted out. At once, Belinda heard the sounds of two men scrambling to join them.

"Captain? That you? Are you hit? You okay?" One of the men held up a torch.

"Yes to everything," he responded. "Just get me out of here."

Belinda turned to leave, saying she had best hurry to get back to her own people.

"Hey, there's nobody out here," one of the newcomers advised her. "We saw a wagon pulling off. Talked to the men on it. Said they were from Johnston's company. They also said they'd had a woman with 'em, but she'd wandered off and they weren't waitin' on her. That be you?" he asked suspiciously.

"That'd be me!" Belinda confirmed with a weary sigh.

"Well, don't worry. You can go with us."

She turned back around. "I suppose I have no choice—"

Belinda was paralyzed with horror.

In the light from the lantern, she could see the wounded soldier in the fire's eerie glow—and also his green-gold eyes.

Cat's eyes.

Captain Ryan Tanner stared up at her in bemused wonder. While he was delighted to again see the face of this woman he could not forget, he was again bewildered at the realization that the very sight of him provoked sheer loathing—and terror.

Chapter Six

"I demand to be either taken back to General Johnston's company or escorted to Richmond," Belinda irately told the officer. "I don't wish to stay here. You're in the midst of a war, for heaven's sake. It's no place for a lady."

They were seated in a tent adjacent to General Beauregard's command headquarters. The night before, when Belinda had been stunned to realize she'd actually been ministering to Captain Ryan Tanner, she had forced herself to recover quickly, lest her behavior trigger his memory as to who she was. She had passed off her strange response as simply exhaustion and stress from the horror of the day of battle. Even then, she had pleaded with the men to take her back to where she'd come from, but they had refused, saying they had other wounded on their wagon and needed to get them back to their own hospital.

She had been quartered in a tent and given food, but had spent a restless night due to the macabre situation in which she found herself. At the first bugle call, she had been up and requesting an audience with General Beauregard himself, but it was a Lieutenant Danson who'd finally agreed to hear her out.

"According to my men," he was saying, "you didn't let your femininity prevent you from being in circumstances where other women would certainly have swooned. As for the officer you helped, Captain Tanner can't sing your praises highly enough. He said you never hesitated to minister to him. The doctors who treated him afterward are also impressed. One of them is on his way here now to talk to you."

Belinda was tightly clasping her hands in her lap so that he wouldn't notice how they were shaking. "You don't understand, I was there by accident. I was driving a wagon for the medical corps, and I was waiting on them to return. When I heard someone calling out in obvious pain, it was instinct to want to help. But that doesn't mean I belong in a war, Lieutenant. Any other woman would have done the same thing—"

"I beg to differ..."

Turning, she saw a tall man stooping to enter through the flap opening of the tent. He was wearing an officer's tunic of cadet gray, with black facings and a stand-up collar. The trousers were dark blue with black velvet stripes and gold cord edging. There were stars on the collar of the tunic, and a sash of green silk net was wrapped about his waist. General staff buttons denoted his status of a surgeon, and the cap he removed had the letters MS—for Medical Staff—embroidered in gold.

He held out his hand to her, eyes alight with pleasure, a wide grin on his bearded face. "I heard what you did last night, Miss Coulter, and there aren't many women who'd have their wits about them at such a time and remember flour and salt can be used for something else besides baking biscuits...

"Like keeping a man from bleeding to death," he added with a respectful nod. "Now tell me—" he sat down in the chair beside her "—what's this about you wanting to leave us and go back to Johnston's army? Surely you don't think we're going to let you go now that we've found you."

Lieutenant Danson hastily interjected, "She says she'd rather go back to Richmond."

"Richmond? Oh, no, no, we can't allow that," the doctor went on, making *tsk*ing noises as he firmly shook his head. "We've got too many wounded from the dreadful fighting of the last few days, and we need all the help we can get. We can't allow it. Why, it's your duty, Miss Coulter. The South needs you."

Belinda opened her mouth to protest, but he rushed on without giving her a chance to speak.

"Now, I'm Major Whitley and I'm the chief surgeon, and the fact is—" his tone became quite serious "—we do need you, and because we need you, I will have to insist you remain here with us, whether you like it or not."

Belinda bit down on her lower lip. The two men were watching her anxiously and she knew that, despite Major Whitley's stern edict, they'd have to let her go if she pressed hard enough. She wasn't a prisoner, for heaven's sake, and they'd not hold her against her will.

"Please..." Major Whitley pleaded quietly, reaching to cover her hands with his. "I've got patients stacked and waiting, and I need to get back. Men may be dying because I had to take time to come over here and persuade you to do your duty as a Southerner...and a Christian. So come with me. Now."

With both men staring at her, faces mirroring their desperate hope, Belinda knew she could not refuse. "All right," she said with a sigh of finality. "But I warn you—the last field doctor I worked with said I was only fit to empty bedpans."

"We'll see about that." Major Whitley laughed, slapping his knee, then leapt to his feet. "Let's go."

Belinda told herself she was in no danger from Captain Tanner, even if he did remember who she was, not when they were surrounded by people this way.

She doubted there'd be time to worry about it, anyway.

Major Whitley had warned there was no telling what she'd be called on to do, and she assured him that she was not squeamish over any detail. She had told him on the walk from the tent to the hospital compound of her experience following an old mountain doctor on his rounds and how she hadn't turned away from any chore.

"I imagine you saw it all," he remarked, seemingly impressed.

"From birthing babies to gunshot wounds. From carelessness with an ax resulting in part of a foot being chopped off to attacks by wild hogs. Snakebite. Burns. Bee stings. Broken bones. I saw it all."

"But you'll see new things here, I'm sure," he predicted grimly.

Belinda quickly learned he was right.

She stepped inside the tent and blinked at the garish scene before her. Major Whitley had disappeared, and she found herself standing alone and wondering what she was supposed to do.

She saw a surgeon standing beside a table. A soldier lay before him, mercifully unconscious due to the chloroform dripping into the paper cone held over his face.

Mutely she watched as the surgeon swiftly amputated the soldier's leg, then snapped to the steward holding the cone to stitch the flaps closed.

She stepped to the next table, where the surgeon was visibly annoyed to find the waiting patient still conscious. "Why isn't he asleep?" he barked. "We've got to move faster around here."

The steward gave him a bewildered glance and tersely demanded, "Which do you want me to do, Captain Hepplewhite? Sew up this one's stump, or put the other one to sleep? We're shorthanded, sir. Two men passed out a little while ago from exhaustion."

"Sew him up. Maybe this one will faint—"

Hearing that, Belinda exploded. "That's barbaric and cruel! You can't just start sawing on a man's arm and hope he'll pass out from the pain. What kind of monster are you?"

At the unexpected sound of a woman's voice, the surgeon sharply turned around, further infuriated at her audacity in daring to admonish him. "Who are you?" he demanded, nostrils flaring, eyes narrowed with anger.

"Belinda Coulter," she told him, lifting her chin in a defiant gesture. "Major Whitley asked me to come here and help."

"Then help!" he snapped. "Instead of interfering." He regarded her coolly, the corners of his mouth finally turning up in a contemptuous sneer. "Which do you want to do? Sew up the flap or administer anesthesia while I amputate an arm?"

Belinda did not flinch, returning his gaze with steady green eyes. "I can do either one, Doctor."

Exchanging an amused look with the steward, the doctor cocked his head to one side, and, with hands on his hips, snickered. "Okay, *Doctor* Coulter. Let's see you sew up that flap. I can always repair that, but there's no bringing a man back from the dead if you drown him with chloroform."

Without hesitation, Belinda approached the table. She had stitched up a few minor cuts for Doc Jasper, but nothing as major as the aftermath of amputation. Yet she'd seen him do it enough times, and she felt she knew the procedure.

She worked fast, meticulously stitching the skin closed with curved needle and silk thread, leaving a small opening for drainage.

At last she stood back, realizing by the stiffness throughout her body just how intensely she had been working.

To the attending steward, who had watched in wide-eyed stupor, she said, "Fan his lungs to purge the anesthetic while I bandage the stump. If he doesn't respond, give him a quick sniff of liquor of ammonia to bring him around. Then we can move him to a bed, if there's one available, and I'm sure the doctor will want him dosed with bromine to stave off gangrene, and—"

"I don't believe it!"

She looked up to see Major Whitley staring at her, a strange combination of anger and wonder on his face.

"Miss Coulter, what are you doing?" he asked thinly.

Simply, bluntly, she told him, careful to let him know she had not just walked into the tent and taken it upon herself to close an amputation. "Captain Hepplewhite suggested I prove my worth," she added frostily.

"I don't believe it," he repeated, then turned on his heel and strode over to where Captain Hepplewhite had just finished severing an arm at the elbow. "After great persuasion on my part, Miss Coulter agreed to help us. I'd like to know why you took it upon yourself to attempt to humiliate her?"

Captain Hepplewhite was frowning as he made the same type of fold Belinda had just completed. "I'll be there to clean up after her in a minute. I should have had more sense than to let her do it, but she was acting so damn smug, as if she could do anything. I had no business letting her work on a helpless man. I'm sorry. I hope she didn't make too big a mess."

"Quite the contrary," Major Whitley informed him. "It appears she did a very nice job, but that's beside the point. She's not a doctor, and she has no business practicing medicine unless it's an absolute emergency."

Captain Hepplewhite motioned to his assistant to take over so that he could attempt to defend himself. "You don't understand. It was a joke. I didn't think she'd do it. We were very busy and I got involved over here, and I assumed one of the assistants would take over when she swooned."

"I told you, she didn't swoon. She very neatly closed the wound. But the fact remains, I intend to see that you are reprimanded for your inexcusable behavior."

At that, Captain Hepplewhite flared. "Wait a minute, Major. *She's* the one who needs reprimanding. In fact, she needs to be kicked out of here for daring to pretend she's a doctor—"

Belinda had heard enough. Swiftly moving to join them, she furiously told Captain Hepplewhite, "I never pretended to be anything. I told you Major Whitley had asked me to help out, and you were indignant. You were trying to make me look like a fool.''

"Which you are!'' he roared, face reddening. "A woman has no business—''

"Stop it,'' Major Whitley commanded sharply. "This is a hospital, for heaven's sake, and no place to discuss this. Miss Coulter is going to be with us from now on, and I expect her to be treated respectfully. She will take her orders from me and no one else. Is that clear?'' He swept the faces of the medical staff, for all had stopped what they were doing to witness the interesting scene between a woman and a physician. At once they returned to their tasks.

And so did Captain Hepplewhite, who dismissed Belinda with an indignant sniff.

"That won't happen again,'' Major Whitley assured Belinda, "and I sincerely apologize. I'm afraid some of my associates have very prejudiced views on women in medicine, in general. But you did do a marvelous job.''

Belinda was given the task of nursing the wounded who had already received medical treatment. The hours melted away as she changed bandages, spooned cool water through parched lips, bathed sweat-soaked faces and, when time permitted, heard prayers or wrote hasty notes to families to assure them that their loved ones were still alive.

There were heartbreaking moments, too many to count, and Belinda tried not to dwell on them. Occasionally she would come across a man who had quietly died. She would close his eyes with gentle fingertips, cover his face with either sheet or blanket, then fetch an orderly to take him out for common burial to make room for yet another recuperating soldier.

She hated nights the worst, for then the hospital resembled dim caverns of the catacombs; but instead of the dead in their final rest, there were wasted figures burning with fever and tossing restlessly from side to side. Oil lamps cast a ghastly light, only half dispelling the darkness and bringing out dim shadows everywhere to render the gloom even more spectral.

Belinda was always exhausted, napping at intervals when there was time. Always, however, she was alert for the appearance of Captain Tanner. She inquired the second day after the battle, and was told he was not in the hospital. One of the stewards who had helped bring him in recalled that he'd left shortly after being seen by a surgeon. Tanner, the steward said, wanted to round up what was left of his cavalry unit and start recruiting new members to train, in order to be ready for the next battle.

"A real brave man," the steward had declared reverently. "Everybody respects Captain Tanner."

Belinda had bit back a sarcastic retort, thinking how quickly opinion would change if it were known that Tanner was a rapist.

In the confused, harried days immediately following the battle at Manassas Junction, Belinda concentrated on her work. She had no quarters in which to change clothes, but that didn't matter, because when Bart had taken off, he'd taken her trunk with him. As a result, she was looking quite wretched when General Beauregard himself visited the hospital one morning. He was shocked, not only to see a female nurse, but also by her appearance.

That afternoon, she received a summons from Lieutenant Danson, who got right to the point. "The general was dismayed, Miss Coulter, to see you look so…" He gestured helplessly, wondering what to say without hurting her feelings.

Belinda helped him along. "Wretched? Dirty?" She wrinkled her nose in shared distaste. "I agree, but the fact of the matter is, I have no clean clothes, and no place to bathe and change if I did. I live, eat and sleep in the hospital tents."

Danson looked uncomfortable and did not meet her belligerent eyes as he said, "Well, that's a problem that must be rectified. The truth is, Miss Coulter, General Beauregard reminded me how it just isn't considered proper for women to serve in our hospitals. An occupation involving such intimate contact with strange men just isn't fit for self-respecting Southern women.

"Of course," he added hastily, "you are certainly worthy of respect, by all means. What I'm trying to say is that it's best to use convalescent soldiers, those who aren't strong enough for field duty. Volunteers such as yourself should busy yourself with more menial tasks, such as cooking and cleaning."

Belinda felt her ire rising. "Need I remind you that Major Whitley practically ordered me to work at the hospital? It wasn't my idea, but..." She placed her palms on his desk and leaned forward so he'd have to look at her as she said fiercely, "...I happen to like what I'm doing. I actually don't mind being dirty and going without sleep if it means I can help ease the suffering of even one wounded soldier. Now if you'll provide me with clothing—trousers and shirt, if that's all you've got—and a tent of my own where I can bathe and sleep, my appearance will vastly improve, I assure you.

"As for the prejudice against women working in the hospitals," she added tartly, "that doesn't concern me in the least. As long as I do my job and know my place, I can't see where anybody has a right to say a damn word."

He blanched at her profanity, cleared his throat and nervously began to shuffle papers on his desk. "Very well. Since the General didn't actually forbid you to work there, and Major Whitley finds your services invaluable, and the medical director said he had no objection, we'll leave things as they are for the time being. I was going to offer you safe passage back to Richmond, but if you insist on staying..." He allowed his words to trail off, glancing at her hopefully.

Belinda shook her head.

"Very well. I'll see you are provided with quarters of your own and clean clothing. You're dismissed."

She gave him a mock salute, turned on her heel and hurried back to the hospital.

Ryan flexed the muscles in his shoulder, wincing only slightly with the pain. The wound was healing, and soon he'd have full use of his arm. Already he was shooting, anxious to get back in shape. But, while the injury was annoying as he sought to train new members of his unit as sharpshooters, he knew he was lucky to be alive. He'd gotten through the whole damn battle, he irritably mused, only to be picked off by a wounded Yankee lying on the ground, who wanted to use his dying breath and his last shred of energy to put a ball in the enemy. Ryan had ridden right by him, thinking him dead, and had been several yards beyond when the single shot rang out. He'd managed to turn and fire once, hastening the man's departure from this world with a bullet between the eyes, all the while feeling himself being hurtled backward off his horse. He could remember hitting the side of the ravine, then tumbling and rolling all the way to the bottom. Nobody had seen it because he'd sent his men on ahead while he took one last turn through the area. By the time they'd realized he was missing, it was dark, and he was unconscious, so couldn't call out for help. And if Belinda hadn't been nearby later, when he did wake up...

Ryan shuddered to think of the consequences. He had lost a hell of a lot of blood and couldn't have lasted much longer. He owed her his life, and he had wanted to find her and tell her so. Asking about her whereabouts, he'd learned General Beauregard had received the message he'd sent, advising she be assigned to hospital service. Ryan had thought it best, however, not to seek her out before leaving to express his gratitude—because it had happened again. When the steward had held up a torch and she'd realized who it was she was ministering to, the reaction had been just as before—stark terror, hysteria, fury, all combined in an obviously overwhelming flood of loathing. Only this time, she'd managed to control it a little better, he'd noticed. As though she'd been thinking about it a lot, preparing herself for the possibility they might one day meet again.

Ryan was bewildered by it, as well as angry. He racked his brain constantly in an attempt to figure out why he evoked such a violently emotional reaction. There was still something vaguely familiar about her, and more and more he got the feeling he'd seen her somewhere before, because never would any man be able to easily forget those jade eyes and that fiery red hair.

But where, damn it? And why did she hate him? He didn't know, but he'd made up his mind to find her and confront her.

"Hey, Captain . . ."

His furious brooding was interrupted by one of his men calling out as he came up the ridge where he'd gone to escape the constant activity of the camp below.

"How's your arm?" Sergeant Lucas wanted to know.

Ryan ignored his solicitousness, instead irritably asking, "You weren't at roll call this morning. Somebody said you were up and gone before day. Where were you?"

"Sick call."

"You know it's a rule my men come to me first. I have to know where everybody is at all times."

Lucas dropped to sit beside him, plucked a blade of grass and began to chew on it as he apologetically explained. "Sorry, Captain, but you didn't want me wakin' you up in the middle of the night to tell you I had the trots, did you?"

Ryan had to chuckle at that, but he still said, "Yeah, I did. What did you do, stay in the woods all night?"

"I went to the hospital to get help, that's what I did."

"Sick call isn't till fifteen minutes after reveille," Ryan reminded.

Lucas nodded, but told him, "There's a lady working at the hospital now, and she don't mind gettin' woke up at night to treat dysentery. She ain't like them surgeons who raise hell if you get them up. Since they finished hackin' off arms and legs till the next big battle, they're real cantankerous if they don't get to sleep all night.''

Ryan's interest was piqued. "What's the lady's name?" He was pretty sure he already knew.

"Miss Belinda. I tell you, Captain," he continued, anxious to convey how impressed he was, "she's really amazing. They say she can do about anything the doctors can, and she ain't scared of nothin'. Pretty, too. But the strange thing is," he added with a perplexed frown, "she's only nice to sick soldiers. Won't have nothin' to do with a man if he's able-bodied—acts like she purely hates 'em, she does. Hard to figure out...."

Ryan was getting to his feet.

"Where you goin', Captain?"

Ryan's smile was mysterious. "Why, to figure out a few things, Sergeant. What else?"

Chapter Seven

The calm spell after the battle was short-lived.

After General McDowell's forces were so badly beaten at Bull Run, President Lincoln turned over command of the Army of the Potomac to General George McClellan. McClellan was then ordered to push toward Tennessee by seizing Manassas Junction in Virginia and Strasburg, Kentucky, in the Shenandoah Valley. President Jefferson Davis was also urging further action in Virginia. He advised General Johnston to take advantage of the weakness surely to be felt by the Union forces after their defeat. Consequently, skirmishes continued to erupt in the vicinity, keeping the medical services busy day and night.

Belinda followed orders implicitly, doing whatever tasks were required, no matter how dirty or distasteful.

She'd learned that the medical services had been authorized by the Confederacy's Provisional Congress at Montgomery back in February, eight days after Jefferson Davis was inaugurated as president. Surgeons were to have the rank of major, and assistant surgeons that of captain, which meant that even though Major Whitley and Captain Hepplewhite were both doctors, Major Whitley had the most authority. And it was obvious that Captain Hepplewhite resented that fact. His disapproval of her presence in the hospital had been intensified by Dr. Whitley's endorsement, and she found herself constantly sidestepping confrontations with Hepplewhite whenever Whitley was not around.

The camp was being plagued by an outbreak of measles. Belinda knew the doctors were prescribing a solution of ammonium acetate in doses of forty to fifty drops, three times a day, in a cup of warm tea. She took it upon herself to brew the tea in her own tent, from roots and leaves of sassafras. In cases of extremely high fever, she went into the woods to find a slippery elm tree. Peeling away the bark, she would pound it into a concoction that she then placed in tiny bags to put over the patient's eyes. Always she asked Major Whitley for permission to try her mountain remedies, and his standard comment was "It can't hurt to try."

There was also a problem with what was being called, simply, camp itch. Belinda had a balm for that, also, a strong concoction of poke root after washing twice a day. For severe cases, she applied either crushed broom straw or slippery elm, and she made her own ointment from the inner bark of the sweet gum tree, combining with olive oil and sulfur flour from the cook's wagon.

It was late one evening when Belinda stifled a groan at finding herself at the same operating table with Captain Hepplewhite. From the way he glared at her, she knew he didn't like the situation, either, but there wasn't anything either of them could do about it at the moment. There had been a big skirmish between Union and Confederate patrols about a half hour's ride from camp, with many injuries. Major Whitley had gone out with the ambulances, having first instructed Hepplewhite to be ready to receive the first transport of victims.

Belinda had another reason for disliking Hepplewhite, besides his unpleasant disposition. Though she did not dare say so aloud, for to criticize a doctor, she knew, was a cardinal sin, she felt he sometimes amputated too hastily. Soldiers knew that once they were placed on his table they would not leave as whole men. Hepplewhite boasted of taking no chances on gangrene. It was better, he felt, to make a clean wound that would heal nicely, so he didn't blink an eye at reaching for the dreaded capital saw.

It was late in the afternoon when the first wagon arrived. Belinda hurried out with the stewards, anxious to help. As the stewards took the litters, she would quickly check the extent of the injuries to see which ones needed priority treatment, waving those straight into the hospital tent, while the others were placed on the ground nearby to wait their turn.

But while Major Whitley trusted her judgment, Captain Hepplewhite quickly let it be known that he did not. Elbowing her aside, he began barking directions to the stewards amid hysterical screams from the wounded. "This man to the table. His foot has to come off. Cut off his trousers and tie the tourniquet just below the knee. This one's arm has to go. Tourniquet at the shoulder. Both legs here..."

Belinda bit back her own shriek of protest, knowing he was not taking time to make a proper diagnosis. With cleansing and suturing and huge doses of quinine and laudanum, several of the men on the way to the operating table could be spared the loss of their limbs. Sadly, however, there was nothing she could do.

"This leg needs to come off, as high up as possible," Hepplewhite was saying brusquely. "Not much we can do to slow the bleeding, boy, but you look like a hearty lad...." He moved to the next stretcher, ignoring the soldier's ragged screams for mercy.

Belinda, standing nearby, was touched by the boy's youth, guessing him not to be much over fourteen or fifteen. With compassion, she went to his side and clasped his hand.

He squeezed her fingers so tight it hurt, his eyes wide with desperation, as he begged, "You gotta help me, lady. Don't let him take off my leg. It ain't no bullet wound. It was ripped open by a cavalryman's saber. It's bleedin' bad, I know, but the bone can't be smashed. You gotta stop him.

Everybody's heard of Hepplewhite. They're callin' him Doctor Blood, for God's sake...."

The two stewards, expressionless, lifted his litter from the back of the wagon, and his hand was torn from hers as they swiftly moved him into the tent. Belinda felt drawn to follow, and when he was placed on a table in a far corner, she felt a rush of excitement at the thought that Hepplewhite would not be getting to him right away.

"You're gonna help me?" His face, slick with perspiration, shone with a glimmer of hope as she moved beside him once again. "You stop the bleedin', and he won't take my leg off. Do it, lady, do it, for God's sake...."

Belinda bit her lower lip thoughtfully as she looked around to see where Hepplewhite was. The tent was rapidly filling with casualties. Some had died after being placed on tables to await treatment, and the stewards were trying to move the dead out fast to make room for those who were waiting. No one was paying attention to her. She could see Hepplewhite, his back turned, starting his first amputation, the soldier choking on his own screams as the chloroform cone was forced over his face to render him mercifully unconscious.

"Do something for me, please...." The young soldier reached out to clutch her sleeve. She felt the fabric tear, but paid no mind.

"I'll try. But be still, and don't make any noise. If they catch me doing this, I'll be in a lot of trouble."

He obliged, and she took a pair of scissors from a nearby instrument tray and hurriedly began to cut off his left trouser leg, beginning at the ankle. She had to slice all the way to the crotch, for the saber wound was almost to the lower abdomen. "You're lucky for two reasons," she told him as she reached for lint to soak up the blood so that she could see the extent of the wound. "If it had been your right leg, you'd probably already have bled to death. There's a big artery on that side. Also, an inch or two higher and it would have gone into your abdomen, and no telling what would have been punctured."

She saw he was right about there being no injury to the bone. The stab was clean, going all the way through the thigh. If the hemorrhaging could be stopped, there'd be no need to remove the leg.

Remembering a remedy Doc Jasper had used when old Ben Trucaby was gored by his bull, she told the soldier she'd be right back and rushed out of the tent to find the first armed man in sight. She cupped her hands and held them out to him. "Give me a half dozen of your rounds."

He was bewildered, but the intensity in her voice and the desperation gleaming in her eyes moved him to oblige.

Without offering an explanation, she turned and ran back inside.

She tore open the paper cartridges, tossing aside the piece of lead, then poured the powder into a small container. With that done, she moved fast to remove the soaking lint from the hole in the thigh and rapidly packed it with the gunpowder.

Finally she stood back and bluntly told him, "All we can do now is wait and pray, soldier. If cauterizing with gunpowder works, you'll live."

He managed a wan smile, for his strength was waning from loss of blood. "You got a nice touch, lady, so I'm sure it's gonna work. And I want you to know I'm beholden to you...."

"How about closing your eyes and trying to get some sleep?" she urged, brushing a shock of dark blond hair back from his face. "What's your name, anyway? And where do you come from?"

"Private Tommy Parker, from Beverly, Virginia."

"And how old are you?"

His grin was impish. "Fourteen. I lied, 'cause I wanted so bad to kill Yankees."

"Well, they almost killed you," she softly chided."And I suggest when you're over this, you head back to Beverly, because I'll wager your mother is worried sick."

He nodded. "Might just do that. I killed two of the bastards today, anyway...." He closed his eyes and drifted away.

Belinda was thankful to see that the gunpowder was apparently doing its job, because the bleeding was slowing. She applied a loose bandage and was just finishing when Captain Hepplewhite appeared, accompanied by a steward carrying a tray with the instruments needed for amputation.

At first he didn't realize what she'd done, and merely said with a frown, "Why did you waste bandages, Miss Coulter? There's nothing to be done here except amputate and seal quickly. Maybe tar is called for to sear the wound shut, and—"

He yanked back the covering strips and gasped. "What's this?" He looked from Belinda in wide-eyed horror to the gummy mass of bloodied gunpowder protruding from Tommy Parker's thigh. "What in hell have you done?" he roared.

"Stopped the bleeding," she told him, not flinching beneath his searing glare. "No bones are broken. It's a clean wound. All the way through. Suturing will take care of it. There's no need to amputate." There, she thought, feeling sweat break out on her upper lip as she squeezed her hands together to keep them from shaking, she'd done it. She had overstepped her position and dared advise a surgeon how to treat a patient. In that frozen moment, Hepplewhite looked as if he was using every bit of restraint he possessed to keep from strangling her then and there.

"What did you say?" He managed to choke the words past the rising anger in his throat. "Are you telling me you took it on yourself to decide this man's leg did not need to be amputated? Are you telling me you took it on yourself to fill his leg full of *gunpowder*, for God's sake?"

She swallowed hard, aware that those around them had turned to stare. "Surely you've heard of the treatment."

"It's crude and barbaric—"

"But it worked this time," she was compelled to advise him. "And the important thing is, a fourteen-year-old boy doesn't have to lose his leg. And that's all that matters."

Hepplewhite firmly shook his head, "No, Miss Coulter, what matters is that you once again took charge, forgetting your place, and I'm sick and tired of it." With veins standing out on his neck, face red with fury, he pointed a trembling finger and hoarsely ordered, "Out. Now. Don't show your face in this hospital again when I'm on duty. As a trained and skilled physician, as well as a respected officer of the Confederate army, I will not tolerate your opinionated and domineering behavior. Now get out, or so help me, I'll have you thrown out bodily."

She knew he would do just that, knew she had no choice but to obey, but with a stubborn, determined lift of her chin, defiantly demanded to know, "Will you still insist on removing this boy's leg?"

He took a menacing step forward. "Get out...."

Awash with humiliation, Belinda ran out, blinking back furious, scalding tears.

A steward stopped her to say sympathetically, "You're right, Miss Coulter. The man is a butcher, and I know everybody admires you for standing up to him like you did."

As always, she felt an inward shudder. Strangely, she could feel comfortable around a man only when he was incapacitated; otherwise, she was unnerved.

Others were waiting to express their sympathy, but suddenly Belinda felt the need to be alone with her thoughts.

Turning off the path that led to her private tent, she hurried into the woods and found her way to the creek. During the day, it was used for bathing or washing out clothes, but now the banks were deserted, bathed in the silver glow of a full moon.

She sank to the ground, covering her face with her hands. She sobbed quietly, allowing the tears to come. Why did it have to be this way? She could have returned to Richmond, but instead had chosen to remain and help the wounded. Never had she meant anyone any harm. She didn't even feel as though she'd overstepped her authority. It had been an emergency situation, and she'd done what seemed proper at the time to stop the bleeding. Even if it hadn't worked, Tommy Parker was no worse off. But now she'd been banished from the hospital, and what was left? She didn't want to work at the kitchen, for that was not her calling. In fact, if things had worked out and she'd married Harmon Willingham, she would have had to admit she could not cook. Jessica had been in charge of preparing meals back home, and that was one of the reasons she'd been free to tag along after Doc Jasper the way she had. She'd had no responsibilities around the house. So now she wanted to serve where she felt she was most efficient, but the prejudice of people like Captain Hepplewhite stood in her way.

Suddenly the sound of someone approaching made her tense, and as if by magic her mind tortured her by instantly taking her back to the night she'd been ravished. The image leapt before her, and she was on her feet and backing away, hands clutching at her throat, trying not to scream, all too terribly aware of how vulnerable she was in such a remote spot.

Ryan saw her standing there, knew she was on the verge of hysteria, and quickly attempted to soothe her. "Hey, don't be afraid. I'm not going to hurt you."

When she saw who it was, Belinda's eyes grew even wider, and she began to retreat farther. She remembered the creek was behind her when she stepped into the cool water, felt it rushing about her ankles, soaking the cuffs of the baggy trousers she was wearing. She had dared to hope he truly did not know her, but now she knew it had all been an act, otherwise why would he have come looking for her?

"It's me. Captain Tanner, remember? You saved my life. I've been wanting to find you so that I could thank you, and I got to the hospital in time to hear what just happened...."

A trick, her terrified brain screamed in warning, another trick to catch her off guard. "Don't come any closer," she warned, fingers of anger squeezing her spine. "If you do, I'll..." She remembered the scissors she'd absently stuck in her pocket, and she whipped them out to menace him with them. "I'll kill you. I swear I will, you bastard. Now get away from me and leave me alone—"

"What the hell is wrong with you, woman?" Ryan stopped in his tracks and laid his carbine aside to place his hands on his hips and stare at her in astonishment. "Are you crazy, or what? Now I think it's high time we got to the bottom of all this. The first time you laid eyes on me, you acted like someone struck insane. And the second time, as well. You tried to hide it out there in that ravine in front of those men, but I could tell, as weak as I was, you were having a hard time keeping from going all to pieces again. Damn it, I want to know why.

"I don't know you," he continued in a heated rush, nostrils flaring, nerves in his jaw tightening with his indignant anger, "but I'll admit I've got a strange feeling I've seen you before, someplace, sometime, but what I could have done to make you hate me so, make you so damn scared of me, I can't figure out. But you're going to tell me. Here. Tonight. I'm not moving till you do."

"Bastard!" she hissed between clenched teeth, waving the scissors menacingly. "You can pretend you don't know me all you want, but did you think I'd ever be able to forget what you and your friends did to me?"

Ryan slowly, firmly, shook his head from side to side. "Lady," he said quietly, evenly, "I swear to God I don't know what you're talking about."

Slashing at the air with the scissors, she screamed, "The hell you don't! Or do you rape so many women you can't remember them all?"

Ryan's heart slammed into his chest. "What?" He was incredulous. "I have never raped a woman in my life...."

"Liar! I'll help you remember. Last winter. Buncombe County, North Carolina. Late at night. I was riding a mule, and—"

"Miss Coulter," Ryan interjected sharply as the initial jolt of awareness subsided, "I think we need to have ourselves a long talk."

Chapter Eight

Ryan had been getting a Confederate regiment together back home near Franklin, North Carolina, and he had gone over into Buncombe County to recruit his cousin, Tully Hodgkins. Tully had agreed, since most of his kin came from near Franklin, too. To celebrate, they were having a night of revelry with Tully's friends the Hardin brothers, who'd indicated that they, too, were also willing to join up.

Ryan recalled how Tully had said the brothers were riled up over their father having been injured in a fight earlier, resulting in the loss of one eye. Jake and Rufus Hardin were bent on revenge, but Tully convinced them it was best to cool off and wait a spell, because the man they were after, Zeb Coulter, would, no doubt, be laying low for the time being.

So they'd all had a bit too much to drink and wound up sitting on a ridge where Jake and Rufus had a sweeping view of the road that led to the Coulters' farm. They were still hoping to waylay him when he came in from his hiding place.

Ryan had settled away from the others because he did not care for the Hardin boys, and was not terribly fond of his cousin, either. Ryan had not planned on a drinking binge, but had gone along with the revelry to take his mind off the building anger within him. Recruiting had made him all too aware of the fact that many Southerners just didn't realize the seriousness of the coming war. They all thought it wouldn't last long and the South would easily win. Ryan thought different. He had talked with officers of high rank and also men learned in government, and shared the opinion that a confrontation between North and South was going to be expensive in both money and lives. And it was always disturbing to listen to hotheads rave on and on when they didn't know what the hell they were talking about. So, that particular night, Ryan had drunk more than usual, but had made up his mind that as soon as his head stopped pounding he was going to ride on into Asheville and get a room at a hotel and sleep off the liquor before heading on back to Franklin.

At first, when he'd heard the commotion, he'd been too fuzzy headed to comprehend what was going on. It had taken a few moments to get himself together, and then he had found his horse, mounted, and headed off in the direction of the screams. By the time he'd ridden down the steep ridge, Tully and the Hardin brothers had been wrestling on the ground with a girl.

In the glow of moonlight, Ryan had noted that she had the reddest hair he had ever seen. And, when he had shoved the others away, he had known she was also the most beautiful.

Mercifully, she had fainted. And while names had not registered, Ryan remembered Rufus had told him she was the daughter of the man they were after, and if they couldn't get to Zeb Coulter, they'd just take their revenge on her.

Ryan had been quick to ax that idea, and Tully, suddenly ashamed, had joined him in convincing Rufus and Jake to leave her be.

Tully had said it was maybe a ten-minute ride back to her house, so Ryan had lifted her in his arms and placed her gently on the mule she'd been riding.

And the last he'd seen of her, she'd been on her way home.

He knew that was not the end of the story, and he attempted to say as much to Belinda, because now he knew exactly where he'd seen her before.

She continued to glare at him in fury as he spoke, still gripping the scissors. When he finished, she cried vehemently, "I don't believe you! You're lying. You were part of it. When I looked up, I knew I'd never forget your eyes. And when I saw you back in Richmond, it all came flooding back. I dared hope maybe you didn't remember me, but then you came looking for me, there, and now here, and you just want more of the same, but this time I'm ready for you, damn you!" The bile rose in her throat, almost choking her, as she recalled all that happened.

"Belinda, stop it. I can see why you think I was a part of it, but you've got to remember you'd fainted, and you must have woken up while I was lifting you onto your mule. You saw me then, so it was my face you remembered. After Tully and I left, the Hardin boys must've gone after you, and in your terror and hysteria you just thought I was a part of it. You've got to believe me..." He held out his hands to her in a pleading gesture. "I never touched you that night except to try and help you. I'm sorry it turned out like it did. If I'd known what they planned once my back was turned, I would've gunned the bastards down then and there."

"My pa did that."

Ryan's brows snapped together.

"He shot Rufus Hardin dead. Shot Jake, too. Maybe he died later. I don't know and I don't care, but where were you?" she asked mockingly, cocking her head to one side. "How come my pa missed shooting you, too?"

"Because I wasn't there. Not when you were raped or when your pa came after those responsible. What happened to him?"

"My sister helped him escape from jail. We never heard from him after that, but I left soon after. I wanted to escape the misery. I never thought I'd wind up looking you in the eye again, mister," she said with a scornful sneer.

Doggedly he told her, "I wasn't one of them. You've got to believe that."

"Just go away and leave me alone, or so help me, I'll go to General Beauregard and tell him everything."

Ryan shook his head miserably and said, "You can do that, and you can sure cause a lot of trouble, but you're wrong, Belinda. Try and remember. Did two men rape you, or three? Surely you'd know, even if you were passing in and out of consciousness...."

"I don't want to think about it," she cried in a thin voice that was barely audible. Anguished tears coursed down her cheeks. "I try to shut it out, but the one thing I can't push aside is the memory of your cat's eyes looking down at me...."

"I can't help having unusual eyes," Ryan said darkly, "and I'll be damned if I'm going to be accused of rape because of it."

"Three men pulled me off that mule. I remember that clearly."

"I didn't know anything was going on till I heard you scream. My cousin Tully was with them then, but he left with me."

"And where is Cousin Tully?" she asked with a smirk. "Not that I'd believe him, anyway. No doubt he'd lie to save you."

"He wouldn't be lying," Ryan stated flatly, "if he were here to tell you. He's dead."

Belinda shrugged. "It makes no difference. I wouldn't believe him, either," she repeated.

Ryan gave a ragged sigh, realizing it was hopeless. "I reckon you're going to believe what you want to, and I'm real sorry about that, because I only tried to help you that night. If you'll calm down and try to recall that night—hurtful to you as the memory is—I think you'll realize there could only have been two men having their way with you that night—and I wasn't one of them." He turned on his heel and disappeared back the way he had come.

Belinda stared after him long after he was swallowed up by the night. Finally she stepped out of the creek, but she did not return to camp and her waiting tent. Instead, she moved into the shadows and lowered herself to the ground, out of sight of anyone who might happen by.

She lay back, the moonlight lacing through the leaves above to pattern her face in dappled silver.

. And, against her will, her mind went spinning back to that horrible night.

With eyes squeezed tightly shut, she sought to remember each and every detail. In a maze of brutality and pain, she thought of how they'd torn into her brutally, laughing at her screams for mercy. She'd seen the faces of Jake and Rufus as she drifted in and out of consciousness. But always there had been the flashing image of those golden eyes. Yet, as perspiration beaded her forehead as memory strained, she could not associate those eyes with the thrusting anguish she'd felt as her body was savagely violated again and again.

She sat up straight to glare into the darkness as she dared to wonder— *Was Ryan Tanner telling the truth?*

She shook her head violently to clear it, to dispel the cobwebs and attempt to clarify each and every vision within. In all honesty, in all fairness, she could associate only Jake and Rufus with the act of rape itself. The image of Ryan Tanner's eyes was distinct, yet it was singular, and void of any attached significance.

Other pieces of the puzzle began to come together. If he was so callous and cruel as to rape a woman, surely he would not be so hypocritical as to come around her and pretend it had never happened. Even if he hadn't remembered her specifically, he would have had sense enough to back away and leave her alone when it became obvious that *she'd* remembered *him*. He would not have doggedly pursued her to try and convince her he was innocent.

Captain Ryan Tanner, Belinda finally, gratefully acknowledged, was not guilty.

She scrambled to her feet, anxious to find him and apologize for all the terrible things she'd said, eager, also, to thank him for having attempted to save her that night.

But the moment she stepped back into the clearing of the campsite, one of the pickets saw her and grabbed her arm, telling her in a rush, "Everybody's been lookin' for you, Miz Belinda. Seems Major Whitley heard about the to-do between you and Captain Hepplewhite, and he's pretty mad."

"I still think I did the right thing," she muttered indignantly, more to herself than to the picket, because she didn't care what he thought. In fact, she didn't care what anyone thought. She would have done it all over again to save Tommy Parker's leg from needless amputation.

The picket said hastily, "Oh, the major ain't mad at you, ma'am. That's why he's lookin' for you. To tell you so. 'Course, I ain't supposed to know that. I'm just supposed to be on the lookout for you, but I heard him and the captain talkin' about what happened, and he sure chewed him out good and proper."

Belinda thanked him and hurried to the hospital, smiling back at the soldiers who waved as she passed. Inside, she did not see Captain Hepplewhite anywhere around, but spotted Major Whitley at one of the operating tables.

She hurried to his side. "You wanted to see me?"

With an ebony-handled instrument, he was probing in the chest of an unconscious man. Absently he nodded to her, but his eyes were squinted with deep concentration as he worked, sleeves rolled up to his elbows. At last, he grinned in triumph and withdrew the probe. "It's as I thought. Minié ball lying against a rib."

Major Whitley nodded to Belinda, who stood next to the instrument tray. "Get that syringe and give him a half grain of morphine mixed with three drops of water. We need to keep him under till I get this sucker out."

Belinda obliged, quickly and carefully. The stewards assisting were only too glad for her to take on the task, for it was obvious her hands were much steadier than theirs after they had exerted themselves out on the battlefield, lifting litter after litter of wounded and the dead.

When the bullet was removed, Major Whitley deftly stitched the wound closed, then instructed one of the stewards to pack it with lint and bandage. "I think we can save our gunpowder on this one," he added with a wink at Belinda as he caught her arm and guided her from the table.

At once, Belinda spoke up to justify her actions. "I was only trying to help, Doctor. I examined the wound and saw it was clean, and I was afraid of a hasty amputation, and—"

"You don't have to explain anything to me, Belinda." He kept on steering her until they were outside in the crisp, night air, moving away from curious ears. "I understand what you did and why, and that's what I told Captain Hepplewhite, but I'm afraid he has a very prejudiced view of women in medicine, especially ones without formal training.

"Let me explain something to you," he went on gently, kindly, his arm about her in comforting, fatherly fashion. "Most of the men helping out in the hospitals are infantrymen detailed against their will. A lot of them are convalescents, chosen because they aren't strong enough for field duty, and they don't have any aptitude or experience in caring for the sick. And, as soon as they're well enough, they're whisked back to their line regiments, so we're really short of help. Women have been volunteering, but very few have ever had any kind of training. You have. Maybe it wasn't much, traipsing around after a doctor, but it was certainly better than no training at all. Still, something like that doesn't mean a hill of beans to a stubborn man like Hepplewhite, who thinks women need to be home making lint for bandages and having bake sales to raise money for the cause.

"Now there's talk the Confederate Congress is going to give women volunteers some kind of status, but it hasn't happened yet. And till it does, there won't be any schooling, and certainly not much respect. Men like Hepplewhite don't care about Florence Nightingale and her tremendous contributions to the health of the British Army in the Crimean War, or how she wound up supervising over a hundred and twenty-five nurses and then went back to London and started up a nurses' training school there. All they care about is keeping a woman in a place they impose on her, and I can talk till I'm blue in the face, but it won't change a thing."

"I suppose what you're trying to tell me is that it would be best if I stuck to emptying chamber pots and doing the laundry," she said lamely.

"Not altogether," he said hastily. "I just think it would be best if you didn't take matters into your own hands. With the Parker lad, you were right to do what you did, but it was wrong of you to assume that Captain Hepplewhite would recklessly remove his leg. You're a hard worker, Belinda. A dedicated worker. I'm happy to have you working with us, but you had no business making that decision on your own."

Defiantly, Belinda countered, "I'm afraid I have to disagree. I've seen him operate countless times without considering any other option, and—"

He held up a finger for silence. "You're wrong to say that. It is not your place to sit in judgment of a trained doctor. Even though the Union is liberal in their views on women nurses, organizing a corps before the echo of the first gun fired on Fort Sumter faded away, I imagine part of their training is learning their place—which you are going to have to do, young lady, if you want to keep working here."

Belinda could have lashed out, indignantly reminding him that she received no pay, just room and board—and meager it was, too. But it would have been a shallow argument, for both of them knew she now had a fevered desire to work in medicine, to help the sick and suffering, and would attempt to surmount any obstacle to prevent her doing so—

even if it meant compromising her feelings about a pompous, arrogant doctor like Captain Hepplewhite.

With a disdainful sigh, she conceded, "Very well. I'll ask before I act, and I'll try to keep my opinions to myself."

"Good." He withdrew his arm from about her to pat her shoulder. "I was hoping you'd agree, because I'd sure like to keep you working with us, dear."

"Maybe the Yankees would appreciate me more," she dared jest. "At least they'd give me formal training and some status."

He laughed at that. "I'm afraid you'd be a real maverick there. I happened to see a copy of the *American Medical Times* with an article about the woman their secretary of war, Simon Cameron, appointed to superintend the women nurses. Her name is Dorothea Dix, and she had a background working with the mentally ill. They say she rules with an iron fist and is working on a circular of rules about any women wanting to train as nurses.

"One of her first requirements is that no woman under thirty need apply. And," he added with yet another chuckle of glee, "they've got to be plain-looking women, and *you*, Miss Belinda Coulter, are not a plain-looking woman."

He turned back toward the hospital, urging, "Now let's get back to work, and next time remember not all doctors are as tolerant as me."

Belinda hurried along with him, anxious to get back to work, for the litters of wounded waiting to be treated stretched out in all directions.

Finding Captain Tanner would have to wait, and that thought pleased her. Talking about the misery only dredged up the memories all over again. She would much rather lose herself in her work. Their paths need not cross again, and that would be best for both. Besides, she had to admit he was an extremely handsome man, and she knew that if she allowed it, the image of those strangely compelling eyes could begin to evoke pleasant stirrings within...stirrings she had vowed never to feel again for any man.

* * *

It was only with great effort that Ryan had been able to walk away from her, because he was getting angrier by the second. To think of what those bastards had done after he and Tully left made his guts burn with fury. *Damn them to hell!*

He hadn't thought anything about it when they'd failed to report at the appointed time to join the regiment from Franklin. Tully said they had never been dependable. Ryan figured maybe it was best, because he'd found them mean and surly, and they could have been a real problem. Later, Tully told him he'd got a letter from one of his cousins saying Rufus had been killed and Jake had been wounded pretty bad. Maybe he had said something about why, but at the time, Ryan hadn't paid any attention. Now he wished he had. And it was just as well, damn it, that Belinda's father had taken care of it, because he'd have been tempted to go back there and do it himself if he'd known about it.

But now it was in the past, best left alone. Belinda was making a new life for herself, such as it was, working in the bloody hell of war. He should go his way and forget about her, because, unfortunately, he only reminded her of the nightmare.

Still, there was something about her that stirred his soul—and made him want to see her again.

Chapter Nine

J uly melted into August. In the oppressive heat came the news that Union president Lincoln had decided that slaves used by the South to fight the North would be freed when captured. Indignant, enraged cries went up, fueling the determination of the Confederacy to teach the Yankees a lesson for having brought about the war in the first place.

Rebels led by General Magruder charged into Hampton, Virginia, where Union general Benjamin Butler was said to be quartering runaway slaves. The town was burned to the ground. Butler, with the approval of the Secretary of War, refused to return the fugitives to the Confederate states.

Ryan had intended to pay Belinda a visit following their encounter at the creek, but was ordered to take his cavalry company into the conflict with Magruder. With skirmishes at Blue Creek and Burlington, it appeared things were heating up, making another major battle likely, and he feared that by the time he returned, she might not be there.

Finally, Ryan received word to report to General Wise, the commander of the western forces. He had hoped the summons meant he was being sent back to Beauregard's army, but he was elated to find the assignment even better. Wise confided that he feared a forthcoming major confrontation with General Rosecrans's forces. Wise had managed to squeeze reinforcements from Richmond, and General Floyd was on the way.

Hearing that, Ryan, with the shameless candor that sometimes got him in trouble, said, "He's more interested in his own glory than he is in winning the damn war. Everybody knows he appointed the editor of the Lynchburg *Republican* as his chief of staff, for God's sake. And why else would he appoint an editor as his aide-de-camp unless he intends for his victories to be set in print as quick as possible?

"And he's got a farmer as his cavalry commander," Ryan raged on, "because he says he knows more about horses than other soldiers. Hell, I can shoe a horse and break a mustang, and I can doctor a horse as good as any man, but I'm a cavalry commander because I'm a *leader,* damn it, and that's the *only* reason any man should be in charge of a unit. And now you're telling me we've got to depend on a man like Floyd to help us whip Rosecrans?" He shook his head in disgust.

General Wise ignored Ryan's outburst and went on to give him his assignment. General Floyd was bringing troops, but he had been unable to gather medical forces, sending word that Beauregard had volunteered a detail from his army. Ryan was to take his men and go after them, giving them safe escort.

Eagerly, Ryan mustered his men, who grumbled about having to move on such short notice, and was on his way in less than an hour.

During the ride, which took that day and most of the next, Ryan deliberated on his planned encounter with Belinda. He would seek her out for a friendly hello. Later, he would ask for a chance to get to know her better. It would be difficult with a war going on, sure, but they could find time. They would *make* time.

He thought, too, how he couldn't help feeling partly responsible for what had happened to her, because, damn it, gut instinct should have told him not to trust the Hardins. He ought to have taken her home himself, instead of setting her unconscious on the mule and slapping the animal on the rump to send it on its way.

Attempting to soothe his conscience, however, was not the reason he wanted to spend time with her. Far from it. Neither was her beauty the motivation. The fact was, there was something different about Belinda Coulter, drawing him to her, making him want to wrap his arms about her and protect her from all harm. He wanted to comfort and safeguard, yes, but he had to admit that he desired the sweetness of her, as well—but later. What Ryan was feeling for her could not be satisfied with a quick tumble in bed.

He wanted more.

Much more.

When Belinda heard that Major Whitley was asking for volunteers to be dispatched to the western part of Virginia, her only thought was to hope he'd get the staff he needed. She didn't think about offering to go herself, for she was quite busy, and satisfied, with her present duties.

With a lull in heavy fighting, they had set up a hospital in a church within a half day's ride of Richmond. Supplies were not hard to come by, and she did not feel so isolated from civilization. Major Whitley had even mentioned that she could go to work at the large hospital in Richmond, Chimborazo, if she really wanted to, but she resisted that idea. Prejudice against female nurses was bad enough in the field, and it had to be worse in the city. In the wilderness there was desperation for help, and few surgeons, she'd found, let their resentment stand in the way of admitting she was useful. Captain Hepplewhite's open hostility was the exception rather than the rule, thank goodness. But in a facility such as Chimborazo, Belinda was sure, she'd be relegated to menial housekeeping tasks, looked upon as no better than a servant.

Thanks to Major Whitley's endorsement and encouragement, Belinda was actually being allowed to train and learn in the field. That had much to do with why she worked hard and diligently, for, with each passing day, she felt herself drawn more and more into the world of medicine. And what a compliment it had been when Dr. Whitley suggested she think about going to medical school when the war finally ended.

A woman doctor?

She had laughed at such a ludicrous idea, assuring him that the struggle she was making for acceptance as a nurse was all the strife she could handle in her lifetime.

Yet she could not wholly dismiss the notion of a career in medicine. Being raped had left her with little sense of her own self-worth, for she had been violated, degraded. Harmon's heartless rejection had left her feeling unfit as a woman, soiled and dirty. But when a wounded soldier clutched her hand in gratitude, she suddenly, miraculously, felt whole again, needed and respected, and that was truly the motivating force that kept her going. It was as though she'd been reborn to her true purpose in life. Despite being surrounded by the tragedies and horrors of war, Belinda felt a strange and wonderful peace—and she was not about to let it go.

So she had not planned to go with Major Whitley, but two things happened to change her mind. First, she was concerned to learn that there had been no volunteers. Apparently no one wanted to leave the relative safety of General Beauregard's encampment and deliberately head into a battle zone. Then, while she was toying with the idea of suggesting he allow her to go, an unexpected visit by a group of Richmond church ladies gave her the final incentive she needed.

At the time they arrived, Belinda was doing her best to care for the men in her care, under less than desirable circumstances. Usually, a convalescent accompanied her to take care of the personal tasks, like bathing those who weren't able to do so themselves and changing dressings on wounds that might be on or around private parts of the body. That particular afternoon, however, there were no convalescents around, for everyone had been discharged earlier in the day to return to their respective units. Those left were far too sick to move around. Compounding an already somewhat sensitive situation was the absence of many of the doctors, because Surgeon General Samuel Moore, head of the Confederate medical services, had arrived the night before and an important staff meeting was being held. She had found herself alone in the little church, trying her best to take care of her daily duties without assistance.

She promised those in dire need of a bath that she would go in search of soldiers willing to oblige as soon as she finished her rounds. She checked dressings, took time to spoon-feed those too weak to feed themselves, and also dispensed prescribed medication.

But at the bedside of one soldier she was assailed by the unpleasant odor of a bandage that could not wait to be changed. Unfamiliar to her, he had come in during the night, and she gently inquired as to the extent of his wound.

With a slight blush, he explained he'd been in a fight with a Yankee picket, with the result that he'd been stabbed by a bayonet. "In my—" he had hesitated, his Adam's apple bobbing as he swallowed against his embarrassment "—my *hindquarters*, ma'am."

Belinda, too, swallowed hard, but she blanched only slightly. Actually, she was more embarrassed for the soldier than for herself, for, despite the obligatory precautions, she had unfortunately been exposed to male body parts from time to time as she had assisted with surgery. Also, on the occasions when she had accompanied stretcher-bearers onto the battlefields to retrieve the wounded, the corpsmen had not allowed the presence of a woman to keep them from doing whatever was necessary to try and save a man's life. If it meant ripping off his trousers to expose a wound that was bleeding profusely, exposing private parts to her as they did so, there was no hesitation.

But, in the particular situation she found herself in that morning, Belinda had no experience. In the past, there had always been a convalescent around to do the delicate work. But when she saw how the sheet beneath the soldier was soaked in blood, she knew she had no choice but to do what had to be done—and quickly. It was dangerous to allow the bleeding to continue.

With a deep sigh of resignation, she reached for her basket of supplies. "That dressing really needs dry lint to stop the bleeding, but I'm afraid there's no one around to do it for the moment, except me. If you feel really uncomfortable about me doing it, we can hope the bleeding stops by itself, and you can wait till someone else shows up. But I have no idea how long that's going to be."

The soldier wrinkled his nose at the odor. He could feel that he was lying in blood, and he was terribly uncomfortable. "Well, ma'am . . ." he drawled, face turning even redder, "as best I can feel, I got stuck on the side of my hip. Ought not be too bad on either one of us if'n I just roll over on my belly."

He proceeded to do so.

And so it happened that, when the good ladies from the Bethany Holiness Ladies' Circle walked into the converted church, they found a young woman bending over a man's naked hip. Two fainted dead away, while three others covered their faces with their hands and ran out screaming. One of those, forgetting to uncover her eyes, stumbled and fell all the way down the steps, sustaining nasty bruises and a slightly injured ankle.

The remaining emissaries, however, exchanged quick, angry looks of shared indignation and, in silent mutual agreement, proceeded to march directly to where Belinda was working over the soldier.

"And what do you think you're doing?" the apparent leader of the survivors demanded irately. Then, seeing the angry wound on the soldier's buttock, she suddenly clutched her throat and thinly gasped, "Oh, my heavens . . ." before stumbling backward to collapse on the floor.

The remaining women, also with choked gasps, promptly fled.

Belinda quickly finished her task, and then, squaring her shoulders, headed outside to a scene of mass confusion and hysteria, stepping over the still-unconscious body of the group leader. The soldiers stared at her sympathetically from their cots.

It was a terrible scene. And by the time each of the ladies got through telling her version of what they'd been so horrified to witness, the tale had grown to depict the wounded soldier as being completely naked while Belinda ogled him under the pretense of changing his bandage.

The officers summoned to try and calm the women down knew better. Of course the situation could not have been as they described; Belinda's reputation, they assured the good ladies, was above reproach.

"She has no business in there," the leader hotly declared after being brought awake by ammonia vapors waved beneath her nose. When she heard that Belinda was working as a nurse, her objections were only reinforced. "No decent woman would want to work around men when they're naked—*except one of questionable morals!*" she added with a sniff of disdain and a contemptuous lift of her chin.

Fearing she was about to lose her temper and tell the women where they could go with their pious sanctimony, Belinda threw up her hands in disgust and went back inside to work. And when Major Whitley came in later, laughing over the incident, she begged him to let her go with him into the field.

"*You* might be understanding about all this," she asserted, "but Captain Hepplewhite will just use it to reinforce his prejudices against women nurses. I'd really like to get away awhile, and I sure don't want to go back to Richmond now."

Major Whitley compassionately agreed, and so, when Ryan arrived in camp, he realized that all his plans for approaching Belinda were for naught. She was standing right beside the doctor, and Ryan realized it was her intent to go out with the medical services.

Suddenly, Ryan knew it didn't matter a hill of beans what he'd said to her that night at the creek, because he could still feel her contempt. He could see, too, how her fingers trembled as she touched her hand to her throat, as though suppressing a gasp of horror at his nearness.

Major Whitley promptly informed him, "We're ready whenever you are, Captain, but I suppose you want to rest up and set out first thing in the morning."

"Dawn," Ryan affirmed, managing to tear his gaze from Belinda to say irritably to the doctor, "Surely you aren't taking *her.*"

Major Whitley blinked in bewilderment, but Belinda exploded. "Of course I'm going, Captain. We're shorthanded here. In case you haven't heard, they've pulled half our staff back to Richmond to handle the casualties pouring in there. General Beauregard said one doctor and one assistant could go—and I'm that assistant because nobody else wanted the assignment." She finished with a curt nod of defiance.

Ryan shook his head; he wasn't about to argue with her. Instead, he addressed Whitley. "Maybe I need to remind you we aren't setting up a field hospital, doctor. All we want to provide is emergency care once the wounded are carried from the battlefield. Any soldier needing convalescence will have to be eventually transported to Richmond, and—"

"Captain," Major Whitley interjected politely, "we'll find a place to set up a hospital. We'll take over a house, or a church, anything where we can do what has to be done. But I need help."

"It's no place for a woman," Ryan declared solemnly.

At that, the doctor's lips curved into an almost mischievous smile. "But, Captain, haven't you heard? Miss Coulter isn't merely a woman. She's a *nurse.*"

"And a damn good one, I'm sure," Ryan conceded, noticing Belinda, too, was smiling. He was glad. At least she had stopped looking like she was about to go into hysterics. "But I still think it's too dangerous for her. We're expecting a major battle at any time."

Major Whitley gave him a friendly slap on the shoulder. "Well, set your mind at ease, Captain. Miss Coulter has been out in the field numerous times. She knows to wait till there's a cease-fire. She knows what to do when she gets there. She doesn't swoon at the sight of blood, and I'm afraid before this war is over she'll be able to amputate a man's leg as well as any surgeon. She learns fast. She's courageous. I doubt you'd find a soldier who could do any better.

"Now then," he finished, "if you'll excuse me, I think I'll try to finish up and turn in early."

He walked away, leaving Ryan and Belinda looking at each other in silent regard. Finally, Belinda moved to follow after the doctor, but Ryan reached out to clutch her arm and hold her back. "There's something I'd like to say—"

"You've already said it." She twisted in his grasp, but he held tight, and she snapped, "You're wasting your breath. I'm well aware of how nurses are held in disesteem."

"Please hear me out." He released her then, lest others see her struggling and wonder what was going on, possibly even move to intervene. "You're being unfair. So is Major Whitley, because my objection has nothing to do with your being a nurse. And, to be honest, I've heard you're every bit as good as he says you are. But you're still a woman, and I'm worried for your safety. I'd also like us to be friends."

She softened, remembering that she'd intended to apologize for the horrid way she'd treated him that night at the creek. But she was exhausted from working endless hours in the hospital. She tried to remember how long ago it had been since the last time she'd seen Captain Tanner, but she honestly could not. Days blended into weeks and she lost all track of time. It was nearly September. That was all she was sure of. Pressing her fingertips to her forehead, Belinda thought of how eager she was for the journey across the state to begin. A soldier would be at the reins, and she could enjoy a rare and precious nap in the back of the wagon during the day. But now Captain Tanner was standing before her, and she did not like the way he made her feel so vulnerable. She could hold her own with the sassiest of men, but this one ignited a different kind of emotion, one she did not wish to dwell upon.

Woodenly, wanting to be done with their exchange, Belinda said, "Listen, I want to apologize for the way I talked to you before. I realize now you weren't one of those responsible, but it's over and I want to try and forget it."

Once more she turned to go, and once more Ryan's arm snaked out to prevent her. "Please," he implored, "understand how sorry I am, because, damn it, I'm angry with myself for not stopping to think those bastards might turn around and head you off. I'd like for you and me to start over," he continued. "That's what I wanted to say to you, that I'd like to be your friend. And if I made you mad just now, I'm sorry, but I still feel it's too dangerous for a woman out there, even though I'd like the chance to be with you—"

"'Be' with me?" she echoed incredulously. "*Never*, Captain Tanner. Not with you. Not with anyone. I'm a nurse now. And that's all I care about."

Helpless, Ryan could only watch her hasty retreat. He had not failed to notice how her voice had cracked at the last as she fought to keep from crying. Nor had he missed the sheen of mingled fear and revulsion in her eyes.

Yet he had also sensed the curtain of loathing descending—not when he'd said he wanted to be with her, but, instead, at the exact moment when he'd first walked up to her and Major Whitley and their eyes had met and held.

He understood, too, that it was not just him, personally, that provoked such feelings. Sadly, it was because he was a man—and he supposed he could understand that.

Belinda had suffered a terrible ordeal, but her body had healed.

It was the wound upon her mind and soul that might never be purged.

They headed out at first light, Ryan's cavalry leading two wagons. Major Whitley rode in one, Belinda in another. Ryan purposely stayed away, hanging back in the formation, as he told himself it was best to just leave her alone. The lady had a problem she had to work out within herself, and since she obviously associated him with it despite his innocence, trying to make friends with her was hopeless for the time being. Still, the more he brooded, the more determined he became. And finally, when they made camp that night, he approached her under pretense of official inquiry.

She was sitting away from the campfire, sipping coffee from a tin mug. He had noticed she seemed only at ease when Major Whitley was around, and he had gone to check on one of Ryan's men, who had been stricken with a bad bellyache. So she was alone, and looking quite nervous, Ryan noted.

With a deep breath of resolution, he walked over and quickly sat down beside her. Whipping her head about, she gave a startled gasp, and he spoke up quickly, lest she run away like a frightened doe. "I wanted to ask if there's anything I or my men can do to make you more comfortable during the ride."

"No, nothing." She gave her head a brisk shake. "I'm fine. Really." She started to get up.

"I think the major was wrong about your courage." He spoke solemnly, staring straight ahead at the fire's gently burning embers, eyes narrowed thoughtfully.

"What do you mean by that?" Belinda asked sharply.

He deliberately did not look at her. "I think you're a coward. Maybe you can go into a battlefield and pick your way among the dead. Maybe you don't faint at the sight of blood. But if you find yourself around a man who's in one healthy piece, you're terrified."

"That—that's not true," she stammered, swinging her head from side to side, red-gold hair flying about her stricken face. "That's crazy—"

"The only time you weren't afraid of me was when you found me wounded in that ditch. You told yourself I couldn't hurt you, the shape I was in. That's what you tell yourself about all the wounded you're around. You revel in it, because it's the only time you feel safe."

"You've got a nerve," she flared indignantly.

"You mean I've *struck* one." He gave a bitter laugh. "Because I speak the truth, and we both know it.

"At first," he went on, ignoring her obviously rising ire, "when you thought I was one of the men who hurt you, you hated me, but even after you were forced to realize I couldn't have been involved, you still don't like me. And the reason for that, Belinda Coulter, is that you've let what happened make you distrust all men. You're scared of them, each and every one, unless they're wounded...weak...vulnerable.... That's what makes you a good nurse. Not courage. And you might as well still be laying on the ground back there in the Blue Ridge Mountains with the Hardin brothers brutalizing you, because you damn sure haven't been able to pick yourself up and get on with your life."

Their gazes locked.

Belinda's emerald eyes mirrored the red-hot embers of the campfire, while Ryan met her stare intently, nostrils slightly flaring, the nerves in his jaw tensing.

Finally, in a voice edged with loathing, Belinda snapped, "How dare you say such a thing? How dare you bring back the nightmare?" Once more, furiously, she attempted to blink away the threatening tears. *She would not let him make her cry.*

"I dare because you needed to hear it." His tone softened, and he reached to caress her trembling hand. She attempted to snatch it away, but he held it tight. "And because I really do want to be your friend. If you'll be honest with yourself, you'll realize having a man for a friend is exactly what you need to make you see we aren't all like the Hardins.''

If only it were that simple, Belinda reflected, a bitter smile touching the corners of her lips. It was easy for Captain Tanner to think her doubts were motivated solely by the Hardins. He did not know about Harmon—and she had no intention of telling him.

Ryan mistook her smile for concession. ''I swear I'll never do anything to hurt you,'' he said gently.

At that, Belinda snapped, ''I know you won't, because you won't get a chance. And I've *got* a friend—Major Whitley.

''You see, Tanner,'' she airily informed him as she got to her feet, with him scrambling to stand beside her, ''you're wrong. I don't distrust or hate all men. Maybe I do feel more comfortable around those who need me, but only because I like feeling needed. As for my hating you on sight, I did believe you were in league with those animals. I'm now willing to give you the benefit of the doubt, because I honestly can't remember every detail of that night, thank God—but I still want nothing to do with you. You make me think of things I don't want to remember. Besides, as you said yourself, you could have prevented it from happening.''

Ryan could only sadly stare after her as she hurried off into the night.

Somehow, some way, he silently, fiercely vowed, he was going to change her way of thinking.

Chapter Ten

"I believe," Major Whitley said one morning as they gathered around the campfire for boiled coffee, "that things will soon start quieting down. Both sides are going to settle in for the winter."

"But hell will break loose in the spring," Ryan opined. "It's not going to be the ninety-day war folks predicted. Bull Run changed all that." He raised his mug to his lips, watching Belinda from beneath lowered lashes. She was standing on the other side of the doctor, clean and sweet smelling, from a morning dip in a nearby creek, he supposed. She had washed her hair and it glistened like spun gold in the crimson sunlight.

Major Whitley shook his head at the memory of the battle. "It might have been a success for our side, but Beauregard's army was more disorganized by victory than McDowell's by defeat. Troops on both sides were ill trained, and the officers weren't used to handling large numbers. Even the opposing flags looked alike, and it seemed everybody had on a different uniform, so nobody was sure who the enemy was!

"I don't know about the Federals," he went on, "but I hear we lost nearly four hundred men, and the latest report listed nearly sixteen hundred wounded."

Ryan gulped down the rest of his coffee. "Well, let's hope this will be the last battle coming up for a while. Where will you be settling in for the winter?'' He addressed himself to the doctor, but continued to surreptitiously observe Belinda.

Whitley shrugged. "Who knows? Where we're needed, we'll go. Right, Belinda?" He gave her a friendly nudge with his elbow to include her in the conversation, and when she only made a perfunctory murmur in response, his brows raised and he asked, "Is something wrong, dear? You've been so quiet since we left camp. You aren't feeling bad, are you? Good heavens, it wouldn't do for you to come down with something...."

"I'm fine, fine," she assured him quickly, not wanting attention focused on her. It was disconcerting enough to be in the company of Captain Tanner. She had inwardly groaned when he had joined them, and she had not missed seeing the way he kept watching her when he thought she wasn't looking.

To her consternation, Major Whitley pressed on. "You aren't still upset by those haughty church women, are you? Don't pay them any mind. They're always showing up at inopportune times, thinking they're doing their good Christian duty, but all they do is get in the way. I had one walk right in once when I was amputating a leg, and, of course, she fainted. If a steward hadn't been there to grab her in time, she'd have fallen right across the patient, with disastrous consequences, I'm sure," he finished with a mirthless chuckle.

Again, Belinda rushed to tell him, "No, no. I don't care about them. Nothing's wrong. I'm just anxious to be on our way. I guess I don't feel really comfortable out here in the open."

"Open?" The doctor hooted, waving an arm challengingly. "You call this *open?* Why, we're having to make our own path as we go. We're in real wilderness now. The men are even having to cut down small trees to get our wagons through, and last night I swear I heard a bear crashing through the woods."

Ryan laughed. "You did. One of the night pickets said he saw him lumbering through the camp. As for being in the wilderness," he went on to explain, seeing the sudden concern mirrored on Belinda's face, "I didn't want to go back the same way we came in. Federal patrols are ever-alert for trails, and they lay in ambush, figuring they can take a supply patrol by surprise. It might take us an extra day to get back to West's camp, but I didn't want to take any chances."

"Makes sense." Whitley nodded, downing the rest of his coffee and turning to go. "Guess I'd better make sure everything in my wagon is secured. Belinda, will you ride with me today? There's some things I'd like to talk to you about, and I fear once we get where we're going, there might not be time for quiet talk."

"Of course." She headed for her wagon to get her things. Ryan was right behind her.

Whirling around, she curtly demanded, "Is there something else, Captain?"

"What did those women say to you?"

"Not much that hasn't been said before—behind my back."

"That bad?" he cheerily prodded.

She couldn't help smiling to remember the pandemonium. "I'm afraid it was worse. Men, after all, try to be a bit gentlemanly in their criticism, but women can be rather brutal when they censure. It didn't help matters any..." she went on to add, green eyes sparkling with mischief, "when they walked in to find me changing the dressing on a soldier's bare hip."

Ryan burst into laughter and cried, "Oh, I wish I could have been there to see their faces!"

She proceeded to describe their reactions in detail, but was careful to explain, "I don't normally do things like that, but I didn't have any choice. The soldier was bleeding badly and I had to get his wound packed with dry lint right away."

"Is he going to be all right?"

"I think so. Major Whitley checked him immediately after he arrived, and he said the bleeding had all but stopped." She shook her head with chagrin. "Seems I'm always getting in trouble by making quick decisions. I never intended to get this involved, really, but I just get so caught up in what I'm doing."

"And you wanted to be a singer."

"That's right," she admitted. "Bart Starkey promised to make me the next Jenny Lind and I was so naive I actually believed him, but all he was after was a pass into the camps so he could gamble with the soldiers in hopes of winning big."

"And he hightailed it when the bullets started flying, right?"

"Right." She giggled to recall the look of panic on Bart's face the day he'd said his hurried goodbyes.

They had lapsed into a bridge of easiness between them in only a few moments. Belinda had begun walking with Ryan beside her, surprised to find she no longer felt desperate to escape his company.

"How is it you went to work with the medical services?"

"By accident." She recounted the story.

He wanted to know if her time trailing after Doc Jasper back in the Blue Ridge had whetted her appetite for nursing.

"Not at the time," she admitted. "But I do remember him confiding he'd rather have me alongside him than his wife, because he'd lost count of the number of times she fainted when she was helping him."

Encouraged by the way she seemed to be warming to him, and in no hurry to bring the encounter to a close, Ryan dared to ask, "What led you to leave home? Don't you miss your family?"

A shadow crossed her face. "I miss my sister. I don't even know if my father is still alive. He probably went to fight for the North. It was him being so outspoken against secession that heaped so much trouble on us in the first place. Folks felt he brought on the feud with the Hardins, so there wasn't much sympathy for what happened to me."

Ryan was aghast to hear such nonsense, and said so. "I can't believe anyone wouldn't sympathize with you, Belinda. An innocent young girl . . ."

"Folks get pretty riled up when anybody takes sides with Yankees in our part of the country. You should know that, being from Franklin. That's not so far from my home."

"It isn't an excuse for condoning those men for what they did. I'm glad your pa shot them."

She nodded, and she felt no remorse whatsoever when she declared bluntly, "I just hope Jake died from his wounds. I don't intend to ever go back there, but I'd like to know I don't have to worry about ever laying eyes on him again."

Impulsively he touched her arm, and she did not draw away as he told her fervently, "As long as I'm around, Belinda, you don't ever have to worry about anybody hurting you."

As their eyes met and held, Ryan was warmed to realize that he could sense her growing confidence. He smiled with pleasure, and, to his further amazement, she responded with a small smile of her own.

When he left her, Belinda went inside the wagon to gather up her personal belongings. There wasn't much. A canvas medical knapsack packed with tourniquets, lint, bandages and tins of medication. Her bedroll. The dirty dress she'd changed out of earlier, ready to be washed when there was an opportunity. But she took her time, wanting a few moments alone with her thoughts after the brief but pleasant time with Captain Tanner—no, *Ryan,* she thought, correcting herself. If he addressed her by her first name, then she could take the same liberty with him. It struck her that he hadn't asked if it would be permissable, but then, she had the impression that he was a man used to asserting himself without concern for decorum. Yet he was also a gentleman, for he'd done nothing to make her feel less than a lady when in her company. Unlike some of the soldiers, who forgot she was around and used foul language, Ryan was ever-polite.

What she found puzzling, however, and now sought to ponder, was why he took it upon himself to make her acquaintance and attempt friendship. With a frown, she wondered at any secret motives he might have; perhaps he thought that, since she had lost her virginity, she had no reason not to give herself freely. Well, if that was the case, he had another thought coming.

She allowed herself to think of Harmon; it was something she always fought against, for the pain was still too deep. If only he hadn't found out, if only she could have kept it a secret from him, they would now be married and blissfully happy. He'd said he needed time, but Belinda knew, desolately, that she'd never hear from him again. He was a decent man and he wanted a decent, untouched woman for his wife. Why would Ryan be any different?

With a vicious shake, she cast aside the happy glow he'd left her with, for it was a waste of time to dwell on the possibility that he might truly be interested in her for herself. Still, she had to be honest with herself and admit that she found him appealing and charming—and, she realized dolefully, she wished their relationship could be otherwise.

When she joined Major Whitley, he had made a comfortable sitting area for them in the back of the wagon. One hand rested on an unmarked wooden box, and there was an excited, eager air about him. "I've got a surprise for you," he greeted. "I've been waiting for a chance to show you, but we haven't had any spare time, so when you volunteered to come along, I made up my mind we'd get together. Sit down."

She did so, curious. The other boxes were all marked MS—for Medical Services—so the one he was being so mysterious about had to belong to him personally.

He began, "Remember what I said about how you ought to think about studying medicine when this infernal war finally ends?"

"Yes, and I told you it was a crazy idea."

"That you did, my dear, but the fact remains there is a fine women's medical college in Pennsylvania. They graduated their first class of lady doctors in 1857, and I'm sure that with my recommendation, along with some others, you would be accepted as a student."

Belinda shook her head and reminded him, "I don't have much education."

He dismissed her argument with a chuckle. "Not many medical students do, my dear. Up until a few decades ago, men learned medicine by trailing around after doctors, just as you did back in North Carolina. And the fact is, you are an intelligent woman and I can see you have a natural aptitude for medicine. Most of all, it's obvious you enjoy it. And no matter what you might think, your becoming a doctor is not an unreachable goal. But we'll worry about that later. Right now, we've got to familiarize you as much as possible with medical procedures, because there's no telling what you're going to be called on to do in the near future."

He opened the box. Belinda saw that it was filled with books. "You brought all these with you?" She was amazed.

He laughed. "You didn't think I memorized everything I learned in school, did you? Even a skilled surgeon like me needs reference once in a while. Besides, I like to keep up with the latest developments and discoveries, so I read everything I can get my hands on.

"These are invaluable." He held up a two-volume text entitled *Operative Surgery*. "They also have illustrations of most of our surgical instruments, and you can familiarize yourself with those you haven't seen used." He reached for another book.

Belinda was thrilled to be able to peruse a textbook on anatomy and physiology. There was also the latest pamphlet on gunshot wounds, and even a medical dictionary, and yet more books on the diagnosis and pathology of urinary deposits, as well as a pharmacy digest.

He urged her, "If you read these, and learn what's in them, you'll have a good working knowledge of medicine, Belinda. Now understand, I'm not giving you a license to practice. Not by any means. I could lose my own—as well as my rank—and get myself in all kinds of trouble. All I'm saying is that you need to know as much as possible, because in an emergency situation, you might save a man's life. Frankly, I think you've done so a couple of times already. And I, for one, wouldn't bat an eye at you taking a situation into your own hands, if me or one of the other surgeons weren't around to take charge. So you get to reading, girl—" he patted her hand and then the stack of books "—and we'll talk about this again when the war is over, because I intend to do everything I can to make a doctor out of you."

Belinda laughed, but she was flattered by his faith in her. He settled back to use the traveling time for a coveted nap, and she picked up one of the books, intending to glance through it before dozing off herself. Yet, as she read and pored over the drawings and illustrations, she found herself enraptured, caught up in the exciting world of medicine. She could not put the books down, and her hands were trembling with enthusiasm.

Eventually she took down Major Whitley's surgical bag, opening it to display the tools needed for amputation, comparing each with those pictured in the book. Engrossed in what she was doing, Belinda was not aware of how he watched her through half-closed eyes, his mustache wriggling as his lips spread in an approving grin.

Before she knew it, darkness was falling, the day had ended, the stack of books had been devoured, and the company had reached their destination.

They found casualties waiting, and Belinda followed Major Whitley to the hospital area, where he reported for duty. Then they offered their assistance to the medical services and found themselves swamped with work. By midnight, Belinda had assisted with three amputations, and only when handed a steaming mug of coffee did she remember that she had not had any supper.

But Ryan had not forgotten.

She felt a gentle hand on her shoulder and she looked up, gasping, as always, at the sight of those familiar golden eyes.

"Will I ever see a day you don't panic at the sight of me?" he teased lightly, though there was a touch of annoyance in his tone.

"Sorry," she murmured. "You startled me, and I'm tired."

"Tired? I'd say exhausted is more like it. I'll admit I don't keep up with what goes on with the medical services, but frankly I'm surprised you found so much work needing to be done."

"Old wounds, but dangerous. You see," she began, "as Major Whitley told me, it's important to amputate right away, say within the first twenty-four hours after injury. It's proven to reduce the chance for infection, which means more lives saved. He said, anything beyond that time, the mortality rate rises to fifty percent. Unfortunately, whoever initially treated those men was overly optimistic. The major took one look and knew the affected limb had to come off.

"It's always sad," she continued, "to see someone lose an arm or a leg, but till somebody else comes along with a better technique, amputation is the best hope for a soldier's survival."

Ryan would have liked to converse with her longer, but he saw how pale she looked and knew she needed food and rest. "I had the cook warm a plate of stew for you, and the major, too. If you can break away, I'll show you the way to the mess tent."

With the fondness of a daughter gazing at her father, Belinda looked to where the doctor had collapsed on a cot in deep slumber. "I've an idea he'd rather sleep right now, but I'd be obliged," she said wearily.

All was quiet. The card games had long ended, for the playful spirit was not abiding in the midst of battle rumors. Pickets were on patrol, but the only soldiers awake were lost deep in thought, and they did not so much as glance up as Belinda and Ryan passed by.

Ryan got her stew and a glass of milk, then led her to a slight rise, where, beneath the moon-laced leaves of a spreading oak, they could see the tent city sprawling before them.

Famished, Belinda eagerly ate, but slowed to ask the reason for the buildup of troops in the area. "Since Manassas, everything seems to have slowed down except here."

"A lot of folks in this region didn't want to join the rest of the state in seceding, so there's a lot of dissent," he endeavored to explain. "The Federals know that, so they're concentrating their efforts here, hoping to secure the entire western section to give them a foothold in Virginia. I'll be taking my men on reconnaissance at dawn to try and get an idea of how many troops Rosecrans is moving in."

"Reconnaissance is dangerous. I've heard some patrols have been slaughtered."

With his usual candor, Ryan told her, "My men are some of the best. I trained them to be sharpshooters and expert riders. We'll make it unless we get trapped somewhere.

"*You're* the one who'd better be careful," he added warily.

"I'll be fine. We never go into the field till both sides signal a cease-fire. They want their wounded as bad as we want ours."

"True..." he agreed, but then he felt compelled to warn her, "But sometimes you can run into enemy stragglers who don't give a damn about cease-fires. They'll shoot anybody on the opposite side, and they don't care whether they're a soldier or a steward—*or* a female nurse," he grimly added. "That's why I had reservations about your coming along. I think I can fix it with our head surgeon, though, for you to stay behind, and—"

"No, don't do that," she said in a rush. "I was accepted to do a job, and I intend to do it. Now don't worry. I know what I'm doing."

He breathed a conceding sigh. He supposed he'd known all along it was useless. "Well, I tried," he said with a shrug and a grin. Seeing how she tried to stifle a yawn, he reluctantly offered, "Guess I'd better show you where I had my men set up your tent. You're dead on your feet, and I've got to grab a few hours' sleep before we start out, or I'll be falling out of the saddle."

She did not protest, and even allowed him to help her to her feet.

As they walked through the night, Belinda was stunned to realize that an easy warmth was spreading throughout her body. Gone was the shimmer of panic she had experienced previously, and in its place were the beginnings of the same kind of complacency she experienced in the company of Major Whitley—though something told her she was feeling anything but fatherly affection for Captain Ryan Tanner.

Outside her tent, which had been positioned a distance away from the soldiers but near the hospital for convenience and protection, Ryan hesitated before bidding her good-night. Fighting the desire to draw her into his arms, he dared ask, "Would it be all right if I come by to see you when I get back from reconnaissance? I know you made it pretty clear how you felt, but I guess I don't give up easy...." He paused to flash her a wry grin, eyes twinkling. "You see, I still think we could be good friends, and I'd appreciate the chance to prove it to you."

A part of her yearned to say yes, but Belinda was still wrestling with the ghosts of the past. She could also see something besides friendship in Ryan's gaze, could sense that he wanted a man-woman relationship, and, regretfully, despite everything she was feeling for him, she knew she had nothing to give. "A war doesn't leave much time for fellowship. Maybe one day..." She let her voice trail off.

"I'll take what time you can spare, Belinda. Like I said, I don't give up easy."

And he turned to hurry away before he yielded to the temptation to take her in his arms.

As weary as she was, sleep did not come easily to Belinda. It was not her uncomfortable cot that made her toss and turn and stare into the darkness of the tent. The truth was, thinking about Ryan was keeping her awake, for he had managed to ignite feelings within her that she had long ago pronounced dead.

But she knew it was useless to think of Ryan in a romantic way. After all, the Hardin brothers had robbed her of her virginity and her innocence. And Harmon Willingham had destroyed her heart.

She had nothing left to give.

Chapter Eleven

In the strange, hallowed glow twixt darkness and dawn, Ryan and his company of twelve cavalrymen quietly saddled their horses. It was not necessary for him to move among them, for he was confident that each had the essential gear—rifle, ammunition, sword and scabbard, a canteen filled with water, and a haversack packed with a blanket and a supply of hardtack.

Unlike the columns of infantry preparing to move out on foot, the cavalry took no medical-services wagons with them. They were the elite corps, moving fast, hitting hard, usually deep behind enemy lines, where usually the only aid, if a man was wounded, came from the other side. And on this particular mission it was necessary for Ryan and his men to move stealthily in hopes of not being observed.

General Floyd had told Ryan late the night before that word had been received that General Rosecrans was moving south from Boone's Court House, heading over Kreitz and Powell Mountains. Rosecrans was said to have left a force under command of General John Reynolds at Cheat Mountain to keep General Robert E. Lee occupied.

Floyd still wanted to know the size of Rosecrans's army, though Ryan thought it was too late to worry about it. The fact was, Floyd had all the men he was going to have, and it didn't matter if they were outnumbered. But Ryan's orders were to locate the enemy and report back with an estimate as quickly as possible. Meanwhile, Floyd was going to advance on Carnifax Ferry, where he expected to meet a division under the Federal general Cox.

Ryan strained in the waning darkness to see in the direction of the medical wagons lined up at the rear of the troops. He ached to go to Belinda one more time and... *And what?* Remind her to be careful? He would look like a fool. Last night's encounter had been the best, by far, but he still had to go slow. She was still leery, still suspicious—and, sadly, with good cause. Surrounded by men in the camp, she was safe. No one would dare treat her as anything less than a lady. Out there, in the wilderness, she was definitely in danger. She had been warned, knew the risks, but that didn't make it any easier for him to accept, because the reality was that he cared about her and his heart was refusing to listen to the arguments from his brain over how he was wasting his time.

Swinging up into the saddle, Ryan turned to appraise his men. Each was mounted and waiting for his command to move out. They sat with a practiced ease, legs well down, backs arched, sabers hanging on a loosened sling to their left, carbine suspended from the belt swivel to their right. Though they appeared impassive, Ryan knew each man was a turmoil of emotion within, wondering if this might be the day he died. Ryan knew with a grim certainty that they could all die. After all, reconnaissance was a very perilous business, because they had to grope their way along, perhaps unknowingly stumbling right into the midst of the enemy, to be wiped out en masse.

The guidon waving colorfully from the pole affixed to his stirrup socket, the guidon corporal trotted his horse into position.

"Move 'em out." Ryan barked the order with a wave of his gloved right hand.

The point scouts went forward and the flankers dropped back. Behind him, Ryan could hear the off-key clinking of metal gear, the almost methodical slap of canteens. There was murmuring among the men, and now and then the chuffing of a horse. Once they were out of sight of the camp, however, a tense silence descended once again.

Ryan had studied his crude map and knew they should spot the scouts from Rosecrans's army, if the information received was accurate, around midmorning. The scouts would have been sent to secure the area around a creek which would have to be forded. If everything went according to plan, all Ryan and his men had to do was hide among the trees and take a count as Rosecrans's army crossed. When that was done, they would hightail it to Carnifax Ferry in hopes of catching up with General Floyd. Ryan estimated they could do so, for they were on horseback and would be moving at full speed then. The infantry would be walking doggedly, and there would be artillery—and medical wagons.

Ryan's brow furrowed as he thought of Belinda being involved. He'd rather envision her back home, sitting by a cozy fire, writing him letters while she rocked a cradle with her toe, as his son peacefully slept and—

Stop it, he silently, fiercely, commanded himself.

Not only did he not have any business having romantic notions about a woman, but he also had to remember he was in the midst of a war and could be blown to bits at any second. But, most of all, he had to remember that Belinda Coulter was, herself, wounded, and even when the time came that she might be able to open her heart to loving a man, it was doubtful she could ever stop associating him with the night she was raped.

"You okay, Captain?" The guidon corporal reined his horse in behind him. "You look mad enough to bite a cannonball in two."

Ryan rubbed at his forehead, shook himself in an attempt to clear out all thoughts of golden red hair and misty green eyes and the face of an angel. "I'm fine. I'll just be glad when we're done and can join back up with Floyd."

"You really think there's gonna be another big battle, like the men are sayin'?"

"Afraid so." Ryan began to converse in a monotone, reciting all he'd heard, for he was anxious to speak of anything to take his mind away from Belinda. "Lincoln didn't like Sherman getting his butt whipped at Manassas, especially in front of all those picnicking newspaper reporters and highfalutin women from Washington society circles who thought they were out for a day of sport. Clearly, he's out for revenge and intends to take it by having Rosecrans secure the western part of the state. Wouldn't be at all surprised if the Federals didn't have in mind making a separate state out of it on down the road. Maybe call it *West* Virginia."

"Funny how you always call them Yankees 'Federals,' but then, I notice all the officers do."

"We've been asked to use the gentlemanly term. Frankly, Corporal, I think of some of them as sons of bitches, just like every other Southerner does."

They rode on, and after nearly three hours, the point men reported that the creek was dead ahead, and, as expected, Federal scouts had been sighted.

The points hurried ahead, fading into the timber. Ryan continued to move at a steady pace, waiting till they were within a hundred feet or so before waggling his hand left and right. His cavalrymen knew their business, and they spread farther apart as they approached the forest. Carefully they threshed through, finally dismounting to leave their horses behind as they made their way through a loose thicket to fan out across the top of a small bluff overlooking the creek.

From their vantage point, they could observe the advance scouts below. They seemed restless—and as time passed, they became even more so. Finally, when he and his men had been in position nearly two hours, Ryan signaled for Sergeant Alton Bucker to come to him. He secretly considered Bucker his most dependable man. "Can you sidle down there and try to hear what they're talking about? It's obvious they were expecting Rosecrans before now. Something has happened and we need to know what it is.''

Without hesitation, Bucker took off.

Ryan watched with interest as a third scout appeared below, obviously having just arrived on the scene.

Bucker was back within a half hour to report excitedly that he had overheard that Rosecrans had abruptly diverted from his course to Carnifax Ferry to instead do battle with a Confederate unit stationed at Summershill. His voice shook with bitterness as he angrily continued, ''The Confederates were driven back. Now Rosecrans is force-marching his men straight to the Gauley River. He won't be coming this way.''

Ryan had seen the Yankees take off and he was disappointed, not only to hear of the defeat of a comrade unit, but also because he wouldn't be able to give a report to General Floyd as to the numbers he'd be facing.

He gave the signal, and it was passed on down. Everyone rushed for their horses. Once mounted and ready, Ryan told them they had to ride hard and fast. ''We won't be able to tell Floyd what he's up against, but it doesn't matter now, anyway. What does, is that we get there in time to fight with them.

''Let's go!'' he cried, and he moved them out.

Word spread through the ranks.

General Cox's division was not at Carnifax Ferry, as expected.

Orders were subsequently given by General Floyd for his infantry to cross the narrow bridges, but when they reached the other side, they were surprised and dismayed to realize that Cox's men had sunk all the ferry boats when they'd taken off. His artillery was still on the opposite side, unable to get across without boats, for the bridges were too narrow for the large wagons and heavy equipment.

Major Whitley told Belinda, ''We're stuck over here, too. The river is too deep for our wagons to ford, and we'd never make it across the bridge, either. Damn!'' He smashed an angry fist against his open palm. "I don't like this one bit. It was planned for the artillery to be trapped. The general needs to get the infantry back over here and rethink what to do next.''

They were sitting on the wagon seat. Just then one of the artillery officers rode by and overheard Whitley. He said, "Don't worry. The general has sent for engineers to get some boats built quick. We should be able to start crossing by morning.''

Belinda groaned, shading her eyes against the blazing midday sun. They were in for a long wait.

"Maybe we should go for a walk," the major suggested, pointing to a distant ridge. "It's cooler up there beneath those trees. I'll get a canteen.''

All around them, anxious artillerymen were pacing. They did not like being separated from the rest of the regiment, and a few were quite vocal in their protests. Belinda knew Major Whitley wanted to spare her hearing their cursing, but she would still have preferred to stay behind, even if it was hot inside the canvas-covered wagon. She'd brought along several of the books he had given her, and was anxious to get back to her reading.

As they walked, she noticed that Major Whitley seemed nervous, talking incessantly about his family, how much he missed them. He spoke of anything and everything but the war, and finally Belinda sensed what he was trying to do and said bluntly, "You're afraid of what all this means, aren't you?'' They had reached the top of the ridge. She turned to face him, and at once saw the truth in his eyes.

"I'm afraid so," he admitted raggedly. "I think somehow the Federals had advance word Floyd was headed this way.''

"Then it's logical they'd burn the ferries so the artillery couldn't get across the river. But at least they're gone and, for now, we're spared a battle. So what has you so worried?''

"It just doesn't seem logical they'd ride on off without a fight. Looks like they would wait in ambush. I don't know. Maybe I'm worrying needlessly, but I've just got this uneasy feeling—"

The sound of rifle and musket fire exploded through the woods on the hill opposite, and Belinda and Major Whitley watched in horror as Union troops moved from among the trees. Below, taken by surprise, the artillery soldiers scrambled to defend themselves.

Roughly, instinctively, the major grabbed Belinda's hand and began jerking her along behind him to crouch behind a tree. "I knew it! I knew it!" There was the sound of a bugle charge, and then they could see the enemy riding in.

Belinda whirled toward the river to see that their infantry was already rushing across the bridges to retaliate.

"That's why I wanted to bring you up here," the major tersely confided. "I sensed something like this was going to happen."

"And all we can do is watch the slaughter," Belinda whispered in anguish.

Around them were wild screams of the charging Yankees, and from Confederates who had fallen and lay dying. Soon the entire landscape seemed to come alive as the infantry rushed from the bridges, reloading, firing. Others hurled themselves forward against the enemy, with slashing swords.

Belinda watched in awe as two artillerymen, both wounded and bleeding, managed to load a cannon. With their last shred of strength, they fired, raking the blue-clad lines in a deadly fusillade.

Soon the smoke was so dense it was impossible to see what was going on. Belinda knew, without question, that they'd be forced to wait till there was a cease-fire before going out to collect the dead and wounded. She feared their medical supplies would be destroyed in the fighting. She knew, too, that if the Yankees won the fight, they would confiscate everything they could get their hands on.

The medical services had not been prepared for this. Ordinarily, when fighting was imminent, they stayed well behind the lines. Belinda realized, with a chill dancing up her spine, that had it not been for Major Whitley's premonition they would themselves have been caught in the crossfire.

Running for better position to pick off officers on horseback, they were joined on the ridge by a team of sharpshooters. One of them called, "Stay down! We're getting all the cannons ready to blow them to hell!"

Again the major grabbed her hand, urging, "We've got to find better shelter. Once they realize shooting is coming from up here, this ridge will be overrun with Yankees."

Underbrush tearing at their clothing as they ran, they maneuvered around trees till they reached the gentle slope on the other side. "There!" He pointed to a natural dugout in the side. "We'll be safe there. If our boys lose this one, maybe we won't even be found, but if we are, they won't hurt us. Captured medical personnel are treated real well, we hear.

"As long as they're willing to work," he added grimly.

"Would you do that?" Belinda asked as soon as they were settled inside their damp but protective earthen shelter. "Would you treat Yankees?"

He did not hesitate. "Of course. I'm a doctor, Belinda, first and foremost. I've talked to some others who, unfortunately, don't feel the same way."

"Like Hepplewhite," she remarked with contempt.

"Right. Heaven help the Yankee soldier who finds himself under *his* knife."

Belinda shuddered at the thought.

"When it comes to a man suffering, if I can do anything to ease him, I will. Doesn't matter if he wears blue or gray. That's what medicine is all about."

She felt the same way and knew there was no need to say so.

Even from where they were, the noise reached them—the earsplitting booms of the parrott guns, the larger Napoleons. Now and then, when a shell landed on the ridge, the ground beneath them would shake, and the walls of the natural cave would tremble as dirt rained down upon them. Smoke seeped in, and with it the smell of sulfur, and their eyes began to burn and water. And, amidst the horror, they cringed to hear the agonized screams of wounded and the dying.

The canteen had been dropped in their haste, and Belinda's throat was dry and parched. Not from thirst, she knew, but from grief and fear.

Time had no meaning. It was as though they'd been caught up in a frozen hell, paralyzed and trapped. But finally, mercifully, after what seemed like forever, the sounds of gunfire began to lessen.

Belinda asked fearfully, "How will we ever find our way back? It's nearly night, and—"

Suddenly, the world exploded once more, and she covered her ears in terror. She thought the war was now upon them, but the major said it only meant new guns, new soldiers—reinforcements for one side or the other. They prayed it was theirs.

On and on the battle raged. Finally, a hush descended as darkness finally crept through the smoke to cover the earth and cease the killing for that day.

"I'm going back up on the ridge and see what's going on, see if I can spot any of our men. You stay here," Whitley instructed Belinda, "in case it isn't safe."

"What about you?" she wailed in protest. "You could be shot, and—"

"Then it's all over for me," he curtly stated. "But I want you to stay hidden till you either hear some of our men or you can be absolutely sure it's safe. Take no chances. And don't start acting like a woman all of a sudden," he dared to tease before melting away into the shadows.

Prepared for a long wait, Belinda froze only a few moments later when she heard the sounds of footsteps crunching down the hillside. She had no weapon, could hope only to hide from the intruder, and she began to retreat as far back into the crevice as possible. Maybe if she held her breath, did not make a sound, whoever it was wouldn't know anyone was inside, would go away, and...

"Belinda, are you in there?"

It was Ryan.

"Dear God, I don't believe it...." She tumbled into his arms without thinking, overwhelmed by relief. "How did you know I was here?"

"Major Whitley told me. I'd been looking for you. Unfortunately, when my men and I got here, it was almost over, but at least we were in time to help hold off Rosecrans."

"It was his army that attacked?"

"They were backing up Colonel Tyler. We didn't know what was going on. All we knew was, Rosecrans wasn't where he was supposed to be."

"Neither was General Cox. He'd been here and gone and burned the ferries behind him. That's why the artillery was trapped."

"I know." He was ushering her outside as he hurried to explain, "Rosecrans had to cease fire due to darkness. No doubt he plans to start back at dawn, but this time we're going to be the ones with the surprises. General Floyd has given orders to retreat, and as soon as we've got the wounded and dead and everything else we can salvage across the river, we're destroying the bridges.

"I'd asked where you were when things calmed down," he went on to say, "and somebody said they saw you and the major heading up this way just before the firing began.

"And I'm glad you did," he added warmly. "I wasn't sure what I'd find."

She could feel his eyes upon her in that tense moment, imagined she could even see the strange green-gold eyes in the surrounding blackness. Suddenly, the familiar tense-ness returned, but she dared not pull away from his grasping hand for fear of stumbling in the darkness.

He felt her shudder, however, and abruptly stopped walking to do what he'd been yearning to do for so very long. With strong hands on her shoulders, he pulled her against him in a searing kiss that left them both shaken. "I had to do that," he said matter-of-factly, "to make sure you're really here, and I'm not just dreaming I found you. The fact is, little lady, I've been sick with worry over you."

"You—you shouldn't be...." She was stammering, unnerved and secretly shaken by unfamiliar emotions, for even Harmon's kisses had never affected her in such a way. Covering the dizziness with anger, she added hastily, "And you shouldn't have—"

"Oh, yes, I should...." Before she could protest, he grabbed her and kissed her again.

This time, when he released her, she did jerk free, furiously heading for the halo of light at the top of the ridge. From there, she could see the fires burning below, could observe the medical stewards from both sides as they went about the grisly task of picking up the dead, others rushing about with litters for the wounded.

Joining her, Ryan became a soldier once more, pushing back desire and passion as he scanned the wretched scene. "We've got a little bit of help," he told her. "Just as my men and I were coming in, we came across a half-dozen soldiers in the woods and brought them along. I suspect they were deserting, but they came in handy, just the same. Now we've all got to get busy and clear this field, make the Federals think we're holing in for the night instead of retreating. You get on down there, do what you have to do, and remember we'll be moving out fast. I've already told the major that amputations and any kind of surgery are going to have to wait till we get wherever we're going."

"And where do you think that will be?" Belinda wanted to talk, lest he hear the beating of her heart in the stillness. There would be time later to vent her indignity, to try and reason with the churning emotions within. "We need to know how long before we can set up a hospital tent for treatment, and—"

Ryan said impatiently that he'd spoken only briefly with General Floyd to receive his orders. Floyd had indicated that they were going to try to reach Meadow Bridge, where General Lee was said to be holding on with an army well over thirty thousand in number. "I'll let you know as I find out. Meanwhile, get moving, Belinda, please. We've got to get out of here. We're outnumbered, only the enemy doesn't realize that yet. We put up a good fight in all the smoke, but when that clears, we're in trouble."

He helped her on down the ridge, then left her.

Belinda rushed toward the medical wagons, which had miraculously survived the battle. Gathering her field bag, she rushed toward the nearest moaning soldier.

For the moment, she could not think about Ryan, or the way he had made her feel when he'd held her, kissed her....

The fierce, crackling flames of the burning bridges exploded against the night sky. Once General Floyd had gotten his infantry safely across, and what was left of the artillery loaded on the hastily constructed boats, he had ordered everything behind them destroyed to block any Union pursuit.

Belinda was exhausted from the ordeal of helping collect the wounded and get them into the wagons and ready to move out. Yet she was exuberant in her gratitude to Major Whitley. "Thank God you were worried and got us to safety in time. I'd probably have panicked and frozen where I stood and be with them now...." With a sad expression, she nodded grimly toward the mass grave being hastily dug.

"Nothing we can do for them, but we've sure got our work waiting for us when General Floyd reaches a place where we can set up a tent." He motioned for her to climb up on the wagon, and, before turning to his own, said gloomily, "Nine amputations, by my count."

Belinda blanched and bit her lip to keep from crying. She was going to have to tend those poor souls during the next grueling hours as General Floyd rushed to move his army as far as possible from the Union lines. At least they had brought along what she hoped would be ample supplies of morphine and chloroform.

After what seemed forever, word came that they were stopping, and Belinda gritted her teeth and steeled herself against the sights and sounds of a night that had become a visit to hell.

At last, the emergency surgeries were completed and they immediately moved through the rows of litters placed outside to treat the more-minor wounds. A slow, steady rain had begun to fall, and soon everyone was soaked to the skin, despite the hastily erected canopies.

At the sight of Ryan striding purposefully toward her, Belinda felt a tremor within, and she chided herself for it, though the sensation was pleasurable.

"Is it real bad?" His sympathetic gaze swept her. Like everyone else, she was drenched. He saw, too, how exhausted she looked. "You'd better get some rest."

"Later." She moved to the next man and set down the lantern she was carrying, along with her knapsack. Taking out fresh lint, she asked, "How long do you think we'll be able to stay here?"

"I'm afraid we'll be moving soon. We just heard General Lee mounted a surprise attack on the Federals dug in at Cheat Mountain. Jackson has gone to hit their main position at Elkwater, and General Floyd is supposed to meet up with Lee at Meadow Bridge before dawn."

"Then I've got to keep working as long as I can. Someone just told me a couple of men just came straggling in, and I've got to find out how bad they are."

Ryan sneered contemptuously. "Yeah, I saw them when they got here. They're part of the same bunch my men and I picked up earlier. Probably deserters. I think a couple took off again when they realized they were riding into a battle.

Now they've found themselves caught between us and the enemy and they've decided to drift in and act like they just got separated. There's nothing wrong with them. They just want to ride in a wagon where it's dry.''

Belinda said she still needed to check on them.

"I'll go with you, then...." He paused when he heard someone call to him. Turning back to Belinda, he swore. "Damn, I've got to go."

Belinda had finished changing the soldier's bandage and retrieved her lantern and knapsack. Staring up at Ryan then, she felt a strange stirring at his nearness, but there was no twinge of apprehension. She realized she actually hated to see him leave her. Dear God, what was happening? She shook her head to clear it, then finally murmured, feeling a bit awkward, "Then I'll talk to you later, Captain."

"With pleasure." He dared touch a gloved finger to her cheek before hurrying away.

Belinda was actually trembling as she made her way to where the stragglers were waiting, but with excitement. Maybe, she dared to muse, Captain Tanner was attracted to her for the right reasons. He'd certainly given her no cause to think otherwise. After all, he swore he had tried to help her that night, and she desperately wanted to believe that was how it had been. The one thing she could be certain of, she reminded herself, was that he knew she had been taken against her will, knew her for the victim she was. And never, ever, had he looked at her as though he considered her soiled and dirty... as Harmon had, she was pained to recall.

Maybe, she silently, merrily sang to herself as she approached the three soldiers huddled beneath a tarpaulin, she could actually start turning away from the past, could forget it had ever happened and dare to think of living a normal life, open her heart to love, and—

"Well, well, if it ain't Zeb Coulter's girl."

Belinda froze as the bearded soldier insolently grinned at her in the lantern's glow. He and two other men held the tarpaulin above them against the steady downpour. Her heart began hammering in her chest as she sought to understand who it could be that knew her.

"Yeah, boys, it's her, all right," he cackled to his comrades. "All we was lookin' for was a nice, dry place to keep from marching in the rain, and look what I found for us—an old friend."

Belinda tried to swallow against the rising knot of fear. Her hands began to tremble and the lantern shook, casting a shaky, eerie light over them.

The bearded soldier let out a guffaw and took the lantern from her, holding it up as he gloated, "Yep, I sure have found an old friend. Don't you recognize me, Belinda? Pete Hardin. Culver Hardin is my uncle."

"Dear God!" Belinda cried in horror. Now she did remember Pete. She had seen him numerous times in the settlement, always regarding him with the same contempt she had for the rest of his trashy family.

With a cackle, he went on to taunt her, "I sure as hell ain't forgot you. Nobody could ever forget a fine-lookin' piece of womanflesh like you. Right, boys?"

The others snickered in agreement.

Belinda shook her head, began to take small steps backward, but he reached out and caught her wrist, yanking her toward him. Away from the others, no one saw as his face twisted with rage, or heard as he told her between clenched teeth, "I always wondered what happened to you after you disappeared. Your sister ran off, too—"

"Jessica?" Belinda's terror was momentarily overshadowed by instant concern for her sister. "What happened to her? Tell me, please. . . ." She was twisting her arm, struggling to free herself, but he held tight and she was hurting.

"Nobody knows. Nobody cares. She helped your murderin' pa escape from jail, and everybody figures he's wearin' a Yankee uniform now and gunnin' down his own people." He gave her a vicious shake. "So what are you doin' here, you little bitch? You one of them camp girls now?"

Belinda shook her head wildly from side to side in protest and denial. "No, no, I'm not! I'm a nurse! Now let me go—"

Clearly fearing she was going to start screaming, Pete Hardin handed the lantern to one of the others, then clamped his hand over her mouth as he wrestled her into the shadows. "Yeah, you're doin' your part for the South, ain't you, sweetie? Doin' what you do best, accordin' to my cousin, Jake. He said even though he wound up shot, it was worth it, 'cause you was the sweetest little piece of tail he ever had.

"Got my cousin Rufus killed, though," he went on to snarl, using his free hand to squeeze her breasts roughly. "And I swore if I got the chance I was gonna see if your sweet little tail is worth dyin' for. I doubt it, but I owe it to my cousin's memory to find out, don't I? And you can stop pretendin' you don't want it, too—"

Suddenly, with a cry of rage, Ryan appeared to slam his fist into Pete Hardin's face, causing him to release Belinda as he crumpled to the ground.

Ryan had dared return to spend some time with Belinda, and he thanked God he had as he whirled about to deal with the others. They came quickly to the defense of their fallen comrade, but they were no match for Ryan's savage fury as he lashed out at them.

Belinda stumbled backward, shaking her head from side to side in panic. Turning, she bolted into the dark sanctuary of the woods.

Chapter Twelve

The night closed about her. Belinda stumbled, fell, scrambled to her feet and kept on going. The rain continued to come down in a torrent. Now and then lightning would split the stygian sky to show the way, but only for an instant, and then she was again plunged into darkness. She had no idea where she was, or where she was going. All she knew was that she had to run from the madness that sought to destroy her.

Dear God, her mind screamed as she fought her way through the brambles, she should have known it was bound to happen sooner or later, that she'd run into someone from back home who would know the whole sordid story. And, of course, there was no sympathy for her, which was another reason she'd left. Life there would have been hell—but was it any better now?

And what about Jessica? she wondered frantically as she staggered along. What final horror had befallen her to make her run away from home, too? Jessica had always been the strong one, hardworking, dedicated. And, more importantly, Belinda had never known Jessica to be afraid of anything or anyone.

Belinda had always envied her sister's spirit, while at the same time pitying her for her position in life as a spinster schoolteacher. Jessica deserved so much better.

Belinda stumbled again, falling to the saturated ground and biting back sobs as she rubbed the mud from her eyes. She struggled to her feet, more preoccupied with worry over her sister's dubious fate than with her own present misery.

Their father had arranged for Jessica to marry Reuben Walker, the widower who owned the land adjoining theirs. Belinda suspected Reuben had somehow found out that Jessica was having a secret romance with Derek and told their father. They had set a trap for her, and Belinda had heard her father mercilessly beating Jessica and had intervened. After that, wretchedness and woe had descended.

Belinda had never known quite what had happened, only that Derek Stanton never came around anymore, and that Jessica had withdrawn from everyone, seldom leaving the farm. She had even stopped going to church.

Then, after the tragedy Belinda suffered, things had really gotten bad, and they had grown even worse when Jessica helped their father escape from jail to keep him from being lynched. They had found themselves cruelly ostracized and condemned by people they had known all their lives.

Belinda had been living for the day when Harmon Willingham would come to take her away. But, to her absolute horror and dismay, he had wanted nothing to do with her once he heard she'd been raped. And so she had left, quietly, in the night. . . .

And now it was needling to wonder what had made Jessica, also, leave, and she wished she could find her, cling to her, because, sweet Jesus, there was no one else.

She could not go back to the camp. Ryan, bless him, had saved her, but Pete Hardin would waste no time before telling everyone about her, spreading lies that would brand her a harlot. She would be embarrassed and humiliated, and Ryan would, no doubt, not want to be associated with her, despite having come to her rescue in her moment of need.

She stumbled into a tree, hard, sliding dizzily to the ground and feeling a roll of nausea as she envisioned what

Pete was capable of saying and doing. There was no way she could return to the camp now. She had to find her way to... where?

With a jolt, she realized she really had no place to go. Maybe she should head north, she dared ponder, offer to work for the Union. What difference did it make, as long as she was good for something?

Somewhere in the distance, she could hear the sound of water running. A creek? A river?

Leaning back against the tree and gasping for breath, she tasted blood and realized she had cut her lip when she'd crashed against the bark. Soaked to the skin, she began to tremble in the cool night air. Her head was aching terribly, and so were her legs and feet. Still, she forced herself to stand, wanting to keep on going. Maybe she was lost, but at least she was putting distance between herself and Pete Hardin. She would not have to be a witness when he repeated his filth to Major Whitley, would not have to endure the look of contempt in the eyes of a man who had been more loving to her than her own father. Neither would she have to see Ryan's face when he realized that his men regarded her as no better than a whore....

Suddenly, in the far distance, above the sound of the steady rain, Belinda heard footsteps crashing through the brush. At once, she leapt to her feet, straining to see into the misty darkness as the terrifying thought struck her that there had been three of them, that they might have bested Ryan and charged off after her before others could come to his aid.

With a shudder at the thought of the horror if they should find her out here in the wilderness, she plunged ahead, hit another tree and fell. Then terror ripped from head to toe when she heard her name being frantically called.

"Belinda! Where are you? Answer me...."

"No," she whispered under her breath. *"I won't let it happen. This time, I'm not unconscious. I didn't faint. I'm braver now. I've been to hell and back, and I'm strong. They*

won't catch me, they won't torture me. I'll get away. I can do it."

Talking to herself to build her confidence, Belinda felt her strength and energy revitalized. She was able to move faster, yet with an uncanny sense of projection and awareness. She would dart behind a tree, pressing against it to wait for a streak of lightning to illumine the way to another. Then, when darkness closed in once more, as thunder made the ground beneath her quiver and quake, she would streak to the next tree to wait for the sky to explode again. The thought that she could be struck and killed never crossed her mind, for she was too engrossed in getting farther away from whoever it was trying to find her.

Then, abruptly, she found herself perched precariously on the bank of a rain-swollen creek. In a flash of lightning, she could see the angrily churning waters below.

"Belinda..."

She jumped, startled, nearly lost her footing, and reached out desperately to wrap her arms around the nearest tree. She pressed against it tightly, oblivious to the scraping pain as the bark rubbed against her face, her bare arms.

"Belinda, where are you? For God's sake, answer me!"

He was nearby. She dared not move. She stifled a scream as she felt the ground beneath her slip, and managed just in time to dig in closer to the base of the tree. But she could not retreat, for she was now helplessly, hopelessly trapped—unless she gave up her hiding place. Otherwise, the bank threatened to give way to the raging creek, and would probably take the tree, and her, when it did. She would be swept away to drown....

But what difference did it make? she silently, dismally asked herself. Maybe death was the only way she would ever find peace from the misery of her life. All she had to do was close her eyes forever on the haunting past and allow oblivion to take her away....

"Belinda, thank God!"

She felt strong arms around her, and she released her grip on the tree to cry, "No...no..." as she lunged toward the awaiting peace.

He had seen her in the latest flashing bolt, just in time to grab her and keep her from plunging into the waiting tempest.

He felt her go limp, and he swiftly lifted her in his arms and carried her away from the dangerous bank. "Thank God, thank God," he repeated breathlessly. "Another second and I'd have been too late. Didn't you hear me calling you?"

Belinda kept her lids tightly closed, barely able to hear his voice over the giant roaring in her ears. Finally, at the precise moment when another streak of lightning tore across the heavens, she looked up and once again found herself gazing into *cat's eyes*.

"Ryan. You..." Her chest rose and fell as she fought for calm, fought against the hysteria churning within her. "Oh, thank God. I was afraid the three of them had beaten you and were after me...."

"I wasn't about to let anything happen to you again," he said, a wave of guilt washing over him. Then he asked worriedly, "Are you all right?"

"As soon as I stop shaking." She managed a feeble smile, then told him, "That was Pete Hardin back there. A cousin of the bastards that raped me, and he was saying filthy things, and he—" She paused, then forced herself to continue. "He was touching me, threatening to take revenge for his kin getting shot, and if you hadn't come along..." Her voice trailed off as a shudder swept her from head to toe.

She began to sob brokenly, and he laid her down on the ground, crouching beside her to pull her into his arms as he attempted to soothe her. "I swear to you, I'd kill any man who tried to touch you. Don't you know that? It will never happen again.

"I'm going to make it all up to you," he went on hurriedly, sensing that she was starting to get hold of herself.

"Remember when you said it was my fault for leaving you that night? Well, sweetheart, I can't live with that kind of guilt, and that's why I made up my mind, as long as I'm around you, I'll do anything I can to protect you...if you'll let me."

She clung to him in desperate gratitude. Something told her that he meant it, that as long as she was with him, she was safe. "Just hold me," she whispered, as her heart began to pound tremulously at his nearness. "Just hold me, Ryan, and don't let me go...."

And he did so, pressing her back against the ground, then lowering himself on top of her in an attempt to shield her from the continuing downpour.

As he held her, his mouth warm against her ear, he began to talk in a continued effort to relieve all her doubts. For nearly half an hour, as he waited hopefully for the storm to abate, he rambled on about himself, where he'd come from, the kind of home life he'd had. He told her, too, of his dedication to the Confederacy, how he believed in the cause of states' rights, how he was willing to die, if need be, and maybe, until then, death was not to be feared, anyway, because he really had no reason to live. There was no family. And the only woman he'd ever thought he could love had betrayed him, so he really hadn't cared what happened to him.

"Till now..." he somberly concluded. "You've come to mean a great deal to me, Belinda."

She pushed him away from her a little so that she could see his face in the intermittent flashing of the heavens. Then, with chagrin, she confided, "For one instant back there, I went a little insane and actually thought about throwing myself into the creek, thinking I had no reason to live, that no man would ever care about me after what happened...."

"That's crazy," he told her with a chuckle. "And even though you let me know from the first that you despised me, I couldn't help feeling drawn to you, and I knew I had to make you change your mind and see I'm not the son of a bitch you thought I was."

She reached out to stroke his rain-soaked face tenderly with her fingertips. "I think I care for you, too, Ryan, but I'm frightened. I don't know if I can ever let a man touch me that way again...."

Ryan knew he had to kiss her. He ran his fingers into her hair, feeling the wet tendrils clinging to his flesh, and held her in a gentle vise as he lowered his mouth to hers. "You can, Belinda...." he whispered fervently. "I'll teach you that you never have to be afraid, not when you give yourself in love...."

Belinda felt the tip of his tongue flick gently across her lips. From deep within came the familiar roll of terror. He felt it, too, and he pulled away, lest she yield to hysteria.

"You don't have to be afraid," he repeated, with added force in his voice. "I'm only going to kiss you. Nothing more. And anytime you want me to stop, let me know and I will. I'm not going to force you to do anything you don't want me to do, Belinda, I swear it...."

When she made no move to protest, he began to slowly make love to her mouth. Only after dancing his tongue across her lips, slowly, deliciously, did he dip inside.

Belinda was oblivious to everything around her. Though the rain continued to come down in torrents, and the sky still periodically split apart with dazzling splits and bolts of lightning, there was no world but the one encapsulated in Ryan Tanner's shielding arms.

Wind whipped mercilessly through the trees, sending small branches and leaves slapping about their bodies as they lay on the ground. But they did not feel the attack of nature. Neither were they annoyed by the mud and mire in which they lay. There was no storm, no night, no day or sun or breath of life, for they had removed themselves from the spheres of misery that had brought them together.

Ryan could sense not only that Belinda was yielding to the gentle assault of his mouth, but also knew that her excitement was building. Despite her wet clothing, the chill both of them felt in the inclement weather, heat was emanating from her, and she pressed closer, her breathing coming faster as she clung to him, accepting the sweet violation of his kiss.

He drew away to nuzzle her throat, fingertips dancing across her face, and repeated, "I *do* care about you, Belinda. More than you can know, because I think I'm falling in love with you...."

Belinda's breath caught in her throat. Somehow she knew he was sincere, and this new awareness of her own feelings came as violently as the storm spinning above them. She had not allowed herself to dwell on the possibility of anything romantic between them during past encounters, for fear that he could never see her as worthy of that kind of emotion. But now the dreams she'd forced herself to cast aside were actually starting to come true. It didn't matter to him. Any of it. He regarded her as a shining, virtuous woman, a woman worthy of a man's love, without blemish upon either body or soul.

She drew a ragged breath and pressed even closer to him. "I think I've been fighting this, afraid you'd think the worst of me...."

"Never," he whispered huskily, silencing her with another kiss, this one deeper, more intense. "Never will I think of you in any way except to cherish you with all my heart." He felt the heat of his loins as he grew hard. As much as he wanted her—it was like a stabbing ache in his gut—Ryan did not dare make love to her here. Not now. Not like this. Especially in her state of mind. She'd had a terrible experience earlier, and now was not the time for her to try to overcome her fear of having a man touch her in that way. Lovemaking had to come at the right time and place, and only when they were both ready. To do otherwise might frighten her into rejecting him forever.

With a reluctant sigh, he drew away from her, forcing himself to turn to practical needs for the moment. They had to find shelter, dry clothing, warmth. "You're going to be sick," he murmured, wondering where the hell they were. He'd been so bent on following the sounds of her crashing through the brush in the distance that he'd lost all sense of direction. He had been calling to her for quite a while, but she hadn't heard above the sounds of the heavy downpour. He had lost count of the number of times he'd changed directions, and he estimated he'd been pushing behind her for nearly an hour or more. There was no need to hope anyone would be looking for them. Hardin and the other two had probably already deserted again, and if they hadn't, they sure as hell wouldn't report him or Belinda missing. Major Whitley would just think she had retired for the night. His own men, camped away from the others, wouldn't be concerned by his absence. They would think he was conferring with the general or his staff. There was just no getting around the fact that the two of them were out here, lost in a storm, and nobody was going to give them a thought till morning.

Belinda sneezed, and Ryan instinctively moved over her once again in a futile effort to protect her from the elements. "We can't stay here. If we move, we can at least keep warm."

He helped her to her feet, and she could not help sagging against him in her weariness. Yet, despite the miserable creeping chill, Belinda was warmed by what had just happened between them. And, while she wasn't ready to contemplate the future, at least she could feel she had taken a giant step away from the past.

They had no idea where they were headed. "We just keep going till we find shelter," he said. "Maybe we'll run into a farmhouse, or a barn. Anything."

"The rain is slowing," she managed to say, despite her chattering teeth. "I wonder how long before dawn."

"Hours. It must have been near midnight when you ran away, and I figure we've been gone a couple of hours, at least."

"Do you know where we are?"

He'd been hoping she wouldn't ask, but he supposed that by then it was obvious he didn't know the way back to camp. "Afraid not. You really took some wild turns back there," he said in an attempt to lighten the situation. "Our best scout with a map in his hand would probably have got turned around."

She agreed dismally. "I think for a minute there I lost my mind. Pete just brought it all back...." She trembled and Ryan quickly tightened his arm about her in comfort as she unleashed the tension within her. "I had to get away. I don't know what I'll do when we get back. I've ideas he'll spread horrible stories about me, and how can I ever work around those men with them thinking I'm no better than a..." Her voice trailed off, for she could not bring herself to say the word *whore*.

Fiercely, angrily, Ryan assured her he'd take care of Hardin. "But I can almost guarantee he's already left camp. Don't give him another thought. Hey—" He froze, and Belinda, unprepared for such an abrupt halt, stumbled and would have fallen had he not kept his hold on her. Lightning had flashed, and in that brief, dazzling moment, he had seen something. A structure of some kind. "Wait. You'll see it next time there's a flash. To our left, look that way."

She did, holding her breath and silently praying he was right.

And then it came, like fingers of fire across the sky, igniting the darkness in startling white glory.

In the midst of the splendor, she could see it. An old barn, perhaps a hundred yards away. She could also see they had come out of the dense woods and now faced an open field.

"We're going to have to run for it," Ryan told her. "I know you're tired, but with all this lightning popping around, we're lucky we haven't been struck by now, and we'll be a perfect target in that field. Just hang on to my hand. If you fall, I'll be there to catch you—*always.*"

He turned suddenly and closed her in his embrace once more for another kiss, a kiss that left them both shaken. He released her, then caught her hand and yelled, "Now go!"

They raced across the pasture, and Belinda did stumble several times, but as he had promised, Ryan was quick to scoop his arm about her and hoist her up on her feet again. Finally, he just lifted her up and carried her the rest of the way, not wanting to take a chance on her twisting an ankle in the muck and mire beneath them.

"I don't see a house anywhere," he said, finally able to set her down as he pushed open the door of the barn. "And I've been watching each time the sky lit up. From the looks of this old place, the house probably fell a long time ago. We may have trouble finding a dry spot."

Inside, the air was fetid with the odor of rotting manure and sour hay, as well as permeating dampness and decay. Scant light from the storm gave intermittent glances of old horse stalls, most with their gates fallen away. Straw littered the dirt floor. A few rusted tools were scattered about.

Ryan was elated to find a tack room in a far corner. Searching about, he triumphantly cried, "Blankets. Old saddle blankets. They smell terrible—probably full of holes—but they're dry, thank God. Get out of those clothes, quick, and wrap up. I'm going to stir up some hay in the driest stall I can find, and we can bed down there. Soon as it's light, we'll try to find our way back to camp."

Belinda hesitated. As much as she wanted to get out of the miserably wet and sticky clothes, the thought of wrapping herself in a blanket and lying down next to Ryan was disturbing to say the least. She had just escaped a storm outside, and now seemed to be facing another on the inside.

Ryan noticed that she had not moved, and he did not have to wonder why. "Maybe you'd feel better if I bedded down in another stall."

"It—it's not that...." She faltered, not knowing exactly how to explain what she was feeling just then. "It isn't that I don't want you near me, Ryan, because I do. I'm grateful you came after me. I don't like to think of what might have happened if you hadn't. It's just that I'm afraid, and I know I shouldn't be, but I am."

"I know you are," he said, anxious to reassure her, "but you needn't be. I'd be lying if I said I didn't want to make love to you, Belinda, but it's got to happen only when we both want it.

"Let me tell you something, pretty lady...." He found her in the darkness and drew her close once more. She could feel the tickle of his mustache as he sought her lips and kissed her lightly. "I've had all kinds of wonderful musings about you, but not all the time in the way you think. Sure, I've dreamed about how nice it'd be to strip you naked and feel you all over, taste you all over. But I've thought of you in other ways, too—like how it would be if one day you were my wife, waiting at home for me.

"You're more to me than merely a woman to take my pleasure with," he continued in a husky voice, his hand moving to lovingly cup her chin. "And that's why you don't have to worry about me trying to take you here and now, tonight. When it happens and I damn sure hope it does—" he paused and chuckled softly before continuing "—it's going to mean you think of me in the same way, as your husband, as the father of your children, and it's going to be beautiful. Not like what those bastards did to you out there on that road that night—and don't try to tell me you aren't thinking about that every time I hold you, because you are. And it's only natural that you do. But it's not going to be that way, and it never could be, anyway, because I don't make love to a woman like that. Especially one I care about."

He moved away then, suddenly feeling a bit awkward for having bared his soul to her.

"Ryan..."

He whirled about.

"Don't bed down anywhere else."

He smiled, but did not speak. It was, he knew, her first real step toward absolute trust. More than that, for the moment, he could not ask. The two of them had come a long way this night. He would do nothing to diminish the glow.

Belinda undressed in the darkness, then wrapped herself in one of the blankets. It was scratchy but, as Ryan had said, it was dry and that was all that mattered.

He joined her, wrapped in his own blanket, and asked for her clothes so that he could hang everything on the railings around the stall.

"I doubt they'll be dry by morning," Belinda remarked, "but at least they won't be sopping wet."

"And neither will we. I'd like to head out at first light. I imagine you're getting hungry. I know I am. But even if I snared a rabbit and could find dry wood in here to start a fire, I'd be afraid the enemy might see the smoke and come prowling around."

"Do you really think they might be close by?"

"I wish I could say no, just to make you feel better, but I never want to lie to you, Belinda." He drew her into the stall and they sat down side by side as he reluctantly admitted there was a good chance they had stumbled behind Federal lines. "But I think I can get my bearings in daylight. If I can't, then we'll make sure we stick to the woods and aren't seen. Sooner or later, we're bound to run into our own forces.

"But enough worrying." He lay back, folding his arms beneath his head. "Let's talk about something else, like how it was back home in the Blue Ridge." Actually, Ryan wanted only to set her mind at ease so that she'd fall asleep. There was no need for her to lie awake brooding over their plight.

Belinda sensed his motive. But, lying down beside him, making sure they did not touch, she still felt moved to tell him bitterly, "I'm afraid I don't like to think about how it was."

"I'm not talking about the bad things. Only the good." In a voice that echoed the homesickness Ryan could not help feeling at times, he said fervently, "Don't you remember what it was like to watch the sunset from the top of the Blue Ridge? You look out over an infinite expanse of broken country, range after range of mountains just melting into each other, and you can't see where the mountains end and the sky begins. The valleys between have patches of shadows from the soft clouds drifting above...

"And then," he went on, a catch in his throat, "in a moment of absolute stunning glory, the world turns to magic. Shades of color start blending and bleeding into each other as the nearer and farther heights start changing their hues in a kind of eerie rhythm. Then, finally, there's that strange mist that falls over the whole world. Not blue. Not purple. But a little bit of both. And it starts creeping down and falling in all the clefts and gorges. It's as if the earth were drawing a robe around itself and bedding down for the night...." His voice trailed off, and finally he fell silent.

No sound came from Belinda.

Ryan raised himself up on his elbow, just as silvered fingers parted the darkness with a clap of thunder and allowed him to see her face.

She was asleep, long lashes dusting her cheeks in weariness. A contented sigh escaped her slightly parted lips.

He was pleased to see that his ploy had worked—she had drifted away with thoughts of happier days, thoughts that might just inspire peaceful dreams.

He touched his lips gently to hers, and then, careful not to awaken her, cradled her in his arms.

It was not long before he followed her into deep slumber.

And neither of them was aware when the soldiers in blue uniforms crept into the barn.

Chapter Thirteen

Ryan awoke with a start.

Faint light shone through the open doors of the hayloft above. He could see blue skies beyond, promising good weather. Fall was in the air, and a brisk wind drifted in to touch his bare skin, for he had absently tossed the blanket off sometime during the night and he lay naked.

It was not the coolness on his flesh that brought him from slumber, however, but a gut instinct that told him something was amiss. He could just feel the invisible fingers of foreboding creeping up and down his spine.

He saw nothing, heard nothing, yet the annoying, nagging feeling persisted.

Belinda lay beside him in a deep sleep. Her golden red hair was fanned out about her face. She had turned on her side, toward him, arm stretched out, hand upon his thigh. He smiled to think how embarrassed she'd be to realize she was touching him so intimately, but at the same time he felt a tightening in his loins.

God, he wanted her.

She had not tossed her blanket aside, and he found himself boldly wishing she had. Tenderly he tucked the blanket even higher, beneath her chin, unable to resist leaning over to brush his lips across her cheek. She stirred, ever so slightly, and he thought he saw the play of a smile on her lips. One day, he promised himself, he'd awaken to find her snuggled naked in his arms, and she'd be smiling, not in her sleep, but rather into his eyes with adoration... and love.

First things first, Ryan told himself, yawning. He still felt a bit uneasy, but he decided it was due to anxiety. He would not feel truly safe till they were back behind Confederate lines, and they needed to be on their way. First, he would get his clothes on, then he'd awaken her and discreetly go outside while she got dressed, and...

Ryan froze.

He had gotten to his feet, heading for the stall railing, where they had left their clothes to dry. Belinda's were still stretched out in place, but *his were missing*.

"Looking for something, Reb?"

He whipped his head to the left to see an arrogantly grinning face beneath a blue cap. Another appeared from the shadows. Two more from his right. Ryan felt his heart slam into his chest as he realized he was surrounded by Federal soldiers.

The one who'd spoken stepped up on the lower rail to hoist himself up so that Ryan could see the pistol he was pointing straight at him. "We got here kind of late last night and bedded down at the other end. Didn't even know you folks were around till one of my men got up to pee just before day and caught a glimpse of your gray uniform spread out here. Now that woke him up, I'll tell you...." His grin grew wider.

Ryan still did not make a move. Being naked made him feel all the more vulnerable, as well as ridiculous. The Yankee had the drop on him, and he saw the glint of other weapons in the scant light and knew he was well outnumbered. Yet he knew that if they had wanted him dead he already would be.

The soldier's smile faded. "We can tell by your uniform you're cavalry. And an officer. A captain. What's your name and what outfit you from?"

Ryan told him.

"And what are you doing so far away from your outfit?"

A voice from the shadows cackled, "I don't think he even knows where he is, Sergeant Purdy. Maybe you better tell him."

The Sergeant obliged. "Seems you got a real poor sense of direction, Captain. You've got yourself at Gauley River. We're with General Rosecrans's fine army."

Ryan seized the opportunity to probe. "Looks like your general is lost, too, Sergeant. We were expecting him at Sewell's Mountain."

"Aw, he knew what he was doing, didn't he, boys?" He took his eyes off Ryan long enough to glance about and enjoy the approving chuckles of his men. Looking pleased with himself, he turned to Ryan again. "We changed directions and went to Cheat Mountain yesterday, where we soundly beat the shit out of your General Jackson."

At that, the soldiers laughed raucously, and just as Ryan was attempting to absorb the latest bit of jarring information, he heard a sound and remembered Belinda. Whipping about, he saw her look of horror as she awoke to the nightmare. Clutching her blanket to her chin, she sat up, shrinking back, her lips working in a silent scream. Ignoring the sergeant's gruff command to stay where he was, Ryan lunged for her, rushing to put himself between her and the enemy.

"You must be wanting me to prove I mean business, Captain," the sergeant snarled, signaling to two of his men to go into the stall. "Get him out of there. He ought to realize by now the little doxy is what got him into this mess...."

"She's no doxy." Ryan exploded with fury as the two men swooped down to grab him and wrest him away from Belinda, who, for the moment, had been struck dumb with terror as she groggily attempted to grasp the situation. "She—" He hesitated only an instant before crying, "She's my wife, damn you."

"Your wife?" the sergeant echoed with a doubting sneer. "What kind of fool you take me for? What would you be doing out here in a barn with your wife?"

"We just got married."

Hearing Belinda's unfaltering voice, Ryan looked at her, incredulously, gratefully, just before he was shoved out of the stall. He could not help smiling. Bless her, she was going along with the ruse, which, ultimately, might save both of them.

"We didn't have time for a proper honeymoon," she went on, glancing about nervously as the men watched, listened. "It so happens I live near here, and when he sent me word his company wouldn't be far away, we made plans to meet here."

The sergeant lifted one eyebrow. "You from Gauley River?"

"Nearby." She didn't want him to ask questions about the area she could not answer. "But I knew this old barn was here. It seemed the perfect place to meet—till *you* came along," she added with a hostile glare. She was careful, however, to avoid visual contact with Ryan. She had been forced to swallow a gasp at the sight of him naked, and she dared not look again. Now she hoped they wouldn't tear away her blanket to humiliate her, as well.

"Crenshaw, give the Reb his traitor's uniform," the sergeant gruffly snapped.

Ryan bristled. "*Traitor,* did you say?"

"Yeah, *traitor,*" came the quick, fiery reply. "You and the rest of them secessionist bastards that got us into this infernal war."

Ryan decided it was best not to spar with the man, fully aware he could order them killed then and there. He only hoped they had enough honor to take him prisoner and allow Belinda to go free. Lying about her being his wife might just make that possible. He was betting they would think twice about raping a man's wife. He had not heard of such an atrocity happening in the war—yet.

"Allow me to introduce me and my men. I'm Sergeant Jarvis Purdy." He gave a mock bow, and each of his men did the same as they were presented. "Corporal Carleton Crenshaw. And Private Douglas Holley and Private Mortimer Duncan."

Holley and Duncan were the soldiers who had dragged him out of the stall. They released him now as Crenshaw threw his uniform at him. Quickly he yanked it on, all the while keeping an eye on Belinda through the slats of the stall. No matter that there were four of them and he had no weapon. If they made one move to touch her, he knew he'd go at them like a tiger, even if it meant death. He'd try, by God, to protect her as he'd promised, but, for the moment, he was somewhat relieved to hear Purdy addressing her in a more respectful tone.

"Mrs. Tanner, if you'll go with Corporal Crenshaw, he'll take you to that tack room over there where you can get your clothes on."

"And then what do you intend to do with us?" she demanded irately, standing up but making sure she kept the blanket wrapped tightly around her.

Purdy scratched at his beard thoughtfully. "I'm not sure. We were out scouting around, looking for deserters. Didn't figure on running up on a cavalry officer and his wife." He snickered once more. "I'll just take you two back to headquarters. I imagine they'll want to question your husband before they send him off to prison."

Ryan bit back the impulse to ask for assurances they would allow her to go free. He didn't want her held, but he was worried about what would happen to her if she was released. She was lost, had no idea what direction would take her back to safety. If she encountered other soldiers—especially deserters, who were usually reckless and desperate—the results could be tragic. Frantically he wondered if he should attempt to convince Purdy to keep her with them, but how to do so without raising suspicions was tricky. After all, she'd already made them think her home was nearby, so it would not seem logical she would want to go anywhere except there.

Belinda furiously swiped at the cobwebs in the tack room. She hated to have to close the door all the way, plunging herself into darkness, but there was no way she was going to drop the blanket till she could be sure Corporal Crenshaw could not see her. Quickly she pulled on her dress. It was still damp, but at least she was clothed.

She tried to keep from shaking, though she was awash with fear at their plight. Evidently they were planning on letting her go, but she had no idea which way to head. And she was frightened not only for herself, but for Ryan, as well. Dear Lord, they had only begun to grow close, and she could feel herself caring more and more for him as time passed. Now to be torn apart, for him to be sent to some horrible Yankee prison, while God only knew what would happen to her... It just wasn't fair.

By the time she had finished dressing, she was blinking back hot, furious tears of resentment. Damn it, she was tired of life kicking her in the teeth. None of this was her fault, or ever had been, and yet every time happiness seemed within her grasp, it was cruelly yanked away.

She stepped out of the tack room.

Crenshaw took one look and yelped, "Hey, where'd all those bloodstains come from, lady? Were you hurt and we didn't know it?"

Most of the time she wore uniform trousers and shirt, but yesterday she had put on a clean dress before setting out. Staring down, she saw that last night's soaking had not removed the stains from her work with the wounded, and she did look a sight. Without thinking, she told him, "No, I'm not. I'm a nurse and—"

"A nurse?" he hooted, at once turning on his heel to look in the direction of Sergeant Purdy, who was staring and wondering what was causing all the excitement. "Hey, Sarge, she's a nurse. No doubt she was working with the Reb medical services."

"And, no doubt, you lied." Purdy turned to Ryan accusingly. His voice thick with contempt, he went on. "She isn't your wife, is she, Captain? The two of you just sneaked off for some loving and got lost in last night's storm."

"She *is* my wife, damn it," Ryan said staunchly.

"Then how come you lied about her being a nurse?"

Ryan spread his hands in a gesture of contrition, offering, "Can you blame a man for wanting to get his wife out of the war, Sergeant? Hell, I never wanted her to work as a nurse, but like I said, we'd just got married, and her father is a doctor, you see, so she knew about medicine, and my commanding officer at the time said she could travel with us if she'd work with the medical services.

"And you're right," he went on, aware that Belinda had moved closer and was watching, listening intently and incredulously as he skillfully spun the web of deceit. He only hoped she was not standing there thinking how glib he was and starting to wonder how much of what he'd said to her could actually be believed. But desperation was what fueled his ability to sound so honest for the moment. "We did slip off last night to be by ourselves. We were in the battle at Carnifax Ferry and were in retreat. We were both exhausted and wanted some time to ourselves. We got caught by the storm, and when we tried to find our way back we realized we'd lost our sense of direction and wound up here, seeking shelter."

Sergeant Purdy swept first Ryan, then Belinda, with narrowed, suspicious eyes. "I don't know...." he mused aloud. "I don't know...."

Crenshaw spoke up. "About what? She's a nurse, damn it, Sarge, and you know they're needing help back at our hospital tent."

Ryan tensed. He did not want Belinda treating Yankees but he dared not say anything. Hell, the fact was, he didn't know what to do, and, he realized dismally, he had no say in the situation anyway.

Purdy looked at Belinda. "You got any objections to treating our men? If not, we'll take you along with us. Otherwise, we'll leave you here to find your way back to your own company as best you can. We've got to get on out of here, before we wind up being the ones to get ourselves captured."

Belinda did not hesitate. Chin lifting in determination, she crisply informed him, "I'll help any man suffering, regardless of which uniform he wears."

Sergeant Purdy smiled and nodded with both approval and respect. "A fine lady you are, Mrs. Tanner. It's going to be a shame to have to separate you from your husband when he's hauled off to prison for the duration of the war, but that's the way it's got to be. Just think of it as keeping him safe for you, because now you won't have to worry about him getting killed in battle."

Sergeant Purdy placed a firm hand on Belinda's arm as they walked along behind Ryan and the others. "We ought to meet up with the rest of our company before long, and then we'll get to headquarters and get some food for you. I know you're bound to be hungry...."

"And my... husband?" She faltered over the unfamiliar word. "Will he be treated well?"

"Better than he would've been without you. That's for sure. My superiors will be real impressed, as well as appreciative, that you're agreeing to work at our hospital, and I'm sure that will have something to do with how he fares."

Belinda felt a great shudder wrench her very soul.

Outside could be seen the remains of the farmhouse.

"Owner must have died," Purdy remarked as they passed the scattering of rotten boards and logs, the crumbling stone chimney of what had once been a fireplace. "Looks like he had a nice place, too. Old hog pen over there..." He pointed, then swept his arm to indicate a door opening into the side of a hill. "Root cellar. Probably nothing left in it.

"I suppose," he went on, still keeping a tight hold on her, "the old farmer that lived here never had any children to pass the place on to. If his wife survived, she probably moved into the nearest town. Happens that way up North, too, when there are no children. Sad. Place just falls to ruins if nobody wants to buy it and take it over...."

He droned on, but Belinda was no longer listening to him, for he had, unknowingly, managed to cruelly strike a chord of melancholy. Pete Hardin had said Jessica had run off, too, and with Pa gone, that meant there was no one left to take over the farm. And her pa had, indeed, intended to have a large family, especially sons to carry on the name of Coulter. But, even after three marriages, Zeb had been left a widower with only two daughters.

Glancing about at the ruination of what had probably been a dream not unlike her own father's, Belinda found herself wondering sadly if her own home would fall to similar ruin. But maybe Reuben Walker would step in, she thought bitterly. She and Jessica had both figured that was his prime motive in wanting to marry Jessica, that he wanted to get his hands on the land.

They reached the farm's well. Holley was already busy filling canteens. Duncan had gone into a thicket to bring out the four horses the soldiers had hidden there.

"We're not as dumb as you Rebs," Crenshaw told Ryan. "We weren't about to take any chances on anybody sneaking up on us. Guess you were too busy to think about that, huh?" he added with a nasty leer.

"Hey, shut up," Sergeant Purdy at once shouted at him. "I'm not having any such talk around Mrs. Tanner, you understand me? She may be a Southerner, but she's still a lady, and she very kindly has said she'll tend our wounded, so all of you better show her some respect."

Duncan scowled. "Her Reb husband, too? No telling how many of our own he's killed."

"We treat our prisoners as good as we hope they treat ours—at least while I'm in charge. Now, you're going to ride on the back of Holley's horse, and Mrs. Tanner can ride in back of her husband."

Ryan had stood quietly watching as the horses were led out. Finally he swung his head from side to side and declared, "Nobody had better ride that sorrel unless you want him lame permanently."

Purdy stepped forward, brow furrowed with concern. "What are you talking about?"

"Aw, don't pay any attention to him," Duncan said with a sneer. "He's been limping ever since he slung a shoe the other day and I had to put it back on him. Hell, I don't know anything about shodding a horse."

"That's obvious," Ryan snapped. To Purdy, he offered, "Untie me and let me take a look. Maybe I can do something."

Purdy nodded to Duncan to free his hands, ominously reminding, "If he tries anything, shoot him."

Belinda blanched at the thought.

Ryan knelt and lifted the horse's right hoof to inspect it. "He's got a bruised sole. And I can see why. It's a badly fitted shoe and needs to come off. Otherwise, he could go lame permanently and have to be put down." He straightened to look accusingly at Purdy. "What are you going to do about it? Do you Yankees have so many horses you don't have to worry about it?"

"Hell, no," Purdy was quick to tell him. "And I don't guess it's a secret many of our soldiers don't come from farms like you boys. They don't know a lot about blacksmithing, but *you* obviously do. Can you fix it?"

Ryan scratched his stubbled chin, absently hoping he'd be allowed to shave soon. He wasn't anxious to be whiskered and unkempt like his captors. "I'll try. Let me take a look around the barn. Maybe I can find an old pair of pincers left behind. First thing I need to do is get it off, and then he'll need a poultice once or twice a day till the inflammation and soreness is out of it.

"And he'll need to be reshod with a special shoe," he went on. "A light, wide, flat seated-out shoe to help the healing. How far back to your company?"

"Hour's ride. Maybe two."

Ryan shook his head. "That horse can't carry two people that long. Shouldn't even carry one."

Purdy thought a minute, evidently trying to decide whether to risk permanently injuring the horse. "Crenshaw, you and Duncan ride back and bring three good horses. Me and Holley will keep an eye on the Reb while he works on this one."

They moved out, and Holley, keeping his rifle pointed at Ryan, followed him back to the barn.

Ryan paused to deliver a warning to the sergeant. "So help me, if you hurt my wife, you better kill me, because I'll see you dead, Yankee."

Sergeant Purdy tried to laugh at the threat, but he seemed shaken by the fury ringing in the Confederate officer's voice. "Don't worry," he responded with a sneer. "We Federal soldiers aren't as callous as you Rebs. We don't go around raping women."

Belinda winced. Ryan saw, and wanted to convey a compassionate glance. But she turned away and he knew it was because she wanted to keep the others from seeing her face, from seeing the mirror of her own personal horror.

Searching the barn, Ryan was able to find an old rusted pair of pincers in a cobwebbed corner of the tack room.

"You got it, let's go," Holley said irritably, not liking being alone with the man, even if he was the one carrying a gun. The Reb was big, and Holley figured he could be a real mean son of a bitch. He would feel better when they were back outside in broad daylight, with the sergeant nearby should the bastard try anything.

Ryan ignored him, continuing to search the shelves in the dim light, paying no mind to spiders or the sound of rodents scampering in the shadows. At last he found what he was looking for and pulled it out.

"What's that?" Holley asked warily.

"Epsom salts. I figured there'd be a bottle around somewhere. Never been in a barn yet that didn't have a supply. It makes a good poultice."

More to himself than to his guard, Ryan murmured, "Now we need a bucket, and something for a bandage. There have to be feed sacks around here somewhere. Ah, there..." He stopped to retrieve several from under a shelf. "Now we've got everything."

Pausing by the well to fill the bucket, he added the Epsom salts and swished the water to dissolve them. "It should be heated," Ryan told the sergeant, "but this will do till we get to wherever we're going."

They all watched as Ryan skillfully pried off the shoe. Then he coaxed the stallion into allowing him to place his hoof into the bucket of solution to soak for several moments. Finally, he wrapped the feed sack around the leg and tied it off. "If he's allowed to rest," he said when he was done, "he should be okay. But make sure he gets that special shoe I was telling you about. I'll talk to your blacksmith and—"

"We don't have a blacksmith," Purdy said, interrupting him.

Holley laughed. "We do now."

Purdy agreed, suggesting, "Maybe if you agree to shod our horses, they won't send you off to prison. You can stay with your wife. Would you consider that, Reb?"

Ryan did not have to consider. "My wife feels compassion for the sick and wounded, regardless of which flag they fight under. I'm the same about horses. I'll take care of them, even if they do have to bear a Yankee's pompous ass."

Holley let out a low growl and started toward him menacingly, but Purdy stepped between them. "His mouth can't hurt you."

"His mouth is gonna hurt *him*, if he don't keep it shut. I don't give a damn about neither of them, if you want to know. They're still Confederates. Both of them." Holley glared from one to the other, as though ready to spring and attack at the least provocation.

Ryan was standing near the horse, still holding the pincers. Purdy reached to snatch them from his grasp at the same time he exploded at Holley, "Just shut your mouth. We've got ourselves two valuable prisoners here, and they're not to be harmed. Any man who does answers to me. Now let's all sit down and relax till they get back with the horses."

Ryan led Belinda to the well on the pretense of drawing water for them to drink. Aware the Yankees were watching and would attempt to overhear anything that was said, he spoke so low that she had to strain to hear.

"These woods are bound to be crawling with our soldiers. Now that I've got my bearings a bit, I can remember coming through this way on reconnaissance. There's a chance a Confederate patrol could happen by at any time, because I think the sergeant miscalculated how far it is back to his company. He's trying to act confident, but the fact is, I think he's turned around. Those two he sent out are going to have to get their own bearings before they can make any time. And the longer it takes them, the better our chances of encountering our own soldiers. And if we don't, I'm going to be ready to seize any opportunity to get us out of this mess. Just be alert and ready and keep your eye on me."

But Belinda was concerned with neither rescue nor escape for the time being. Instead, she fervently whispered an apology. "I'm sorry. For all of it. If I hadn't panicked back there with Pete Hardin, none of this would have happened. I got us into this."

"Don't worry about it." He was able to say it with a fond wink and a smile delivered straight from his heart. "How else could I have married you so fast?"

And Belinda felt a warm tremor, wishing she could, at that instant, throw her arms about his neck and lift her lips for his kiss. Instead, she had to content herself with a murmured "Thank you, Ryan...."

He saw the emotion in her lovely eyes and could not resist reaching out to trail the backs of his fingertips down her soft cheek. "Someday," he dared to say, "maybe it won't be make-believe."

"Hey, get back over here," Purdy roared, not liking being unable to hear what was being said. Now, more than ever, he wanted to hang on to his prisoners. When his commanding officers learned how valuable they were to the Union army, he was almost certain there would be a commendation for him. Maybe even a promotion.

"Remember," Ryan urged as they turned to go back, "when the time comes, do as I tell you."

The morning wore on, and their stomachs rumbled with hunger. Holley went with Belinda to search the root cellar when she suggested there might be something there. They returned with a jar of beans and a few dried-up potatoes.

"Give them the potatoes," Purdy ordered, greedily reaching for the beans.

Ryan and Belinda declined, and Holley laughed and ate the vegetables himself.

Around midday, Purdy headed for the woods to take care of his personal needs, leaving Holley in charge, with instructions to shoot them if they tried anything. Ryan could tell they were both getting restless, obviously starting to worry over why Crenshaw and Duncan had not returned. "Maybe your men got lost," he said, goading Holley. "Or maybe all of you were lost all along and didn't want to admit it. Maybe you just happened to take us by surprise because you just happened to stumble by here, and—"

"Hey, you shut your mouth." Holley lowered the rifle to point it straight at Ryan's chest.

Instinctively, Ryan positioned himself slightly in front of Belinda, squeezing her protectively behind him as he went on challengingly, "Then why haven't they returned? Your sergeant said two hours. I figure they've been gone nearly five. . . ."

He fell silent.

All three of them heard the sound at the same time.

Horses. Moving slowly. Coming from the woods in the same direction where Sergeant Purdy had disappeared.

"That's them!" Holley leapt to his feet and began waving his arms frantically as he called, "Hey, I hope you boys brought something to eat—"

It happened quickly.

The Confederate point soldier saw a man in blue waving a rifle, and he fired once, striking him dead.

Belinda screamed as Holley pitched forward to the ground.

His arms going about her to hold her tightly against him, Ryan pulled them both to their feet as he yelled, "Don't shoot. He's the only one here, but there's another in the woods near you. Find him." Pushing Belinda behind a tree to shield her should there be more shooting, he lunged to retrieve Holley's gun. "Stay here," he told her as he ran to join the men in gray coming out of the brush.

Belinda watched and waited for what seemed like forever. Finally, Ryan came to inform her that it appeared Sergeant Purdy had seen the Confederate patrol approaching, decided he did not stand a chance against them, chose to save himself and fled. "Now we're going to get out of here before the others get back. I've already told the patrol captain about them, and he agrees we need to move out.

"They aren't from Beauregard's army. They're with General Hill's Regiment from North Carolina.

"Looks like we've been rescued by home folks," he added jovially.

Belinda swayed, her face paling and her heart pounding tremulously.

Ryan was puzzled by her reaction and asked sharply, "What is it? What's wrong?" He stepped forward to clutch her arm. He could feel her trembling.

She could not speak, could only stand there, washed by dizziness. Harmon Willingham was a member of the First North Carolina Regiment . . . commanded by General Daniel H. Hill.

Chapter Fourteen

"Belinda, what's wrong?" Ryan clutched her arm and leaned over to whisper, "Surely you don't think, just because they're from North Carolina, that some of the Hardin family might be among them?"

She shook her head, reminding herself that Ryan knew nothing about Harmon Willingham and that there was no reason to tell him anything now. Besides, she was probably worrying for nothing, anyway. Harmon might have been transferred to another company, or maybe he'd even been killed. She cringed at the thought, for, despite everything, she wished him no harm.

"You're acting strange." Ryan continued to watch her face, his own tight with concern.

She swallowed against her anxiety and covered by explaining, "It's been a terrible day. Everything happened so fast. First the Yankees capturing us. Then standing only a few feet away when a man gets blown apart. And I can't remember when I ate last, and..." She fell silent when she realized she'd been babbling nervously and some of the rescuing soldiers were looking at her oddly. "Just tired...." she finished lamely.

"Sir, is the lady all right?"

Ryan turned to the soldier who had spoken, noting his rank. "Like she said, Corporal, she's tired and hungry. How far away is your camp? I'm Captain Tanner, by the way."

"Corporal Chalmers," the officer countered, introducing himself. "And we're a few hours' ride away, I think. It's a new camp. Just being set up in anticipation of winter quartering in a few months, and I'm not sure how long it will take to get there.

"Actually," he went on, seeming slightly chagrined, "we're trying to round up our regiment. We were backing up General Jackson at Gauley River, and when Rosecrans overran us there was a lot of confusion and everybody got scattered. We don't know how many are dead, wounded, or got captured. That's why we happened by here. We were looking for some of our men."

Ryan frowned. "The fact is, we're lost, too." He had no intention of explaining how that came to be, even though the corporal was obviously interested in hearing about it. Instead, he offered, "I need to get back to my cavalry unit, and Miss Coulter needs to return to medical services. We were with General Wise—"

"We can't help you there."

"What do you mean? We need an escort. These woods are crawling with Federal soldiers. My company can't be very far away. Miss Coulter and I got here on foot, for Christ's sake. We should be able to find our way back by nightfall, but we need your men to ride with us, Corporal Chalmers, just in case we do run into the enemy."

"I'm afraid that's impossible." The corporal shrugged resignedly. "We have our orders to scout this area to the creek, which we've done, and then return to camp. I'm sorry, but we have to start back right away if we want to get there by dark. You're welcome to go with us, if you like."

Ryan looked to where Belinda was accepting some hardtack from one of the soldiers. If it weren't for her, he'd not hesitate to strike out on his own and try to find the way back, but he was not about to risk her safety.

"Another thing . . ."

Ryan turned expectantly to Corporal Chalmers.

"We ran into a scout a while back who told us General Lee and General Wise have been recalled to Richmond and moved out during the night. General Wise, we were told, left Floyd in command, and he's gone into winter quarters. I'm not sure where that leaves you."

"For the moment, nowhere," Ryan said, disgusted. Hell, not only was he separated from his men, but they were on their way into winter quarters, and it was only September. What was Floyd thinking of? Sure, there had been some major setbacks in western Virginia, and things did not look good for the Confederacy there for the time being, but it was too soon to dig in till spring, and he had no intention of doing so. "All right," he said finally, lamely, "I suppose we've no choice but to go with you." He went to inform Belinda of his decision.

She listened, biting back her protests lest he become suspicious and start asking questions. Besides, she told herself, it was of no consequence if they did meet up with Harmon. After all, he'd let her know he didn't consider her worthy of him any longer. He'd broken their engagement. It was all over. Nothing had changed. In his eyes, she was still defiled, soiled. He'd wanted nothing to do with her, but, due to his position as an officer and a gentleman, he would have to provide for her adequately till she could be sent back where she belonged. He'd have no reason to treat her otherwise. Therefore, she feverishly rationalized in preparation for getting her emotions under control, there was no reason to fear being in his company. And he was much too proper to let on in front of Ryan that there had ever been anything between them.

Offering what she hoped was a convincing smile of approval, Belinda finally was able to say, "That's fine, Ryan. We could both use some rest. And it shouldn't take long to get a message to our company where we are. They'll send someone for us."

"More than likely, we'll be reassigned to Hill's regiment," he said, with no enthusiasm. "That's simpler than me trying to find my way back, and if Floyd has gone into winter quarters, I sure as hell don't want to go with him.''

Belinda did not like the idea of not returning. ''Surely we can get back....''

''Maybe not. We'll see.'' Ryan slipped his arm about her waist, pleased to remember the closeness they'd shared during the night, and warmed to think of the feelings growing between them. ''But whatever happens, we'll be together. I don't intend for us to be apart if I can help it.''

''And I want that, too,'' she assured him, pushing back her fears over the possibility of meeting Harmon face-to-face. She wished she could ask one of the soldiers if, indeed, Harmon Willingham was with their regiment, but she didn't dare. If he was, and she inquired about him, he'd hear about it. But if she kept silent, said nothing, it might be that she'd slip right in and out without him knowing she'd even been about. There was no way she was going to call attention to herself.

Ryan took Holley's horse, leading the lame horse, and Belinda rode behind. Doggedly they followed Corporal Chalmers and his men through the afternoon and evening. Along the way, they encountered two more of Chalmers's men. Soon they were a patrol of nearly a dozen.

It was nearly dark. Belinda's arms were around Ryan's waist, her head pressed against his back as she dozed. The horse lumbered along the trail as they slowly moved from the wilderness and began the incline up a gently sloping mountain.

Corporal Chalmers had said their new camp was at the very top. ''It's a wonderful place. Our scouts found it some time ago. There's a small cave with tunnels in all directions. I was in it some months ago, so I know my way around. It's ideal for the winter because there's a vantage point where sentries can see riders coming from miles away. Nobody can slip up on us.''

''Do you have a hospital set up?'' Belinda had wanted to know.

"Not much of one, Miss Coulter," he had told her regretfully. "We're not a big outfit. There's no doctor, but General Hill did manage to get us a surgeon's assistant, and he does the best he can. Of course, when we head into battle with the entire regiment, we know we've got the services of the army's medical personnel. Wagons. Supplies. Doctors. I heard there were quite a few wounded in the fighting yesterday, so I imagine you'll have your hands full if you're of a mind to help."

Belinda had assured him she was, then settled contentedly against Ryan's broad back, weary and wanting to rest, but also reveling in the feel of being next to him.

She awakened to hear a terse command: "Straight line. Single file. The trail narrows just ahead. Room for only one rider at the time."

Darkness had almost completely enshrouded them, but there was enough light for Belinda to see that to their left was a sharp drop down. Instinctively she tightened her arms about Ryan's waist.

"Don't worry," he murmured, intent on staying directly behind the rider in front of him. "I can tell we've got a real surefooted horse, and I get the feeling this isn't the first time he's been on a trail like this. I just feel sorry for the one behind us. He really needs to rest to get the soreness out of that hoof."

Belinda turned, ever so slightly, to look at the limping horse, and that was when she caught the tail end of the conversation between the two riders beyond. They were just moving into single file and one called to the other, "You've got to hand it to Major Willingham for finding this place. It's going to be a perfect hideout, and..."

She could hear nothing more, for the name *Willingham* had provoked a sudden roaring within, shutting out all sound and reason save the anguished screaming of her brain that *Major* Willingham could only be *Harmon* Willingham....

Ryan felt her tension and quickly demanded, "Belinda, what is it? What's wrong?" And, when she did not answer, he promptly swiveled about in the saddle to ask her again.

"Nothing. Nothing. The drop just frightens me, that's all." She struggled to smile in the gathering dusk.

"I told you, my dearest—" he patted her knee where it pressed against him "—I'm not going to let anything happen to you.

"Besides," he said, endeavoring to soothe her, "I'm a good rider. I grew up riding horses on much higher trails than this in the Blue Ridge. We're going to be okay."

And they were, despite Belinda's growing nervousness at the knowledge that she would soon be face-to-face with Harmon. Though she'd tried not to think about it, she willed herself to vividly recall that day last spring.

It had been the first of May, only two weeks after the bombardment at Fort Sumter, which had finally gotten the war going full steam. Spring had been bursting in the mountains, and the ridges had been ablaze with pink and purple laurel and rhododendron blossoms. The popcorn blossoms of the dogwood trees had dotted the valleys and hills.

It had always been her favorite time of year, but anxiety hung like a shroud, obliterating the usual joy at this lovely season. Not only was she trying to overcome the horror of what the Hardins had done to her, but she was also living in fear that Harmon would hear about it. His last letter had said he'd be coming for her soon, to marry her and take her to Raleigh to live with his family while he rode off to war with then Colonel D. H. Hill and the regiment he had formed from the military institute in Charlotte, North Carolina. Foolishly, she had reasoned that once they were married and safely moved away, there'd be little chance Harmon would ever find out what had happened.

But that day she knew her hopes were for naught.

"Why didn't you write me about it, Belinda?"

At the sound of his voice, she whirled to see him standing there, the thrilling rush melting to a chill of foreboding as his words washed over her. "I—I don't know," she stammered, swaying as she stood there, holding her apron filled with potatoes and turnips.

"Did you think I wouldn't hear?"

Even in the vague shadows of the root cellar, she saw how his handsome face tightened with contempt as he stared at her so very coldly.

"I—I suppose I hoped you wouldn't..." She managed to choke out the admission, while trying to think of words to make him understand how she had been living for the hope that, if he did find out, he'd love her enough to not let it matter. But, even as she stood there, Belinda knew in that sickening moment that it was all over.

"It would have saved me a trip had you written to me." He stood with legs apart, left hand holding the white gloves he methodically slapped into the palm of his right. "I don't know the whole story, Belinda. Perhaps it's best I don't. But I heard enough when I stopped by Gaither's store on my way here to know it's a sordid mess. First, you get yourself ravaged by those animals—"

"*Get* myself ravaged?" she echoed, aghast. "Why, you make it sound like it was my fault, that somehow I caused it to happen, and that's not true. I was on my way to Asheville, to your aunt's, because I'd made up my mind I couldn't live here anymore, not with all the scandal and—"

"Enough, enough..." He waved his gloves at her, closing his eyes momentarily, as though attempting to shut out the ugliness. "Spare me the details now, please. I've had quite enough for one afternoon. Bad enough I have to hear it from someone else that my fiancée has been raped, without also hearing my intended father-in-law is a murderer who has escaped from jail—thanks to my intended sister-in-law—and gone off to fight for the enemy."

"Why do you think I wanted to leave?" she had cried, feeling as though she was suddenly facing a stranger. This was a side of Harmon she'd never seen before. Cold. Distant. Accusing. Suspicious. "Hear me out, please. . . ."

With another wave of his gloves, he took a step backward, in retreat, as though anticipating she was about to throw herself into his arms in desperation. "Please, Belinda, I asked you to spare me the details. What's done is done. And you must realize this has been a terrible blow. I came here today to take you to Raleigh. My mother was getting everything ready for a small wedding, so that we could be married before I leave for Virginia in two weeks, and . . ."

"And *what?*" Belinda had echoed incredulously. "You make it sound as though it's all over, Harmon. I'm still the same girl. Those bastards didn't kill me, though there have been times when I wished they had. But it was thinking of you that kept me going. Through the darkest days, when I just wanted to die, I'd think of you, how much I love you and want to be your wife, about the future we'll have together, our children. . . ."

She loosened her hold on the apron, allowing the vegetables to fall to the dirt floor and roll between them and on into the shadows. Quietly, dismally, she murmured, "So what is it you now want to say to me, Harmon?"

He had been watching a turnip spin into a dusty corner, staring at it as though mesmerized. With a quick shake of his head, he forced himself to meet her accusing glare. "As I said, this is a shock. I haven't had time to really think about it yet, but . . ." He hesitated, glancing away once more.

Coolly Belinda had prodded him, though she already knew what was coming. "But *what,* Harmon? Go on. Tell me."

"I need time to think about all this because the fact is, Belinda, a man wants a virgin for his wife. . . ."

"I *was* a virgin till they *raped* me!"

"But no more. And if I heard about it, others will also. I need time to decide whether I can live with that—others knowing my wife was soiled, defiled, degraded. Surely you can understand that...." He gestured helplessly.

Belinda nodded mutely, afraid to trust her voice in that moment, for she was so dangerously close to tears.

His smile was forced, patronizing. "You know I care about you. I just need time," he repeated. "I'll write to you."

Again she nodded, no longer able to look at him, staring down at her feet instead.

"A pity, because it really wasn't your fault."

Then, suddenly, angrily, he exploded. "*Damn your father!* And your sister, as well. I hear she's got herself talked about, too. The whole family is scandalous, for God's sake. Why, if my mother hears of this... But enough. I've got to get out of here."

He turned on his heel and rushed from the root cellar.

The encounter had lasted less than five minutes.

Belinda doubted he had given her another thought after that day. And, if he *had* written, she would not have known, for she'd left that very night.

"We're here."

Ryan's announcement brought her back from the miserable past with a jolt.

Quickly, anxiously, she scanned the soldiers standing around. She did not see Harmon anywhere. In fact, there was not an officer in sight, only Corporal Chalmers, who came to say that their horses would be taken care of and they should just follow him into the cave.

The opening was small, situated behind a large, concealing rhododendron. A perfect hideout, Ryan was saying, but Belinda could only make perfunctory noises of agreement. She wanted only to get it over with—to see Harmon, then turn away and stay as far away from him as possible during the time they were there. "How long do you think it will be?" she asked Ryan.

"What?" He looked at her, bewildered.

She realized she'd been thinking aloud. "How long do you think we'll have to stay here?"

"I've no idea, but right now you need some rest—"

Corporal Chalmers rushed up to them. "I'm afraid that's going to have to wait awhile. They need help with some of the wounded, and when I told the surgeon's assistant we brought a nurse in, he said he could use you."

Belinda did not hesitate, tarrying only long enough to ask of Ryan, "Will I see you later tonight?"

"Don't worry." He gave a mock salute. "I'll be close by, and whether they like it or not, I'm going to see to it you get a decent meal and a good night's sleep."

Chalmers had hold of her elbow, was pulling her away.

He described the cave as they hurried along in the eerie glow from the torches set in the wall. Most activities went on in the entrance chamber, which was large enough for the men to bed down in for the night, as well as eat in when the cook served up their rations. "The medical facility has been set up in a big chamber to the rear. There's a waterfall running down the wall, which is a big help, I'm sure."

As they went deeper into the cave, the air grew colder and damper. "A terrible place to put the sick," she remarked disapprovingly.

Chalmers dared to agree, confiding, "No doubt Major Willingham had something to do with it. He says he doesn't like to have his men exposed to the wounded. Says it's bad for their morale, because they might start thinking they're going to wind up the same way, so they aren't so eager to go into battle.

"Nobody would dare tell him to his face, of course," he went on, "but most of us think it's *him* that doesn't want to be around the wounded. We call him a rear-end officer, anyway."

Belinda was listening to every word he was saying, realizing there was a lot she had never known about Harmon and, so far, it was all unpleasant information. "What is a 'rear-end' officer?"

His laugh was scornful. "Pardon me, ma'am, but it means two things. A rear-end officer is one who does his commanding from the rear. Always looking at maps and charts and giving orders but staying as far from the battlefield himself as he can.

"The other thing is—" he hesitated "—he don't know his rear end from a hole in the ground."

Belinda blanched. Not with embarrassment for herself over Chalmers's impropriety, but for Harmon, to think his men should regard him so disrespectfully.

Stepping into the chamber, Belinda saw that torches were set along the walls to provide ample light. She could see the wounded, perhaps two dozen, lying on the dirt floor on blankets.

Nearby, ringed by torches, a crude operating table had been set up—boards placed between ammunition barrels. Corporal Chalmers pointed to the man standing next to it. "That's Captain Staples. He's considered a surgeon's assistant. He's had medical training, enough so's he's allowed to operate in an emergency, which looks like what he's doing now."

They waited till he had finished, and then Chalmers took Belinda to introduce her.

"They tell me you're a nurse," Captain Staples said.

She took note of his sideways glance as he carefully scrutinized her, and she sensed his hostility, for she'd encountered it from doctors all too often in the past months—except Major Whitley, of course. "That's right. I understand you need some help."

"We sure do. I've only got one steward to help me with twenty-six patients. Bedpans need emptying. Bandages need changing. A couple need to be spoon-fed. Plenty for you to do, Miss Coulter, so just do it and stay out of my way. I've got two more amputations to do right away."

"I've had experience with amputations."

Over the unconscious man on the table, Captain Staples exchanged an amused glance with his assisting steward.

"The last thing I need now is a woman fainting over my patient, Miss Coulter. See to the bedpans, please."

"Yeah," the steward snapped. "They're stacked back there by the waterfall. Get 'em washed out so I can take them around soon as we finish here."

Belinda did not mind washing bedpans. Neither did she mind changing soiled bandages or feeding by hand men too ill to do it themselves. What she *did* take exception to, however, was being considered unqualified to do anything other than the most menial of tasks.

She noticed that Corporal Chalmers had quietly disappeared, leaving her alone.

Captain Staples, seeing she had not moved to obey his instructions, irritably thundered, "Well, what are you waiting for, Miss Coulter? I thought you said you were a nurse. Are you going to just stand there?"

"No," she responded with a sigh of resignation, "I'm going to do what you asked me to, but if you find you do need help operating, I assure you, I can assist, and you don't have to worry about me swooning."

He ignored her.

The steward snickered.

And Belinda turned to her tasks.

Major Harmon Willingham pushed aside the blanket hanging over the opening to his small chamber of the cave. Glancing about at his surroundings, he smiled with pleasure to see that everything had been set up just as he had directed. It had been sheer luck to pass by the farmhouse near Sewell's Mountain. The family living there had been told the armies of Rosecrans and Lee were about to engage in a fierce battle, so they had taken their personal belongings and fled to safety elsewhere. When they returned, they would find a bed and mattress missing, as well as a table and two chairs. He'd had his men tear the bed down, bring it here and set it up.

And, when the owners went to their root cellar to fetch a bottle of muscadine wine, they would find their supply of spirits missing, too.

He sat down on the side of the bed and pulled off his spit-polished boots. Life in the army, he had decided, was not so bad. All he had to do was either plan the strategy for his troops or carry out orders given by his superiors; thus far, he'd managed to do so at a safe distance from actual combat. His reasoning was that he would be of no service to either his men or the cause if he were wounded, or, God forbid, killed.

He reached under the bed and pulled out a bottle of wine, uncorked it and took a big swallow. He hated drinking that way, but his aide had not yet brought in the glassware he also had confiscated. Well, he would see about that later. For the moment, he was tired and wanted to nap before dinner. He smacked his lips at the thought of dinner. Two nice fat hens had also been taken from the farm, and right about now, he figured, they should be simmering in a pot with drap dumplings.

Leaning back on the soft pillow, he was glad he'd had it brought along, too. Goose down, no doubt. Well made. As comfortable as his own bedding back in Raleigh, North Carolina.

A frown touched his forehead as his thoughts turned to the recent Yankee victory in his own state. A Federal squadron, consisting of seven warships with 149 guns mounted, had steamed out of the harbor at Hampton Roads, Virginia, on the twenty-sixth of August. With the squadron had been a fleet of transports carrying close to nine hundred soldiers of the Ninth and Twentieth New York Volunteers. They had arrived off Hatteras Inlet on the afternoon of the twenty-seventh to do battle with Colonel W. F. Martin's Confederates, who numbered less than four hundred. The Yankees had laughed about how they were being sent to clean out what they called "the Hatteras Hornets' Nest."

The Yankees had begun their assault on the twenty-eighth with heavy bombardment of Fort Clark. A colonel named Max Weber had taken three hundred soldiers and two guns and landed on the beach. The surf, according to the reports, had been very high, and they had been afraid to take any more men in. But alas, by noon, the Confederates had run out of ammunition. Spiking their guns, they had abandoned the fort and withdrawn to Hatteras, and Colonel Weber's men had declared victory.

It shouldn't have happened that way, Harmon ruminated with an annoyed grimace and a deep swallow of wine. Afterward, Colonel Weber had admitted he had worried all night long that he would ultimately be beaten, because, unbeknownst to the Confederates, two Federal ships supposed to lay near the beach had been forced to withdraw for fear of being wrecked on the coast. Weber had been at the Confederates' mercy, figuring the Rebels would regroup during the night, reinforce their forts, repair damages, take them prisoner and whip the hell out of all the Federals at first light.

But, Harmon recalled with a pang of regret, the sun had risen on Yankee ships moving into position in a calm sea, without a cloud in the sky. They had proceeded to bombard Fort Hatteras, where Martin's men had taken refuge with Commodore Barron and over four hundred men.

Sadly, within three hours it had been all over. Barron had surrendered the fort and all his troops.

And it was a loss that could have been prevented, Harmon fumed. Nearly eight hundred Confederate soldiers had spent the night within six hundred yards of only three or four hundred men and had let them walk right in and take them. Now the valuable approach to the outer banks had been secured by the Federals, and the blockade of the South was growing ever tighter.

Harmon was snatched abruptly from his reverie by a voice calling to him from the other side of the blanket that afforded him a measure of privacy in his cubicle.

"Major... sir. I have a report for you."

Harmon sighed at the intrusion but responded, "Very well. Come in and get it over with. I'm trying to rest."

Corporal Chalmers pulled the cover aside and entered to offer a perfunctory salute, which Harmon waved away. Then he proceeded to tell of the rescue of the female nurse and the cavalry officer.

Harmon listened with interest. He liked the idea of a woman being around, though only if she was comely, of course. It had been nearly a month since he'd last enjoyed a woman's favors. Dahlia Burdette had been sheer delight. They had met shortly after the first land battle of the war, at Big Bethel, Virginia, back in June. He had commandeered her family's house for his headquarters, and the very first night she had found her way to his bed. When he and his men moved out, she had gone along, but then General Hill had heard about it and sent word that he did not want "camp women" among his ranks. Harmon had been due for promotion to major along about that time, so he'd sent her on her tearful way. But damn, he silently cursed, he missed having a warm body to lie with at night.

"What does she look like?"

"Huh? What?" Chalmers did not understand the query at first, for he had been in the midst of telling about Captain Tanner's blacksmithing skills. Immediately after arriving at the cave, Tanner had gotten busy, not only with the lame stallion he'd treated earlier, but checking the hooves of all the men's horses, as well. He had found just about every one poorly shod, and already the big fire necessary for his craft was roaring and he had started removing shoes to reheat in the flames for molding to proper fit.

Harmon waved the wine bottle impatiently. "The *woman,* Corporal, the *woman.* What does she look like?"

Chalmers managed to keep a straight face. The major's womanizing was common knowledge among the troops. "If she was cleaned up, I'd say she'd be a real beauty, sir, but right now she's wearing dirty, bloodstained clothes and her hair's a mess."

"Where is she?"

Chalmers explained, "Captain Staples has her working back in the area set up for the wounded. Once he found out we had a nurse around, he couldn't wait to have her sent to help out."

"She's there now?" Harmon was getting to his feet, his interest piqued.

"Yes, sir."

Harmon set his wine down and walked out of the chamber. He had chosen the best area for himself, of course. It was situated at the top of a short flight of natural stone steps, so he could observe both the front and the rear portions of the cave. Now he could see soldiers scurrying about, laying out bedrolls, staking claim to where they'd be sleeping.

He was aware that Corporal Chalmers was right behind him as he made his way down the narrow corridor toward the hospital area.

"She's over there...." Chalmers pointed as they stepped through the arched entrance, ducking an outcropping of hanging stalactites.

Harmon drew a sharp breath and stopped short. It couldn't be—*or could it?* he wondered in astonishment.

He was looking at her profile as she spoon-fed broth into a wounded soldier's mouth. It certainly looked like Belinda. There was no mistaking the fiery red hair, and there was no denying how the lush, full breasts strained at the constricting bodice of the filthy dress she was wearing.

"Sir, what's wrong?" Chalmers was puzzled by the way his commander had frozen in his tracks, his expression one of surprise and wonder.

"Nothing...nothing..." Harmon backed away from the opening, lest she glance up and recognize him. "Tell me, does she know who's in command of this company?"

Chalmers was even more bewildered. "I believe your name was mentioned, sir."

Just then, Belinda finished what she was doing and got to her feet. As she turned to the next soldier in line for care, she was momentarily facing in Harmon's direction, but, intent on what she was doing, she did not notice him standing so far away.

With a slamming jolt of his heart, Harmon knew in that instant that, despite the dirt-streaked face, the limp, stringy hair falling about her face, it was, beyond a doubt, Belinda Coulter.

"Sir, what is wrong?" Chalmers repeated. He'd never seen the major behave so strangely. "You look like you've seen a ghost."

Harmon smiled, absently touched the tip of his mustache. "I have." Then, before the corporal could annoy him with yet another prying question, he said, "Give her another hour to finish feeding the soldiers, then tell Major Staples I have invited Miss Coulter to dine with me tonight because I know she's bound to be very tired, as well as hungry.

"Miss Burdette left one of her gowns behind," Harmon continued as he headed back to his chamber, with Chalmers right behind him. "I believe it should fit Miss Coulter nicely. I want you to deliver it to her with my invitation to dinner and suggest she clean herself up before being brought to my quarters."

Chalmers could not resist asking, "What about the man she was with? Captain Tanner? You want him for dinner, too?"

Harmon withered him with a look of disgust before disappearing behind the blanket to the privacy of his stone alcove.

Chalmers snickered. The major wasn't fooling him. He knew what he had in mind.

But one thing puzzled him. . . .

How had the major known the female nurse's name was Coulter? Chalmers was positive he hadn't mentioned it earlier. . . .

Chapter Fifteen

At last, all the patients had been taken care of and bedded down for the night. Belinda was exhausted. She was also anxious to take her leave, not only to be with Ryan, but also to escape the very pompous and very arrogant Captain Staples.

Looking at him across the chamber, she was struck by the thought that Major Whitley was probably the only doctor in the entire Confederate medical services who wasn't prejudiced against female nurses. Throughout the evening, Staples had criticized everything she did. Bandages were too loose or too tight. She was much too slow in scrubbing out bedpans and spent far too much time coddling the patients.

He had become especially irate when she had comforted a soldier who was crying over the death of the man who'd been lying next to him. Staples said crying was a symbol of weakness; only the strong could survive a war. Belinda had bitten her tongue to keep from reminding him tears were also self-soothing, allowing grief to flow, instead of being kept locked inside to fester and torment.

But she had kept silent, attending to her duties, anxious to finish.

Meanwhile, she had been hoping—no, praying—that Ryan would get them out of there swiftly, before she encountered Harmon. Despite her fatigue, she found herself pondering her present feelings for the man she had once fancied herself in love with and had hoped to marry. It all seemed a lifetime ago, and it was hard now to ever imagine herself as a giddy-headed young girl with no other ambition in life except to marry well and have a family. The past months had changed her into a mature woman, and not altogether because of what the Hardin boys had done. No, it was more than that, for she had found herself thrust into a world of desperation, suffering and death. Life had taken on new meaning, and Harmon's cruel rejection now seemed trivial by comparison.

And yes, she remembered with a sudden smile, Ryan had turned her feelings around, as well. Tender, kind, understanding, he had made her realize she was wrong to withdraw within herself, shutting her heart to love forevermore. There was a chance for happiness out there, somewhere, and, if God so willed, the two of them would make a future together. There was no room left in her mind, or heart, for regret over Harmon, and it was best they not meet.

"Tomorrow morning, first thing, get back here," Captain Staples snapped to Belinda as he turned to retire for the night. "I expect we'll have more wounded coming in."

Knowing he would not like it, she still dared ask, "How long do you plan on keeping these men here? These aren't the best of conditions—a damp, drafty cave. They need to be taken somewhere else. A church or a house down in the flatland. Surely—"

"Surely," he interrupted with an impatient scowl, "you should know it isn't your place to question anything about these men, Miss Coulter. Frankly, I'd like nothing better than to get out of here myself. Major Willingham may think this cave is an ideal place for winter quarters, but I don't. You, however, should learn your place and keep your opinions to yourself."

Belinda continued nonetheless. "The doctor I've been working with said a hospital is being constructed at Petersburg. It might already be operating. You could send a scout to find out, move these men there..."

He threw his arms up in the air in weary dismissal. "It's not up to me. And for the next few hours, I don't care what happens to anybody. I've got to get some sleep."

Belinda looked around her. The steward was bedding down nearby, so the men would not be left alone and unattended during the night. She could not stay, anyway, for it wouldn't be proper for her to lie down and sleep around the men.

She turned to go, and that was when she saw Corporal Chalmers waiting for her. She was puzzled to see that he was carrying what looked like a dress of some kind, but what truly baffled her was the strange, almost apologetic expression on his face.

She approached him, and he held the dress out to her with a hurried, almost embarrassed explanation. "Major Willingham said he thought this would fit, that you'd probably want to clean up before dinner. I'll take you to your quarters now. It's a small chamber, but the major had confiscated an extra mattress, so he had us put that in for you. You should be quite comfortable. We're heating water for you, for your bath. The major is having a nice dinner prepared, and when you're ready, I'll take you to him."

Belinda stopped walking to stare at him incredulously. What was he talking about? A borrowed dress? A confiscated mattress? Hot water? She shook her head to clear it, felt indignity rising at the realization that Harmon obviously knew she was there, but instead of rushing to say hello and politely inquire as to her well-being, he wanted her cleaned up, properly dressed, as though preparing to meet royalty, for heaven's sake.

She thought about refusing the dress, but she knew she did need to change. Besides, she reasoned, perhaps it was best just to get it all over with. No doubt that was what Harmon intended, to justify to her all over again his reasons for ending their engagement, to remind her that she was soiled and tainted, and, most of all, to let her know that merely because fate had brought them together again, she should not get her hopes up that he would change his mind and want to marry her.

Stiffly she took the dress, thinking it a bit gaudy for her taste—bright red satin, for heaven's sake!

Chalmers led the way, and she was surprised when he cut off from the main rock corridor and into a narrow passageway. A torch hanging from the wall cast eerie, mellow shadows over the outcropping of stalagmites along the floor. Carefully they stepped around them, finally reaching the hanging blanket that gave privacy to the tiny cubicle on the other side.

Within, a lantern had been placed on the floor, and she could see a mattress, covers, and a pail of what was obviously hot water, as evidenced by the steam rising from it.

"How long do you think you'll need to get ready?" Chalmers wanted to know.

"An hour." Then, with a sharp pang of anxiety as she thought of Ryan, asked, "What about Captain Tanner? What's become of him? He was going to bring me food, and I don't want him to go to the bother if I'm not here...."

Chalmers laughed. "Don't depend on him to keep you from being hungry tonight, Miss Coulter." He proceeded to tell her how Ryan had plunged right into checking shoes on all the horses, how he seemed indefatigable. "You best be obliged to the major for seeing you don't go to bed hungry."

With a bitter flash, Belinda was reminded of how she wouldn't be in the predicament she was in, anyway, if it weren't for Harmon. She'd be in Raleigh now, cozily living with his parents in their huge, luxurious house and—*stop it!* She gave herself a mental shake. No need to think like that now, for it was only torment. Far better, she furiously told herself, to get it all over with, let him ease his guilt by offering her a nice meal. Then they could both get on with their lives.

Corporal Chalmers left her, saying he'd return in an hour, and Belinda quickly stripped and enjoyed a warm sponge bath from the pail. As she did so, she tried not to feel anger or disappointment for Ryan, telling herself he'd just gotten caught up in his work, the way she had. And, if he'd thought of her at all, no doubt he'd assumed others would see to her needs for the night. Still, it needled her that he could dismiss her so easily, especially after all they'd been through together the past night and day.

She had dipped her hair in the basin to rinse it, and it was still damp about her face when she struggled into the dress. Thank goodness she'd taken time to scrub out her own things, which would, she hoped, be dry by morning. With the bar of lye soap provided, she'd managed to get most of the bloodstains out. She certainly did not wish to wear the horrid red dress any longer than necessary. The bodice was cut low and, due to her large bosom, more cleavage was exposed than she felt comfortable with. Never had she flaunted her body, not even when other girls had told her she should be proud enough to do so. And the dress also reminded her of her miserable days as a saloon singer.

Corporal Chalmers was right on time. He took one look at Belinda and could not help gasping, "My God, you're beautiful...."

Belinda thanked him demurely, self-conscious about the way her breasts were practically spilling out. She wished she had a shawl. Still, she found that if she allowed her shoulders to slump a bit, the effect was less dramatic.

Doggedly she followed him through the cave, and, at last, they reached Harmon's quarters.

Chalmers called out to him.

With a sudden swish of the blanket, Belinda found herself staring into the divine blue eyes she'd once adored, as Harmon smiled down at her with the same smile that had once melted her heart.

He took both her hands in his, kissing each in turn, as he devoured her with his intense, burning gaze.

Chalmers discreetly retreated.

"My God, Belinda, you're even lovelier than I remembered." He drew her inside, and the blanket closed behind them.

She pulled her hands from his as she glanced about her to see that he'd lit more than a dozen candles. The little stone cubicle glowed cozily in a mellow, romantic light. On a small wooden table, there were settings for two. She could smell the delicious aroma of the chicken and dumplings. There was a bottle of wine and glasses.

Harmon saw her surprise and hastened to explain that he'd confiscated everything from a farmhouse. "They're going to wish they hadn't been such cowards and run off," he told her, laughing, "because now I'm set for the winter."

Belinda stiffened, feeling uneasy. She could understand his hospitable offering of clean clothes, a bath and a nice meal. After all, he was the commanding officer of his company, and any woman happening along, especially one ministering to his wounded, should be afforded certain courtesies, but she thought he was overdoing it a bit.

He gestured to one of the chairs. "Please, Belinda, sit down. I know you must be famished."

She was, and, despite the way her stomach was churning with nervous apprehension, she eagerly accepted the helping of chicken and dumplings covered with thick gravy. "This is very nice of you, Harmon," she told him graciously, sipping her wine.

"Yes, as I said, all compliments of cowards," he airily bragged.

"Did you also confiscate material we can use for lint? Bandages? Any supplies at all that we might be able to use in the hospital?"

His voice lost its imperious confidence as he said defensively, "No, that's not my department. Medical services—"

"Is vastly overworked," she cut in, "and I thought it was standard procedure for troops to search houses for anything of medicinal value."

He raised his brows, annoyed by her censorious tone. He wanted nothing to do with blood and suffering, and the last thing he wanted to talk about this night was her disgusting involvement in that part of the war. Still, he yielded to his own nagging curiosity and asked, "Tell me, how on earth did you wind up in such a degrading situation?"

Belinda kept reminding herself that she was eating too fast, but dear Lord, she was famished. Between mouthfuls, she endeavored to explain that it had been quite by accident, but assured him, "I don't regret it. I just wish the Confederacy were more tolerant of women in nursing. The prejudice is a great hindrance to me in trying to do a good job. I'm treated no better than a slave in some instances, and never allowed to take any initiative. It was different with Major Whitley, though...." And she proceeded to give a full recitation on her respect and admiration for the man.

Harmon listened, growing more and more resentful with each word she spoke. Their reunion was not turning out at all as he had planned. It had only been—how long? Since the end of April. Now it was nearly October. Only five months since he had left her absolutely brokenhearted and devastated. But when she looked at him now, across the table, as she had when she'd first seen him, her lovely emerald eyes no longer shone with love and devotion. It was as though he were no more than a casual acquaintance, someone she merely used to know. Five months ago, damn it, they had been engaged to be married, and now he was nothing more than an officer politely feeding her.

He shoved his plate away, food untouched, and lifted his wineglass to down the contents in one gulp.

"...so I'm thinking perhaps we'll go back to Richmond, where I can work at Chimborazo for the winter, and—"

"Enough, Belinda." He slammed his glass down on the table.

She jumped, startled, eyes widening.

"I'm sick of all this talk about your being a nurse, damn it. What happened after I left? What made you leave home?

I should think after you were attacked you'd want to stay out of sight for a while, to give people a chance to forget.''

Her voice shook with bitterness. "To hell with other people, Harmon. I'm the one who has to forget. It's obvious *you* haven't," she said stiffly.

His face tightened with furious contempt. "Don't curse, Belinda. It isn't ladylike. And, of course, I haven't forgot. How could I? I've thought of nothing else. Day and night." He refilled his glass.

"Is that why you asked me here tonight? To remind me of all the pain you caused me?"

He gasped. "*I* caused? Dear Lord, woman, you dare blame me for what those savages did to you?"

"You thought I was soiled, defiled, not worthy to be your wife. Did you think that caused me no pain when I fancied myself in love with you?"

Harmon told himself to tread carefully, to think before he spoke. One wrong word and she would be out of there in the time it took to snuff out a candle, and he'd be spending another night alone. There was no denying that he wanted her. He always had. In fact, when they had been engaged, desire had been as miserable as a throbbing toothache. He thought of the nights in Asheville, when she had been a guest in his aunt's home. Just being near her had set him on fire, and, after a few proper kisses, he'd had to run to the nearest whorehouse to unleash his pent-up passion. Now, however, it was different. Belinda Coulter was not the vestal virgin he'd placed on a pedestal, untouchable till she was his lawful wife. She'd been had by those rednecks who'd raped her, and there was no telling how many others since. This was war, damn it, not a cotillion, and men didn't worry about things like proper courting. If a woman was around—especially where she didn't belong, like an army camp—she was good for just one thing. And, through no fault of her own, Belinda fitted the category in war, or peace. She had been defiled, and he damn sure didn't want her for his wife, much less for the mother of his children. But he did want her—and fiercely.

"I suppose," he began finally, framing his response slowly, carefully, "I knew I was causing you pain, but it was nothing compared to my own. I loved you, Belinda. I still do. But you have to understand I was in a stupor that day. I'd just come from Gaither's store, and the men in there were only too glad to be the ones to tell me my fiancée had been raped. How do you think that made me feel? Think about it. Consider *my* feelings. You should have written me and told me about it. It wasn't fair I should hear such horror from strangers."

"Maybe..." she conceded. Then she yielded to curiosity and asked, "Did you ever write to me afterward?"

"Of course, of course," he assured her.

She had no way of knowing whether he had or hadn't, so she could not dispute his word—and she no longer cared, anyway. She finished her wine, satisfied that she'd had enough to eat. All she wanted was to get back to her quarters and out of the gaudy dress. She did not want to sit and listen to Harmon's whining. The truth was, and she'd been too long in realizing it, he was spoiled, selfish, and self-centered. And if any good at all had come out of the horror inflicted upon her by the Hardins, it was that she had been spared becoming Mrs. Harmon Willingham. Thank God she had grown up and realized there was more to life than marrying a man solely for social position and financial security. Maybe she would go to medical school. If she could make it through this infernal war, by God, she could do anything. "I'm really tired, Harmon. I think I'll go to bed." She stood.

He leapt to his feet so quickly that his chair tipped over, and he rushed to take her in his arms and protest, "No. You can't go. Not yet. We have to talk."

She pulled away from his embrace, self-consciously tugging at the bodice of her dress as she did so, scolding him mildly. "Please don't touch me, Harmon. We've nothing to discuss. It was nice of you to invite me for dinner. While I'm here, I'd like nothing better than for us to be friends.''

"*Friends?*" he echoed blankly, his eyes widening. He lifted his glass from the table, drained it and poured himself another, reeling all the while. He had been drinking all evening, anticipating her arrival, and now he felt mellow, relaxed, anxious to win her favor. Despite her request that he keep his hands off her, he danced his fingertips up her bare arm, finally reaching her cheek to tenderly caress her as he whispered, "Oh, my dear, I want to be more than friends. It's as I told you, I've thought of you constantly. You're like a fever in my blood. I can't stop thinking about you, regretting how things turned out. I want us to start over, to put the past behind us...."

Belinda bit back a giggle, for it was all she could do to keep from laughing in his face. Did he really think she was so stupid and naive that she would believe him? Swallowing hard, struggling to keep a straight face, she allowed him to draw her into his embrace. Just as he lowered his lips, about to kiss her, she cocked her head to one side, fluttered her long lashes, and demurely asked, "Will you be able to get leave so you can see me safely back to Raleigh?"

Harmon had closed his eyes in ecstatic anticipation of the kiss, but now they flashed open as he stared down at her in wonder to demand, "Raleigh? Why do you want to go to Raleigh? I thought you said something about Richmond, Chimborazo..."

She playfully touched fingers to his nose and lightly tweaked. "That was before you changed your mind about marrying me, silly. Your family will want me to live with them, where I'll be safe. That's what we planned before, remember? I'll move in with them and—"

Her words jolted. His arms fell away and he took a staggering step backward, swinging his head from side to side as he laughed nervously. "No, no, I didn't say anything about getting married, Belinda. I told you before, I need time to think, and—"

She made her eyes go wide with feigned surprise. "But you just said you regretted how things turned out, that you wanted us to start over, put the past behind us."

"Oh, I do, I do," he assured her hastily, gathering her close once more as he attempted to explain, "but I wasn't talking about marriage. Surely you can understand the need to wait, to get to know each other all over again. And that's what we're going to do. Forget what happened. Start fresh.

"I'm going to hole up in here for the winter," he continued in a rush, "and you can stay with me. You see how cozy it is, and—"

"Where did you get this dress?"

He blinked. "Huh?"

Belinda lifted her skirt ever so slightly, pulling away from him to turn around. "Where did you get this dress? It seems strange for an officer to be carrying around a lovely red dress like this in a war. And it doesn't look like one a farmer's daughter would have, so don't try to tell me you confiscated it along with all the other things here."

"No, no..." He licked his lips in agitation, reaching for her again, this time roughly. Nuzzling her neck, he whispered fiercely, "It doesn't matter...."

"It *does* matter. Maybe you're married," she said petulantly, jerking away again, mustering a look of hurt and horror. "Oh, Harmon, you didn't marry someone else, did you?"

"Of course not, damn it!"

She wagged a finger at him. "Don't curse, Harmon. It's not gentlemanly. Now, if you don't have a wife, where did you get this dress?"

He had lost all patience. The tantalizing sight of her luscious breasts, exposed almost to the nipples, was more than he could bear. He could feel himself growing hard, the ache beginning in his loins. Those other bastards had taken what was rightfully his, he raged within, something he'd never had and, by God, he'd waited long enough. "Don't worry about it." He grabbed her, his hands clamping over her breasts and mauling. "She's gone now. And I never married her. And she *was* a farmer's daughter, damn it. I bought her the dress, but it's yours now."

"I don't want the dress, Harmon." Gone was the pretense of coquettishness. "I want you to marry me, like we'd planned." She did not mean a word of what she was saying; she only wanted to see how far she could push before he exploded.

She did not have long to wait.

"I don't want to marry you, damn it!" he roared, giving her a rough shove that sent her sprawling backward across the bed. "I just want you to give me what the Hardin boys took. It was rightfully mine, anyway...."

He fell across her, fingers dipping inside the bodice of her dress. She felt the fabric tear, and her breasts tumbled forth into his eagerly waiting hands. His hot, eager lips covered hers, smothering her scream, and he was oblivious to the frenzied pounding of her fists against his shoulders and back.

A shroud of hysteria descended, and Harmon disappeared within its foggy depths. In his place came first Jake Hardin, then Rufus. Belinda was no longer in the cave, but *back there,* on the side of the road to Asheville, being savagely ravished on the ground.

She kicked wildly, twisting from side to side in a futile attempt to buck him off, but her struggles only incited him more. In his drunken state, Harmon was beyond reason, beyond caring about anything except satiating the lust he had harbored for Belinda Coulter since the first time he had laid eyes on her.

He twisted to one side, long enough to wrestle her arms behind her back and pin them down. She fought to breathe against his tongue, which he had forced inside her mouth, his face mashing into hers, hurting and bruising. With his free hand, he squeezed her breasts, lifting his lips long enough to warn her hoarsely, "Don't make me hurt you, Belinda. You know you want it, too...."

Again he silenced her cries, reaching to yank up her dress and attempt to spread apart her tightly squeezed thighs.

"I'm going to have you...." he promised between choking, stifling kisses and thrusts of his hot, eager tongue. "Again and again...night after night.... My woman... always have been ... Not fair they took it first...."

Belinda welcomed the new curtain descending, one of black oblivion. She felt herself being pulled away from the repeated nightmare, felt herself yielding. No matter that she'd promised herself that she would always fight back, that she would never again allow herself to be a victim. He was hurting her, with his mouth and hands. He would ultimately win, just as the Hardins had, and it was so much easier to just drift away, to leave the horror and seek peace in the dark abyss awaiting...

No, don't give up, her brain was suddenly screaming, making her resist surrender. *Fight him, fight him....*

Ryan held a torch in one hand, and in his other the bowl of stew he'd talked the cook into warming. Time had slipped by. He had lost count of the number of horses he'd examined. A few were so bad he'd gone ahead and shod them properly. The others would have to wait till tomorrow, but at least he'd gotten the poorly fitting shoes off with pincers and bar. He felt bad to think how hungry Belinda must be, but told himself that others had surely seen to her needs. And, even though it was late and he was bone weary, he did not want to turn in without telling her good-night, without making sure she was okay.

A smile touched his lips. What was happening between them was wonderful. He had to go slow, he knew, because she'd been through a hell of a lot, but the way things were going, he was optimistic things would work out.

"Captain Tanner, where are you going?"

He stopped short as Corporal Chalmers called from where he was playing cards with some of the other soldiers.

He explained that he had promised Belinda he'd take her something to eat, but had gotten caught up in his working with the horses. "I just hope some of you thought about her before now and took her something, because she hadn't eaten since yesterday."

As he spoke, Ryan noticed Chalmers looked uncomfortable, but before he could wonder about it, one of the other men spoke up with a sneering grin.

"Don't worry, Captain, somebody thought of it."

The others, all except for Chalmers, began to snicker among themselves.

Ryan tensed. Something strange was going on. "What are you talking about?"

"Let's just say..." The soldier paused to pick through the cards he'd just been dealt, discarding one, indicating he wanted one more. "...that Major Willingham is real obliging when it comes to the ladies. I helped set up his little love nest in that private little alcove of his, and I have to say, it's real cozy. And he had the cook make chicken and dumplings just for him and the lady. He's even got wine—"

"Shut up, Rathbun," Chalmers snapped, digging at him with his elbow. He could tell Tanner was getting riled. The cords were standing out in his neck, the nerves in his jaw were tightening, and those strange cat's eyes of his were near to glowing with sparks of angry fires.

The soldier called Rathbun continued to pick through the hand he had been dealt, and did not see Ryan's building rage. The others around him, however, like Chalmers, did observe, and they began to exchange uneasy glances, instinctively moving away from Rathbun in an effort to disassociate themselves from the explosion sure to come as he dared to continue his goading. "Ah, nothing to get upset about, Corporal. Everybody knows Willingham is quite the ladies' man. Hell, if he weren't, he wouldn't have that pretty red dress his last one left behind, so's he could give it to his latest filly. Looked real pretty in it, too, she did. I saw her when you was leading her to his quarters. My, my..." He made smacking sounds with his lips. "She sure is a sight to behold when she's cleaned up, ain't she—?"

The bowl of stew smashed into his face.

"What the hell—?" Rathbun began to rake viciously at the hot gravy, the bits of vegetable stuck in his hair and beard. "You crazy son of a—"

But he had no time to finish his cursing epithet, for Ryan Tanner had stepped directly into the middle of the pile of cards and ante money to reach down with one hand closing about the soldier's throat and lifting him straight up from where he sat. Ryan held him high, with his toes dangling, barely touching the dirt floor, as he hoarsely demanded, "All right, big mouth, since you want to talk, you can tell me where I can find this hospitable major and his little love nest."

The others had scrambled to their feet and backed as far away as possible. Several had fled to alert others that the visiting cavalry captain had gone berserk.

Rathbun's eyes were bulging and his face was turning red as he struggled to breathe. Ryan released him and he fell to the floor in a heap, choking and gasping for breath.

"Talk," Ryan ordered.

"That...that way..." Rathbun was clutching his throat, wheezing between the painfully forced words. "Up...up the narrow...steps...that way...." He unclasped one hand long enough to point, then grabbed at his neck again.

Ryan took great striding steps, continuing to hold his burning torch to light the way. Shadows leapt out at him as he made his way to the natural stone steps leading upward.

He raced up to find himself at the beginning of a long, narrow corridor laced with stalagmites below to step over, hanging stalactites to duck beneath. In the distance, he could see what looked like a blanket hanging over a small opening in the wall of the cave.

And that was when he heard it—a scream of terror, abruptly cut off.

All at once, he was slammed back in time to that night last spring when he'd heard a similar sound, and suddenly he knew Belinda's nightmare had returned....

He dropped the torch and ran the rest of the way, kicking at the stone outcroppings below, smashing at those above with angrily flailing arms, oblivious to the tearing of his flesh by the sharper stalactite points.

With a howl of rage and a mighty lunge that tore the blanket from its holdings, Ryan crashed into the chamber. In an instant, he had torn Harmon from where he lay on top of Belinda, attempting to force himself on her.

"You bastard!" Ryan held him by the nape of his neck with one hand and smashed his fist into his face. Again and again he hit him. Harmon's nose was spurting blood, and his knees were buckling.

Ryan was vaguely aware Belinda had scrambled away from the bed to back away in terror. At the same time came the sounds of shouting, yelling, as soldiers poured through the opening to grab at him and pull him away from Harmon.

"You're killing him!" somebody yelled.

"God, look at his face," cried another.

And, above them all, Belinda's voice, pleading, "Don't do it, Ryan. He's not worth it...."

He was torn away at last, but it took four soldiers to hold Ryan back as others attempted to minister to his victim.

"He's coming around...."

Ryan recognized the soldier he'd choked holding Harmon in his arms and calling his name, trying to get him to rally.

Harmon blinked dazedly.

"Lordy!" Rathbun gasped, "his face is a mess...."

Hearing that, Harmon shouted furiously, "Get the doctor in here right away. He's got to fix my face. As for him—" he glared at Ryan with scorching fury "—I want him executed at dawn. He tried to kill me, an officer. I have the right to have him executed."

"You stupid, arrogant son of a bitch." Ryan swept him with a gaze of contempt. "If I'd wanted to kill you, you'd be dead. I could have broken your worthless neck with the snap of two fingers. And you're damn right, I beat the hell out of you for trying to rape her...." he nodded toward Belinda, who continued to watch, eyes wide with terror, hands pressed across her mouth to stifle the bubbling sobs of rising hysteria.

Harmon's face was on fire with pain, and his head was throbbing furiously, but he managed to conjure up a hasty lie. "That's not true. I invited her here for dinner, as a courtesy and a thank-you for helping out at the hospital, but the woman is daft. Evidently working around so much tragedy has caused her to become touched in the head...."

As the tale rolled easily off his tongue, Harmon became caught up in his own creative deceit. He began to talk faster, excitedly describing how Belinda had suddenly gone to pieces and said she couldn't take it anymore, that the terrible, terrible war had taken too great a toll. She was going to smash the wine bottle, use the glass to cut her wrists. He had only tried to get her to calm down, to keep her from harming herself. "And that's when he came charging in here like a madman and tried to kill me!" He pointed an accusing finger at Ryan and tersely, furiously ordered, "Tie him up. He goes before a firing squad at dawn."

Ryan struggled and fought valiantly but there were too many overpowering him. Belinda, having been momentarily stunned by the audacity of Harmon's lies, suddenly came alive to scream in furious protest, "You can't do that!" She lunged for the men dragging Ryan from the chamber, but was roughly shoved away as she cried, "Harmon is lying. He was trying to rape me. He thought if the Hardins could, so could he. He thinks I'm good for nothing else. That's why he ended our engagement...."

"She has gone completely mad!" Harmon bellowed. "I know nothing about this woman. I never saw her before tonight—"

"You're lying, Harmon...." Belinda started toward him but a soldier caught her by the waist and held her back. She began to claw at him, kicking and screaming and repeating her protests. "We were engaged to be married, back home in the Blue Ridge, but I was raped and he wouldn't marry me then, and tonight he said he was going to take what had always been his, and I was fighting him off when Captain Tanner came in and saved me. You can't execute him. Your major is the one who deserves to be shot...."

Ryan was angrier when he heard Belinda's diatribe and, damn it, he cursed to himself, he wished she had told him about Willingham, their engagement, all of it. Now they were both in one hell of a mess. He was being hauled off to await execution for striking an officer, and she was left at the mercy of the lying, scheming bastard. But somehow, some way, he had to find a way to escape and get them both out of there.

Just then, he saw Corporal Chalmers with a sleepy, harried-looking man holding a leather bag. They pressed themselves against the wall of the cave as Ryan was being dragged past.

No doubt, Ryan quickly reasoned, it was the doctor, but it was Chalmers he tried to make eye contact with. He hadn't missed the way the man had seemed embarrassed over Belinda's vulnerability at the hands of his commander, and now Ryan sought to plead with him visually, silently, for help.

Chalmers looked horrified, but gave no sign that he could discern Ryan's silent, desperate appeal.

"Damn it, can't you give her something to calm her down?" Harmon yelled over Belinda's screaming.

Dr. Staples did not need to be persuaded to put an end, for the moment, to her hysteria. He quickly took a syringe from his bag, and a measure of morphine, and injected it into her arm while she was being held. "We use morphine for pain," he said to no one in particular, "but its effect will put her to sleep. I gave her a good dose."

"Good. Now get her out of here," Harmon directed. "She's obviously lost her mind, gone hopelessly insane. Put her in chains so she can't harm herself or anyone else. We'll have her taken to an institution later.

"Now, Doctor..." he said with a ragged, hopeful sigh, "please see what you can do about my face."

Chapter Sixteen

Hands and ankles tightly bound, Ryan was carried out of the cave.

Placing him on a rocky ledge, Private Rathbun taunted him, "Better be real still or you'll go rolling off the edge. But maybe you'd prefer that to the firing squad. It sure don't matter to none of us. We're just not going to lose any sleep guarding you, so you can stay out here."

Ryan watched him go, and, even though there was no one else around, he knew there was no point in trying to free himself. The ropes were so tight they were cutting into his flesh; there was just no way he could wriggle out of them. And he hadn't failed to notice the sheer drop below during the daylight hours. The only thing he could do was remain perfectly still and hope that, by some miracle, Belinda would find a way to get to him and free him.

A cool wind blew across the ledge. Every so often the moon would peek out from behind the thick layers of clouds, allowing him to see the surrounding mountains. The trail downward would be precarious in the faint light, but he was willing to chance it. Still, Ryan knew, even if he could untie himself, there was no way he would leave without taking Belinda with him.

As the night passed with agonizing slowness, he found himself wishing he had killed Harmon Willingham when he'd had the chance. At least then he'd not have to go to his grave worrying about Belinda being at the bastard's mercy. If only she had confided in him about having been engaged to him, if only he'd known they were walking right into Willingham's bailiwick, none of it would have happened, because he would not have let her out of his sight. Not for a second.

He could not sleep, for every nerve was raw, tense, as he tried to figure a way out of his predicament. Harmon would make good his order to have him shot. There would be no trial. No hearing. Just a quick execution after which Harmon would, no doubt, have his way with Belinda till he tired of her, then send her to an insane asylum so that no one would ever believe her when she tried to tell the truth about what had happened. He'd managed to hear Harmon's accusations of madness as he was being dragged out.

The more Ryan brooded, the angrier he became, and when he spotted a soldier stealthily creeping toward him in the shadows, he was quick to challenge furiously, "What the hell do you want? Are you going to roll me off this ledge to save bullets?"

"Shut up, Tanner, or the picket will hear you."

Ryan tensed, recognizing Corporal Chalmers as he dropped to his knees beside him. "What are you doing here?" he whispered, daring to feel a ray of hope.

Chalmers quickly rolled him on his back, and, with a quick slice of the knife he was holding, cut the ropes, first at his wrists, then his ankles. "I'm not going to be a party to your murder, Tanner. I know Major Willingham for the lying bastard he is." He sent the ropes flying to disappear off the ledge and into the black abyss. "They'll think you rolled off, and with the wilderness below, they won't even look for your body. If they do, they'll think it was dragged off by animals. Now go."

Chalmers got to his feet, turning to leave, but Ryan was right beside him, grabbing his shoulders and spinning him around. "Not without Belinda. You're crazy if you think

I'm going to leave her here with him. We both know what will happen to her.''

"You don't have any choice. He had her drugged and she's sound asleep. You'd never get in there to get her without someone seeing you and sounding an alarm. Then *I'd* be in trouble.''

"Isn't everyone else asleep?''

Chalmers frowned. "Yeah, but it's too risky, Tanner. If she was awake and could walk, I'd lead her out myself, but—''

Ryan was already on his way to the mouth of the cave. "Come on. Take me to her.''

Chalmers knew it was useless to protest. The man's mind was made up, and there was nothing to do but go along with him and keep an eye out should anybody happen to be up and about.

They moved quickly. When they got to the chamber that had been prepared for Belinda, Ryan had to grope his way in the darkness. At last, he had his hands on her. He paused to hear her deep, heavy breathing and knew that Chalmers was quite right in saying she had been drugged. He picked her up effortlessly and slung her over his shoulder, then stepped out into the narrow corridor. There was scant light, for the torches placed in the walls had almost burned themselves out and cast only a faint glow.

"They're going to know you escaped now," Chalmers fretted, once they were again outside the cave. "If you'd gone on, like I told you, they would've thought you were dead. Now they'll be out searching at first light, or whenever you're discovered missing. I just hope they don't suspect me of helping you, or I'll be taking your place before that firing squad.''

"You'll be fine. They've no reason to think you had anything to do with it. As for us, once I've got us down off this mountain, I'll cover enough distance by morning that they won't be able to follow." He instructed him to stay with

Belinda while he went to get ammunition, a gun, and his horse.

Again, Chalmers had no choice, as Ryan disappeared into the cave once more. Returning with his weapons, he then hurried into the shadows, heading to the corral where the horses were penned.

When he was ready to go, Ryan shook the corporal's hand and thanked him. "If we ever meet again, I owe you," he vowed. Then he took Belinda from his arms and brought her up on the horse.

Carefully he picked his way down the trail, reining the horse tightly into the side of the mountain. But, as he'd suspected earlier, the animal proved to have trail prowess, plodding along surefooted.

Finally, thankfully, they were off the mountain. The first fingers of dawn were starting to streak the eastern sky. Holding Belinda firmly against him, he urged the horse onward, heading back in the direction from which they had come.

When they came upon a creek, Ryan led the horse straight into it. If Willingham's men did try to follow, they'd lose the trail in the water, for sure.

On and on he rode, every so often speaking to Belinda, trying to get her to awaken. Once in a while she would softly moan, and he cursed the doctor for giving her such a heavy sedative. He needed to have her alert, damn it, and perched behind him on the horse's rump. They could make better time, for it was difficult to travel at a fast pace when he had to cradle her in his arms across his lap.

When the sun was high in the sky, Ryan decided they were far enough away that he could breathe a little easier. They had been following the creek, and when they reached a spot where the bank cut high, he spotted a washed-out area that formed a small grotto. Tethering the horse in a nearby grassy area beneath a grove of oaks, he carried Belinda inside and laid her down on the sandy bottom.

For a long time, he held her, touching her tenderly now and then, whispering to her, calling her name. But she continued to sleep deeply, and, finally, Ryan succumbed to his own weariness and fell into slumber, arms about her, her head cradled on his shoulder.

The afternoon faded peacefully. At last, Belinda stirred. Ryan was instantly awake, soothing her. "It's all right. You're with me, and we're a long way from Willingham."

Hearing Harmon's name, Belinda attempted to sit up, eyes growing wide in sudden panic, but Ryan held her tightly against him, continuing to attempt to soothe, till, at last, she yielded to his embrace.

"How did we get here?" she wanted to know, calmed by his strong arms about her. "The last thing I remember, Dr. Staples gave me an injection of morphine."

He explained that he owed his life to Chalmers, adding pointedly, "You owe him a lot, too. I imagine by now Harmon would have you wishing you were dead."

"I should have told you," she lamented quietly. "But I was ashamed to talk about it."

"Ashamed to admit the man you were going to marry is an insensitive clod? No need to be, sweetheart. If he'd truly loved you, it wouldn't have mattered to him. I think you know that now."

"Oh, yes," she assured him. Then she went on to tell him of the scene before he'd arrived, how she'd foolishly driven Harmon into a rage by pretending she still wanted to marry him. "I should have torn out of there the minute I realized what he had in mind. It was stupid of me to think he was feeling guilty over how he treated me. Sadly, he still thinks I'm unfit for anything except what he intended...."

"Belinda, stop it," Ryan sharply ordered, rolling onto his side and reaching to cup her chin in his hand so that she would have to meet his steady, burning gaze. "All men aren't like the Hardins and Willingham. I know you've been raped, but that doesn't make me not want you just because I know you're no longer a virgin. What if you had been married and were now a widow? I'd still want you, because you're the most beautiful and desirable woman I've ever met and I love you...."

His lips brushed against hers, ever so lightly, for he was not about to pressure her. Actually, despite the great roaring of desire that had exploded within him, Ryan was not trying to seduce or persuade her to give in to his passion. All he endeavored to do in that heated moment as their gazes locked in assessment of one another was to make her see that his longing had nothing to do with her past. Had he never met her before, had he no reason to think she was not a virgin, he would still want her... desperately.

Belinda looked into his strangely beautiful eyes as she felt a hot wave spreading from her head to her toes, bedazzled by his profession of love. Never had a man looked at her with such intensity, and never had she felt such a heated glow in her belly. Without her realizing it, her fingertips danced up his arms and across his shoulders, touching the firm lines of his jaw. She could not tear her gaze from his. She felt mesmerized, hypnotized, frozen in that clarifying moment when she could not deny her own feelings.

Ryan made no move to kiss her, determined that she had to take the initiative. Otherwise, she might feel he had coerced her into doing something she wasn't ready for. He realized he had been holding his breath, and he sucked it in raggedly, chest heaving.

Belinda rolled easily to her side. She could feel his hardness pressing against her, hot and pulsating. At the same time, she felt herself becoming moist between her legs. Impulsively her hands went about his neck to bring his face close to hers. He had been the first man ever to kiss her with his mouth open, and she had reveled in the feel of his tongue melding against hers. She wanted to feel it, taste it, again.

Moaning deep in his throat, Ryan obliged, but not all at once. Slowly, ever so slowly, he brushed his lips against hers, and she wriggled with delight at the feel of his teasing mustache. His tongue moved to lick her lips from side to side, then in outline. Tormented by the desire to feel his mouth claim hers, Belinda attempted to pull him closer, straining higher.

With a slight, teasing smile, Ryan continued his ecstatic torture. Cupping her breast, he began to knead gently. Then, because she was still wearing the red dress with the deep, dipping bodice, he lowered it easily, exposing her to him. Touching fingertips to each nipple in turn, he felt them grow hard.

Belinda gasped at the sheer glory of his sweet assault, arching her back to bring herself closer, and at the same time eagerly seeking the surrender of his mouth.

He slipped his tongue between her lips and she began to suck hungrily, eagerly, as he worked her breasts rhythmically, milking desire that soared to her loins.

He raised himself to declare huskily, "It's got to be because you want it, Belinda. I'm not forcing you. I'll stop now, if you're afraid—"

"No, no..." She swallowed hard, shaking her head wildly against the flashing images of Jake Hardin, Rufus Hardin, grunting and laughing at her pain. But this was tenderness. This was love. And it was good and wonderful and she wanted it with every fiber of her being. "Please," she begged, "be gentle, Ryan, because I do want you so... love you so...."

But Ryan was not about to give in to his own anguished lust. He wanted to make sure she was ready for him, knowing that one wrong move could send her straight back into her shell of rejection of the world around her. He continued to assault her breasts, finally dipping his head to devour with his mouth. Her fingers clutched his hair and she made no effort to hold back her whimpers of pleasure and her pleas for more.

She wrapped her legs around his, attempting to pull him closer, wanting to feel his pulsating hardness.

"Touch me if you want, Belinda," he urged, slowly pulling up her skirt, reveling in the feel of her bare thighs. "Don't be afraid. Do anything you want. I'm all yours...."

Hesitantly, slowly, she dared move her hand downward to caress his manhood. It did not feel like a weapon, as when the Hardins had so cruelly violated her, but instead, like a tender symbol of Ryan's profession of love for her, and she knew she was prepared to give him all there was to give.

He touched her in that nucleus of pleasure, felt her wetness, gently moved his finger upward. She whispered hoarsely, feverishly against his ear, "Yes, yes," and he caressed and teased, driving her into a frenzy of desire. Yet he wanted her total surrender, wanted her to look back and see that she had been the aggressor, for it was important that she realize the man was not always the savage, that a woman, too, could be driven mad by her own lust.

Fastening his mouth on one breast again, sucking hard and almost painfully, he maneuvered himself out of his trousers. Her skirt was, by then, bunched up around her waist, rendering her naked and vulnerable to his assault, but he was not about to give her what she was so wantonly, brazenly, begging for. Her breasts were exposed, and he devoured them in turn, licking and sucking in rhythm with his hardness, which he pressed between her thighs. He allowed the tip to touch her in that most sensitive of places, yet did not penetrate her. Again and again, she arched her back, thrusting her buttocks upward in an attempt to fill herself with him, but he held back.

Finally, when Belinda thought she must surely die from wanting him so much, he rolled over onto his back, taking her with him to straddle him. "Take me if you want me, Belinda. As much as you want. As hard as you want. I'm all yours...."

She felt as though her body suddenly had a will of its own, raised her hips, then lowered to slowly impale herself upon him. A low, ragged cry of delight slipped past her trembling, tightly pursed lips as she allowed herself to take all of him. For an instant, there was pain, discomfort, but then pleasure overshadowed it, and soon she was trembling, whimpering with sheer delight to at last feel him inside her.

Releasing her breasts, he clasped his hands about her waist, reveling in the sight of her upon him. Again arching her back, her neck, she trailed her fingertips first down the sides of his dear face, then to his shoulders, then dancing through the thick mat of hair on his broad, rock-hard chest. Her eyes were half-closed. She felt dazed, transported to another plane of existence, leaving the reality of this world behind as she soared, both in spirit and in body, to bliss untold.

Gently, ever so gently, Ryan began to thrust up and down. Her hands left his body to slide into her long golden red hair, lifting it up in wild ecstasy as she rode the gentle saddle of passion. "Never..." she breathlessly whispered, "never did I think it could be like this...."

"Forever," he vowed tensely, tightly, gritting his teeth to hold back his climax. "Forever, if you want it, Belinda, it can be like this. Tender. Sweet. Never will I hurt you...."

But, in that moment of divine delectation, Belinda would not have winced with pain had he actually turned savage. A honey-sweet shroud of happiness and joy had wrapped her in its cocoon, holding her imprisoned as the endless ecstasy seemed to lock her in its velvet embrace. "More," she begged. "More... for always...."

At last, when he felt her softness squeezing against him, knew she was about to reach her own pinnacle of glory, Ryan maneuvered her onto the side, then onto her back. Then, spreading her legs and pressing them back against her chest, he gripped her waist once more, this time pounding into her relentlessly, furiously, slamming her body into the sand. Her nails dug into the hard flesh of his back as she cried his name over and over, wanting the moment never to end, wanting to remain a part of him forever and always.

Finally, at last, he could hold back no longer, and he filled her with his hot nectar at the same time her scream ripped through the air. She sank her teeth into his shoulder in un-bridled rapture, but he felt no pain, only fruition never be-fore known in any woman's arms.

And, as he collapsed against her, to roll onto his back and take her with him and hold her tight, Ryan knew why the ultimate happiness had been achieved. Before, with other women, the motivation had only been lust, never love, and, yes, in that crystalline moment, he knew he was truly in love with Belinda Coulter.

"Hold me," she begged, snuggling closer. "Hold me, Ryan, and never let me go. I want us to stay this way for-ever."

He nuzzled her forehead with his lips. "So do I, sweet-heart, so do I...."

For a long time, they lay together, too overcome with emotion to speak. Then Belinda felt the need to apologize again for how she'd initially treated him. He tried to shush her, but she insisted on explaining. "I need to talk about it now, more than ever. I need to get it all out of me, Ryan, once and for all, from beginning to end. I want to tell you about Harmon, and I want to tell you about Pa, and Jes-sica, all of it."

And she proceeded to do so.

Ryan listened intently to the story of Zeb Coulter, and how after losing three wives in succession he had come to believe God had placed a curse on him. His last, Melissa, had died in childbirth, along with their baby daughter, when Jessica had been seven, Belinda three. From then on, Zeb had vowed that, till God sent a sign the curse had been lifted, he would never marry again.

Every Sunday morning, Belinda said, her father would be in church, looking for that sign. In between, he had drunk himself into a stupor, which meant the farm was neglected. Jessica had been forced to grow up quickly to take on as many chores and responsibilities as possible. She had re-fused to let Belinda help. "So I didn't have a serious thought in my head. I suppose that's one reason I was so attracted to Harmon. His family was rich and I figured I'd have a perfect life in Raleigh. Little did I know..." She shook her head in bitter dismay.

Ryan smoothed her hair back from her forehead as he confided, "I've made my mistakes, too, sweetheart. No need to feel bad. We all have to endure unhappy experiences in life, but it's worth all the suffering when we realize it all happened for a reason."

She reached for his hand, kissed his fingertips, then proceeded to tell him again what had led up to the Hardins' attack. He'd heard some of it before, but understood that she wanted to purge herself for all time, so that there would be no secrets between them. And when she'd finished at last, tears were streaming down her cheeks as she turned to him in adoring gratitude to declare, "Thank you, Ryan, for making me realize I didn't have to live in that pain. It's over. The future is waiting, for both of us."

"Both of us, indeed," he assured her, laughing. Then he eagerly went on to share some of the plans he'd made during the morning's brooding ride. "In a little while, I'll go forage for food, and we'll stay here tonight. Tomorrow, we'll continue to work our way back to our lines. Then I want to get you home, back to Franklin. I've got an aunt still living there. We were never close, but I'm sure she'll take you in and give you shelter till the war is over—especially when I introduce you as my wife," he added with a warm, caressing smile, leaning over to kiss her.

Belinda squirmed and protested teasingly, "Are we still going to tell people we're married, Ryan?"

"No," he said, almost curtly. "We won't be lying at all, Belinda."

She looked at him in silent wonder, unsure of what to say next. She did love him, did want to be his wife, but the thought of going to live with a stranger while he was off fighting in the war was disconcerting. And how could she abandon her service and commitment to the Confederacy? She'd learned much in the past months, but, most of all, she'd found out something about herself, as well—that she did not want to be subservient to any man, did not want to relinquish her spirit to the preordained concept that a woman's lot in life was to be a wife and mother. She wanted to continue working in medicine, and more and more lately she had actually been thinking she could go to school and study to be a doctor.

Ryan noticed the shadow that fell across her face and asked tightly, "What's wrong? I thought you wanted to marry me."

"I do," she quickly confirmed. Then she took a deep breath while framing how to put her feelings into words. "But you have to understand why I think we should wait awhile. There's a war going on. Like it or not, we're both now a part of it."

"*I'm* a part of it," he reminded her tersely. "Not you. It's no place for a woman, and I'm getting you out of it."

"But I don't want out of it."

He released her and sat up to glare down at her with rising anger. "Belinda, you don't know what you're talking about. You got into this by accident. Surely you've got sense enough to realize the danger you're in. I want us to be married as soon as possible, and then I'm taking you home. I'll come to you as soon as I can, but I've got to get you out of all this."

Firmly she shook her head. "No. I may have gotten into it by accident, as you say, but now I'm staying. You have to understand, Ryan . . ." She touched his arm beseechingly, but, stubbornly, angrily, he shook it away. "I'm good at what I do. They might resent saying so, but any doctor I've worked with will tell you I've done a better job than most men. Right now, I'm a nurse. But Dr. Whitley gave me some books on medicine, surgery. He said I should consider going to school to become a doctor—"

"Belinda, no!" Ryan turned to her then, aghast at the thought. "That's ridiculous. Why would you want to do that? I told you—I'm taking you home to the Blue Ridge, and when the war is over, I'll build us a house and we'll take over my family's land, get a farm going. We'll have children.

"Maybe..." He paused to smile and tenderly caress her cheek. "...we'll get started on the babies right away. Maybe before I know it, I'll get a letter from you saying I'm going to be a father, and that would give me extra reason to hurry home to you."

Doggedly she continued to try to make him understand. "That's something I want, too, Ryan, but not now. For the moment, I want to get back to medical services and do what I can till the war *is* over, and then I'd like to look into going to medical school. You could go with me, get a job nearby doing something, somewhere. Afterward, we could go back to the Blue Ridge. Maybe by then I could even go back to Pa's farm, and all of us—you, me, and Jessica, if I can find her—we can make a home there. And I can practice medicine, too...."

"Between having our babies," she went on cajolingly, snuggling closer once more.

Ryan bit down thoughtfully on his lower lip. Maybe things had been happening too fast. After all, a few days ago they had still been like strangers to each other. Now they had been through a couple of life-and-death situations together, meanwhile discovering a newfound awareness, a love. She had opened her heart to him, sharing all the pain and anguish of the past, as well as confiding hopes and dreams for the future. In turn, he had professed his love, his devotion, and his own desire for a future together. He had asked her to marry him, by God, which was no trivial matter. Still, they might both need time to get to know each other even better. As it was, he knew Belinda was not the sort to be lightly dissuaded once her mind was made up, at least not by anyone else. She had to decide things for herself, and, if she did return to the misery of the war, perhaps she'd come to realize that being a nurse, or a doctor, was not what she wanted after all. And he would damn sure make sure he was around often enough to remind her she had an option—as his wife.

"All right," he said finally, with false conviction and a forced smile that he did not truly feel. "For the time being, my headstrong young woman, go ahead with your plans. But remember—I'll be around, waiting for you to come to your senses, understand?"

For answer, she slipped her arms about his neck and offered him her lips. He melted against her, pressing her back against the sand. Quickly the smoldering embers of passion just spent ignited once again into hot, furious flames of rekindled desire. They were soon lost in each other, attempting to quench this burning hunger that seemed to defy satiation.

They did not hear the horses as they came down the other side of the creek bank, were not aware when their own mount was spotted peacefully grazing nearby.

Ryan took his time, wanting the tenderness to last. It bothered him immensely that Belinda obviously did not love him enough to give up thoughts of pursuing another kind of life to commit to a lifetime with him. Perhaps, he dizzily reasoned against the wildly flowing ecstasy exploding between them, she was still tainted by the nightmare of the past. Maybe her explanation about studying to be a doctor was actually a way of covering up for her own hesitation in being able to truly love. If that was the case, then his only hope was to make her love him so damn much she'd move heaven and earth to be with him, casting aside thoughts of any other kind of life. First, he would show her with his body how much she meant to him, and then, in the coming days and weeks and months, however long it took, he would show her how happy he could make her in many other ways. Eventually she would come to realize he could make her feel whole and complete as his wife and the mother of his children.

Again he drove into her with a frenzy, making her crazy with the heat of desire.

She clung to him, crying and sobbing and begging him once more for the sweet release of climax, but he teased her into a frenzy. He wanted her to taste again and again the tenderness of the bonding of their bodies, for soon he would endeavor to bond their spirits, as well.

At last, they came together, and Belinda reveled in the sheer wonder of it. Clinging to him, not wanting the moment, the closeness, to end, she thought how much she loved him. Yet, as she slowly returned to earth from the awesome and ethereal pinnacle of bliss, she found herself jolted by the nagging question of whether she would ever be ready to bind herself to him completely. Passion was only a momentary, fleeting joy. And what else did they have together? He obviously did not share her dream. But, she wearily told herself, perhaps she was worrying for nothing. After all, they had been through a lot and were both exhausted. With a tiny shiver, she was reminded that the danger was not yet over. They were still lost, still separated from their own people.

Ryan could sense that she was cooling, and that it was not just due to passion spent. It was as though she was drawing away from him once more, an invisible curtain dividing their spirits. But he was undaunted. Damn it, he was going to *make* her love him.

With a sigh of resignation, he stood and pulled on his uniform. "First, we've got to get you some clothes," he said, nodding toward the red dress she wore, still bunched up about her waist.

She yanked it down, quickly shoving her breasts back into the bodice. "Maybe when you go foraging for food you can find a farmhouse where someone will give you another dress. I'll even take overalls, trousers, anything to get me out of this horrid rag—"

"How about a nice blue uniform?"

Ryan whipped about, reaching for his gun, but the Yankee swiftly kicked it out of his reach as Belinda screamed in terror.

"Yeah, I reckon you'd look good in blue." The Yankee raked Belinda with lust-filled eyes, keeping his rifle trained on Ryan. "But actually, I think you'd look better with nothing at all. Suppose you just get out of that dress, so's I can see and make up my mind."

Ryan bit out the warning: "You touch her and I'll kill you."

"Oh, you will, will you?" the soldier laughed as several of his cohorts crowded around him. "Well, I reckon you're gonna have your hands full, Reb, 'cause I got a feeling my men are gonna want to share the booty."

Another man stepped up to shove the others out of his way. He looked from Belinda to Ryan and then threw his head back and laughed loudly, raucously.

The first soldier who had entered asked, bewildered, "What's so damn funny, Sergeant?"

"Well, for one thing, you aren't going to rape a man's wife, are you?"

"She's his wife?"

"That's right. This here is Captain Tanner, and this little lady is his wife." He turned to Ryan. "Isn't that right, Captain?"

Ryan knew, in that stricken moment, that his only hope of protecting Belinda was to return to the pretense that she was his wife.

With a curt nod to the man from whom they had been rescued only the day before, Ryan murmured, "That's right, Sergeant Purdy."

Chapter Seventeen

Once again, Ryan and Belinda found themselves captives of Sergeant Jarvis Purdy, who was delighted to have recaptured the duo. He considered both prize booty, excitedly telling his men of Ryan's skill in blacksmithing and Belinda's experience in nursing. "General Rosecrans will be real happy to hear about these two prisoners," he crowed, hopes again rising that his success would result in a promotion.

Belinda's anger had quickly overshadowed her terror. Falling easily into the pretense of being Ryan's wife, well aware that it was probably all that would save her from being ravished, she spunkily responded to Purdy's taunting by lashing out. "You disgust me, Sergeant. Tell me, do you make it a habit spying on married couples making love?"

His men guffawed behind his back, which infuriated Purdy. "Hell, no, you haughty snippet, but you two seem to make a habit out of ruttin' anywhere, anytime. You'd think by now you'd have realized it gets you into trouble.

"A pity..." he went on, looking to his men for their laughing approval, "the whole damn Rebel army ain't as randy as you two, or this war would be over in no time."

Coldly Ryan changed the subject by asking, "What are you still doing in the area, Sergeant? The way you high-tailed it yesterday when you saw our troops coming, leaving your man to die, I figured you'd be on the other side of the Potomac by now, still running."

Purdy's grin faded and his face went tight with furious contempt. "He's lying," he snapped to no one in particular. "They tried to kill me, too, but I ducked and dodged, barely got out of there. Let's go...." He gave Ryan a rough shove, then yanked Belinda to her feet. "This time, you two aren't getting away. There's work waiting for both of you, and if you don't cooperate, I promise you'll go straight to prison."

When they were mounted on the horse, Ryan whispered to Belinda, "Just do as they say. You're in no danger as long as they think you're my wife. We're also valuable to them, like Purdy said. My blacksmithing should keep me out of a Federal prison, and maybe they'll let us stay together if you agree to nurse their wounded."

Belinda merely nodded and settled against his back, clinging to him. She realized she really wasn't frightened, because what he said was true—she would be treated with a minimal amount of respect by virtue of being with her "husband." She would also be helpful to their medical-services unit, and, while she dared not admit it to Ryan, she had no qualms whatsoever about treating the enemy. She did not consider it disloyalty to the South, the Confederacy, but rather loyalty to mankind, in general. God had given her a natural aptitude for nursing, and she intended to use it, no matter what color uniform a sick or wounded man wore.

It was nearly dark, and Ryan found himself wishing they were moving north faster. Despite being in the hands of the enemy, he hoped they outmaneuvered Willingham's troops, which were, no doubt, trying to pick up their trail. He might not know what awaited them with Purdy, but one thing was certain—there was a firing squad in his future if Willingham caught up with them.

They realized almost as soon as they left the creek that they were deep in enemy territory. Ryan told Belinda he hoped they camped soon, because they might have a chance of escaping before they were too far north. However, Purdy rode on into the night till they reached a large campsite.

"A hornets' nest of Yankees," Ryan remarked dismally, surveying the men in blue uniforms gathering to gawk at them. He felt her tense, reached to pat her leg to comfort. "It will be all right. They've got bigger plans for us than killing me and raping you, sweetheart. Just don't say anything to get them riled. Let me do the talking."

But, as it turned out, there was no talking to be done. Purdy ordered them taken into one of the tents and posted two guards outside. They were given food and water, but no conversation. Ryan's questions as to where they were headed went unanswered.

Lying together on the blankets they'd been given, Ryan held Belinda close, but did not attempt to make love to her. He not only knew she was exhausted, but could feel her nervousness and apprehension, as well.

"What's going to happen to us?" she asked, swallowing against the lump of fear that had settled in her throat from the moment of their capture.

"They'll probably take us to Rosecrans's encampment, wherever that is. I'll be sent to the stables, and you to the hospital. Let's hope we'll be given quarters together, since they think we're married. Maybe it won't be so bad. In fact, we have to look at the bright side—we'll be together." He pressed his lips to her forehead.

Belinda snuggled closer. She had no regrets over the consummation of their love, for several reasons. First of all, she had wanted him fiercely, and had needed the melding of their flesh as an avowal of their feelings for each other. But, equally important, she had wanted to cast aside all the ghosts of the past, especially the fear that she would never be able to give herself to a man without reservation. Now she could truly start forgetting the filth and degradation the Hardins had inflicted upon her, for she knew now that lovemaking could be tender and beautiful, something to be treasured and savored.

As the clutching fingers of slumber began to drag her away, despite her worries over their present situation, Belinda also was grateful for having said goodbye forever to any regrets over the loss of Harmon Willingham. If anything good had come out of her ordeal, she knew, it was being spared a miserable life married to him.

Surprisingly, they did not move out of the camp the next morning. They were given a breakfast of coffee, fried fatback and boiled eggs, and Sergeant Purdy arrived while they were eating to tell them they would not be moving out for some time.

"No harm in telling you why," Purdy said airily. "We're waiting on our troops to arrive from Greenbriar. There was a big fight there yesterday, and the dispatcher sent by General Rosecrans said they routed the Rebs there and took lots of valuable cattle and horses. They're driving them this way, and we're going to wait on them.

"They're going to be real happy to hear we got a blacksmith waiting," he added, goading Ryan.

Ryan could not resist firing back, "If they're stolen *Confederate* horses, they're no doubt properly shod and won't need a blacksmith."

At that, Purdy flared. "Well, I tell you what, Tanner, the horses here aren't Confederate horses, and I expect they all need looking after. So you best hurry up and eat, because you've got some hard work ahead of you.

"As for you—" he scowled at Belinda "—we're going to find out how good a nurse you are. We've got five men down sick, and no doctor. The one we had got killed, so we're going to let you tend to them till a new one gets here."

Ryan was quick to bark a reminder at him: "She's not a doctor, Purdy. You can't expect her to know what to do."

"I can try." Belinda was already on her feet, anxious to begin. "Do you have the doctor's medical bag?"

Purdy nodded. "I'll have it taken to the tent where the men are."

He walked outside into the crisp fall morning, with Belinda right behind him.

She was unaware of Ryan standing at the entrance to their tent, glowering with quiet rage.

As they walked through the camp, Belinda noticed that once they were away from Ryan, Sergeant Purdy was no longer hostile. He explained that the men were suffering from acute diarrhea, obviously embarrassed to speak of such a delicate matter. "They can still eat, but everything runs right through them. I saw one of them being carried into the tent a little while ago, and he looked real weak and bad."

"Don't give them any more solid food," she quickly advised him. "Only liquids. Milk or beef tea for at least a day. Tomorrow, soft-boiled eggs and rice. We have to get their insides calmed down...." She could have closed her eyes and heard Doc Jasper's voice repeating the same declaration the summer a rage of diarrhea had swept through their mountain settlement.

"And I really need the doctor's bag," she repeated as they reached the tent.

Inside, Belinda moved among the men and confirmed that each appeared seriously dehydrated. A young soldier she guessed not to be over fifteen or sixteen, ordered to help her, hovered about looking frightened and unsure of himself. She told him to go to the cook and have him start brewing beef tea, knowing it was important to get liquids into each man as quickly as possible.

Sergeant Purdy brought the worn leather medical bag himself, and Belinda immediately opened it, quickly rummaging through it to learn what medicines and supplies were available to her. She drew out a bottle of pills marked Sulfate of Copper, counting out a dose of one-twelfth of a grain. Then, relieved to also locate a supply of opium, she added a quarter grain to the other drug. "We start with this," she said, more to herself than to Sergeant Purdy, as she continued to search through the bag. "Then this." She took out a bottle of aromatic sulfuric acid. "Ten drops in water sweetened with sugar four times a day."

She prepared each dose. Then, just when she was about to begin administering, the sergeant gripped her arm. Almost apologetically, he asked, "Are you sure you know what you're doing, Mrs. Tanner? I mean..." He swallowed hard. "You wouldn't deliberately kill my men, would you? Maybe poison them because you consider them the enemy?"

Infuriated and indignant, Belinda jerked away from his grasp. With chin lifted, she glared at him, crying, "If you can even remotely suspect me of being so cruel, Sergeant, please don't allow me to treat your men!"

"I'm sorry." He shook his head, stepped back. "It's just that you *are* a Southerner, married to a Confederate officer, and it's only natural to assume—"

"That everyone is as cruel as you are? Thank God, that's not the way it is, Sergeant, or all mankind is lost."

Sergeant Purdy didn't seem angry at the way she berated him. He watched her tenderly minister to the soldiers, and, Belinda thought, it must surely show on her face that it made no difference to her which side they were on, for she spoke to each with kindness and compassion. Purdy certainly seemed glad he'd been able to capture her for the Union; after all, they needed all the medical help they could get.

Belinda stayed with the men throughout the day and, by suppertime, was satisfied each was on the mend. "Rice tomorrow," she promised with a smile, and they all called out their gratitude for her having tended them.

Sergeant Purdy had delivered to her uniform trousers and shirt, with the almost-apologetic explanation that he figured she'd rather be in an enemy uniform than continue to wear the red dress that made the men stare at her.

She accepted gratefully and hurried to the creek to change. Ryan was not at the tent, and she assumed he was still working with the horses.

He was still not there when she returned.

However, Sergeant Purdy was waiting to extend an amiable invitation to join everyone for a supper of fried trout. "A few of the men went fishing in a nearby stream today and came back with quite a catch."

The thoughts of delicious mountain trout made her mouth water, but she wanted Ryan included, as well, and asked where he was.

"We'll send him some," the sergeant assured her, motioning to her to follow after him. "He's real busy with them horses. Says he feels sorry for 'em, so I doubt he'll want to quit to eat."

It was a pleasant meal, despite the fact she was dining with the enemy. The soldiers were all polite and sociable. There was no cursing, no obscene remarks. Conversation was actually pleasant, as they talked about the beauty of western Virginia. A few made a point of expressing their thanks to Belinda for her help with the sick men. And she was impressed. Sadly, her nursing for the Confederate army had not been met with any acceptance, much less any enthusiasm.

It was late when she returned to the tent. Ryan was lying on his blanket, arms folded behind his head. As she held aloft the small lantern she'd been given, he muttered an oath at the sight of her in the loathsome Federal uniform.

"It's all they had for me to change into," she said defensively, not liking the way he viewed her with such contempt mirrored in his eyes. "I couldn't keep on wearing that awful red dress."

"I suppose not," he conceded.

She lay down beside him, wanting, needing, his closeness, the comfort of his arms. He made no move to touch her. Hesitantly she touched her fingertips to his cheek and whispered, "Ryan, what is it? Did something happen you don't want to talk about?"

He made no move to touch her. "I don't like the idea of you nursing Yankees back to health so they can go out and kill our people. It's not right."

She gave her long hair a disdainful toss. "Well, aren't you making sure their horses are properly shod so they'll have a way to ride out and kill our people?"

His gaze snapped to her face and she recoiled in shock at the scorching fury in his golden eyes. "It's not the same, and you know it, damn it. Those horses can't help what they're used for. Why punish them by crippling them with poorly fitted shoes? They're dumb animals, for Christ's sake. The soldiers are out to slaughter."

"I—I just don't look at it the same way you do," she stammered.

"That's obvious."

For long moments, they lay side by side, not speaking or moving. Tension hung over them like a shroud. Finally, Belinda timorously offered, her lower lip trembling, "Maybe if you tell them we aren't married, they won't keep you here. Maybe they'll send you somewhere else—"

"Stop it!" He rolled onto his side, fiercely drawing her into his arms as his eyes searched hers in the mellow glow of the lantern. "Don't even joke about a thing like that. And don't worry. I'm going to find a way to get us *both* out of here. It's just going to take a little time. We didn't have a choice when we were running from Willingham, and I knew all along we were taking a chance on running into Yankees, which we did. Next time, I'll have a plan. A map. I'll know where the hell we're going, and you can believe it will be straight into our own lines. Till then, we're going to be together, because I never want to let you go...."

With an almost vengeful savagery, he tore the uniform from her. Then, slowly, languidly, he kissed every part of her, wanting to savor the touch and taste and scent of her delicious flesh. In turn, her fingertips danced across his broad, muscular back, and she curved herself against him, arching her back to bring herself yet closer.

"God, how I love you," he whispered raggedly, positioning himself on top of her as she spread her thighs in offering. "I can't wait for the day when you really are my wife, and then heaven help anyone who tries to take you away from me...."

Her arms twined about his neck, and she gasped softly as he entered her. At first, he was rough, almost brutally forceful, as he sought to claim her, possess her, but then, realizing what was happening, he slowed to a gentle, rhythmic pace, rocking her to and fro in a gentle, yet firm, coupling. She clung to him happily, wanting the moment never to end, wishing they could always be bonded together, one flesh, one love, one being....

A few days later, the livestock confiscated at Greenbriar arrived. Ryan was kept busy checking the horses' hooves, while the cattle were slaughtered and prepared for drying for winter food.

Belinda, introduced to the arriving medical staff, was overwhelmed by their pleased reaction to her presence. When a skirmish nearby resulted in the need for several amputations, Assistant Surgeon Harvey Woodward insisted she work at his table. Afterward, he raved to everyone that a male steward could not have done a better job.

With so much work to be done during the day, Belinda and Ryan were together only at night, and they lived for the moments of deep, tense lovemaking before they fell asleep in each other's arms.

The days melted into weeks, then blended into months, and suddenly they found themselves on the move toward Washington and winter quarters.

Their accommodations were much better, though Ryan grumbled it made no difference. All he wanted was to find a way to escape and head south, and not a day went by that he did not repeat his vow to Belinda that they would, eventually, have their freedom.

But Belinda was not really concerned about their plight. Though she dared not admit it to Ryan, she was secretly happy with the way things were going. The nights with him were heaven, of course, and she reveled in the love they shared. The days, however, were also special, for, upon arrival in Washington, Sergeant Purdy delivered her to the hospital that had been set up in the Odd Fellows Hall.

There, she was introduced to Miss Dorothea Lynde Dix, whose appointment to superintend the women nurses volunteering for duty as Union nurses gave her sweeping powers. She had the authority to organize hospitals for the care of all sick and wounded soldiers, to appoint nurses wherever and whenever she wanted, and to take care of receiving, control and disbursement of special supplies that were donated by individuals or humanitarian associations. Most important, however, was her duty of organizing a corps of female nurses.

Belinda remembered what she'd heard about the circular Miss Dix had sent out stating that no woman under the age of thirty need apply, that all nurses had to be plain looking. The rules as to simple brown or black dresses being required, and the forbidding of bows, curls, jewelry, and especially hoop skirts, did not concern her. Belinda reported to her wearing blue trousers and shirt, the only clothes she had.

Upon meeting, Miss Dix thoroughly scrutinized Belinda with sharp, piercing eyes, finally conceding, "You come to me highly recommended, Mrs. Tanner, not only by Assistant Surgeon Woodward, but by former patients, as well. I have to say I'm impressed, but," she coldly, warily added, "I am somewhat concerned about the fact you're being held against your will. I have to question your devotion to your duties to what you, no doubt, consider enemy soldiers."

Belinda stiffened, meeting Miss Dix's challenging gaze with her own. "You just said I come highly recommended. I think my record speaks for itself. When I'm ministering to the sick and wounded, they aren't soldiers. They're merely men suffering and in need of care."

Miss Dix pursed her lips and nodded. "I suppose the fact that you're married will allow me to bend my own rule about having nurses under the age of thirty. As for your clothing—" her sweeping gaze seemed somewhat amused "—I think we can remedy that right away."

Dorothea Dix went on to explain to Belinda that she would be required to go into formal training for several weeks. Afterward, she would be given legal status as an employee of the army and receive a salary of forty cents and one ration in kind each day.

"I suppose," Miss Dix commented, "you're already well aware of how most surgeons resent the presence of women nurses."

Belinda gave a curt nod. "And I already know my duties—to be assigned to any housekeeping job that needs to be done, like scrubbing the wards or supervising the laundry. And I'm only to be called upon for direct patient care in moments of crisis, such as when a trainload of wounded troops arrive and there are so many to be washed and fed and quickly put to bed."

Miss Dix smiled to see how Belinda was frowning and happily corrected, "That's in the *Confederate* army, Mrs. Tanner. We do things a bit different in the Federal army. Of course, you'll have the duties you just mentioned, but I also ask my female nurses, along with the male nurses, to dress wounds and administer medications. That will be part of your training."

She went on to explain that there were already three hospitals operating in the Washington area. In addition to the Odd Fellows Hall, facilities had been set up in the National Hotel and at Georgetown College.

After their meeting, Belinda termed it a pleasant experience. She looked forward to her association with the respected Miss Dix.

* * *

Throughout the bleak winter months, Belinda devoted herself completely to her training. Ryan did not like it, but he had little choice, as he was kept busy working at the national stables. Both lived for their moments together at night, and, due to Belinda's being favored by those in authority, they were provided with comfortable quarters.

"Our first home..." Belinda whirled about the living room of the small cottage the first night after they were taken there. "Parlor, bedroom, and a separate kitchen where I can prepare all our meals."

Ryan did not share her happiness, curtly protesting, "No, don't call this our home, please. It's still a prison. We're inside a Federal compound. There are guards all around us. We can't go and come as we please. I have to be escorted to the stables, and there's always someone to take you to whichever hospital you're assigned to for the week. We're given rations, like the soldiers, and what can you do but try to make them palatable with seasoning?

"No, sweetheart..." He shook his head adamantly from side to side as he drew her into the circle of his arms. "This is not our home. When we're properly married, then we'll have a place to call home, and there won't be any guards or shadows or clouds of war hanging over our heads. Till then, we just have to be grateful we're together.

"I've thought of a way we might be able to get out of here," he confided eagerly, lowering his voice lest one of the guards posted outside overhear. He then went on to tell her that he figured they would have no choice but to endure their situation through the winter. But he was confident that in the spring the Federals would once again launch an offensive into Virginia. By then, he would have given everyone the impression he was content to sit out the war, far from actual combat. What more could a soldier ask for, anyway? He worked as a blacksmith, while his purported wife worked as a nurse. They had comfortable quarters, enough to eat. Everyone would think him a fool to want to escape and head south and back into the fighting, and that was exactly what he intended for them to think.

"But," he continued excitedly, "I'll be ready when they head out of winter quarters. I've managed to hide that Federal uniform you were wearing when they gave you those brown dresses to wear. All I'll have to do is put it on and slip out with a large regiment, one where nobody knows me. Between now and then, I'll figure out a way for you to meet me right outside Washington, and then we'll slip out together. I'll have a sense of direction, and this time, we won't get caught."

Belinda bit down on her lip, forced herself to speak the words he expected: "That's wonderful, Ryan, just wonderful."

But all the time she was haunted by the reality that perhaps that was not what she wanted, after all. She was doing what she loved, here, among people who accepted her more readily than her own ever had. She was treated with respect, and, more and more, the doctors were allowing her to assist with surgery. No matter that she'd already had experience; they'd had to accept her for the first time, in her status as a paid Federal employee. And she had never dared admit that to Ryan, either, for fear he would explode with fury. He thought she was still dutifully, doggedly, performing menial tasks, having no choice but to obey. He did not know she was undergoing formal training and was actually one of Miss Dorothea Dix's prize nursing students.

Perhaps, she mused later, when he held her in his arms after a torrid lovemaking session, he would eventually realize how much better off they were. To go back into the war was dangerous. One of them could be killed. Far better, she hoped he would see, for them to remain where they were. Later, when it was all over, they could go back to the Blue Ridge. Or, if she could convince him to agree, she could go to medical school. Maybe he could start his own black-smithing business. There were so many wonderful possibilities for a confident, secure future—if only she could persuade him to stay out of the war.

Diligently, Belinda learned the edict for hospitals handed down by the Federal surgeon general, William H. Hammond. Nurses were under the direct supervision of the stewards and the chief wardmaster. Patients were to obey all lawful orders and instructions given by the nurses, and their conduct had to be exemplary. Any patient swearing or using vulgar language or guilty of indecent exposure would be severely punished. Wards had to be thoroughly ventilated and cleaned once a day. Nurses were to guard against fires and not use lights in their wards when not required, and they had to report to the surgeon in attendance anything unusual that happened.

Also, if a patient needed medical or surgical attendance, the nurse was to go to the medical officer of the day to request that he visit the person who was complaining. If a patient not in sound mind was troublesome, the nurse had to bear with him, but, if he was rational and conducted himself improperly, he had to be reported.

There would be no lounging on the beds, and smoking in wards—by anyone—was not tolerated. Beds, when not occupied, had to be covered with clean bedding, which had to be thoroughly changed at least once a week.

Patients were to bathe at regular intervals, and there would be no excuse for vermin.

Most important, female nurses would not be allowed in the wards after tattoo, and, while all lady friends and relatives of patients were to be treated with proper courtesy and respect when visiting the hospital, they also were not allowed in any of the wards after dark, except by special permission from the surgeon in charge.

Belinda managed to keep her status as a Federal employee from Ryan until the latter part of February, 1862. Then, one night, he came in earlier than usual from the stables because the army posts, along with all government offices in the capital city, were shut down in a period of mourning for President and Mrs. Lincoln. Their twelve-year-old son, Willie, had died of typhoid fever.

"Even if I can't stand Lincoln, I'm sorry about his son," Ryan said, pulling off his boots and preparing to relax for the evening. Then, remembering that Belinda, too, was supposed to be at work, he remarked curiously, "I didn't think they'd close the hospitals down. What are you doing home?"

Belinda gave a nervous shrug, wishing all the while she could share her wonderful news. But suddenly, the situation was taken out of her hands when someone pounded on the door.

Ryan went to answer, and frowned at the sight of Assistant Surgeon Woodward, who made it a habit to stop by every so often to pay a friendly visit to Belinda. Ryan didn't want to socialize with Yankees, and had tried to make that obvious without being outright rude. Apparently it wasn't working, and he could only motion the doctor to come on in.

"I just heard," Dr. Woodward cried, crossing the room to clasp Belinda's hands. "Congratulations. What an honor...." He turned to Ryan to exclaim, "You must be very proud of your wife, Tanner."

Ryan's brows snapped together in apprehension. Something told him he was not going to like what he was about to hear. "Suppose you tell me. Belinda hasn't got around to it yet."

"Why, she's been placed in charge of her own ward at the new hospital that used to be a Georgetown tavern and hotel. There are accommodations for about three hundred patients, and Miss Dix has given Belinda charge of a ward of forty beds."

Woodward turned back to Belinda, continuing to squeeze her hands. "You deserve it. And I had to come by and say so. I went by the hospital, but they said you'd left early because you're working tonight."

"Tonight?" Ryan echoed, stunned, his anger creeping into his tone. "Since when do nurses work at night?"

"When they're in charge of wards." Woodward grinned and winked at Belinda. "But it will all be quite proper, I assure you. She's also going to have a steward working with her.

"I've got to be going...." He turned to the door, calling over his shoulder, "By the way, Margaret says she's baking a cake for you to celebrate. She'll stop by in the morning when you get home."

A tense silence descended as Ryan and Belinda faced each other.

"You want to tell me about it?" he asked darkly.

And she did so, explaining how she'd kept it all from him, knowing he would neither understand nor approve, defensively adding, "But it's something I want, Ryan. Can't you see that? I'm accepted here. I've been given training and hired as a nurse. I'm not treated like a slave. I'm respected—"

"You're also working for the damn Yankees," he reminded her furiously, careful to keep his voice down. It was imperative, despite his burning rage, for the Federals to continue to think him docile, and ambivalent toward the war.

Stubbornly, defiantly, Belinda shook her head. "It doesn't matter. I'm doing something that makes me feel good inside, and worthwhile. That's important to me after what I've been through. Can't you see that?" she beseeched him with tear-filled eyes.

He, too, shook his head from side to side. "No, I can't, and if you were honest with yourself, you'd realize just why you're so damn satisfied here."

"And why would that be?"

"You're a coward."

Belinda was quick to scoff. "How can you say such a thing? How many women would have been able to do the things I've done without fainting dead away?"

"That's not what I'm talking about. The blood. The gore. The pain and suffering. You can handle all that. I'm not denying you're a nurse, and obviously a damn good one, too. But the fact is, you want to stay here because you feel safe. You don't have to worry about running into folks from back home who remember you were raped by the Hardin brothers. You don't have to worry about running into Harmon Willingham again—"

"I should think *that* would even appeal to you," she curtly pointed out. "He's waiting to put you before a firing squad, you know."

"I'm not worried about that. When I get back, I intend to go to someone a lot higher up than he is and tell the truth about what the slimy little bastard was up to. And I'm confident that my unblemished record as a Confederate cavalry officer will bear credence over anything Willingham claims.

"But you..." he harshly rushed on to accuse, "you're not only a coward, Belinda, but a traitor to your own people. Next thing you know, you'll be rooting for the Federals to win the war."

"That's not true, Ryan." Her lips were trembling, and the tears she could no longer hold back were spilling down her cheeks. "I hope the South does ultimately win, but I don't mind saying if it means less lives lost for the North to take victory quickly, then so be it."

For an endless moment, their gazes locked in burning fury and defiance. Finally, with a slight, mocking inclination of his head, Ryan said, "Well, I suppose I'd better keep my plans for escaping to myself, now that I find myself living with a traitor."

Belinda blanched, jolted by his cruel accusation. "Don't worry," she said in a shaky voice, for he had hurt her to the core. "I would never tell, but from now on, I think it's best if we live separate lives."

She went into the bedroom and closed the door with finality.

Ryan stared after her, clenching and unclenching his fists at his sides as angry bile surged up in his throat. He was right, damn it. She'd never admit it, but she *was* a coward. Maybe she had given herself to him, and maybe she truly loved him, but the fact was, she was still running from the nightmare of the past. And, till she could face reality, and the future, there was no hope that their love could survive.

He knew he would make his plans to escape, and when the time came, he would go. He did not want to leave her behind, but he had no choice.

He still loved her. Of that he had no doubt. But he was still a soldier, an officer, and, by God, even if it did mean they might never see each other again, he had a war to fight....

Chapter Eighteen

Belinda told herself repeatedly that Ryan was wrong in his accusations.

The problems they were having, she felt, were caused by his loyalty to the South and her devotion to helping the sick and wounded of either side—not by any lingering ghosts of the past. And, if the war would only end, everything between them could be resolved. She was sure she loved him. Yet, as days turned to weeks, and the wall between them remained, she began to suspect that his feelings for her had changed.

It was easy to lose herself in her work, and she welcomed the long, grueling hours when there was no time to think about anything except the moment at hand.

All that changed, however, in late March, with the clash at Kernstown, Virginia. The Union dead numbered well over a hundred, with 450 injured, and most were transported into Washington for treatment. Once again, Belinda found herself working almost around the clock, assisting in surgery or wherever else she was needed.

So it was that it was nearly four in the morning when the buggy driven by Dr. Woodward pulled to a stop in front of the cottage to deliver Belinda. "Thanks for staying with me through that last surgery," he wearily said, helping her alight in the chilly night air. "But frankly, I don't see how you do it. The stewards who had been working all day were barely able to stand on their feet.''

Belinda gathered her woolen cape tighter around her in the brisk March wind. She could not explain it, but it was as though God gave her just the strength needed to carry on as long as necessary; then, when it was over, she was ready to collapse. ''I'm glad to do it,'' she told him. She planned to sleep in her clothes, for she was too exhausted to make the effort to change.

''Have someone pick me up at seven,'' she requested with a yawn, turning away.

Dr. Woodward was quick to object. ''Absolutely not. A buggy won't be here till noon. You're going to get some rest, whether you like it or not.'' He climbed back up and popped the reins over the horse's rump, not giving her a chance to protest.

Belinda knew she'd find her own way to the hospital should she awaken much before noon, but she feared she'd sleep the day away if given the chance.

The guards had gradually been removed from the immediate vicinity of the cottage, as she and Ryan were no longer considered likely to escape. But, while she was only too glad to have escaped the prejudice she'd experienced in the Confederate medical services, she knew that he was only pretending to be content to escape combat. Still, it was nice not to feel that eyes were constantly watching.

Quietly she let herself in, not wanting to awaken Ryan. He, too, was busy and tired lately, getting all the military horses ready for the spring campaigns that were sure to come with the good weather. They had little time together, and when they did make love, it was over quickly, and so many nights Belinda had cried afterward to think of how they were drifting apart.

She fumbled in the dark, not wanting to strike a match to a lantern. She made her way to the bedroom, and was about to collapse on the bed when Ryan startled her by stepping from the shadows to pull her into his arms. "What are you doing awake? I thought—"

"Shh," he whispered urgently. "No questions. Just listen. We don't have much time. I've got to get you out of here right away. I've a horse waiting for you. All you have to do is ride straight across the Potomac. If you get stopped, all you have to do is show your pass as a nurse and say you've been sent to minister to a government official at his home. They won't ask questions."

She attempted to speak, to protest. "But, Ryan—"

He rushed on, cutting her off. "There's a barn on the left, about a quarter of a mile on the other side of the river. I checked it out when I was over there the other day looking at some horses corralled nearby, and the owner said he was leaving to go up to Canada to bring more back. Nobody will be around. It's a perfect place for you to wait on me. I'll be leaving here with the troops in a few hours, but I'll have to stay with them awhile till I can slip away and double back.

"They've got orders to march into western Virginia. I accidentally found out earlier tonight that Rosecran's command has been handed over to General Fremont, with orders to march on Middlebury. They expect to encounter a Confederate cavalry detachment under General Hill. We're going to have to get there first, to warn them of impending attack. But we can make it, because I've got a crude map I stole from one of Rosecrans's cavalry officers' saddlebag. You just be ready when I get to the barn, and—"

"Ryan, no!" Belinda cried sharply, pushing him away from her, feeling a wave of hysteria at the thought of returning to the South. "I can't. They need me. . . ."

"So do your own people," he lashed out then. He had feared she would react just this way. "Damn it, Belinda, you aren't staying because of your work, and you know it. You're just scared to go back, scared you'll run into the Hardin family, or Willingham, but it's time you realized you can't run from life. You've got to face it, good times and bad."

She turned away from him. "I won't go."

"Then I'll go without you."

She did not respond, for she had known all along it would come to this. There was nothing left to be said.

"We'll probably never see each other again, Belinda. Is that what you want?"

Blinking back hot tears of pain and frustration, her voice quivering, she told him, "You know it isn't. You know I want you to stay here with me. And you can, you know. The...the Federals..." she stammered, swallowing against the sorrowful lump in her throat, "they've been good to both of us. You weren't sent to one of those awful prisons. They've given us a nice place to live, good food to eat—"

"And worked us to death and stripped us of our pride," he roared, striking the air with his fist as rage exploded within him. "Damn it, Belinda, they're the enemy! They invaded our homeland and they're destroying it, and I'm sick and tired of seeing you killing yourself, standing on your feet day and night, ministering to them. And I'm also sick of shoeing their horses so that they can trample my own people.

"No! Hell, no!" he repeated forcefully. "I won't stay! And if you love me, you'll go with me!"

She turned to face him then. She was barely able to make him out in the darkness, but she could feel the heat of his fury as she tried to tell him, "No, Ryan. It's just the opposite. If you love me, you'll stay here with me. I need you...."

"You don't need anybody," he snapped. "You've got your precious wounded to keep you company, and it's them you love, because you don't have to be afraid of them."

He picked up the knapsack he'd packed earlier. He was wearing the Federal uniform Belinda had been given by Sergeant Purdy to replace the red dress so many months ago. It had been much too large for her, and she'd had to roll up the trouser legs, as well as the sleeves. On him it was tight, and, as soon as he broke away from the troops he was smuggling himself into, he planned to change back into his gray cavalry outfit.

"Write to me," she said in a suffocated whisper. "Let me know you're alive and well. You know where I'll be."

He did not respond, afraid to trust his own voice in that heart-wrenching moment. And he knew that if he dared touch her again, he might not be able to leave her, after all.

He hurried on his way, and did not look back.

Chapter Nineteen

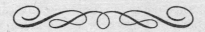

When the man believed to be her husband was discovered missing, Belinda truthfully admitted that she had known when he left, but refused to give any further details. Due to the fact that she had not herself escaped—and on the recommendation of Dr. Woodward and others who knew and respected her—she was allowed to continue her work at the hospital and was not placed under any kind of additional guard. She was, however, ordered to vacate her quarters and move into a boardinghouse with other nurses.

There were times when, despite her weariness, thoughts of Ryan would steal into her mind. She would remember the comfort of being in his arms, the ecstasy of his kisses, but, more and more, she missed just being with him, sharing his life. Despite the bad times, the strife caused by his wanting to leave and her refusal to share his dream, they had had many wonderful hours together. And these memories she cherished.

It was in the early part of June that Dr. Woodward called her into a private office to inform her, "I've been told our troops are getting ready to move on Richmond. Things are heating up for a major confrontation and I've been ordered to get a medical unit ready to help out. I wanted to know if you were willing to go along into the field."

Belinda gripped the arms of the chair she was sitting in, felt a terrifying shudder at the thought of going back into the South. "I...I can't...." she whispered raggedly, swinging her head from side to side. "I just can't."

Dr. Woodward did not miss the flash of horror in her eyes. He had sensed, as had others who worked with her, that there was something very painful in her past. Everyone figured that was why she was so content to remain in Washington. It was also speculated that it had something to do with why she had not seized the chance to escape with her husband. Steepling his fingers, he looked at her, noting that her face had paled. "I'm sorry," he said finally, quietly, "but if you aren't willing to volunteer, then I have no choice but to force you to go with us. We need you, Belinda. It's that simple. And you have to go with us. Your services as a trained surgical assistant will be invaluable to me. You and I work well as a team.

"And I promise," he went on with a gentle smile, "whatever it is you're afraid of, you don't have to worry. Every effort will be made to keep all of us well behind the lines of combat."

"Very well," she said finally. "I'll go with you. Just tell me when, so I can train someone to take over my ward."

"It's hard to say. The latest word I had was that bad weather is keeping General McClellan's forces from pushing farther toward Richmond, but I think we'd better plan to move out first thing in the morning, so we can be there by the time we're really needed."

Belinda blinked, stunned at the notice of immediate departure. "But I won't have time to train anyone—"

"That will be taken care of. We have other nurses. Not as competent as you, of course," he said pleasantly, "but your patients won't be neglected, I assure you. And you'll have time to bid them all farewell this afternoon. Tonight, I'd like your help preparing field kits."

With a sigh of resolve, Belinda got to her feet, murmuring, "I'd better get started."

"There's something else." He reached slowly into the pocket of his vest and took out a folded envelope. He laid it on the desk before her.

Her heart slammed into her chest as she picked up the letter and read the scrawled name: Mrs. Ryan Tanner. Astonished, she looked to Dr. Woodward for an explanation.

He gave a careless shrug. "I don't know when it was mailed, or from where. I don't even know how it got here. It was passed along to me to give to you if I deemed it proper to do so. Those above me in command were afraid hearing from your husband might provoke you into running away to join him. I disagree, because I think you've proved your loyalty to the Union.

"And besides," he added, "he doesn't say where he is, anyway, only the regiment he fights with. Under Major General Ambrose Hill. A highly respected officer. Even if he *does* wear the wrong uniform," he added, unable to resist making the small joke.

Belinda was unamused. "The letter has been opened," she remarked in annoyance.

"Surely you didn't think it wouldn't be."

She turned to go, wanting to be alone to read it.

Dr. Woodward called out for her to be ready to help with the field packs after dinner.

She did not respond, but kept on going, all the way out of the building and into the warm June afternoon.

She waited till she reached a shady spot beneath a tree, with no one else about, before taking the single sheet of paper from the envelope.

With misting eyes, she read:

My dearest Belinda,
This is to let you know I made it safely through enemy lines and am now, once again, fighting with the proud Confederate States of America.

My cavalry unit is assigned to Major General Ambrose P. Hill and the Thirteenth Virginia Volunteers. I could not find a North Carolina unit to attach to when I needed one but am satisfied here, as long as I am fighting for Dixie.

I miss you, and I hope you are safe and well. Maybe one day we will be together again.

> With my love,
> Ryan

Folding the letter and putting it in the pocket of her apron, Belinda bowed her head and wept.

Her face swam before him again. He had sworn to put all thoughts of Belinda from his mind. Then, just when he thought he'd succeeded, the memories would creep up on him again. In the darkness, he could see her emerald eyes, the way they shimmered with passion when he held her. And, yes, he could almost feel her body, warm, supple, giving and taking. How honestly and freely she had come to him, desire created by the closeness that had developed between them, born of friendship, not lust, though God knew, he'd never wanted a woman more.

Maybe, he reasoned, he should have left well enough alone and not sent the letter. His argument to himself had been that at least she would know where he was if she did change her mind. Sadly, he doubted that would happen. She could not, would not, see it for herself, but she still had not let go of the past, even though she professed to love him.

He had to admit, if only to himself, that there had been times when he had actually contemplated turning his own back on the Confederacy in favor of staying with this woman he loved more than life. But he had known that was not the answer. It would be a miserable existence, to be sure, he reasoned, if their future together was spent with him constantly yielding to her insecurities and fears.

No, he had had no choice. He had had to let her go.

And, if she loved him, she had to come to terms with herself.

Only then could they find the right kind of happiness together.

And, as much as he adored her, Ryan knew he could not share her with the ghosts of the past.

He was proud of how he had gotten through enemy lines in time to warn Major General Hill that Fremont's cavalry was on the way to attack in huge numbers. Hill was thus able to retreat in time to keep his troops from being slaughtered, for his company was vastly outnumbered.

Hill had welcomed Ryan heartily, only too glad to assure him that any charges against him filed by Major Harmon Willingham would be dismissed. A few weeks later, Hill reported that he had sent telegrams requesting an investigation of the incident and had learned that there was no record of a formal accusation. A jealous tantrum, Hill opined, best forgotten.

Ryan silently knew he would never be able to cast aside the reality that, had it not been for Corporal Chalmers, the execution would have been carried out. But he said nothing else about it, well aware that Hill felt it important he turn all his attention to the war.

Given command of a cavalry force, Ryan was urged to get them ready for immediate combat. Rumors were flying of a big impending battle, and, all too soon, they found themselves moving out of Virginia and heading for a place in Tennessee called Shiloh.

Southern advance scouts excitedly reported that they could not believe what they saw while spying on the Union encampment at Shiloh. It appeared the Union commanders had no idea a Confederate attack was imminent. Although there had been some skirmishes between the pickets of the two forces, the scouts recounted that there was an almost festive spirit in the Federal camp. There were no fortifications, and the scouts had managed to hear an officer say that entrenching might make them look weak and lower the morale of the troops.

Now the word was spreading throughout the Confederate camp to make ready for battle, and Ryan was ecstatic over how he'd managed to bring with him a half-dozen Spencer repeating rifles he had stolen from the Yankee soldiers the second night out from Washington, when he'd crept away in the middle of the night. The tubular magazine could be removed and replaced by a full magazine of nine cartridges in a few seconds. He smiled to think how one of his men had laughed and said, "Now we got them Yankee guns you can load on Sunday and shoot for the rest of the week."

So Ryan felt he was ready for combat, and he only hoped his men felt the same. He had left them to go off by himself, to be alone with his thoughts, and, as always, he could think only of Belinda.

Maybe, he dared muse, if he got out of the war alive, one day he would go and look for her. She said she would like to go to school to be a doctor. There weren't that many places she could go, and it would not be hard to find a woman student. He would only be trying to assure himself that she was all right before heading back home to the Blue Ridge to try and make a new life for himself. He owed it to her, being as he still felt a bit guilty over what had happened to her in the first place—what had brought her into the infernal war.

But Ryan knew he also owed it to himself—his own peace of mind.

Because no matter how hard he tried, he knew he would always love her.

"You out here, Captain?"

Ryan got to his feet as one of his men came through the patch of woods where he had sought refuge with his musings. "Here, Private. What is it?"

"Major General Hill wants to see you right away."

In the scant moonlight, Ryan could see the anxious look on the soldier's face.

"I reckon he's gonna tell you we're movin' out first light."

"And I reckon," Ryan fired back with a reckless grin as he fell into step with his man, a comradely arm around his shoulders, "that's what we're trained for, soldier, so let's go...."

Chapter Twenty

It was Sunday, April 6, 1862. With over forty thousand infantrymen, Ryan and his band of cavalrymen bore down on the Union camp at Shiloh. The ground beneath them trembled with the distant sound of the cannons booming in cadence like the very drums of hell.

The Rebels were formed into four lines across three miles of front. Ryan thought, as they headed into the hastily assembled Union lines, that it was an almost medieval kind of formation.

They were told they would be joining General Albert Johnston, who was bringing in his troops from Corinth, Mississippi. Their surprise clash against Union general Benjamin Prentiss was to take place behind the main camp.

Finally, proudly, with a wave of a gloved hand, Ryan led his mounted soldiers in a charge against the main line. When they fired the stolen repeating rifles, blue uniforms fell in waves. It was like riding into a hornets' nest as the cavalrymen closed on the enemy to finish their initial thrust with slashing swords and stabbing bayonets.

Ryan saw two of his men fall and charged to bring down the soldiers responsible with a hard thrust of his sword, then grabbed up his rifle to quickly reload and take down six Yankees in quick succession.

All around him, they were falling, but he scarcely had time to glory in the gallant performance of his regiment, for it was a scene of blood and gore and carnage unlike anything yet witnessed in the war.

Hour after hour, the battle raged on, but finally someone called out to Ryan, "They're surrendering, Captain...."

But Ryan had seen something else and shouted, "That's Prentiss's forces...." He pointed at the Federal soldiers attempting to get through a ravine that would take them to a boat landing and escape. "We've got to head them off. Hit the ravine."

Horses thundering, Ryan and his men leapt over the rim and into the chasm, charging to meet the hysterically scrambling foe. Realizing they were beaten, the Federal soldiers threw down their weapons.

But Ryan's glory was short-lived, for word soon came that General Johnston had been killed.

"And they're driving us back," came the frantic word from another officer. "Union gunboats just got here and they're firing over the heads of their own soldiers to push us back."

"We've got to pull back and regroup." Ryan grimly gave the order: "Pass the word. Head back to that peach orchard over there."

Someone cried fearfully, "Two of our men, Harper and Knight, are down back there, Captain. We need to pick them up."

Ryan would not allow his men to risk their own lives, especially when it was a hard-and-fast rule not to chance picking up the injured in the field. A cease-fire would doubtless be called at dark so that both sides could send in ambulances and medical staff, but often the delay meant the difference between life and death. "I'll get them. The rest of you head for the orchard." He sliced the air with his sword to send them on their way.

As he rode, ducking grapeshot as he sent his horse galloping over piles of dead bodies, Ryan was struck by the thought of how Belinda might one day be back out in the thick of battle. God, he hoped not. Surely her fear of being anywhere near the South, her painful memories, would keep her safely in the Union capital. Still, he feared there might come a time when she would yield, out of her sense of duty to the suffering.

He felt a zinging pain against the side of his face. He realized, as blood began to stream down his cheek, that he'd been grazed by a bullet. He shivered at the horror of having been so close to death and sharply, angrily, reminded himself to think about what he was doing, not dwell on a woman who obviously didn't love him enough to want to be his wife.

He froze at the sound of someone calling his name.

"Tanner . . . Tanner, for God's sake, don't leave me here. . . ."

He could see a man in gray uniform, lying on his side perhaps a hundred feet away, one bloodied arm outstretched.

Ryan knew it was suicide for him to ride straight into the charging enemy, but he could not desert a comrade, and especially when he saw who it was—the man to whom he owed his own life, Corporal Chalmers.

Digging his heels into his horse's flanks and pressing hard against his neck, Ryan gave up the reins as he shouted, "Keep that arm up, Corporal, I'm coming in. . . ."

He did not try to slow the horse, but galloped at full, furious speed, praying all the while that the animal, trained to respond to knee and foot signals, would obey. And, just before he reached the fallen man, he dug in his knees to urge it into a leap. The horse conformed, thrusting directly over Chalmers, and Ryan swung down and grabbed him by his arm. With every ounce of strength he possessed, he jerked up and across him, at the same time signaling the horse to turn abruptly and race in the opposite direction.

Bullets were coming closer, but the mighty horse stretched out to outdistance them, and finally, mercifully, the peach orchard they had left closed about them again.

"Keep moving," Ryan shouted, fiercely holding on to Chalmers and charging by his men. "They're right behind us...."

The cavalry unit wasted no time before riding off in hot pursuit, expertly guiding their horses around trees and jumping fences in their path.

At last, they reached the area where the infantry had pulled back to gather and regroup. The atmosphere was jubilant, for even though it was being reported that both sides had sustained crippling losses, it appeared the Federals had been stretched to the breaking point. Victory was predicted by the battle weary but happy Confederates.

Ryan headed for the hospital tents that were hastily being set up. Reining in, he cried out to the nearest steward, "Give me some help here. I've got a wounded man."

Chalmers was taken from his arms and placed on a litter, then swiftly carried inside. Promising he would be back later to talk to him, Ryan then hurried to find General Beauregard, whom he knew would be taking command after the tragic death of Johnston.

He found him in his headquarters tent, surrounded by his staff. All were somber, obviously distraught over the death of a general they loved and respected.

With an absent nod to Ryan as he quietly entered, General Beauregard went on with his briefing. Grimly he advised the assembled officers that a scout had reported that General Lew Wallace's division was en route to give the Federals reinforcement. "We have also received word the divisions of Nelson and Crittenden from Buell's Army of the Ohio, will be here by morning. I estimate that will bring their strength up to over fifty thousand. Right now, we've got just over thirty thousand. But," he went on, "we are expecting Earl Van Dorn to bring in reinforcements."

"And if he's not here by morning?" Ryan wanted to know.

"We pull back to Corinth, Mississippi, and declare Shiloh a draw."

Ryan shook his head in disapproval, but no one was paying any attention to him, for the focus was on General Beauregard.

The fact was, Ryan sadly reasoned, Shiloh would *not* be a draw. Strategically, it would have to be regarded as a Union victory, since retreat would leave the Federals in possession of a strategic section of the Mississippi.

Going back outside into the night shadows, Ryan wrinkled his nose at the smell of sulfur in the air, along with the stench of smoke from burning trees and wagons.

He was anxious to hear news of Chalmers, but he knew he had to have something in his stomach.

And it wasn't food he had in mind.

His horse was where he'd left it, outside the hospital. He reached into his saddlebag and took out the bottle of whiskey he carried for such wretched times.

After a deep, burning swallow, he felt a little better, but not much.

In the distance could still be heard the sound of gunfire. The troops were trying to shut all the fighting down for the night, but there were diehards on both sides who would keep shooting for a while to come.

Rations were being passed out, but he declined, preferring whiskey to beans and bacon and boiled peanut coffee. Surrounded by suffering and death, Ryan wanted numbness within, not nourishment.

At last, he felt enough time had passed that he could seek out Corporal Chalmers. Locating the steward he remembered having helped take the wounded man inside, Ryan asked about his whereabouts and condition.

The weary steward pointed to an area ringed by campfires, where those already treated were being taken. "If it's the one I remember, he'll be all right. They didn't have to amputate, 'cause the ball went through the muscle in his calf. I don't imagine it will even earn him a trip home," he added with a smile of mock sympathy.

Ryan hurried over.

Corporal Chalmers, his left leg swathed in bandages from knee to ankle, was sitting up. "I was hoping you'd show up, Captain. I want to thank you for saving my life out there. Those Yankees would've finished me off, for sure."

"Now we're even," Ryan said brusquely. "Thanks to you, I wasn't executed.

"So tell me..." He dropped to the ground beside him. "What happened after they found out I didn't stick around for breakfast?" He gave a wry grin and tipped the bottle once more, then handed it over to Chalmers, who gratefully helped himself before responding.

"Rathbun was the one to sound the alarm. Then, when they found Miss Belinda missing, everybody assumed Doc Staples hadn't given her a strong enough dose of morphine and she'd woke up and untied you so's the two of you could escape.

"The major was breathing fire, to be sure," he added with a laugh. "Stomped all around, cursing and swearing. He sent a patrol out looking for you, but they didn't stay long. The place was swarming with Yankees, so we had to lay low for several days."

"So how did you wind up fighting with Beauregard?"

Chalmers made a face. "I always hated Willingham. We were in school together at the military institute in Charlotte. Hill was the commandant, and he organized the First North Carolina Regiment, and I joined up with him and so did Willingham. Willingham's daddy was a rich doctor and he knew the right people to help him get promoted right on up. I had to work my ass off to make corporal.

"Anyways..." He lay down again, wincing with pain from his wounded leg, "Like I said, I couldn't stand the son of a bitch, and that mess with you and Miss Belinda was the last straw. We had a talk, all of us, and Doc Staples, he said there wasn't any way he'd ever agree with Willingham that she was crazy, not after the way she helped out at the hospital. Said she was real smart, able to do anything a steward could.

"Then," he went on, his face tight with remembered anger, "Willingham got drunk one night and started talking about her and told everybody how he was engaged to her once upon a time but some men back where she used to live had raped her, and after that, he didn't want her for his wife."

Ryan felt an angry lurch in his gut and found himself wishing for the second time that he had killed Harmon Willingham when he'd had the chance.

With a sigh, Chalmers continued, "Well, it wouldn't have made no never mind to me if she had been *my* fiancée, and after hearing him talk like that, I knew I had to get away from him, before I wound up putting my fist in his face like you did. So I put in for a transfer and I got it, thank God.

"But you needn't worry," he added hastily. "Willingham didn't make any formal charges about you attacking him. Between you and me, I think he knew none of us would've backed him up, unless it would have been Rathbun, but you don't even have to worry about him anymore. He's dead. Got shot a few weeks after that."

"Good. Saved me the trouble."

Suddenly Chalmers wanted to know, "Whatever happened to Miss Belinda, anyway? Is she still a nurse?"

"I suppose so...." Ryan soberly replied, getting to his feet. He saw no reason to confide the story.

"Hey," Chalmers called after him, "thanks again...."

"We're even," Ryan reminded him one last time, and kept on going.

At dawn, after a sleepless night, word was passed that they were to retreat to Corinth. The expected Confederate reinforcements had not arrived, and scouts had seen more Union gunboats coming up the Tennessee River.

Shiloh was over, with nearly two thousand Confederate dead and over eight thousand wounded. Nearly a thousand men were missing, thought to have been taken prisoner.

What was left of Ryan's unit headed out to reunite with Hill's division. All the while, his heart was heavy at the thought that he was moving farther and farther away from the only woman he could ever love.

Belinda moved with the Union medical services into the fringes of battle.

Despite the praise of all those with whom she worked, she did not consider herself a stoic heroine, and, all the while, she feverishly wondered when the nightmare of war was going to end.

It was mid-August and stifling hot, and Belinda was more than a little upset to realize that they were within only twenty-five miles of Richmond, having followed McClellan's Army of the Potomac since early summer. In a way, it seemed strange to be so close to the place where she'd once fled in panic in the hope of finding a dream, but that was all past and dead now. There was no time for looking back, for every moment was spent ministering to the wounded soldiers who came in by droves.

She'd had less than four hours of sleep when, reporting for duty, she was surprised to find everyone preparing to move out. One of the stewards hurriedly told her that McClellan had received orders to join up with General Pope's army in another attempt to drive toward Richmond.

"But what about the men not fit for travel?" she cried in protest. "We need to get them to a hospital base for recuperation—" She stopped short when she realized that the patients were nowhere in sight.

The huge tent was being dismantled, and gone were the men she'd left a few hours ago.

Whirling to face the steward, she demanded, "What's going on here?"

He shrugged, brushed by her with an armload of field kits. "Orders came down fast, Miss Belinda. We didn't want to leave them here, and, like you said, they couldn't travel, so we did the only thing we could do—moved 'em back to Washington."

"Well, why wasn't I notified? Why didn't someone wake me up and tell me what was going on?" She stamped her foot in exasperation.

Dr. Woodward arrived just then to inform her crisply, "Because you needed the rest, Belinda, that's why. You had gone nearly two days without sleep, and you know it. And, like the man said, the orders came down fast."

She threw up her hands in defeat. "So onward we march...." She turned away, shaken by frustration.

"Not if you don't mind treating Confederate soldiers instead."

She faced him once more, struck not by his words, but by his tone of voice, which was challenging, even taunting. "What are you talking about? We aren't about to be overrun, are we?"

"Quite the contrary. I was just informed that a group of prisoners of war will be arriving here in a little while, en route to prison back North. A couple of them are hurt bad, and we've been asked if any of us are willing to hang back and treat them. I understand a few may not make it."

She did not blink an eye. "And you're asking me if I'll volunteer?"

"Nobody else seems to be interested. They'd rather ride on to help our men than treat the enemy."

Bitterly, she fired back, "I'm not at all surprised. Of course I'll stay."

"You won't have much to work with," he warned. "Fact is, I can't even spare a steward, but I will leave an escort to bring you to catch up with us. I'm afraid you'll just have to rely on them and the guards traveling with the Rebs for any assistance you might need, though I don't anticipate you'll want to do more than change bandages.

"You can't be expected to do much more than that," he added pointedly.

With eyes narrowed, she asked frostily, "Then why leave me here? Why not just let them pass on through?"

He did not respond, and suddenly looked quite uncomfortable.

Belinda coldly, bitterly, answered for him. "I think I know. The Union army just doesn't want it said it wouldn't provide medical care for Confederate prisoners. It doesn't matter if the care they do give is inadequate. It's the attempt. Am I correct?"

With a tired glance, he spread his hands in a gesture of defeat. "What can I say? I was asked to find out if anyone wanted to stay behind. Now I've got to get going. You'll be held back maybe half a day, at best, because—"

"Because I'm only supposed to go through the motions of helping them, right?" she interjected sharply. "Very well. I'll stay. What supplies and equipment may I have?"

"Take what you want, damn it." He turned on his heel and left her, not liking her in that moment for the way she was making him feel about himself.

Belinda hurried to one of the wagons about to leave and grabbed out a surgeon's bag, as well as several field packs. Whatever needed to be done, by God, she intended to do, and, though she'd never admit it to anyone—and especially Dr. Woodward—she was secretly looking forward to the chance to do something for the Confederacy.

The others had been gone almost an hour when wagons bearing a dozen prisoners arrived. One of the soldiers left behind with her, Private Deaver, told her he had heard that all those captured were officers. "That's why they're bothering with them. Otherwise, they wouldn't care whether they lived to make it to jail or not."

Belinda hurried to direct that the men be brought in in order according to the urgency of their wounds.

She had been left one tent, and all she had for a treatment table was the door from a nearby log cabin, which had been placed across two empty ammunition barrels.

Within two hours, all the prisoners had been treated, including one whose arm had to be quickly removed.

As the guards began to move the litters back onto the wagons, Belinda protested, "Can't you wait till morning? Give me the night to keep an eye on them?"

Sergeant Lorche, who was in charge of the prisoner detail, was quick to respond. "Afraid not, ma'am. If we stick around here, we're liable to wind up *their* prisoners. This place is going to be crawling with Rebs before long. We've wasted enough time as it is. We're leaving as soon as we're loaded."

Private Deaver chimed in anxiously. "He's right, Miss Belinda, and we've got to be moving out ourselves, if we're going to catch up with the others. We wait much longer and we won't be able to."

Belinda had to agree. "At least let me check the amputee before you move him. Did he wake up all right?"

"Yeah, but he's groggy." Duncan led the way to where he'd had the litter placed near the wagons.

As they approached, she saw him moving his head slowly from side to side, could hear his soft moans of protest and anguish. "No doubt he's realized his arm is gone," she said, biting back tears of sympathy. "That's got to be a horrible experience to wake up to."

She knelt beside him, first checking to make sure there was no unusual amount of blood soaking through the bandage, then placed a hand on his forehead and said gently, "You're going to be all right. It was a clean amputation. You can be fitted with an artificial limb and—"

Belinda fell silent, reeling as though a giant fist had slammed her in the throat, rendering her speechless.

Private Deaver, stunned by the way she was acting, rushed to ask, "What is it? What's wrong? He ain't dead, is he—?" And he, himself, was staggered to see the way the man on the ground was looking at Miss Belinda, as if he'd kill her with his bare hands if he had the strength—and two of them to do it with.

Instinctively, protectively, Private Deaver clutched her shoulders and tried to pull her away, but she resisted.

She drew a sharp breath, managed to speak despite the panicked constriction of her throat. "I didn't know it was you. Dear God, I didn't—"

"The hell you didn't." He snarled the accusing words between clenched teeth. "You did it on purpose, you bitch!"

Belinda lifted her chin in firm defiance, spine stiffening with courage. She felt no guilt. No matter what he said, she had not taken a close look at him, had not recognized him with his heavy beard and his filthy, bedraggled appearance. "No," she told him again, voice becoming calm and assured as she coolly repeated, "No, I didn't know it was you, and if I had, it wouldn't have made any difference in my decision. The arm had to come off to save your life."

"Damn you...." He raised his remaining arm. It was a feeble attempt, due to his weakness, and the arm fell to his side. His head lolled back and he stared upward, tears streaming down his cheeks as he declared in a guttural whisper, "Damn you to hell, Belinda Coulter. You should have left me to die...."

"That's not up to me to decide. I did what had to be done. The rest is between you and your God."

She got to her feet and walked away—leaving Harmon Villingham behind.

She did not look back.

And her conscience, thank God, was clear.

It was another part of her life, and it was forever over. A challenge met, and honorably satisfied.

But still, regret smoldered and needled, for more and more she was coming to realize that Ryan had been right. She *was* a coward when it came to dealing with the past.

But now—mercifully, thankfully—she was one step closer to courage, for she had been able to face Harmon, as well as his bitter accusations, without faltering.

She had stood up to him, had stood up for her convictions. She only wished Ryan were here to share her triumph.

And the love she held for him, so deep in her heart.

Chapter Twenty-One

With Private Deaver leading the way, they rode hard and fast, catching up with the rest of their unit just as darkness was spreading across the Virginia countryside. Tents were already being hastily set up for the night, and they learned they would be moving out at first light, heading for the planned rendezvous with General Pope north of Richmond.

Although Belinda beseeched Private Deaver to keep silent, he could not wait to tell everyone how she had skillfully performed an amputation. As a result, she was summoned to Dr. Woodward's tent before she even had time to settle in.

"Tell me about it," he commanded brusquely, brow furrowed, obviously piqued.

And she did, sparing no details except the fact she had once been engaged to marry the patient. All that had been resolved within herself, anyway, and she knew that if she had it to do all over again—if she recognized Harmon from the first instant—she would change nothing. The arm had had to come off, and that was precisely what she told Dr. Woodward. "If you want to reprimand me, that's your privilege," she said, green eyes flashing with spirit and deep resolve. "I realize it was taking a chance, but I had enough confidence in myself that I thought I could do it. And I did."

"You had no right to make such a decision, Belinda."

"Maybe not, but it was either perform the amputation or let the man die. There is no way it could have been saved. The amputation should have been performed when he was first captured, by a Union doctor," she added pointedly, accusingly.

He leaned back in his chair, fingers steepled, lips pursed, as he contemplated the situation. Finally, he declared, "We'll just forget it happened, since it was the enemy, but make sure you never dare attempt such a thing with one of our own."

At that, Belinda's ire exploded. Leaning forward, hands pressed against the table that served as his desk, she cried, "I think that's a callous and coldhearted statement, Harvey." Normally, she never called him by his first name when they were working, only in private social situations with him and his wife, but suddenly she could not find it in her to address him as "Doctor," and she said so. "You shouldn't even *be* a doctor if you have such callous disregard for human life. There's such a thing as mercy, compassion, and you obviously don't have it.

"And I'll tell you something else," she raged on, not caring who heard and ignoring the way he leapt to his feet, face turning red with indignant anger. "I think what guided me to success was the fact I was dealing with a human life that I wanted to save. And it didn't make a damn bit of difference to me whether he was in gray uniform or blue."

Furious, he fired back, "If everyone had your attitude, there'd be no need for the damn war, Belinda. What's the point in *Union* soldiers shooting *Confederate* soldiers if Union doctors and nurses are going to go running out and try to save them so they can go back into battle and try to kill our own men?"

With hands on her hips, she cocked her head to one side, and, with a bitter laugh, said, "Frankly, I've never seen a need for the war in the first place. All this useless killing and maiming, and why? Brother against brother, father against son. Where's it going to end? And when? And in the meantime, do I just turn my back on a dying man because he happens to believe in a different cause?

"And what *is* the cause?" she raged on, voice edgy as she fought to hold back tears of frustration. "What is the real reason Americans are fighting Americans, Harvey? Do any of us really know? We talk about the slavery issue, but it's deeper than that, isn't it? Something about states' rights, and the North trying to tell the South how to run their business—"

"I think maybe you're working on the wrong side, Belinda." Woodward slammed his fist on the table so hard it collapsed, but he continued his diatribe without a pause. "Perhaps leaving Washington was the wrong thing for you to do. Perhaps coming south has stirred your Southern blood to the point it might be best if you didn't serve the Union any longer. Frankly, after this, I don't think I'd like to entrust our soldiers to your care."

Belinda's eyes widened in astonishment. "How can you say such a thing? You know different. You know I've always done my best for every soldier in my care."

"But now I question your loyalty, and I am going to immediately send a telegram to the surgeon general, Dr. William Hammond, as well as to Miss Dorothea Dix, recommending you be relieved of your duties immediately."

"Don't bother," Belinda cried with a furious toss of her hair. "You can have my resignation as of now."

"Fine. That will save me the bother of having you formally removed."

Meeting her fiery glare with one of his own, he went to the entrance of his tent and called to the guard right outside and ordered, "You will take Miss Belinda to her quarters, where she will remain till morning, with a guard posted outside. At first light, she'll be escorted to the Confederate lines under a white flag.

"Since she likes experimenting on human lives," he added with a sneer of contempt, "let her do it on the damn Rebels."

Belinda was livid with indignant rage and she rushed out, wanting to end the conflict before she lost all control and slapped his arrogant, sneering face. Dear God, back in Washington she had considered him and his wife her friends, but in the space of only a few minutes he'd become an irrational stranger.

"You really going over to the other side?" the soldier asked shyly as they walked through the camp.

"I guess I have no choice."

He shook his head. "A real shame. Private Deaver has been telling everyone what you did for that Reb major, and I think that took lots of courage, Miss Belinda."

Her laugh was brittle. "You mean you don't think it was a waste of my time because he wore gray?"

"Not me," he lowered his voice, glancing from left to right, clearly anxious that he not be overheard. "I got a cousin who went to fight for the Rebs, and my sister married one. Every time I fire my gun on a battlefield, I'm afraid I might actually be shooting at one of them. It's not a good feeling, I tell you, but there's nothing I can do about it. They got their opinion. I got mine. Each man does what he thinks in his heart is right. I just want the whole dang mess to hurry up and be over with and stop all this killing."

"You and thousands of others, soldier," she said with a wistful sigh.

They reached her tent, which had been hastily set up. She had planned to report straight to the hospital to see if she could be of any help, but she knew there was nothing for her to do after what had happened but retire for the night.

Almost apologetically, her escort offered, "I'll go get you some supper and bring it to you, Miss Belinda, being as you aren't supposed to be out and about no more." He signaled to another soldier nearby to stand guard till he returned.

He brought her a plate of boiled beef and potatoes, but Belinda could not eat. Though exhausted, she was too excited to sleep. Instead, she passed the time making plans for the future. As soon as she was turned over to the Confederates, she would ask to be taken to a medical-services headquarters. There, she would tell the whole story of how she'd been captured and remained to work for the Union. If Major Whitley was still alive—and, dear God, she prayed he was—she was confident he would want her transferred to work with him. Meanwhile, she would request to go to Richmond and volunteer her services at Chimborazo Hospital.

And maybe, she thought happily, heart pounding, she could locate Ryan. He had said he was fighting with General Ambrose Hill, and even though it might take a long time for a letter to reach him, she could try, by God, and—

Her excited reverie was interrupted by Dr. Woodward calling to her from the other side of the closed tent flap. He sounded nervous, edgy, and when she looked out she saw in the glow of the lantern he carried that she was right. His face was the very mirror of chagrin.

With an uncomfortable glance at the hovering guard, he softly asked her, "Can I come inside and speak with you for a moment?"

She nodded and stepped back.

Upon entry, he wasted no time in getting to the point of his visit, beginning contritely, "I want to apologize. I don't know what came over me. I guess it's all getting to me. I'm overdue for leave, but it looks like we're gearing up for another big battle once McClellan meets up with Pope and they move on Lee and Richmond...." His voice trailed off and he shook his head in despair. "I'm sorry. I don't mean to go on so. I'll get to the point. I *do* apologize, and I'd like to forget the whole thing happened. We need you, Belinda."

"So does the Confederacy."

He had been staring down at his boots, but he instantly jerked his head up to look at her in disbelief and cry, "You don't mean that. My God, woman, you let your husband go back without you because of your loyalty to the Union. Surely you aren't going to let our little disagreement send you running back—"

"He wasn't my husband," she admitted with a sad little smile. "But I wish he were. I hope—" her smile grew broader "—one day he will be.

"You see, Harvey," she went on, her face calm and serene, for she'd come to terms with all the turmoil she'd carried since the nightmare began, "I was never really loyal to the Union. I just wanted to help where I was needed, and since I was running from something that hurt me very badly, I didn't want to go back where it all began. That's why I didn't leave with Captain Tanner. I wanted to stay in Washington and hide from the past. But no more.

"And it's not because of what happened between us," she rushed to advise him, seeing that his distress and dismay were increasing with each word she spoke. "Sooner or later, I think I would have wanted to go back. Our disagreement just made me realize it sooner."

"Is there no way I can change your mind?" he asked in obvious anguish. "My God, I'll never forgive myself if you go."

She reached out and clasped his hand. "I want to share something with you, Harvey, to make you feel better. By the way, I'm really glad you came to see me, because even though we'll never agree on many things, you were once kind to me, when I was a newcomer to your world, and I'll always be grateful to both you and your wife for how you befriended me back then.

"But," she continued, "I have to tell you about me and my life, and why I think this is all happening. You see, my sister, Jessica, and I had different mothers. Both died when we were infants. Our father married for the third time, and when his wife died in childbirth, along with her baby, one of my aunts told me about the funeral. She said he came into the room where the coffin was lying and kissed his wife on her cheek, and then, after telling everyone there he thought God was mad at him about something and that was why so much grief had befallen him, he turned to me and my sister and said, 'You little ones won't have a mama, but I reckon that's your destiny.'

"I never forgot that," she went on to confide. "I thought of it so many times, wondering why he said that, and then, when I grew older, I found out what destiny meant, how it's really a person's fate, an unseen power that predetermines what happens in your life. Now I can look back and see that everything that happened to me was all leading up to this time. Can you understand that? It's my *destiny* to return to the South, to the Confederacy, and there's really nothing you or I can do about it, Harvey. It was just meant to be."

He stared at her for a long, thoughtful moment. "Then God bless you," he said finally, moved by all she had told him. He was not going to stand in judgment for her having lived with a man who was not really her husband. He held her in the utmost respect and esteem, and he endeavored to say so, but she pressed a fingertip to his lips and told him there was no need.

"At least we part friends," she cheerily reminded him, "and that's all that matters."

"God bless you, Belinda...." he repeated. Then he shook his head and laughed. "I'm not even sure if I'm calling you by your right last name."

"Coulter," she told him. "Belinda Coulter. Mrs. Ryan Tanner was only make-believe."

But, by God, she silently, firmly vowed in that moment, *if there is a way in the world to find him, I will, and if he can forgive me for ever letting him go, Belinda Tanner will be my real name for the rest of my life....*

Chapter Twenty-Two

The Confederate pickets looked at Belinda and exchanged bewildered glances. The Yankees had waved a white flag and yelled that they had a woman to turn over to them, and, not knowing what else to do, they, too, had raised a flag of momentary truce and stepped out into the open.

"My name is Belinda Coulter," she told them, carrying a small bag with one clean dress and an apron, her sole possessions in the world. "I'm a trained nurse. I'd like to be taken to your commanding officer, please."

One of the soldiers regarded her suspiciously and told his companion, "Jed, we better not take no chance. She might be a spy." Of Belinda, he demanded, "What you got in that bag, little lady?"

She showed him. "I promise you, I'm no spy."

"Well, we'll let the major decide," he snapped, nodding to his partner. "Get her on back to camp and have somebody take her in, but be sure and keep an eye on her."

Belinda resigned herself to their skepticism. After all, it had to be an unusual event, one that they seldom, if ever, encountered.

Major Thomas Jacobs listened politely to her story, saying that he would agree to send her back to Richmond, but also that she would have to be kept under surveillance until her story was checked out. "We can send telegrams to the generals and doctors you have mentioned to get verification that what you say is true, but you understand, Miss Coulter, until then, we have to take certain precautions.

"It isn't every day the Yankees turn a lovely lady over to our keeping," he added with a warm smile.

She thanked him for his kindness, confident that all would turn out well, then offered, "There may be some questions you'd like to ask me, Major. After all, I just came from McClellan's army, which is en route to meet General Pope for their march on Richmond."

Face expressionless, he responded, "I'm afraid I could give no credence to anything you have to say, until I hear from my inquiries about you."

She told him quickly, "To be perfectly honest, Major, I wouldn't tell you anything that would jeopardize one Union soldier, anyway. I want to heal people in this war, not hurt them. But I will tell you there's word of an impending battle, and that's why I'd like to get there as soon as possible, to be ready to help with the casualties."

"We know about that," he informed her smugly. "And I see no harm in telling you just how we came by this information, since you're to be closely guarded and won't have a chance to get word back if you are, indeed, a Union spy.

"Two nights ago, the Sixty Virginia Cavalry, under our illustrious Major General Jeb Stuart, got behind Union lines and managed to penetrate Pope's headquarters at Catlett's Station. They seized several staff officers, and, more important, they were able to get Pope's dispatch book. Now we know the exact situation of the Federal army, its need of reinforcements, and the time they are expected to arrive.

"And yes, Miss Coulter," he cheerily concluded, "there is going to be a big battle, the second one at Bull Run, and that's why, if you are what you say you are, a trained nurse, I'd like to get you to Richmond and Chimborazo as soon as possible."

She smiled. "I'd like that, too, but perhaps I can ask you a question now."

He frowned. "I'm not sure I can answer."

"How would I go about getting in touch with a captain in the cavalry? The last I heard, he was with General Ambrose Hill's army."

With a shrug, he told her, "I suppose you could write a letter and address it that way, but I would suggest you wait till you get to Richmond. You can ask someone at headquarters who might be willing to give you more specific information."

"And when will that be?"

"You're leaving right away." He stood to indicate that their meeting was over, boldly adding, "I do hope you're telling the truth, Miss Coulter. It'd be a shame to lock away a pretty girl like you."

With a patrol escorting her, Belinda was rapidly whisked back through the Confederate lines. Heavy rain had raised the level of the Rappahannock River by nearly eight feet, sweeping away bridges and making fords unusable. As a result, they were forced to go farther upstream in order to cross, which meant an extra day's travel.

At last, they reached their destination, and Belinda was awed by how much Richmond had changed in hardly a year. The streets were jammed with soldiers and civilians alike. Horses and wagons made a near impassable mire of the roads. Everywhere there was an air of tension and excitement.

She was taken to the Confederate headquarters. One of her escorts explained that she was to be kept at the stockade until a response was received to the telegrams the major had sent out. "But don't worry. He had 'em on the way before we was even out of spittin' distance from the camp, and if you ain't lying, then you should be outa here before you know it."

They signed her over to a bored-looking corporal, and she said goodbye to the patrol and wished them Godspeed.

The corporal motioned to her to sit on a bench that ran along the wall. "Somebody will be here to take you over in a little while," he said, not looking at her as he leafed through the stacks of papers on his desk. "May be a while, though. We're pretty busy."

"I'm in no hurry to be taken to jail," she said primly, sitting down and folding her hands in her lap, preparing to wait.

"Oh, you're not going to jail. You're going to Chimborazo Hospital, soon as somebody gets here to take you."

With a startled gasp, she asked, "But why? I thought there was to be an investigation—"

"Lady, I don't know what you were told, and I don't care," he curtly interrupted. "All hell is fixing to break loose, and we got new soldiers being processed through, and it's all I can do to keep up with them. I really don't have time for your problems. Now like I already told you, it may be a while before somebody is free to take you over there."

She lifted her chin, miffed by his abruptness. "Would it help you out if I found my own way over there?"

He brightened, looked up at her to ask hopefully, "Do you know the way?"

"I can find it."

He waved his hand in dismissal. "Then go."

She paused, and he glared at her, snapping, "Yeah, is there something else?"

Coolly, she informed him, "It might simplify things if I knew who I was reporting to."

"Oh, yeah, yeah." He nodded, clearly annoyed, shuffling through more papers, then pulled out a piece of paper and skimmed it. "Okay. Here it is. You're to report to one of the chief surgeons, a Major Whitley...."

He stared after her, shaking his head in wonder at the way she lifted the hem to the skirt of her plain brown dress and took off running out of his office.

And he could have sworn she was laughing and crying at the same time.

People stared at the beautiful young girl running through the streets of Richmond. Her golden red hair flew wildly about her face, and her emerald eyes sparkled with happiness as she danced her way. Pausing to ask directions every so often, having to get her bearings, she at last rounded a corner and saw the hospital building just ahead. With a joyful cry, she sprinted the rest of the way, holding her dress above her ankles as she splashed through the mud, not caring that eyebrows were raised as she displayed shapely ankles for all to see.

She took the steps two at a time, but had to force herself to slow when she reached the porch, lest she give the appearance to those inside of someone gone mad. Taking a deep breath, smoothing her skirt and rubbing at the prim collar that always scratched her neck, Belinda took a deep breath and pushed open the doors of Chimborazo Hospital.

A pinched-faced woman, hair pulled back in a tight bun at the nape of her neck, peered at her curiously over the rim of glasses perched at the end of her pointed nose. "Yes?" she inquired with apparent disdain at the way Belinda was panting, out of breath, eyes still wide with excitement and cheeks red from running so far. "May I help you?"

"Dr. Whitley," Belinda gasped, clasping her hands together in anticipation of seeing again the man who'd been like a father. "He's expecting me. Belinda Coulter. I—I'm a nurse," she added hesitantly, well aware that she must not look like one at the moment.

There were others in the big waiting room, obviously inquiring about, or waiting to see, loved ones, and Belinda knew they were all staring at her. She felt like crying aloud in exasperation. Good heavens, if they only knew how long she'd waited for this moment, they'd know why she was so excited. "If you'll direct me, I'll find him myself."

The receptionist was starting to overcome her initial shock over how the young woman had burst into the room and was about to remind her she was in a hospital and there were certain rules, but just then the doors at the end of the hall swung open. A gray-haired man with a neatly trimmed beard, wearing the uniform of a Confederate medical officer, came striding down the hall.

The receptionist watched as he held his arms open to the nearly hysterical girl running to meet him. Making a *tsk*ing sound, she shook her head. So many strange things went on these days. She just didn't have time to worry about all of them....

"Dr. Whitley, it *is* you...." Belinda threw herself into his arms, unable to hold back tears of delight. "I was so afraid I'd never see you again."

"What are you talking about?" He laughed and gave her a big hug before holding her at arm's length to say chidingly, "What about *you*, young lady? You just disappeared, along with a cavalry officer, I believe. No one heard a word after that. I didn't know if you'd run off to get married or if the Yankees got you."

"The Yankees," she confirmed quickly. "It's a long, long story, and I've got so much to tell you. But how on earth did you know I was coming to Richmond? I thought they were going to put me in jail till they made sure I wasn't a Union spy."

With his arm about her waist, he led her back through the doors and on into the hospital. As they walked down a long corridor with rooms on either side, he told her that when the telegram addressed to him had arrived at headquarters it had been sent on to the hospital. "As soon as I read it, I went straight over there and told them they didn't have to check any further, that I'd attest to your loyalty and anything else you said."

"But what are you doing here instead of in the field?"

"Actually, I came in to learn something about this new procedure they're wanting us to use on the dead to embalm them, in an effort to preserve the body so it can be shipped home for burial. There have been so many requests from families that it's been necessary to come up with a system of preservation.

"Anyway," he went on, giving her another hug, "I'm glad you're here, because I need a good hand in the field. I'll be going back at the end of the week, and it's a good thing, too, because all hell is breaking loose, Belinda. We're sorely needed."

She slowed, hesitation washing over her as she lamely echoed, "The *field?*"

"Yes, of course." He looked at her with narrowed, thoughtful eyes. "Is something wrong? Has something happened to make you not want to go back into the combat areas?

"And where *were* you all these months, anyway?" he suddenly wanted to know. "Have you been away from medicine so long you've lost interest? But no..." He chuckled at the absurdity of the idea. "Not you."

"No, no, nothing like that. Actually, I've been working in Washington, at a Union hospital there. They found out I'd been a nurse for the Confederacy, so they were willing to let me work, and I wanted to. I even studied nursing under Miss Dorothea Dix herself."

"I'm impressed. And you *have* got a lot to tell me, don't you? But why don't you want to go back into the field?"

Belinda was not about to tell him she wanted to stay in one place so that if and when the letter she planned to write Ryan caught up with him he would know where to find her. Otherwise, he might never be able to locate her. But then, she dismally reminded herself, he might not even want to. He'd written that one letter, but that had been long before. Since then, he might have found someone else. After all, he was handsome and charming, and she knew that when officers went on leave, especially in large cities like Richmond, they were entertained in elegant homes, and there were probably lots of pretty, and lonely, young girls around, desperate for husbands. She might be getting her hopes up for nothing. Maybe nursing, medicine, was to be her ultimate future, her *destiny*.

Finally, just as they reached another door with a sign proclaiming Doctors Only, she told him, "Of course I'll go back in the field with you. Everything has just been happening so fast lately, I really hadn't thought about it." She offered what she hoped was a convincing smile of enthusiasm.

"Wonderful, Belinda, just wonderful," he cried jubilantly. "I've managed to put together a good staff for us, and having you along will make it absolutely perfect. We'll be attached to the Army of Northern Virginia, under General Robert E. Lee himself.

"Come on along and let me introduce you to some of the others." He pushed the door open and stepped back so that she could enter. "We've got another lady going with us. Actually, she's a cook, but she helps out in the hospital when we need her, which is often. Her husband serves as company chaplain, and he'll be with us, too."

Belinda murmured, "That's nice, Doctor—" She turned her head to view her surroundings, and that was when she stopped short, reeling, stumbled and would have fallen had Dr. Whitley not been beside her to grab her arm and hold her steady.

"Belinda, what on earth—?" he cried.

But she was already wildly pulling away from his grasp, exploding with a shriek of joy that shook her to her very soul. She forgot she was in a hospital, forgot anything and everything except that she was running, with arms open wide, to meet the sister she had missed so very much.

Jessica Coulter Stanton had been checking off items to be packed in the field kits, with her husband, Derek, beside her.

They both heard the cry at the same time and whirled around.

"My God!" The paper Jessica was holding fell from her trembling hands as she tremulously whispered, "Belinda— my baby sister!"

Chapter Twenty-Three

Belinda wept as Jessica told her of their father's death at the battle of Shiloh the past April, describing how she'd gone out in the field to look for Derek and found him holding Zeb Coulter in his arms.

"He said God had given him the sign he had been waiting for, that He had taken the curse away, and he was going home, to the *real* Blue Ridge—in the sky."

Belinda shook her head in pity, swiping at her eyes with the back of her hands. "God rest his tormented soul...."

"He asked forgiveness."

"I can understand why. I hate to speak ill of him, because despite everything, he was my father and I did love him, but we both know he could be very cruel."

"That he could," Jessica agreed. Then she went on to explain, "But he wanted me to forgive him for how he had schemed to keep me and Derek apart." She proceeded to recount how Zeb had intercepted a letter from Derek asking her to meet him to run away and get married, substituting one he'd had written by someone else confessing that he had to marry a girl who was having his baby. To make sure Derek did not come looking for Jessica, he'd also had a letter written to him, supposedly from Jessica, telling him she had married Reuben Walker.

Belinda gasped. "That's terrible. But how did you and Derek get together?"

Jessica told how life back in the Blue Ridge had become so unbearable she'd had no choice but to leave. "When word came Pa was seen wearing a Federal uniform, everyone took out their anger on me. I decided I had nothing left there, anyway, so I went to Richmond to search for you, but couldn't find you anywhere."

"When was that?"

"Summer. June."

"I wasn't there then. I'd already left with Bart Starkey, with dreams of becoming the American Nightingale." She gave a wry grin, pushing back her grief at the news that her father was dead, instead directing her interest to Jessica's story, urging, "Go on. What happened then?"

"I wound up staying at a church just down the street from Libby Prison. In exchange for my room and board, I helped out in their kitchen, and it fell to me to take food to the prison hospital every day." She paused, closed her eyes in momentary wonder to relive the awesome moment when it had happened, then blinked back her own tears to share the glory. "I found Derek there. At first, I hated him, believing he'd betrayed me, especially when I thought he used me to escape.

"And, don't forget," she reminded Jessica bitterly, "All the time he was thinking I had betrayed *him* by marrying Reuben, so he had his own animosity toward me. We had a lot of obstacles to overcome, especially with him being a Yankee soldier, but we made it." She smiled. "Derek gave up fighting and started preaching again, and, after we took Pa home for burial, we got married. Ever since, I've been working between the kitchen and the hospital, and Derek has been ministering to the troops.

"But what about you?" Jessica was anxious to know. "I have to know everything that's happened since you left home."

And Belinda told her, from beginning to end.

Jessica was aghast to hear of her encounter with someone she had thought at first was one of the men responsible for raping her, and fascinated to hear that she had fallen in love with him after realizing he was innocent. "Where is he now? Do you have any idea?"

"With General Ambrose Hill. That's all I know. I had planned to write him and tell him he could find me here at Chimborazo, but Dr. Whitley asked me to go with you all, and I couldn't refuse."

"No, you couldn't," Jessica agreed somberly, reaching to draw her into her arms, kissing her forehead as she held her. "When the war is over, then you can search for him. Till then, we've got to do what we can to help our soldiers.

"At least," she added, attempting to lighten their mood, "I've kept one promise to Pa. With his dying breath, he asked me to find you."

At once Belinda was curious. "What else did he ask you to do?"

"Keep the Coulter land."

With a shake of her head, Belinda murmured, "That's probably gone forever by now—probably sold for taxes."

"Oh, no," Jessica brightly disputed, and she described the deal she had made with Reuben Walker before leaving home. Papers had been drawn up and signed giving him permission to farm the land as a tenant in exchange for paying the taxes. And there was a clause saying he would vacate if any of the Coulter family returned. "When we went back to bury Pa, Derek let him know we'd be going home one day. I have to say Reuben was actually nice about it, but Leona was not at all happy."

"Leona?" Belinda asked, eyes widening. "Leona Billingsley? Why, she had eyes for Derek back when he was the circuit rider...."

"Exactly, but she wound up marrying Reuben. I think they deserve each other."

Dr. Whitley and Derek heard their gales of laughter and peered in curiously. At once, Belinda opened her arms to her brother-in-law, and then Dr. Whitley apologized for put-

ting an end to their reunion, but reminded them that there
was work to be done.

In the following days, Belinda and Jessica were insepa-
rable. They had so much catching up to do, wanting to share
each and every trial and tribulation encountered since last
they'd met. Finally, when they were all talked out, they
agreed that when the war was over they would all go home,
back to the Blue Ridge, and farm the land and keep it in the
family, just as Zeb Coulter had wanted.

"And I can find Ryan, and if he still wants me," Belinda
fervently vowed, "we'll get married and start filling all those
rooms upstairs with babies, and make sure that for genera-
tions to come the land will belong to Coulter blood."

Jessica shared her dream. "It's going to be wonderful. All
of us living together, working together, making a future together. I can't wait...." Her voice trailed off as she took note
of the shadow that crossed Belinda's face. "We'll find him.
Don't you worry. And he'll still want you."

"How can I be sure of that?"

"Do you believe he loved you once?"

Belinda nodded, regretting to have to admit, "He even
asked me to marry him then, saying he wanted to take me
back to Franklin to live with his aunt till the war was over.
He wanted to get me out of the fighting. But I refused because I was afraid to go back where it all started."

"But you aren't afraid anymore," Jessica pointed out.

"No. Not since Harmon Willingham."

When she finished the astonishing story of how she had
successfully amputated Harmon's arm, Jessica's mouth was
hanging open, and her face had turned chalk white.
"That—that is incredible," she stammered. "My God, Belinda, you are wonderful."

Belinda shook her head. "I had a job to do. I did it. And
I wouldn't have done anything different had I known it was
Harmon I was working on."

* * *

In mid-September, word came that General McClellan had fought his way through the passes of South Mountain, in Maryland. As his forces converged on Lee's, the medical services braced themselves for the heavy casualties that were sure to pour in.

Finally, the sound of artillery fire echoed all around. The sky was thick with smoke, the sun trying to break through the clouds. The air was heavy with the smell of sulfur.

Belinda found herself once more caught up in a world of horror as she worked to help the wounded.

Now and then Jessica would pass by, carrying supplies, sips of water for those patients able to drink. Always she looked at Belinda with awe to see her working so stoically, side by side with Dr. Whitley.

Eventually, however, it became obvious that they were falling behind badly. "We've got to move faster," Dr. Whitley fretted, wiping perspiration from his brow with bloodied sleeve. "At dark, when the firing stops, we've got to go out in the field and bring those in we haven't been able to get to yet. Then they're really going to stack up on us."

Belinda nodded in weary agreement and asked, "Can any of us do anything we aren't already doing?"

"I think," he said suddenly, "we need to get you doing something else. I can drag some soldiers in here to swab and bandage, but it will save time if we can divide the stretchers as they come in."

Motioning to someone else to take over her task, he took her by her arm and led her to the entrance of the huge tent. "From now on," he directed, "I want you to examine each and every man that comes through here. The ones that have to be amputated, send to my side of the tent. Resections, trephining and simple gunshot wounds, you send them to the other side. We can stabilize them for a while and then get to the intricate procedures hopefully tomorrow, after we get caught up with all the emergencies that will be coming in between now and daylight."

Belinda swallowed hard, took a deep breath to mask an inner shudder as she pointed out in a thin voice, "That's placing a big responsibility on me, Dr. Whitley. I'm not a doctor, and—"

"I know that," he said, exasperated, for there was no time to argue. "I've got every available surgeon, surgeon's assistant and steward working to their full capability. But you've seen enough wounds. You ought to be able to tell the difference between an arm or leg that needs to come off right away and a simple gunshot wound that only needs cleaning and bandaging. Why waste everybody's time having a man put on an operating table?"

"And what if I make the wrong decision?" she fretted. "What if you realize the limb should have been directed for immediate amputation instead of waiting in hopes of resection?"

"Believe me—" his tone softened and he clasped her shoulder affectionately "—it's far better to make a wrong decision to resection, rather than to amputate. I can always correct that mistake, but once the limb is gone, it's gone."

He left her to her duties, and Jessica, having overheard, rushed over to offer Belinda encouragement. "You'll do fine, Belinda. I've seen you work and I'm amazed at your knowledge and skills. And Dr. Whitley is right. It is going to save a lot of time, having you sort them as they come in."

"I hope so," Belinda mumbled, turning to her task.

The hardest part came when those who were lying on litters, waiting to be admitted, realized that their fate was up to Belinda. Those with serious wounds began to cry and beg, or curse and demand, that they be sent to the "holding" side, as it came to be called. To be sent the other way meant amputation, and they fought against it ferociously.

Intent on what she was doing, she had paid no attention to one man who was staring at her venomously. It was only when he spoke that she felt a chill spread throughout her body.

"It don't matter whether it's bad or not, you'll send me straight to them butchers, won't you?" And he spat out her name with contempt, *"Belinda Coulter."*

Reeling, suddenly feeling as though a fist had slammed into her stomach, she found herself looking into the ugly, sneering face of Jake Hardin.

"Yeah, you'll send me to the knife, for sure," he continued to taunt. "I reckon it's the only revenge you'll ever get. No matter your son-of-a-bitch daddy, the goddamn traitor, killed my brother. I reckon you want revenge, too...."

Suddenly, as Belinda looked down at him in horror, she felt something happening deep inside. The instant fright was rapidly fading, and, in its place, came a kind of ambivalence. It was like awakening from a bad dream, a nightmare, and looking back on the shreds of memory with a veiled kind of terror, all the while aware that it was not real, could not hurt, that there was actually nothing to fear.

And in that frozen moment she knew, at long last, that she had no reason to be scared of Jake Hardin.

It was over.

She could, at long last, let the past completely go, could let her hatred go.

"No, Jake, I don't want revenge. You have nothing to fear from me." Dispassionately she examined his leg and made the decision without hesitation. To the waiting litter bearers, she gave the directive, "Take him to holding. That leg can be saved by resection."

She turned to the next patient, and Jake suddenly burst into tears of gratitude. "Thank you, Belinda. I'm sorry... real sorry...." He was still weeping when they carried him away.

A hand touched her shoulder, and she found herself looking up into the admiring eyes of Derek Stanton.

"That was a good thing you did, Belinda. I know who that must have been. Jessica told me what he and his brother did to you. You could have sent him to have that leg removed. In their haste, the surgeons might not have noticed it could be saved. You'd have had your revenge."

"Revenge isn't my job." She managed a tired smile. "I leave that up to God."

With a quick hug and a kiss on her cheek, he left her to her grisly task with a whispered "Bless you."

Night came, and there was a temporary lull as the stewards headed out onto the field to try to retrieve the dead and wounded. Derek went with them. It was a habit he had developed that worried Jessica; he felt called to minister to those who would not live to make it back to the hospital, to hear their last prayers and comfort them as much as possible.

Belinda munched on hardtack and sipped coffee, the staples of her diet of late, for there was no time to enjoy a regular meal. She knew the brief rest period would end with the arrival of the first litters. Then everyone would work on through the night—and longer, if need be.

She stepped outside into the darkness, wincing now and then when the shriek of a dying soldier pierced the stillness.

"You all right, Miss Coulter?"

She blinked in recognition of Major Thomas Jacobs, the dubious officer she had encountered when she was first turned over by the Federals. His left arm was in a sling, and he was sitting beneath a tree, sipping coffee.

She joined him. "I'm fine, but how about you? Were you wounded badly?"

"No. Flesh wound. Ball passed right through. I'll live to fight again." He flashed a grin in her direction. "By the way, I hear all my doubts about you were for naught. You are, indeed, a nurse, and, according to Dr. Whitley, a very good one. Sorry if I treated you like you were a criminal."

"You were only doing your job, but, quite frankly, right now I wish I were a spy. Then maybe I'd know what's going on out there."

"Oh, I can tell you that much," he offered, tossing down the rest of his coffee and leaning back in weariness. "Lee had his back to the Potomac and was hopelessly outnumbered by McClellan, but Stonewall Jackson got there in time with nine thousand troops to turn the tide.''

Belinda asked hopefully, ''Then it's our victory?''

''We're holding the line. Tomorrow will tell the tale. One thing for sure, we owe a lot to A. P. Hill's division. They marched the seventeen miles from Harper's Ferry in time to deliver a surprise attack at four o'clock to save Lee's right flank, and—'' He stared after her in wonder, for she had suddenly scrambled to her feet, and, with skirt lifted above her ankles, was running off to God knows where. Now what in thunderation, he wondered curiously, had he said that had set her off so?

She ran all the way to where the soldiers were staggering wearily in from battle, asking each and every one, fighting to keep hysteria from her voice, if they'd seen Hill's division. ''The cavalry,'' she specifically requested. ''Have you seen their cavalry?''

But no one knew anything, and, finally, she had to return to the hospital tent with a heavy heart.

Ryan was nearby.

She knew it for a fact, but was powerless to do anything about it.

Thursday morning, September 18, 1862, dawned with the armies at Antietam still in position. Yet no firing began.

The day wore on, and finally it was late afternoon. Belinda and Jessica were helping feed the recuperating soldiers when word came that two fresh Union divisions under Generals Couch and Humphreys had arrived, but apparently General McClellan would not send them out to fight until they had time to rest properly.

Hearing that, the recuperating soldiers enjoyed a hearty laugh. Someone yelled out, ''It's a good thing Hill didn't feel the same about his troops, marching them seventeen miles yesterday, or we'd all be dead.''

"Some of his cavalry may be," a steward passing by commented. "There was a skirmish over near Middle Bridge. We're going to pick up some wounded now."

Belinda, heart pounding, was right behind him, crying, "I'm going, too."

Jessica knew it was futile to try to stop her, did not even want to, for well she remembered the searing desperation she'd felt back in April, when she'd gone out looking for Derek. And, laying down the kettle of soup she was carrying, she hurried to look for him again, this time to ask him to go with Belinda, to be there should she find Ryan dead.

Derek, praying with a dying soldier, saw the distraught look on his wife's face as she approached, knew he was needed, but did not hurry the lad to his final whispers.

When the soldier breathed his last, Derek tarried only long enough to hear Jessica's request, then rushed to oblige.

He held Belinda's hand in the back of the wagon. Together, they listened to the stewards discussing the bloody battle that was Antietam. A rumor was spreading that Lee was going to withdraw during the night.

Belinda was only half listening, intent on finding Ryan before it was too late.

Suddenly they reined up, and she cried, "Are we here? Is this the cavalry wounded?"

One of the stewards called back, "No, ma'am. We've got some injured, though. We're going to have to take them back first."

She did not dare protest, knowing at a glance that these poor souls needed immediate treatment. Ryan, if he was injured, would, sadly, have to wait.

When they started out again, Dr. Whitley rushed over to tell them, "Make this a good run, boys. It's got to be the last. We're pulling out."

Derek saw the anguish on Belinda's face and squeezed her hand tight.

Finally, they reached Middle Bridge, and Belinda scrambled out of the wagon. Darkness was spreading like a giant unseen hand, and it was difficult to see. Everyone was given a torch, and they spread out in search of wounded cavalrymen.

Two were found and verified as part of Hill's army. One was unconscious and near death, but the other was lucid enough that Belinda was able to ask, "Your Captain Tanner—was he with you?"

"Yes, ma'am..." he replied feebly as he was lifted up into the wagon, blood oozing from a head wound. "I saw him get hit, just before I went down. He fell in the water back yonder...."

"The water!" she cried, turning to Derek, who was right beside her. "We've got to find him."

"Miss Belinda," the steward at the reins anxiously yelled down, "I don't know why you're so desperate to find this man, so I hate to be the one to tell you, but if he fell off that bridge, he's dead. It's powerful deep there, and we just don't have time to look for him. You heard Dr. Whitley. General Lee is getting ready to move out—"

"I won't leave without him," she cried furiously. She was about to turn away, but Derek held her back.

"You can't go tearing off by yourself," he cried. "You want to get captured by the Yankees again? Maybe killed? We've got to get back, Belinda—*now!*"

"I told you, I won't," she screamed, beating at his chest with her fists. "Let me go—"

Her sudden fury took him by surprise, and she was able to break free of him and take off running in the direction of the bridge. It was little more than a vague shadow in the smoky twilight.

"Preacher, I'm sorry," the steward declared tersely, "but we've got to get out of here."

Derek wasted no time. He began to unharness one of the horses. "You can get by with one," he said, his tone of voice indicating it would be best not to argue with him right then. "Now get on back. We'll catch up with you." He mounted and rode off after Belinda.

The steward did not hesitate, reining the remaining horse around and heading back to camp.

Belinda called Ryan's name over and over again, wildly, frantically.

Derek caught up with her, and together they searched up and down, climbing around the bank. Then, just when Derek thought he would have to force her to give up, they heard a sound.

"It's him!" she cried, scrambling down the bank in that direction.

Derek murmured, "Thank God..." and followed after her.

In the light from the glow of distant fires, Ryan looked up into the eyes he'd thought he'd never see again. "Belinda," he raggedly whispered, reaching for her. "Belinda, my darling, is it really you, or have I gone to heaven?"

"You're here, with me," she assured him, her tears falling on his face as she quickly examined him while Derek held the torch high. His only injury appeared to be a nasty gash on his forehead, suffered when he'd fallen from the bridge when his horse was shot out from under him.

"Then I *am* in heaven...."

"No, Ryan, not in heaven," she told him tenderly. "You've just met your destiny, like me, and sometimes, thank God, it seems like heaven...."

He touched her cheek. Then, mustering what strength he had left, he pulled her against him for the kiss they had both been dreaming of for so very, very long.

* * * * *

THE TAGGARTS OF TEXAS!

Harlequin's Ruth Jean Dale brings you
THE TAGGARTS OF TEXAS!

Those Taggart men—strong, sexy and hard to resist...

You've met Jesse James Taggart in FIREWORKS!
Harlequin Romance #3205 (July 1992)

Now meet Trey Smith—he's THE RED-BLOODED YANKEE!
Harlequin Temptation #413 (October 1992)

Then there's Daniel Boone Taggart in SHOWDOWN!
Harlequin Romance #3242 (January 1993)

And finally the Taggarts who started it all—in LEGEND!
Harlequin Historical #168 (April 1993)

Read all the Taggart romances!
Meet all the Taggart men!

Available wherever Harlequin books are sold.

If you missed *Fireworks!* (July 1992) and would like to order it, please send your name, address, zip or postal code, along with a check or money order for $2.89 (please do not send cash), plus 75¢ postage and handling ($1.00 in Canada) for each book ordered, payable to Harlequin Reader Service to:

In the U.S.
3010 Walden Avenue
P.O. Box 1325
Buffalo, NY 14269-1325

In Canada
P.O. Box 609
Fort Erie, Ontario
L2A 5X3

Please specify book title with your order.
Canadian residents add applicable federal and provincial taxes.

HE CROSSED TIME FOR HER

Captain Richard Colter rode the high seas, brandished a sword and pillaged treasure ships. A swashbuckling privateer, he was a man with voracious appetites and a lust for living. And in the eighteenth century, any woman swooned at his feet for the favor of his wild passion. History had it that Captain Richard Colter went down with his ship, the *Black Cutter,* in a dazzling sea battle off the Florida coast in 1792.

Then what was he doing washed ashore on a Key West beach in 1992—alive?

MARGARET ST. GEORGE brings you an extraspecial love story next month, about an extraordinary man who would do anything for the woman he loved:

#462 THE PIRATE AND HIS LADY
by Margaret St. George
November 1992

When love is meant to be, nothing can stand in its way . . . not even time.

Don't miss American Romance
#462 THE PIRATE AND HIS LADY.
It's a love story you'll never forget.

PAL

Take 4 bestselling love stories FREE

Plus get a FREE surprise gift!

Special Limited-time Offer

Mail to Harlequin Reader Service®

In the U.S.	In Canada
3010 Walden Avenue	P.O. Box 609
P.O. Box 1867	Fort Erie, Ontario
Buffalo, N.Y. 14269-1867	L2A 5X3

YES! Please send me 4 free Harlequin Historical™ novels and my free surprise gift. Then send me 4 brand-new novels every month, which I will receive months before they appear in bookstores. Bill me at the low price of $3.19* each—a savings of 80¢ apiece off the cover prices. There are no shipping, handling or other hidden costs. I understand that accepting the books and gift places me under no obligation ever to buy any books. I can always return a shipment and cancel at any time. Even if I never buy another book from Harlequin, the 4 free books and the surprise gift are mine to keep forever.

*Offer slightly different in Canada—$3.19 per book plus 49¢ per shipment for delivery. Canadian residents add applicable federal and provincial sales tax. Sales tax applicable in N.Y.

247 BPA ADL6   347 BPA ADML

Name _____ (PLEASE PRINT) _____

Address _____ Apt. No. _____

City _____ State/Prov. _____ Zip/Postal Code _____

This offer is limited to one order per household and not valid to present Harlequin Historical™ subscribers. Terms and prices are subject to change.

HIS-92   © 1990 Harlequin Enterprises Limited

WELCOME TO

The quintessential small town,
where everyone knows everybody else!

Each book set in Tyler is a self-contained love story; together,
the twelve novels stitch the fabric of the community.

"Scintillating romance!"
"Immensely appealing characters...wonderful intensity and
humor."
Romantic Times

Join your friends in Tyler for the ninth book,
MILKY WAY by Muriel Jensen, available in November.

Can Jake help solve Britt's family financial problems and win her love?
Was Margaret's death really murder?

GREAT READING...GREAT SAVINGS...AND A
FABULOUS FREE GIFT!

With Tyler you can receive a fabulous gift, ABSOLUTELY FREE,
by collecting proofs-of-purchase found in each Tyler book.
And use our special Tyler coupons to save on your next
TYLER book purchase.

If you missed *Whirlwind* (March), *Bright Hopes* (April), *Wisconsin Wedding* (May), *Monkey Wrench* (June), *Blazing Star* (July), *Sunshine* (August), *Arrowpoint* (September) or *Bachelor's Puzzle* (October) and would like to order them, send your name, address, zip or postal code, along with a check or money order for $3.99 for each book ordered (please do not send cash), plus 75¢ postage and handling ($1.00 in Canada), payable to Harlequin Reader Service, to:

In the U.S.

3010 Walden Avenue
P.O. Box 1325
Buffalo, NY 14269-1325

In Canada

P.O. Box 609
Fort Erie, Ontario
L2A 5X3

Please specify book title(s) with your order.
Canadian residents add applicable federal and provincial taxes.

TYLER-9

· HARLEQUIN ·
HISTORICAL

CHRISTMAS

· STORIES · 1992 ·

Capture the magic and romance of Christmas in the 1800s
with HARLEQUIN HISTORICAL CHRISTMAS STORIES
1992—a collection of three stories by celebrated
historical authors. The perfect Christmas gift!

Don't miss these heartwarming stories, available in
November wherever Harlequin books are sold:

**MISS MONTRACHET REQUESTS by Maura Seger
CHRISTMAS BOUNTY by Erin Yorke
A PROMISE KEPT by Bronwyn Williams**

Plus, this Christmas you can also receive a FREE
keepsake Christmas ornament. Watch for details in all
November and December Harlequin books.

**DISCOVER THE ROMANCE AND MAGIC OF THE
HOLIDAY SEASON WITH HARLEQUIN HISTORICAL
CHRISTMAS STORIES!**

HX92R